Acknowledgements

A couple of years ago Barbara Wilson, then Editorial Director of Women in Translation, suggested that I update and expand *An Everyday Story: Norwegian Women's Fiction* first published in 1984. For that initial impetus and for her thoughtful criticism and suggestions throughout the various stages of this project I am deeply grateful. I would also like to thank Brita Butler-Wall for her careful reading of the new translations and June Thomas for guiding this edition to its completion. I am particularly indebted to Judith Messick who generously gave her time, her critical eye and her sure sense of the English language. Much appreciated support has come from institutions and individuals in Norway as well. The Norwegian Information Service awarded me a travel grant which enabled me to do necessary research; the Information Office for Norwegian Literature Abroad provided cheerful and efficient assistance from beginning to end; and there were many people who offered me valuable advice. To all of them I extend my heartfelt thanks. And finally, my husband, Michael Schick, deserves special thanks as always for his patience, good humor and ever incisive commentary!

Katherine Hanson
Portage Bay, Washington
December, 1994

Contents

AN EVERYDAY STORY

Introduction

Katherine Hanson

One hundred and thirty years ago, in 1854, Camilla Collett published *Amtmandens Døttre,* the first feminist novel in Norwegian literature. The book, which came out in two parts separated by six months, appeared anonymously, though the author was not able to keep her identity secret for long. Camilla Collett belonged to a prominent Norwegian family and accordingly had been brought up in a manner befitting young ladies of her class; they were taught to be passive and unobtrusive, obedient and dutiful. Young women were deprived of the opportunity to develop skills or acquire knowledge, but were encouraged instead to direct their talents toward attracting a husband. This is precisely the situation Collett depicts in her novel about the Governor's four daughters. She levels her criticism at the superficiality and injustice of their marriages which, arranged for them by their parents, were based on social and financial status, with little regard for mutual love and respect. And she concludes with the demand that marriage be determined by love, for which woman, with her greater emotional capacity, is the best authority.

Amtmandens Døttre provided a model for many women writers and since its appearance feminist literature has grown and flourished in Norway. It is, of course, neither desirable nor just to isolate literary works by women authors from the greater body of Norwegian literature. Like their male counterparts, female writers have followed literary movements or, in some cases, led them: Camilla Collett's aforementioned novel anticipated the social realism that dominated Norwegian literature in the 1870s and '80s; Amalie Skram made important contributions to the naturalistic novel in Norway; and in the 1980s the experimental writings of Cecilie Løveid and Karin Moe place them among the avant-garde. As this suggests, Norwegian women have from the outset been well informed regarding ideological and literary trends beyond their national borders. And for this reason they should also be viewed in a context with their European and American contemporaries: Camilla Collett, for example, acknowledged the inspiration she received from reading the works of George Sand; Cora Sandel has said much the same about her encounter with Colette, and Karin

Moe's current writing shows the influence of French feminist literature.

Naturally, not all women writers are feminists and even those who consider themselves as such do not always write feminist books. The literature written by Norwegian women is rich and varied. Inasmuch as their greatest contribution has been to the novel and short story, the prose pieces contained in this anthology provide a representative sample of their writing. The authors included span the mid-nineteenth century to the 1980s, thus offering the reader a historical survey. With few exceptions, the stories have been arranged chronologically according to the date of the author's birth. There are stories depicting rural life, urban culture and the various classes within society. Women or girls figure centrally in each of them and they are also linked by common themes and motifs and can be grouped accordingly.

Folktales, legends and ballads—Norway's national treasure handed down orally from generation to generation—have been one of the strongest influences in modern Norwegian literature. Inspired by the work of the Grimm brothers in Germany, P. Chr. Asbjørnsen and Jørgen Moe started collecting and publishing folktales and legends in the 1840s. At that time Norway was struggling to shape her own cultural identity after four hundred years under Danish rule, and in the humor, tone and narrative style of Asbjørnsen and Moe's folktales, Norwegian writers recognized a voice distinctively theirs. At the heart of this tradition is the storyteller, of course, such as the one we meet in Camilla Collett's story about Sara Sandmark. Besides her own tragic story, which Collett relates, Sara possessed a wealth of tales which she left to her daughter, Lisbet Marie, who in turn became one of Asbjørnsen's sources. In this anthology the authors most clearly showing their indebtedness to Sara's legacy are Regine Normann, with her tale of love charms from Nordland, Ragnhild Jølsen and Ingeborg Refling Hagen, whose stories are set in eastern Norway, and Magnhild Haalke who tells of an ill-fated love on a lonely coast far to the north.

Norway is a mountainous country with a long, convoluted coastline where communities are separated from each other by deep valleys and fjords. The first decades of this century saw the appearance of many novels and stories documenting life in these various regions. The stories by Ragnhild Jølsen and Ingeborg Refling Hagen can also be characterized as regional literature, inasmuch as they are realistic depictions of a specific milieu. Jølsen's tales give the reader a glimpse of an early attempt to industrialize forest and farm land and Hagen's story describes the lot of poor rural families where hard work and responsibilities were assumed at an early age. Two additional examples included here are the excerpt from Gro Holm's *Løstølsfolket,* a novel about farm life in the western fjord country, and Åsta Holth's story about Finnish immigrants in eastern Norway.

Although the story by Inger Hagerup is also about a farm family, its focus is not on rural issues but on feminist ones—specifically, woman's expectations and disappointments in marriage. Novels treating the problems within marriage represent, in fact, the strongest current in Norwegian feminist literature. In the nineteenth century the most important exponent of the marriage novel after Camillå Collett was Amalie Skram. She is represented here with an excerpt from *Constance Ring,* an intimate portrayal of married life treating the sexual ignorance and immaturity of young brides and the shock they experience when confronted with marriage's double standard. According to Skram's contemporary, Dikken Zwilgmeyer, the oppression and humiliation suffered by married women was "An Everyday Story" and there have been many renditions of this story up to the present day. As women's social and economic conditions have improved, the search for freedom and fulfillment within a relationship has become more introspective, as exemplified in "The Breakup" by Bjørg Vik and the excerpt "Viviann, White" by Kari Bøge.

Feminist concerns in Norwegian literature have not been limited to the sphere of married life. Implicit in the criticism of marriage in nineteenth century novels is the fact that women had few opportunities to support themselves outside of finding a husband. The lonely, often difficult situation of the unmarried woman was treated with frankness and sensitivity by Dikken Zwilgmeyer in a collection of stories from 1895 and this theme was taken up by many authors in the first half of the twentieth century. Gro Holm has described the lives of unmarried women in rural communities as fraught with drudgery and a sense of shame. In "The Charity Ball," as well as in other stories from the same collection, Sigrid Undset depicts the strained circumstances of single working women in a Norwegian city after the turn of the century. The constraints on the Landsrud sisters, in the story by Nini Roll Anker, are not so much economic as emotional, having been allowed no independence by their strict and domineering father. And Cora Sandel illustrates in "A Mystery" that, although she has escaped the bonds of marriage, the divorced woman will nonetheless have limited freedom in a society that regards her as an outsider.

Fortunately, the conditions for women, married and single, have improved in Norway, though complete equality has yet to be achieved. In literature of a more recent date dealing with single women, the focus has shifted to different problems. Torborg Nedreaas gives a devastating account of sexual manipulation in "Achtung, Gnädiges Fräulein." In the stories by Ebba Haslund and Margaret Johansen we are shown that while a woman may not feel pressured to enter into marriage and is able to maintain financial independence, she still has to contend with a society dominated by men.

Norwegian women have regarded literature as a forum for debating issues and raising awareness, but this represents only one level of their fiction. The authors in this volume have produced a number of excellent studies in feminine psychology—Sigrid Undset's *Kristin Lavransdatter* and Cora Sandel's *Alberte* trilogy are two examples which are available in English translation. Interest in female development, from childhood and through adolescence to adulthood, has a long tradition among Norwegian women writers going back to Camilla Collett who wrote about her own girlhood in her memoir *I de lange Naetter*. Amalie Skram has shown great sympathy with children in her fiction and Dikken Zwilgmeyer has written about childhood and puberty with sensitivity and insight. Many of the authors in this century, writing under the influence of psychological realism, have explored the formative years of the personality, and the outstanding example of such writing is the trilogy about Herdis by Torborg Nedreaas. The first of these books is a short story cycle, the other two are novels with chapters that read like short stories. In these, Nedreaas charts a girl's development from the time she is a pre-school child, still very attached to her parents, until she is a teenager experiencing sexual awakening and a longing for independence.

Cora Sandel and Bjørg Vik, previously noted for their portrayal of adult women, have also written with compassion and intuition about children. These three authors, Sandel, Nedreaas and Vik, are masters of the short story and they have each been represented in this anthology with two selections, one about growing up female, the other about dealing with the complexities of adult life.

The young writers whose books have appeared in the 1970s and '80s are investigating new areas at the same time they continue to explore traditional themes. There is a political awareness and a concern for lower economic classes in much of this writing. Karin Sveen has written about the relationship between a mother and daughter in a working class milieu and interwoven into the story is a protest against economic and political inequality. In "Scum" Tove Nilsen raises questions about human dignity and social injustice with her depiction of a woman who knows no home but the streets. These are by no means the first examples in Norwegian women's fiction dealing with lower class women—Amalie Skram, Nini Roll Anker and Torborg Nedreaas, to mention only a few, have made notable contributions. Bjørg Vik has also written about working class people, as exemplified in "The Entryways." But unlike their predecessors, Sveen and Nilsen are writing from an inside perspective—they are writing about their own class.

Even among those authors who are experimenting in form and style, there are threads linking them with the past. Kari Bøge's book *Viviann, hvit* is a marriage novel in terms of content, but in structure it bears little resemblance to the realistic novels that have preceded it. In the selections by Cecilie Løveid we read about human relationships and interactions, a daughter's search to understand her ties to her father—familiar themes that nonetheless take on new dimensions due to Løveid's innovative use of form and style. Thematically and stylistically, Karin Moe is breaking new ground in her prose texts, but even here we can hear echoes of an age-old tradition: the little girl in "The Lady in the Coat" imagines her mother as a fairytale princess and herself as the troll in the mountain. And this brings us right back to our starting point, the magic and the tradition of the folktale, the legacy of Storyteller Sara.

AN EVERYDAY STORY

Camilla Collett

(1813-1895)

Camilla Collett is among the most important and influential writers in Norwegian literature. During the first half of the nineteenth century Romanticism was the prevailing ideology shaping Norwegian culture. Perceiving romantic ideas and attitudes as stifling and detrimental to a young woman's development, Camilla Collett wrote a *realistic* novel in which she exposed social injustices, particularly within the institution of marriage. *Amtmandens Døttre* (1854-55) was the first Norwegian novel to present a realistic and critical view of contemporary society. It was an impetus and inspiration not only to many women but also to important male authors (most notably Henrik Ibsen) who became staunch supporters of women's rights. In the 1870s and '80s Collett, an increasingly outspoken feminist, published several volumes of articles and essays. She addressed the need for social and political change, but this was overshadowed by her greater concern for the personal emancipation of women: a woman's right to assert her personality and develop her abilities, her right to be respected as a woman.

Strong opinions and sharp criticism notwithstanding, Camilla Collett is an author possessing great warmth, as evidenced in "Storyteller Sara." This piece first appeared in a collection of stories published in 1860 and was later incorporated into *I de lange Naetter* (1862), a series of autobiographical sketches recorded during sleepless nights.

Storyteller Sara

The parsonage garden at Eidsvoll is situated close to the church, at a fair distance from the parsonage, with which it is connected by a long, angling path. The garden was laid out on a grand scale around the turn of the century by the then pastor, Professor Leganger, who chose the spot more for its beauty than its practicality, since he wished to incorporate a patch of woodland with a striking view of the Vorma River.

This distant location, and perhaps also the churchyard's rather stifling proximity, meant that in my time the garden was seldom visited by the pastor's family, who preferred the pleasant terrain near the duck pond for their pilgrimages. A worker was rarely seen in the garden. The only life to be detected on a summer afternoon when the giant trees along the wall enveloped it in early shadows, was the sound of a spade from the churchyard, or the tread of a hound sniffing out the trail of a master who had recently bounded over the stile, or perhaps a rustling in the garden's single, large apple tree, a signal that the local thieves "were taking a shortcut" as they liked to say when again caught in the act, though this "shortcut" passed in lemming fashion right through the apple tree.

I had for many years not visited the garden when I walked through it one beautiful and warm July afternoon. It had always been a lonely place, yet filled with "potential." Now it seemed desolate and lifeless. I did not feel inclined to look around but walked straight on into the churchyard through the little gate in the wall. Here, too, it was silent, only graves—green graves, sunken graves, naked graves. Peasants are little interested in landscaping for the living, let alone for the dead! The east side of the cemetery is, however, quite beautiful and well-kept, as the more genteel families of the district have chosen it for their resting places. I found the graves I was seeking and I left them deeply moved and grateful that they had been preserved and decorated by loving, anonymous hands. I strolled on amidst the other graves, all old acquaintances from childhood; nearly each one is linked with memories and impressions that will never fade. But alas, everywhere, even here in death's immutable realm, time leaves its traces. Some of the familiar mounds had sunk down to fertile lawns; others had given way to new mounds, freshly adorned. Alas, did I say? No, the Lord be praised! Precisely here in death's silent domain, time should triumphantly and most joyously celebrate its transformation!

Yonder lies the young and lovely maiden who so delighted in dancing; she died of measles. By that bank I stood as a six-year-old, the youngest of those who strewed flowers. I still can visualize my little paper basket with chokecherry blossoms and yellow cowslips. The inscription on the wooden frame is no longer legible. Here rests Mathilde, dear, talented pupil, the widow's joy, buried already at sixteen, alas, with so many tears and flowers!

I still feel compelled to read the long, pompous inscriptions on the three iron tablets that cover the dust of the von Krogh family. Husband, wife, daughter buried here 1800, 1801, 1802. The last-mentioned died first, in the flower of her youth and beauty, of heartbreak, it is commonly said. She loved a man from the bourgeoisie, but that era's strict class prejudice did not permit her to marry this loved one. On her death bed, happiness was at last promised her. How often I have stood here and spelled out the long description of her virtues; between each of the cold, stiff lines, the secret sorrow which consumed her shines through in invisible runes! It was always with a strange, holy awe that I approached this grave. I never dared to tread on it, whereas I tramped quickly away across the other iron tablets.

Night had already begun to fall, as I walked back through the dreary, naked part of the churchyard where the common folk lie buried. An oddly shaped wooden cross caught my eye. In the middle was a little door, which appeared to open a cabinet and which bore the tantalizing inscription:

Open the door
See what it doth say
Close it again
As you go your way

Naturally, I did as I was bidden. Inside it said: *Sara Sandmark,* born 1760, died 1836. Sara Sandmark! Sara Wooden-Nose! Storyteller Sara! So here you rest, old Sara! Memory had grabbed hold of my skirt hem and would not release me; overcome, I sank down in the grass and surrendered to the new scenes and images this name awakened in me. Sara was the mother of our nursemaid, our splendid, un-equalled Lisbeth Marie. Now and then she visited her daughter, or we children and Lisbeth paid a visit to her up on the mountain on the other side of the river. She was always the object of fear-tinged curiosity. Her wooden nose aroused neither our scorn nor our laughter; on the contrary, we viewed her with the deepest respect. How clearly I remember one episode:

My younger brother and I had begged permission to go to Sara's on an errand. It was a lovely summer day and when we had finished the errand, we walked farther on into the forest to pick blueberries. But before long we returned, sobbing, to tell Sara of our plight. My brother's new cap had landed in the middle of the bog and attempts to reach it had ruined both my shoes. The instigator of the deed, our black poodle Murat, had done no more damage to the cap than to drag it out there. For quite some time Murat had been an outlaw. After a series of minor crimes—of which I will only mention a fatal attack on the Captain's duck, which resulted in tension between the two families—he had just the previous day committed a new offense, which truly damned him. I cannot help telling this little tragicomic incident, while at the same time appealing to everyone's own child-hood memories, for they can indeed take on considerable im-portance.

Mother was the embodiment of friendliness and courtesy and she sought to adapt to the prevailing standards of rural hospitality and resign herself to its many vicissitudes. Whether she succumbed to an attack of human frailty or that day had an urgent task to perform is beside the point; when the old, stupid and quite difficult Lieutenant called, she pretended not to be at home and locked herself in the side parlor with her sewing. While the Lieutenant entertained his captives in the parlor, Mother had to watch from her prison window with the imperturbability of a martyr while Murat tore to ribbons the three pairs of snow-white curtains that had been spread upon the meadow to dry. He soon finished the job, leaving behind only a pile of rags. During the ensuing trial, we children of course defended him with all conceivable eloquence. We argued that the Lieutenant's presence and Mother's own passivity, which almost could be taken for acquiescence, ought to be regarded as extenuating circumstances. Our logic proved useless. The case, pleaded in front of the household's additional courts – Father, Tutor and Housekeeper – lost in them all, and Murat was sentenced to death. And this is how he had rewarded us!

Old Sara heard our lament, at once put aside her spinning wheel, and went to the rescue. Just then a barking Murat appeared and, feeling greatly consoled by Sara's intervention, we frivolously began the familiar game of tossing sticks for him. A stick flew over the picket fence and landed in Sara's garden. Murat followed, kicked about after it; alas, that was not all, our cries and incitements were to no avail – he did not stop as long as there was a bush or plant on which to practice his wild destructive urge. The bed of peas ringed with sage and the flower bed, as big as a *flatbrødleiv* with poppies, marigolds and southernwood, . . . reduced to a dirty heap of grass. My little brother scurried away as fast as he could, terror-stricken. I stood as if nailed to the spot and tremblingly awaited Sara's return. As far away as the gate she could survey the destruction; but what I had expected, the crude outburst of complaint, shock and scolding typical of an old woman did not occur. Calmly, almost majestically, she strode down the path, bringing with her, as if to make my humiliation complete, not only the lost cap but also some fresh, plump cloudberries, which she handed me without a word. Then she walked over to the fence, viewed the damage silently for a moment, and finally burst out in the words of the porter in the Arabian Nights: "Oh, woe is me! Oh, woe is me! My two hundred pieces of gold! Oh, woe is me!" The heart-

---

flatbrødleiv: a round piece of unleavened bread; it can be as big as 2½ feet in diameter.

piercing pathos of this outburst I did not fully understand, but her calmness made a deep impression upon me.

You perhaps doubt that Sara knew the Arabian tales? Oh, yes, she knew them and many others besides – Norwegian, Spanish and French—though she seldom told them herself. She had deposited the entire treasure in her daughter Lisbeth Marie. Here could be observed a phenomenon that marks the lives of most great masters. Mother Nature needs several generations in order to prepare and produce perfection—genius—and once produced, it is also exhausted; genius does not reproduce its equal. Lisbeth stood in relation to Sara as Raphael to his father or as Bertel Thorvaldsen to the old woodcarver Gotskalk. To her mother's remarkable memory and clean, correct, I would almost say Classical delivery, Lisbeth added a creative aptitude, more imagination, and a certain Romantic intensity. I need not offer more striking evidence for Lisbeth's great talent than to say that for ten whole years she had the job of nourishing a flock of children who were as greedy and insatiable with regard to stories as swallow fledglings are to worms. She performed this task so cleverly that we always believed we were hearing something new, even when she told an old tale. A good number of *Asbjørnsen's* legends stem from our nursemaid. He even allows her to appear in some of them, if I am not mistaken, under the name of Anne Marie. During my trip to Eidsvoll in 1858 I was deeply saddened to learn that she had died. This kind, devoted soul had finally passed from this land of sorrow and toil; for her it had particularly been a land of sorrow, trouble and toil, ever since the day she left our home to marry.

Mechanically, I closed the little door on the grave marker and soon daily life with its manifold impressions had crowded out thoughts of Sara Wooden-Nose and her daughter.

One nice sunny day some time later, I went riding on the other side of the Vorma River up toward the gold mine, which lies at about the same height as the ridge that, in a straight line from north to south, parallel with the river, separates Eidsvoll from the district of Northern Odal. Up there the well-trod forest path swings in broad, even curves and in certain moods this monotony is extremely comforting. Nothing can be more conducive to lonely meditation than a horseback ride or hike on monotonous, closed paths; the spirit is refreshed by the motion and the soul unconsciously absorbs the

---

Asbjørnsen: contemporary of Camilla Collett who collected and published several volumes of Norwegian folktales and legends.

quiet beauty all around. If you really wish to nurture your thoughts and let them flourish, you will avoid panoramic views and choose instead to wander up and down a tree-lined avenue.

My goal, a ten-kilometer ride into the forest, was reached almost before I knew it; the spot known as the gold mine simply happened to be there. No gold mine actually exists, nor do I believe there ever did exist one except in the dreams of the visionary Bernt Anker. At any rate there is now only the name and a cluster of miserable huts. I was already halfway home again and feeling somewhat despondent when I saw the town come into view and realized that my little excursion soon would be over. My mind was now alert to the surroundings; the weather was lovely. Why that little cloud topping the mountain ridge was nothing more than a fair-weather cloud! Graycoat, my fair hunting horse—on every large farm there should be such a horse—did not stumble too often, even though he was not used to mountain terrain. I therefore decided to extend my ride. By following a side road to the left, I would arrive at the main road, about five kilometers to the south, and could follow it back to the ferry landing on the river, thus completing a semi-circular route.

But I had not gone far before I had reason to regret this plan. The road, which initially gave a good impression, deteriorated more and more until it looked like a cattle trail or a logging road that only gets used in winter. In many places it was steep and almost impassable and it was, unfortunately, all too obvious that this was not the right road. Nevertheless, I stubbornly followed it in the hope that it would somewhere lead me down to the river. Keeping myself in the saddle and protecting myself from the trees gave me enough to do, so I let my horse have free rein and trusted in his instinct. Threats also appeared from above. The little "fair-weather cloud" proved itself an advance force, a spy if you will, for a serious shower that was gathering over the forest. Facing the unenviable prospect of losing my way in the forest during a storm, I continued to urge the horse forward, or to be more precise, accepted his lead. How long this went on, I really cannot say. Perhaps it was not as long as it seemed, for in circumstances like these, when the psyche is under a certain stress, one loses perspective on time and place. At last, it began to lighten. The path opened up upon a clearing where trees had been cut; part of the wood was already stacked in enormous piles, other trees lay felled and stripped, a desolate forest battlefield. No person was to be seen. A woodpecker made a low sweep and let loose a penetrating cry, warning of rain. Over the mounds and tree-tops, across the roots and trunks, through the heather and brush, I finally managed to gain the fringe of trees on the other side. Here the path—just wide enough for a horse's hoof—twisted steeply down to a large bog. There we stood, Graycoat and I, with no sign of a path beyond!

With that our distress also ended. On the other side of the bog I heard an axe; and before I had attempted to maneuver around toward it, an old gray-bearded man with an axe on his shoulder came walking toward me. With few words and no obvious astonishment at meeting such an apparition on horseback in the middle of the marsh, he took hold of my steed's bridle and led it a fair distance back along the path. He was, as mentioned, an old man of few words. In his peculiar laconic way he relayed instructions to me. Without any pictorial or misleading expansiveness, these reduced themselves to the two landmarks I was to follow: "the big birch" and "the timber gate." These were naturally etched on my memory. It was impossible to forget them. "If you make the gate, then you are saved," he called after me for the tenth and last time. He was barely out of sight when the shower broke. The large spruce trees began to rustle and the tiny forest streams grew so animated and vocal that one would have thought a waterfall lay nearby. But in my joy at having regained the road I now paid little heed to the rain, especially since I felt it fall upon me, weary and warm as I was, like a refreshing bath.

Glorious was the evening! The rain had ended and the forest vegetation exuded its most powerful aromas after the shower. Two song thrushes, one quite close, the other more distant, warbled with such melancholy power that their notes reverberated through the entire forest and echoed from the nearby ridges. The other birds grew silent at this powerful song; only the crows paid no attention, cawing they rose up from the wet branches as though anticipating the rich booty of insects and worms seduced forth by the rain.

The sun came out just as I reached the gate at the outskirts of the forest. Below, the countryside with its mighty river lay reposing in the sudden light. The rain clouds were headed off to the north and had just formed a broad, slanting, whitish-gray stripe over Lake Mjøsa. The most beautiful rainbow I have ever seen planted one foot in the Vorma River and buried the other in the distant, unfamiliar forests that stretch toward the east. Inside this magnificent arch, the marvelous, pointed mountain peak Ninabbe ranged above the wooded hills, lit by the brilliant evening sun against a backdrop of murky sky. It was a lovely sight. I hopped off my horse and while it grazed, I stood entranced, leaning on the gate. This gate! The steep, burned-off clearing below! Between the black, charred stumps I saw, you could not really call it rye, but rye grass, perhaps two spikes for every stone that had been cleared away. And on the right there was a spruce root where the blueberry bushes grew green and fertile. I should know this spot. Yes, of course . . . Sara, old Sara, once again I meet your shadow. The roof down there in the birch grove beneath the clearing, that is the roof of her cottage. Through this gate she came, the day Murat destroyed her garden; down there I stood with my fear and bad conscience. I had often seen Sara before, but at the moment she strode down the path, her personage etched itself permanently in my memory.

She was old, yet still tall and erect. Her clothing did not distinguish itself from the typical garments of cotter women except in its extreme cleanliness. She wore an expression of shrewdness and resigned patience, which strangely enough suited her wooden nose so well that it never seemed especially conspicuous. Only when she told a story did her composure give way to such liveliness that this immobile part of her face, cold and passive as it was, produced a most curious effect. Whether this nose was Greek or Roman, Circassian or Mongolian, was not an easy matter to determine; old Ola Tømte, who modeled it, probably did not concern himself much with the question. In her speech Sara displayed the maxim-rich, laconic-reflective, often brilliant style that one sometimes finds in peasant women when they have aged from great sorrow and harsh distress. The almost poetic way in which she expressed herself was heightened by a diction as delicate and cultivated as could be desired; she even referred to us children by the formal pronoun "De." I want now to tell her story, just as I have often heard it.

She was the daughter of a *klokker* in Eidsvoll; her father had studied at the university, without, however, obtaining the clerical robe he sought. While quite young, Sara took a post in Copenhagen. There the pretty, lively Norwegian girl won general favor. She received several proposals and eventually became engaged to a fine young man who had a good post as a wallpaper maker. Happy and content, she returned to Norway to bid farewell to her old home before exchanging it for her new one. During this visit, she was without question the most decorous young woman in the district. It is said that her bearing was as refined as that of the Judge's daughters, but her friendliness and courtesy toward all resulted in no one taking offense. I have not heard her beauty mentioned; judging from certain signs it must have been of a nobler sort, too seldom observed to be popular.

The date of her departure had been set when she was invited to a

---

klokker: a lay person whose job it was to assist the pastor during the worship service and other church ceremonies.

wedding at the neighboring farm. Since she was to leave the next day, Sara wished to return home at an early hour; the Lieutenant, who had glorified the wedding with his presence, still was asking for a *polsdans*. He begged and she finally consented. In front of them Hans Østgaarden was dancing; he had sworn he would touch the ceiling hook with his foot . . . A wild cry and a violent throw of the body shows that he is serious; an iron-shod heel glitters against the rafters . . . Dust, confusion . . . When the Lieutenant turns to grasp his lady, she lies unconscious on the floor. She is carried away; the dance continues as though nothing had happened. What had happened for that matter? Poor Sara! A future was ruined—a future, a lover, a nose.

When Sara regained her strength after a long and painful illness, she was maimed for the rest of her life. A letter arrived from her beloved; it was full of concern about her silence and contained the most tender assurances of his steadfast fidelity. She informed him of her misfortune, released him from his vow and asked for her ring back. Her lover had boldly challenged fate but had not dreamed that it would take him so literally. It was an awful test—too difficult for any man, and a wallpaper maker is no more than a man. He sent her ring back. Don't you suppose Sara smiled bitterly then? For a secret hope that he would not accept her sacrifice was perhaps hidden in her heart. A number of years passed in her joyless home. During this time she suffered greatly and pondered the life she had in store. Then the old widower from the cottage down there proposed to her. He owned not a handful of land, but many hungry children, and Sara moved in with him. He made mats from heather and she raised his children kindly but strictly, so they acquired decent habits and a fear of God. Oh, impoverished people like that are honorable creatures who deserve more admiration than the virtuous well-fed products of wealth. Sara's husband recognized her worth. He did not drink; he never beat her; indeed, his loving care extended beyond these negative demonstrations. It was old Ola who skillfully designed the wooden noses from which her nickname derived. He made two— one for everyday and one for Sunday. The first was simply painted; the other was polished and more carefully carved. As long as old Ola lived, he always took care of this object. After his death, Sara had to limit herself like so many widows; she then could not afford the luxury of two noses and had to do away with the fancy one.

This was Sara Sandmark's external life. Your life, poor Sara, was true to your name—a sandy field, a barren Sahara, where every

---

polsdans: a folk dance in which the couples whirl around in ¾ time.

footstep was marked by sweat and tears! Only in your fertile memories and precious imagination, which thrived as innumerable legends and folktales from your lips, did you create oases and trickling streams. Who has a true sense of life in a cottage up on a naked mountain? It was always a mystery how she could survive with her family and not go begging. It is the secret of noble paupers that cannot be grasped. Even if someone does reveal to us the pitiful mystery, can we comprehend what it is like to eat gruel for breakfast, gruel for lunch and gruel for supper? The only variation that might occur is having no gruel to eat at all. Sara's daughter has told us that on such evenings, when they had nothing to eat, their mother told them fairy tales and they forgot their hunger amid the enchanted castles and marvels of the "Thousand and One Nights." Oh, this daughter must often have gone hungry, for she knew a great many tales.

The sun hovered on the ridge, when I arrived down at Sara's former cottage. The large birch tree, beneath which I many times had seen her sit and work, had been chopped down and the garden transformed into a potato field. Two or three sooty, fair-haired boys, clad only in shirts, stood by the door staring out at me from beneath their shielding hands as I hurried past.

Original title: *Eventyrsara og hendes Datter.* Translated by Janet E. Rasmussen

Amalie Skram

(1846-1905)

When *Constance Ring* was published in 1885 it was received with shock and outrage in Kristiania (former name of Oslo, until 1924). Never before had a woman written so frankly about marriage and sexuality in a Norwegian book. Amalie Skram's major contribution to feminist literature centers around *Constance Ring* and three subsequent "marriage" novels: *Lucie* (1888), *Fru Ines* (1891) and *Forrådt* (1892). The protagonists in these novels, having been inadequately prepared for the realities of married life—the double standard, isolation and inactivity, subservience—become victims of unhappy marriages. Crisis leads to the recognition that a wife's complete economic dependence on her husband reduces her to a sexual object, and that as long as she stays in such a marriage, she forfeits her freedom. However, unable to cope with disappointment and disillusionment, the Skram heroine does not free herself, but ultimately suffers psychological breakdown.

Amalie Skram has written a number of short stories, but her greatest achievement is in the longer format of the novel—it is generally agreed that her finest work is the four-volume *Hellemyrsfolket*, the story of a family through several generations. The two chapters here are taken from the beginning of *Constance Ring*: Constance has been married to Ring, a man sixteen years her senior, for two years; these have not been happy years for Constance, and in the hopes it will improve his wife's humor, Ring has invited her mother for a visit.

Constance Ring

A telegram arrived from Ring's father-in-law, Judge Blom, announcing that Constance's mother would arrive on the next steamship.

Constance counted the days, busying herself enthusiastically with redecorating the guest room, putting the house in perfect order so that her mother would be pleased with her housekeeping.

Ring had never seen his wife so lively and energetic. She actually looked happy bustling around the house.

The two of them went on board to welcome Mrs. Blom. All day Constance had been distracted and silent, darting repeatedly into the guest room with some trinket for the dressing table, making first one change and then another in her arrangements.

When suddenly she saw her mother on the deck, she burst into tears and clung to her.

Ring looked annoyed and muttered that a steamship was hardly the place for Constance to make a spectacle of herself.

Mrs. Blom quieted her with gentle words and affectionate caresses, and as the carriage moved toward home, directed casual questions to Ring about the name of a street or about a new church that they were passing.

There were more than enough things to ask him about; she had not been in Kristiania for sixteen years.

When she thought Constance had recovered her composure, she began to talk about home—small things, for the most part—the doves and chickens; the beloved old horse that soon would have to be shot; the dining room they were painting; the old curtains she and Constance used to mend every spring and that now, finally, were going to be thrown away. And there were all the people who had sent their greetings; her father and sisters, the boys and the coachman, the old servant Ane, friends and cousins and lots of others.

But this chatter about things at home wrenched Constance's heart. As the memories came crowding irresistably back, she struggled against tears.

"You certainly look happy—fine way to show your appreciation," Ring said suddenly, clicking his tongue in displeasure.

"Why, Constance," Mrs. Blom reproached mildly when she saw the tears sliding down her daughter's cheeks. "What is the matter, child?"

"I can't help it, Mother," came the choked, imploring voice. She pressed a handkerchief to her eyes.

"Well, this certainly is uplifting for a man," Ring said, shifting his body angrily as if looking for a more comfortable position, then resuming exactly the same posture as before.

When the carriage arrived at their door shortly thereafter, they were all relieved that the ride was over.

Upstairs, Ring conducted his mother-in-law through the rooms. He wanted to show her the whole apartment right away. He pointed out which things were gifts and which were not, confided what the paintings were worth and what he had paid for them, opened the door of the buffet so that she could see the silver and fine crystal, pulled her into the bedroom so that she could admire the fabric of the bed curtains. He pulled out his violin and played her a few bars, then seized by a sudden desire to show her the linen closet, dashed into the kitchen to get the key from Constance, who was preparing a salad. At last it occurred to him that Mrs. Blom might be tired and want to sit down. In an instant he had settled her in an armchair and was piling albums and illustrated books on the table in front of her, all the while talking in disconnected fragments about anything that popped into his mind. It all made Mrs. Blom's head swim.

At supper Ring was unusually loquacious. He described their homecoming on their wedding evening, when the living room glittered with the vast array of presents. Then he told little stories about the first days of their marriage, laughing uproariously at his own witty delivery. To celebrate his mother-in-law's arrival, he drank three shots of Aquavit with the cold dishes and a couple of glasses of sherry with the home-made apple cake.

Constance was silent and looked as if she were bored. He never seemed more disagreeable to her than when he was trying to be charming. Moreover, on occasions like these he had usually been drinking, and this was glaringly obvious, at least to Constance. She was thoroughly ashamed of him. Everything he said was distorted. To give a story a more impressive ring, he added things that were completely false. She, too, exaggerated sometimes, when she felt like it, but she didn't try to pass it off as something other than it was; whereas he would get furious and stubborn if she protested and accuse her of being quarrelsome. Tonight, for example. Unable to stand it any longer, she objected to something he said about the time they fired their first maid for stealing. He expressed his annoyance and Constance answered him back. Mrs. Blom put in a soothing word on Ring's behalf. Constance was taking him too literally—there was no point in quibbling about words. If someone was having a good time, he couldn't be expected to weigh every word so carefully—he wasn't under oath, after all. Constance answered her mother sharply. Why was she getting involved with something she didn't know anything about? Regretting her words immediately, Constance held her tongue. Ring had the last word. He muttered something about how hard it was for a man when his wife was always criticizing, no matter what he said or did. He shook his head and sighed deeply, with the look of someone accustomed to being misunderstood and determined to bear it patiently.

"You shouldn't contradict your husband so often, Constance," said Mrs. Blom. They had risen from the table and Ring had gone into the next room to smoke his pipe.

"Nonsense!" Constance said with a toss of her head.

"No, I'm serious. It isn't proper."

"Then I should just let him go on telling lies like that?"

"Lies. What an odd word."

"Yes, exactly. Lies. It's infuriating to have to listen to them."

"Come now, behave yourself. You simply must not treat your husband with such disrespect."

"You shouldn't humor him, Mother. He can take care of himself, believe me, and if he sees that you're on his side, it will be impossible to be in the same room with him."

"'On his side,' 'humor him'—those aren't terms that belong in a proper marriage."

Constance stood drumming on the table with her fingertips, her nose in the air, the corners of her mouth pulled down in a frown.

"You certainly haven't had that kind of example at home. Your father and I have never been on a footing like that."

"No, of course not—I know that," she said, her face and voice protesting the absurdity of the comparison. "Can you imagine father drinking and jabbering away in a slurred voice—making himself completely disagreeable?"

"So Ring has a drink or two with his dinner—it's nothing to make a fuss about."

"Nonsense, he drinks brandy after dinner, too!"

"Well, all right, if he doesn't overdo it. But going around with a sour expression on your face is the surest way to drive a husband to it."

The maid came in to clear the table and the two women went into the living room where Ring was smoking, a large glass of brandy and soda in front of him. He offered to bring them some cold punch, but they declined.

Ring had regained his good spirits. He went on blustering and gesticulating without a moment's pause, and Mrs. Blom, the perfect audience, nodded agreement and laughed in the right places.

"Don't sit there like a sourpuss, Constance," he burst out in an excited tone. "Put that trashy newspaper down and come over here and be nice to me." He pulled her up from her chair and tried to draw her to him.

She resisted.

"Now sit down, Constance," admonished Mrs. Blom.

She went reluctantly, and Ring settled her on his knee. He began to caress her and call her pet names. She wanted to sink through the floor. It was mortifying that her mother could watch this, that she could actually approve of it. The reek of tobacco and brandy sickened her; his lips and beard felt moist and disgusting against her burning, dry face.

"Let me go! You're choking me," she cried suddenly, wrenching herself free. She dashed out of the room, wiping her face with a handkerchief.

"Well, now you can see what living with her is like," Ring said, getting to his feet in irritation. "I try as hard as I can to be nice and she's always like that." He paced restlessly back and forth across the room.

"She's just tired and nervous tonight," Mrs. Blom soothed.

"She's exactly the way she always is." He sat down again in a determined manner. "I have to beg for the slightest crumb of affection—she acts as if she's doing me a favor."

"That doesn't sound like Constance," answered Mrs. Blom, appearing to give the situation some thought.

"It's just some whim, of course. Some damned nonsense from those novels of hers—pardon me." He had hiccupped inadvertently.

"Do you really think so?" Mrs. Blom asked skeptically.

"Yes, of course I do! It's the only explanation possible. What else could it be, for God's sake?"

Mrs. Blom heaved a sigh and looked at her fingernails.

"If only I weren't so confounded crazy about her. If I could be cold and indifferent, she'd come around soon enough."

"Oh, Ring, don't do that. Constance will have to be won with love."

"L-love!" Ring said, leaning suddenly toward his mother-in-law. "I don't see how any man could be more loving."

"You have to be sensible about this, Ring. Most young wives are a little unsettled for the first couple of years."

"No, confound ,it, they act like they're in love—Marie, for instance—now there's a wife for you—but Constance is so strange. I swear to you..." He bent closer and spoke in a lower tone.

"Constance is still so young—I'm sure everything will straighten out," Mrs. Blom said confidently.

"Well, in any case, she'll have to change if she's going to make me happy. I have high hopes for your visit—you've got to talk to her."

Constance entered the room and said if her mother was tired, her bedroom was ready for her. Mrs. Blom rose immediately and said goodnight. Her daughter went with her and lit the lamps, puttering aimlessly around the room while Mrs. Blom prepared for bed.

When her mother was tucked under the covers, Constance perched on the edge of the bed beside her.

"It's so wonderful to have you here in this bed—to know you'll be here every single night for weeks." She laughed happily and kissed her, blissfully content.

"I just wish you were really at peace, Constance...Tell me what's wrong."

"It's not something that can be forced, Mother. Your new night-caps are so pretty! Did you make them yourself?"

"Yes. You have a great deal to be happy about, Constance."

"But I'll bet anything Helene did the embroidery."

"Yes, yes, of course. That's right, isn't it, Constance—you do have a great deal to be happy about?"

"Oh, yes, I recognize Helene's stitching. Her work is so beautiful."

"Surely, you are happy with your husband. He's such a kind man!"

"Why do you suppose she chose that boring pattern—scallops are so much faster and prettier."

"Please stop talking about the pattern and listen to me."

She pressed her head against her mother.

"My sweet child, of course you love your husband—you do love him, don't you?"

"I don't know."

"What kind of talk is that? You don't know?"

She lifted her head and plucked at the ribbons of her mother's nightcap.

"I don't think I do," she said slowly.

"You frighten me, child. When you accepted his proposal, wasn't it out of love?"

"God knows. Oh yes, I suppose it was, in a way—I have thought about it, believe me, but, but..." she broke off and looked embarrassed.

"But..." repeated her mother, "go on...but what?"

"I don't like being married."

"What kind of foolish talk is that?" Mrs. Blom asked indignantly.

"Is it so foolish? Can't you understand at all? Isn't it often that way?"

"Well, if a husband is immoral, or cruel..."

"And nothing else counts?"

"Nothing else *should* count."

"Does affection for a man always have to depend on how good or bad he is?"

"Really, Constance. There is no place in a marriage for talk like that. A wife has no right to think that way."

"I don't see why not."

"It's ridiculous, or childish at the very least, and it can destroy a marriage. Don't be a child, Constance, for God's sake."

"All right, we won't talk about it then. Listen to me, Mother—now you musn't say no—I'd like so much to sleep in here with you."

And she slid her hands under her mother's neck and lifted her head toward her.

"With me? Have you taken leave of your senses, child?"

"I'll make myself very small—don't you remember when we used to have company in the country and I would sleep with you," she coaxed.

"Well, in those days, yes—you were just a little girl."

"Oh, well, I've grown a few inches—that doesn't make any difference…and then I can imagine I'm home again and that it's summer vacation and we can talk as much as we want. I'll run and get my nightgown."

She was already at the door.

"It's out of the question, Constance. What would your husband say?" Mrs. Blom sat up in bed looking genuinely alarmed.

"He ought to allow me that much—if he's such a *kind* man."

"Come here, Constance," her mother said sternly. When her daughter was again sitting on the edge of the bed, Mrs. Blom spoke to her in an earnest, admonitory tone. She should not be moody or cold toward her husband. It was her duty to love him and to make him happy. She should think about how lucky she was—the daughter of a poor civil servant and settled now so well in the world—that was really not something to look down upon; such a fine, kind husband, with such a sense of the comforts of home. She should take care that he didn't get tired of her. There was always the risk that he would look for love somewhere else—that was just the way men were. Her words were mild and gentle and as she spoke she stroked the hand clasped in hers. If this was something she could not overcome by herself, she should turn to God and ask His help. She should begin by giving thanks for all His grace and goodness. If she would just turn to the Lord, everything would be blessed and good—and she would be her own dear Constance again, just as she had always been.

It was exactly what her aunt was always saying. Was her mother really going to give her the same depressing speech about how lucky she was—the same insistence that she spend her life on bended knees. They wanted to force her to be glad—to feel happiness. But what did she have to be happy about? She couldn't see it. True, she had plenty to eat and drink, but these were things she had always had. How could she help the emptiness she felt inside—this ever-growing intolerance for her husband. If they would only leave her alone. She never complained or reproached anybody. If it really was so contemptible for her to feel the way she did, surely it was not her fault—she couldn't make herself into a different person. Sitting there on the edge of the bed listening to her mother's long speech, she felt bitter disappointment and a painful sense of abandonment. She had expected so much from her mother's visit. She had drifted along with the vague idea that when her mother came everything would be all right. But now they could not understand each other at all. Her mother had suddenly become a stranger to her, in league with her accusors. A gap had opened between them—a huge room filled with things that her mother walked past without seeing or even knowing existed. She suddenly felt self-conscious with her. If only they could avoid conversations like this. She would be sweet and affectionate to Ring. Then there would be no chance of it. And she would be sure to look happy all right. It would just take a bit of pretending, that was all.

"Isn't that right, Constance, my dear—you will be a good, sensible girl?" asked Mrs. Blom at last, after waiting a few moments for her daughter to reply.

"Yes, I will! I'll be very sensible—you'll see. Good night, Mother." She kissed her and got up and left the room.

The day of Mrs. Blom's departure arrived at last. As Constance was helping her pack, she realized with a feeling of desolation that now she was going to be alone with Ring again.

Her mother's presence had filled a void—not her inner emptiness, but still, they had enjoyed themselves together, and the constant activity had been a distraction. She had been a daily stimulant for Constance. There were times when the superficial character their relationship had assumed pained her a little; it was depressing to think that without this constant activity they would not find anything to say to each other. Occasionally at such moments her mother's presence had seemed a burden, and Constance almost wished she were gone.

But now that the time had come, she realized with horror how lonely she was going to be. She knew perfectly well that her mother had to leave, but she sobbed while they were saying good-bye and pleaded with her to stay just one more day.

She had seen her to the ship and now, sitting at her old spot in the bedroom, gazed out over the fjord in the direction her mother had gone.

She felt so bereft, so bitterly alone.

Her mother was travelling toward home, where life had been so safe and happy, where just being alive had seemed sufficient in itself, and nothing in the world had been dull or difficult.

It was this fatal marriage that had put her at odds with herself and everything else. Why in the world had she gotten married! What for? And to Ring of all people, an unappealing man with whom she could never be in harmony.

She left the window and paced up and down the floor, moaning softly.

Was her life always going to be like this . . . until she was old, old, old . . . never free to be herself again . . . what if he died . . . oh, but he wasn't going to . . . there was nothing wrong with him . . . an accident perhaps, in the sailboat . . . oh, how could she think such a thing . . . where was her shame!

Worn out by pacing, she sat down on a settee and leaned back against the wall, her arms crossed on her breast. The moon was full, and the room was so light that every object could be seen distinctly.

If only her mother would come in through the door, just one time more; she would throw her arms around her neck and cry, cry until the frozen crust around her heart melted away. She would tell her she wasn't happy, that she never could be—no matter how much they tortured her—that she didn't feel, would never feel, that it was her duty and her calling to make this fat, self-satisfied man happy, this man who never asked about her feelings, who treated her like she didn't have a soul in her body—something to be cranked like a hurdy-gurdy.

Someone came into the hallway; it was Ring, she could tell by his footsteps. Now he would come in and pet her, and if she pulled away, get angry and shake his head as if she were a delinquent child. She could hear him walking through the rooms. Now he was in the dining room; now he was calling her—she couldn't stand his voice.

She jerked herself to her feet and took a few steps; it looked as if her legs were fastened to the floor.

Suddenly, just as he was opening the door to look for her, she darted into the corner between the wardrobe and the wall. He retraced his steps and called Alette to ask her if the mistress had gone out. Mechanically, Constance slipped from her hiding place.

"Where the deuce have you been?" Ring asked in an injured tone. "I've been looking all over the house for you."

Without bothering to reply, she placed a shade over the lamp.

"Why don't you answer me?"

"Do you really want me to give an account of myself to you?"

"Good God, Constance, are you going to be difficult again?"

"What a small vocabulary you have; everything is always 'difficult!' "

"It will serve me very well if you're going to start acting like this again."

She started leafing indifferently through a book.

"When it comes to being unpleasant, nobody can touch you," he said in exasperation. "But let Fallesen or anybody else from that crowd of yours come in, you put on a different face then."

"It's your crowd, not mine—I thought they were friends of yours."

"Like hell...they're friends who come to flirt and play up to you. And you certainly make yourself available—with a vengeance."

"You're so vulgar...I won't respond to that."

"Oh yes, certainly—I'm inarticulate, and vulgar and stupid—just say it."

"You may well be right," she said coldly.

"But I am your husband, just the same, and you would do well to remember that I won't tolerate impertinence." He stood there glowering at her.

Her contemptuous eyes slid down over his face and chest; she glanced toward the open book as she turned away.

"Do you hear me?" he asked, gripping her firmly by the chin and forcing her to look at him.

"How could I help it! I'm not deaf, as you know perfectly well. Let go of me," she said furiously, her eyes flashing as she tried to stand up.

"Sit still—I'll teach you." He took both of her wrists and squeezed them until they ached.

"Your fingers are stronger than your arguments," she said disdainfully, without making the slightest resistance.

He slung her hands away violently and began to pace the floor, hands jammed in his pockets, his face flaming.

"Ha!" he said, after pacing a few moments, "What a woman! She could wring tears from a stone." He shot a glance at her as he spoke, as if expecting some response, but she made no reply.

"And that act you put on while your mother was here—she ought to see you now. But I knew how it was going to be when she left."

Ah yes, her mother was gone, and she was left behind with this disgusting, hateful man. What a boor he was!

Her cheeks grew pink and tears rolled down them.

Ring noticed that she was crying.

She's sorry, he thought, continuing to pace back and forth. Satisfied with this fortunate turn of events, he waved his arms and went on talking.

"An angel would lose patience—all my work and my dreams are devoted to her happiness, but it's water off a duck's back."

She had not wanted him to see her tears. Unable to prevent it, she hurriedly wiped her face with her handkerchief.

Ring seated himself in front of her. "If it were up to me, Constance," he said in a conciliatory tone, "there would never be a cross word between us. You could spare yourself these tears."

"I'm not crying," she said obstinately.

"Of course you are, and it hurts me to see it. Now tell me you're sorry and we'll forget all about it."

"Me!" She looked at him incredulously.

He leaned towards her.

"Listen, Constance, let's be friends. Be a good girl and give me a kiss."

She jumped up as if she had been stung and shook herself free.

"Go away!" she cried, "I can't stand you," and she dashed out of the room.

Ring was thunderstruck. He remained paralyzed for a few seconds, staring at the door.

"That bitch!" he growled. "By God, if she thinks she can sweet-talk herself out of this, she's got a few things to learn." He stalked out into the main hall and slammed the door violently behind him. A few minutes later he was striding down the street in the direction of Tivoli.

Original title: *Constance Ring.* Translated by Judith Messick

Dikken Zwilgmeyer

(1853-1913)

For generations, children in Norway have delighted in Dikken Zwilg-meyer's "Inger-Johanne" books. Supposedly penned *by* Inger-Johanne, an independent, spontaneous and mischievous girl of twelve or thirteen, these books were particularly inspiring to female readers for whom Inger-Johanne became a wonderful role model, an antidote to the proper and passive young women they otherwise met in literature.

Prior to the publication of this series, Dikken Zwilgmeyer wrote a number of short stories and novels for adults, including the present story (first published in 1885, later included in the collection entitled *Ungt Sind,* 1978). Her candid depiction of the humiliation and oppression suffered by women, regardless of marital status, was not well received by critics however, and, disheartened by their lack of understanding, she focused her creative energies on books for young people. Toward the end of her career she did return to the feminist concerns of her early fiction, publishing three novels between 1906 and 1908. The women in these later works are not downtrodden; they possess confidence and self-respect, and succeed, to a degree at least, in shaping their own destinies.

An Everyday Story

It was now nearly twenty-two years since little Mrs. Bruvold had, as we say, secured her happiness and married *kirkesanger* Bruvold. She didn't marry out of love. She did it so that she would be provided for. She had, of course, always heard that one should not enter marriage before one had experienced, even ever so slightly, that transient feeling we call infatuation. And she had not been in love with *kirke-sanger* Bruvold. So she waited and thought about it for eight days to see if love wouldn't come after all. But it didn't come; instead, the voice of reason, in the guise of an old aunt, spoke louder and louder, and so she took him.

He got married because he was tired of housekeepers who would quit at moving time just as predictably as moving time came around.

---

kirkesanger: another name for *klokker,* see page 24

He wanted to have one who couldn't quit and so he got married. Furthermore, he was struck by the fact that the sweet little thing he had cast his eyes upon possessed that quality which he considered, above all else, a wife's duty: complete relinquishment of one's own will. And on this premise they had lived together for twenty-two years. She had been given nine children, shelter, food and drink and hadn't quit, and he, well, actually he had assumed no obligations except to bring home the money that kept it all going. But that he had fulfilled this obligation and provided for the children he himself had put into the world impressed him as being the height of respectability and integrity. Not that he ever allowed these thoughts of self-esteem to reveal or even suggest themselves in the presence of the public. No, they lay well hidden in his heart under his large silver watch with the tombac case and his paramatta overcoat. But his wife knew them well enough; indeed she partook of them daily. He could never forgive her for bringing so many children into the world and with each child laying one more stone on the burden he had to haul up life's mountain. And it was also for this reason that he, with every kroner he gave to his timid little wife, seemed to spew forth oceans of honor and conscientiousness down upon her, as she stood there curtsying and thanking him. It never occurred to her that it should be any different. He was the husband, she only the wife. And men were, after all, of another ilk than women. The former shall command, the latter obey; thus has it been since the creation of the world. In silence shall woman suffer and struggle, the minister said so often—and there is something so beautiful in that thought, he added.

Little Mrs. Bruvold had suffered and struggled for twenty-two years now, silent to the world. She did, on occasion, wonder where all the beauty of which the minister spoke could be found. But she had not yet discovered it. She was probably not bright enough to see it.

Still, in more recent years somewhat vague and confused thoughts sometimes entered little Mrs. Bruvold's head, thoughts she seemingly breathed in with the air—she had no idea where they came from. But they were so liberating, she thought. They were thoughts about a woman's right and woman's great cause, which brightened her pitiful, repressed mind like a gleam of light. She didn't comprehend all of it; it came with messages from another, lighter world, where she didn't belong. If she found anything about this in a book or a newspaper, she would read it again and again. Humbug and drivel, from which nothing would ever come, Bruvold said.

Bruvold was a middle-aged, middle-sized man with a peculiarly flat head. His light, yellowish hair was combed down across his neck as smoothly as if it were a wall. There was, as a matter of fact, something unfinished about his entire face. It was as if nature had thrown it together in a hurry, intending to return later to finely chisel and polish it. But then the finishing touches were never added. His nose was thick and broad and his mouth was just like a crack; it served its purpose, but was ugly. Little Mrs. Bruvold was a tiny woman in her forties, small-boned and quite thin, with blond hair and a high, narrow forehead. Once you saw that forehead, you could look at nothing else and the face underneath was forgotten—it all seemed so strangely empty and bare and blank.

This then is what the Bruvolds were like. The little grey house, surrounded by a high wall in back and a marshy low-growing garden underneath, was their home. Across the street on the other side was the city's poorhouse; its long yellow-brown facade with those two rows of dull, narrow windows had been Mrs. Bruvold's outlook for all these years. There was something so hopelessly monotonous about those windows, never any change year out and year in, the same old faces behind the same old panes. The only change occurred when someone died; then white curtains were hung in his room until he was buried. Mrs. Bruvold liked to look at the white curtains. It gave her such a feeling of peace, she thought.

For peace and quiet was something about which Mrs. Bruvold knew nothing. She was always on the go. Ever since the first days of her marriage her dream had been to hire a woman to help her in the house. But that request was always rebuffed by Bruvold, who asked if she meant to ruin him. And that cut off any further discussion of the matter. And so little Mrs. Bruvold toiled and slaved, sewed, darned, knit, patched, cooked and washed her way through seven days each week. Five growing boys could give a poor, exhausted little mother more than enough to do. Almost every day there were trouser seats in need of reinforcement, holes made by elbows and knees in need of mending. Not to mention shoes and boots; those she could not repair and that was her greatest sorrow. Because there was nothing that infuriated Bruvold as much as the sight of a pair of worn-out shoes. There were times when he positively went berserk up in his office and called his wife and children bloodsuckers; they wouldn't give up, he claimed, till they had every drop of his blood. And then she would pick up the little worn-out shoes and descend the stairs from the office. She held the railing with her other hand, a yellow, bony little hand, and her wrist was so very thin—it shook ever so slightly on the well-worn railing.

Little Peder Even was waiting in his stocking feet at the foot of the stairs. She shook her head. "Peder Even, you must be more careful; Father was angry that your boots have holes again." And Peder Even solemnly promised to be careful, but in a few minutes his promise was forgotten. Little Mrs. Bruvold, however, rose at four o'clock the next morning so that she could sew and earn enough money to have Peder Even's boots resoled.

One thing pierced her heart every time she saw it happen, which was often: Bruvold's drinking so much port. What did it matter that it was the corner merchant's home-brew made from blueberry juice and alcohol? To her it was something very fine indeed. How many boots couldn't be resoled and how much help couldn't she hire with that money. But not a sound crossed her lips about this touchy point. He was, after all, the husband; she only the wife. No, it was simply a matter of covering up as best she could and keeping it from the children.

When she lay awake at night, unable to sleep because she was too tired, thoughts came to her. They never came during the day, because then she was too busy. She could lie and think about everything and about what had gone wrong. For she clearly understood that something was wrong somewhere.

Was it that they had so little money? Or was it that she wasn't close enough to the Lord? It seldom occurred to Mrs. Bruvold to think about love; she had met so little of it during her life that she finally began to doubt its very existence. But if there truly was a love that endured, not merely the days of one's youth, but a lifetime; survived a tight budget, children's screaming, toil and drudgery, even those hard, bitter words—then, thought little Mrs. Bruvold, it must be so great and so strong that it is a joy too magnificent for this world. The mere thought brought tears to her eyes.

But recently she had hit upon a brilliant plan and on this matter she would not yield. The plan was that her daughter, Maia, now seventeen, should learn so much that she could be employed and become an independent and self-supporting woman. She sought the advice of the minister's wife one day. "But Maia is such a pretty girl," was the response, "she can be married!" "God spare her from that," the little *klokker's* wife blurted out. The minister's wife looked at her, but said nothing. When Mrs. Bruvold was home again she regretted, for Bruvold's sake, having said that. After all, he was no worse than others and everyone had a cross to bear in this life.

Her most cherished thought was this hope for her daughter. And it therefore caused Mrs. Bruvold the most heartfelt anguish that Maia didn't appear to have any particular desire for the role in life her mother had chosen for her. A young student with a shock of wavy hair had lately been walking by their house suspiciously often. And he cast such longing glances toward the window where Maia usually sat. Maia smiled and hid herself behind the curtain, though never so much that she couldn't be seen. Mrs. Bruvold was beside herself. Whatever would come of this? What did he have to support a wife with? Not even as much as she and Bruvold had had. And she looked back on that long perspective of years, all those many, many burdensome, hopeless days and wakeful nights, a never-ending struggle. And should Maia start all that now? She is so frail and delicate, Mrs. Bruvold often thought, just like a tiny, pink English daisy.

Bruvold had always strictly insisted that his wife go to church. Otherwise people might wonder. She was always hard put to get ready on time. But after she had managed to get through her morning chores and the entire house and all the boys were in their Sunday best, it often felt good to sit in her place behind the broad back of her better half. She loved to sing the hymns, especially those hymns about peace and rest. She was strangely moved by the tranquility; it descended upon her so softly and quietly. And she liked to sit and look at the thin, rainbow-colored rays of dust that quivered in the sunlight across the church, while the minister's voice hovered above the bowed heads of the congregation. And then, as was known to happen, sleep stole in ever so quietly; a gentle hum was all she heard and everything began to sway so peacefully; her hat slipped down across her high forehead and little Mrs. Bruvold nodded and fell asleep. "Look at the *klokker's* wife," said the people down in the church, nudging each other. But they didn't consider her having been up since five o'clock, or all her boys and all her toil and drudgery.

Late in the fall Mrs. Bruvold's health began to fail. This wasn't something one could see from her outward appearance, for she had been so thin and shriveled for such a long time that she couldn't become any scrawnier. No, it was just that she had fainted a couple of times after climbing the steep kitchen stairs with a heavy load. She never spoke about it herself, but the children noticed that she often put her hand to her heart as if she were in pain. But that anything could be wrong with Mother, always ready to drop everything for any or all of them, was something so unheard-of as to be quite beyond belief. Bruvold noticed nothing; but recently he had often had to wait for the coffee, roll, and pipe that were brought to him in bed every morning. And that put a scowl on his face. What in the world was the matter with her? What else besides his comfort and well-being did she have to think about?

But little Mrs. Bruvold was tired and could go no farther. One evening she was standing ironing Bruvold's shirts. It had been a bad day—a notice demanding payment of tax arrears had arrived. Bruvold had snarled and snapped at her like an old tomcat when she went to his office with afternoon coffee. Down in the kitchen Maia sat crying with her head in her apron. She had been promised a new dress and now that money had gone to pay taxes. Outside it was dark and rainy and there were no curtains. Mrs. Bruvold stood right by the window, ironing and on the ironing board was a candle. She moved the candle and suddenly saw her image mirrored in the window and the darkness outside. She was so pale and her cheeks so hollow. She was overcome with a wild, uncontrollable desire to throw herself out into the darkness and hide herself, to run away, just get away from everything, from herself, from life. It wasn't until she smelled something burning that she came to—she had burned one of Bruvold's shirts right through the chest. She fainted again that same evening and the next day she didn't get up.

This took Bruvold by surprise; it seemed an encroachment on his own personal well-being. The whole house was upside down—no one knew where to find this or put that. But Mrs. Bruvold stayed in bed, that day and the next day as well. Most of the time she was alone in the bedchamber, but every now and then the boys came in to show her rips in their trousers or holes in their boots.

She had been in bed for two weeks now. Bruvold had been in to see her in the morning; he was rummaging around and carrying on about a candy dish which was missing and which he always used in church. Mrs. Bruvold had simply turned her head toward the wall and not answered. He looked at her in astonishment: it was the first time in their marriage she had demonstrated such apathy. He turned and walked out and slammed the door behind him. Later on that afternoon Maia rushed in. Her cheeks were warm and flushed. "Mother, Mother, Rørvig and I are engaged!" The student with the shock of wavy hair. Mrs. Bruvold's cheeks turned very white. And finally, "Maia, don't do it. You don't know what you're getting yourself into." Maia began to cry and said that it was horrid of her mother to say such a thing today, when she was so happy—for she was really very fond of him. With great effort Mrs. Bruvold raised herself up in the bed. "If you love him, then there may be a chance after all; but love is not only kisses and loving glances of one's youth, my child, there is so much, much more that follows." Maia wept a little and then left.

An hour later she came in again. The sun setting across the heath was so beautiful and a golden wave of sunlight illuminated the bedposts. Mrs. Bruvold was lying on her side with folded hands, staring directly into the sun. She was dead.

Eight days later she was buried. It was a fall day, wet and cold, water on the ground and a chill in the air. It had rained the past seven days, a constant, grey drizzle. But now it was beginning to clear up a little. Occasional gusts of wind from the sea promised a change in the weather. But the air had turned cold and old people predicted the imminent arrival of winter. The cemetery was situated on low and swampy ground. Between the rows of gravestones the ground was wet from all the rain—a moist, earthy, decaying odor permeated the atmosphere. The grass was brown and matted against the wet earth, with a yellowed blade sticking up stiffly here and there. On the smaller trees and bushes a few leaves still hung; they were grey-brown with black splotches and one heard a strange and mournful sighing when the wind whistled through them. The large maple trees, lined up in a row all the way from the entrance, were bare; high above the enormous branches creaked and groaned.

In the uppermost corner little Mrs. Bruvold's grave had been dug. Beside it the earth was heaped in a mound, black and moist and filled with small, wet stones. The funeral procession was coming up. There were only men, clothed in black and wearing top hats. The casket was small and on it were wreaths of bearberry and partially withered cowberry and artificial flowers. Interspersed were a couple of fresh wreaths, but this was no season for flowers.

The minister and Bruvold walked immediately behind the casket. The minister lifted his black gown as he walked over the grass. The top hats were removed and for a moment everyone stared into them, but a sigh of relief was heard when the hats went back on—the wind was cold and most of them either had thinning hair or were bald. And then the hymn, solemn and ponderous, floated out over the graves and the withering world. Just as the landscape was withered and bare, so too were the hearts withered and bare; devoid of all sorrow and reflection, the strains of the hymn sounded forth. Now and then the wind carried the melody high up into the bare, creaking branches, yet the music continued to labor and lag; the notes seemed unable to reach beyond the clump of people around the grave.

Then the minister stepped forward; he belonged to the good old school and his speech was filled with lots of flowers and beautiful words. Today he dwelt on the quiet housewife's happiness in the shelter of her husband's protecting love. He returned to this frequently: a life shared together in love. He had many lovely things to say about this; in fact, it was his most eloquent theme, which was why he had chosen to speak on it again today. But the wind was cold and he hadn't put on enough clothes under his gown. He could already feel pains in his chest and he thought to himself, "This is a fine how-do-you-do."

The funeral sermon for little Mrs. Bruvold was not long; it ended with a few flattering words about her husband, this noble, manly heart on which she had leaned during life's struggle. And he had no doubt that he could speak for the deceased and give thanks for all the warm, caring and protecting love her husband had strewn on her path. She was one of the quiet and weak ones among us, he concluded, and therefore needed it all the more. Bruvold had folded his black-gloved hands and was humbly gazing down at them. A calm confidence entered his soul and he was filled with good thoughts. Never before had he felt so pious. Later he was to look back on this as one of the best moments in his life—that half hour at his little wife's grave. He had loved her, indeed he had, and she had made a good home and been competent and able in her task. Of course most recently she hadn't amounted to much, but then the Lord had released her, and that was all for the best.

The procession walked homeward. They were glad it was over but, after all, they did owe the *klokker* that courtesy.

And once again the wind began its dance with all the withered leaves. They rustled, flew and leapt up the long boulevard like small, living creatures, but against the fence, in the lee of the wind, they gathered and lay still. During the night it began to freeze over and snow in big soft flakes. And by morning a soft snowblanket lay upon little Mrs. Bruvold's grave. The wind blew across it, sighing and shrieking; each gust of wind a lament.

But little Mrs. Bruvold lay snugly hidden from all the world's harsh and biting winds.

Original title: *En hverdagshistorie.* Translated by Katherine Hanson

Regine Normann

(1867-1939)
Regine Normann was born in the Vesterålen islands in Northern Norway, a place where the sun doesn't set from May to August and where
twilight prevails from November to February. Nature in the far North is
starkly beautiful and there is an intensity and magic about that country
that is mirrored in the people who live there. In novels and stories about
her native Nordland, Regine Normann effectively captures the essence
of the country and its people. She is best known for her collections of folktales and legends and in "Love-Root," taken from the volume *Bortsat*
(1906), there is a strong undercurrent of superstition and folk belief.

Love-Root

A spider lay in wait, suspended from the innermost ring of the web
she had fastened high up in the left hand corner of the loft window.
The little window barely allowed a strip of light from the midnight
sun to shine in across the table. Maren-Lisa sat and puttered with the
love-root. She divided it in two and tossed it into a brown dish filled
with water. Under the slanting roof Morten-Sofia sat on the edge of
the bed, her elbows on the table and her chin resting in her hands,
solemnly looking on.

"Eve sinks and Adam swims," Gypsy-Marja had taught Maren-
Lisa. If a fellow wanted a girl to fall in love with him he was supposed
to give her a bite of Adam, and if a girl wanted a young man to fall in
love with her, she was to give him Eve.

"How will you get them to swallow it? Are you sure it'll work?"
asked Morten-Sofia as she tossed her braids over her shoulder.

"Of course it will work," Maren-Lisa's face flushed bright-red.
How dared Sofia doubt it? Last night they had slogged through the
swamp hunting for the root, because it should have been picked on
Midsummer's Eve, and not far into July, as it was now. If Maren-Lisa
hadn't been absolutely certain where it grew, they might have

wandered aimlessly all night; the plant had long since dropped its blossoms and she had only been able to recognize it by its leaves.

It wasn't for her own sake, but to give poor Morten-Sofia a helping hand that she dug it up. It was just awful to see her go around moping since Mattis, her boyfriend, had gotten tired of her. Men were like that—he wasn't the only one to flirt with a girl, court her with gifts from the market until her heart was captured, and then blow ice cold. But Maren-Lisa would surely teach him a lesson this time.

"Just you wait, Sofia, until he's eaten the root—then you'll see how well it works."

"Do you think it's a sin?" Morten-Sofia asked softly, fingering the button on her nightgown as if she were ashamed to mention it.

"Sin? Piffle!!" Maren-Lisa turned quickly on her stool. In any case the sin wasn't great enough to answer to the Lord for. But the spell must be learned and God's name named, fair and square, at the same time that Mattis swallowed the first bite of his breakfast, because under the cheese on his slice of bread would lie the root.

As a joke, Maren-Lisa would try the charm out on Halvor. He had been born both simple-minded and stingy, and never gave women a second glance.

Maren-Lisa pushed the dish across the table. "See how white it looks!" Morten-Sofia was supposed to cut it in thin slices; she could use the inside cover of the hymnal to slice it on, for the root had to be spotlessly clean.

Morten-Sofia fished the root out of the bowl and set it down on the table in front of her, but her hands trembled and her heart pounded so it could be seen through her nightgown. This was trolldom and witchcraft, no matter what Maren-Lisa said. But maybe the Lord wouldn't be too strict with her over it. He certainly knew how dear and priceless Mattis was to her.

Frightened black eyes flickered in her narrow, pale face as she glanced up at Lisa, who was leaning over the table. "What are the words?" whispered Morten-Sofia.

"You can learn them right now." Maren-Lisa loosened her waistband and breathed more easily.

"Let good fortune follow me, as it followed the Israelites when they travelled from Egypt to Canaan, in the name of the Father, the Son, and the Holy Ghost."

She said the charm slowly and Morten-Sofia repeated it solemnly. Had she gotten it straight?

Yes, Morten-Sofia thought she had gotten it.

"Don't forget it!" warned Maren-Lisa. Of course she would go over the spell again early in the morning, Lisa added comfortingly.

Carefully they scraped the cheese off the bread that the house-keeper had set out for the men, laid the sliced root on the buttered bread, and spread the crumbled cheese over it all again. From the chest in the corner Maren-Lisa fetched a plate with a picture of Petter Dass on it, and put Halvor's food on that. They had to have something to go by, so each would get the portion that was intended for him.

The housekeeper was up early and had taken over the kitchen table to knead the bread dough, while she set the coffee cups and morning snack on the counter under the plate rack. There sat both of the fellows taking the edges off their appetites with a cup of coffee and a slice of bread apiece before they went to work. Morten-Sofia stood by the hearth looking on and repeating the charm over and over again to herself. Mattis looked so handsome sitting there with the sun shining on his golden curls while he flirted with Maren-Lisa. She sat and played with the spinning wheel, never at a loss for an answer to him, loose-tongued as she was. Would Lisa remember to say the charm over Halvor? Surly and grumpy in the morning, he wolfed down his food and slurped his coffee from the saucer so it trickled down his beard stubble. What a disgusting sight! What would Maren-Lisa want with a fellow like him? Even a blind woman could see that he was born to be a bachelor. Now Mattis, on the other hand, was some fellow, so tall and good-looking. My, but he was handsome!

Fervently she recited the charm for the fifth time and said an amen for good measure just as Mattis swallowed the last bite.

The men left and the girls hurried to the counter for milk and sugar for their own morning coffee, but stopped short and stared. The housekeeper had set the Petter Dass plate with Halvor's food on it in front of Mattis, and it was over him that Maren-Lisa had recited the magic words. But it was over Halvor, the ugly beast, that Morten-Sofia had repeated the charm five times, and even added the amen. It surely would have worked even if he were made of stone, she had whispered the spell so intensely.

It was evening, three weeks later. Maren-Lisa slept with her face to the wall. One bare arm was flung over the covers and her head rested on the other. Out of her bright red camisole stuck the corner of a letter. Morten-Sofia couldn't take her eyes off it. She lay beside Maren-Lisa in the bed holding back her tears. She began to cry as soon as it grew quiet, as she had every night since Mattis had turned heart and soul away from her and towards her friend.

Right in front of everybody he flirted, pinched, and fussed over Maren-Lisa, until it was disgusting to watch, and paid no more attention to Morten-Sofia, his old sweetheart, than to her child which wasn't yet born. But she had been his love, and he had sworn by God and all that's holy to remain faithful. He had given her a golden pin and a rose-flowered silk kerchief from the market. Morten-Sofia gave a huge sob and sank her teeth into the sheepskin coverlet.

But she would have her revenge! Morten-Sofia would meet with the pastor and the sheriff and the bailiff, take his letters and show them black on white that what she came with was God's truth. Reveal his faithlessness, and put a stop to his marrying that creature who lay here beside her.

Maren-Lisa didn't fool her any, for all that she pretended to be innocent, and swore that she thought no more of Mattis than a clump of dirt under her shoe. Oh no, his sweet talk tasted too good for that.

It had been a sin and blasphemy to use the root. Mattis had cooled off towards her before, that was so—but now—Now Halvor had gone completely crazy over her!

What could it be that Mattis found so enticing about Maren-Lisa? Morten-Sofia rose on her elbows and looked at Maren-Lisa as she slept.

There she lay with that turned-up nose in her round, false face with the cleft chin, and the curly tow-colored hair that she boasted reached down to her knees. She bragged about it just to get the boys to run their fingers through it, the old sow. Humph. There she laughed in her sleep so her white teeth glistened. Was it Mattis she was dreaming of?

Almost beside herself, Morten-Sofia plucked the letter from Maren-Lisa's bosom, and lay still with her eyes closed, pretending to be asleep.

From the windowsill came the buzz of a fly struggling and fighting for his life while the spider started to weave, taking in a thread here and there, tying and binding, until her victim was secured. Up in the rafters under the gable a magpie chattered to her young and the twigs rustled in the old nest.

Was somebody turning the latch on the door? Morten-Sofia stared with open mouth and flaring nostrils. The door was locked from the inside. They had locked it as soon as they came upstairs this evening in order to escape Halvor's roaming. Two nights in a row he had come sneaking into the loft without Morten-Sofia knowing it, until he was standing by her bed, stroking her cheek. Morten-Sofia almost had a fit she was so frightened. But Maren-Lisa only laughed; it wasn't any of her affair.

And how Halvor rigged himself out! Sunday trousers for everyday wear, and a new tourist shirt with a red silk tie around his neck. Well, he could certainly afford it. He was a well-to-do fellow with money in the bank and a sure prospect of inheriting the farm from his grandfather. But he needn't go to any trouble on her account. She had told him off in no uncertain terms—chased him out almost like a dog last night, so he slunk off clearly crestfallen.

Did Mattis suspect anything? At the dinner table he had gone on and on with talk about sweethearts.

Suddenly Morten-Sofia rolled on her side, turning the coverlet to make a covered space between herself and the edge of the bed, and slipped the letter out of its envelope.

It was—Good Lord!—it was a proposal from Mattis to Maren-Lisa.

"Precious Girl!

While silence surrounds me and my thoughts linger on you, I will take pen in hand and dip it in Anguish's inkwell and write to you. Oh, most precious girl! I must cry out with the words of the Prophet Jeremiah: If my head were of water and my eyes flowing springs, I still could not extinguish love's burning flames. —He had once written words like that to her. She could say them all by heart—

"Only you, my beautiful girl, can relieve my pain. I love you, Lisa Sjursdatter."

Sofia clutched at her breast and gasped for breath, hot tears flowing. She couldn't bear to read any more. Even if it were a matter of life or death, she wouldn't look at one more syllable of his faithlessness. Quickly she stuffed the letter back in its envelope and again tucked it into Maren-Lisa's bosom.

Well, Maren-Lisa could have him, for all she cared! Not even if they brought him to her on a silver platter would Morten-Sofia ever glance in his direction again—the slob—the skirt chaser—he wasn't worth the toe of Halvor's boot. And she would be sure to tell him that first thing in the morning—show him who she thought the most of—Halvor would never do such a thing—Never!

Sofia dried the tears on her burning cheeks and folded her hands. She sought to express her feelings in an evening prayer. She tried to pray, "Lord subdue...," but came to a halt. Her thoughts refused to obey her. They gnawed and churned obstinately: "Practice witchcraft, lie, and deceive...."

Original title: *Kjaerligheds-Roden*. Translated by Torild Homstad

Ragnhild Jølsen

(1875-1908)
Like the women she created in her fiction, Ragnhild Jølsen was a fascinating and controversial figure. As a young woman she was drawn to a bohemian lifestyle and her attitudes toward women's rights, both economic and sexual, are reflected in the strong-willed and highly erotic female characters in her novels. But Jølsen also had deep roots in the land and in family traditions. For generations her family had owned a large estate east of Oslo and during her childhood she witnessed the decline of the old agriculture-based economy and the arrival of industrialism. Where there once had been cotters who tilled the soil, there now were workers who were employed at the pulp mill. In a collection of short stories, *Brukshistorier* (1907), from which the two stories below are taken, she writes about the people who lived and worked at the mill. These stories are realistic depictions, but one can easily hear that the author's style has been influenced by an oral tradition. She had known folktales and legends all her life and as she grew older she began to record them. They were told to her by storytellers in the community and at home – her mother is said to have been an almost limitless source.

In "Fiddle Music in the Meadow" we read about the dead dancing with *hulder*, supernatural female beings in Norwegian folklore who are very beautiful except for long, cowlike tails that they try to conceal when they interact with humans. We also read about an old Norwegian custom – in the week after Christmas young people dressed up in costumes and masks and went around in groups from house to house. These *julebukkene* were welcome visitors and their hosts would treat them with the traditional fare they baked and brewed for the Christmas holiday.

The Twelfth in the Cabin

It was crowded in Sandhytten: husband, wife and nine offspring, aged eighteen to two, lived, ate and slept in one and the same room. Judging by appearances, everyone there was subject to the same law that governs trees growing too close together—the stronger draws strength from the weaker; growth in the south occasions dormancy in the north and vice versa. So it was in Sandhytten, a household in harmony with the wisdom and economy of nature—the lot of them would never succumb to misery and perish, but neither would they all thrive and grow causing the space to become too cramped.

It appeared as if the husband, Lauritz, had thought so long about his length that he became thin enough for the next oldest to squeeze alongside him on the edge of the bed; while his wife, Mattea, who lay on the inside and was short and broad, had room for the youngest in a clothes basket down by her feet. Likewise Jens and Jon, despite being twins, were so uneven that they could lie beside one another comfortably, their feet in opposite directions, without kicking each other in the nose. And then there was Johanne who, although she had turned five, was so short that she could still sleep in the cradle. Jakob, Nils and Ole all slept in the sofa bed; Jakob and Ole, who had the outside, were chubby and broad-shouldered at the expense of Nils, who was in the middle and seemingly hadn't had room to fill out, for he was as long and thin as a string. And finally Karoline, the oldest and the only one who had her own bed—she was so healthy and strong that she was a delight to behold: red lips, ample breasts and a broad waist.

That the bed was solely responsible for this was, incidentally, uncertain: perhaps it was the evening forest life as well, the smell of spruce trees, who knows. . . . She was such a marvelous, high-spirited girl, singing cheerful and lilting tunes when she went to work at six o'clock in the morning and when she came home in the evening, laughing and shouting about everything and nothing. Lord, what spirit and vitality!

Karoline's parents never asked her to keep still or quiet down a little, probably because they had an inkling things would be even crazier then—and besides, they were proud of the girl and it gave them a tremendous lift to listen to her. She was useful too: sometimes when she came home from work she would gather up her younger siblings and, amid great commotion, drag them down to the well and scrub them clean. Other times she heaved the big iron kettle onto the stove and made porridge, so her mother was spared for days from preparing food. Still other times she scoured the cabin and decorated the hearth with birch sprigs she had gathered. But she was flighty too, and terribly lazy once in a while. She could sleep in her bed for two whole weeks without making it; she could wear the same shift until it was as black as a pipe, and so on. . . .

One dusky spring night something most extraordinary occurred in this nest at Sandhytten. It was raining and the waterfall was roaring outside, when Mattea woke up, sat up in bed and, bewildered, asked: "Dear me, where's that coming from?" But since no one in the room answered, she lay down, telling herself it had been an owl or a cat, and fell asleep again immediately.

She didn't know how long she had been sleeping when she was once again awakened by the same sound—one to which she, who had borne many children, was particularly sensitive. "What's going on?" she whispered, wide awake, and for a long time she sat listening. Her husband turned over, having heard nothing: "What are you sitting there like that for, woman? Lie down now," he mumbled crossly, "if you don't have a toothache."

And Mattea lay down.

But she had no sooner done so when out of the darkness there came unmistakable crying and whimpering.

"Come on now, girl, out with it! What is it, what *is* it?" cried Mother Mattea, beside herself with astonishment and fright.

And suddenly, from over by Karoline's bed: "Hush, Mother, don't yell like that!"

"What's going on—what's all this noise?" Now the husband chimed in too and everyone across the room began to stir.

"Karoline," the mother said, "I don't understand this. I do believe it's coming from you!"

"Darned if I do either, Mother," Karoline's voice answered, "I wake up—and all of a sudden I have a baby in my bed."

The old woman was up in a flash, grabbed a match and lit it—there lay Karoline, looking a bit queer and somewhat uneasy. A broad smile spread across her face and then she laughed out loud. "This is the funniest thing that's ever happened to me, Mother," she said.

By morning all was quiet over in the straw bed and Karoline got up, flung on her clothes and went her way as usual.

In the evening, Lauritz and Mattea were sitting on the doorstep when she came home; they wore a peculiar expression and when they spoke, they spoke very slowly and deliberately but didn't appear angry.

"You're awfully pale and quiet today," Lauritz said, "you'd better sit down out here with us." The two of them made room for the girl between them. She sat down, picked a straw up from the ground and began to break it into pieces.

"How did it go at the mill today, Karoline?" the mother asked looking at her intently.

"Just fine, Mother. But they told me I didn't have much energy. Well, I said, if you think I'm moving so slowly you might just as well get me a chair. They did and I *sat* and packed three gross."

"Seems to me you keep peeking inside the cabin," the father said. "Something you have to do in there?"

"Oh," the girl answered, picking away at the straw. But Mother Mattea, turning her head toward the door, said: "It's lying in there, you know what I mean—the thing you got in bed last night. But there are so many here already, you know—this makes the twelfth in the cabin! So I figure you're going to have to be the one to take care of this one."

The girl looked up—her mouth broke into a big, happy smile: "Yes, I guess I am," she said as she got up and walked in.

Original title: *Den tolvte i stua.* Translated by Katherine Hanson

Fiddle Music in the Meadow

One Saturday evening there was fiddle music in the meadow. Low, careful fiddling with mysterious little plunks and snaps. It sounded so eerie in the mist, as if it grew out of the summernight itself. The meadow was still with white flowers on a dark floor, and the trees waved silently, silently. . .

In the middle of the meadow was a hut with light behind the windows. And the strains of the fiddle came from within.

A single twig snapped on the path — a woman with a white scarf approached the hut. She stopped a minute now and then and looked around as if she were puzzled about something. And for a while she disappeared. But when she reappeared, she walked resolutely to the cabin door, lifted the latch and stepped in. The fiddling stopped abruptly. Instead there was boisterous talk, accompanied by something like the noise and commotion of tables and chairs — then it was quiet.

The woman emerged from the door — a shaft of light shot around her, showing her fiery red cheeks — she straightened her bodice, her scarf had slid down around her neck — she didn't take the path back, but slipped away in the bushes.

And once again the sound of the fiddle came from the house. Quiet, careful, with mysterious plunking and snapping.

A new woman came up the path. She was all dressed up — the ruffled frill showed white at her throat — and she walked calmly and assuredly up to the hut and entered. Once again the fiddling stopped and there was a terrible noise and commotion; shadows whirled past the windows, as if someone were dancing round and round, wildly and out of step. Then suddenly it stopped and was quiet.

A while later the woman came out, her hair unkempt — and she breathed heavily from the dancing. Down the path a ways she turned around and shook her fist at the hut, from which quiet fiddling could now again be heard.

Then still more came — this time *two* women together and the grass waved and swayed about them. They laughed and giggled, "Fun — dancing!"

They were inside the hut for a long time; there wasn't any noise, and when they left the one said, disappointed, "There wasn't any dancing tonight, after all."

The other answered, "No, that's what happens when no one comes."

A second Saturday evening there was again fiddle music in the meadow. A quivering melody with deep plunks and snaps. The tune was like red and yellow leaves blown through the autumn evening and had the seductive tones of the dove in the forest. Free-flying webs drifted through the air and the meadow was full of wet coltsfoot. And the eyes of the meadow hut were opened wide; oh, how the light shone from the windows — two lamps had been placed right next to the windowpanes!

There was a crackling in the leaves and a squishing in the mud — an old woman was making her way on the path. She shuffled along eagerly, and in the dusk the feet under her skirt looked like the paws of a bear. She stopped a minute in front of the hut and looked around from left to right.

"Strange! Not a person in sight," she muttered. But then, without further hesitation, dove in and slammed the door behind her. "What — is that you Guri?" No fiddling was heard for a while; instead, shrieks, laughter and coarse insults pierced the silence.

A boy and a girl bumped into the old woman on the threshold, or more correctly, *she* bumped into them: as they were about to go in, she came headlong out the door.

"There won't be anything tonight," she snapped.

"Why is he playing then?" they asked.

"Oh, he's just limbering up his fingers!"

"Well, we may as well leave then." And the three of them took the trail back.

"When did he come back?" one asked. "Seems to me he's been gone a long time. . .I s'pose he'll stay awhile now?"

"He came back yesterday and he leaves again tomorrow — you won't be having a fiddler right away." As they rounded the bend and approached the alder thicket, the girl turned around.

"Say, did someone come after all? Something is fluttering by the window, just like dancing."

"That's only the shadow of the trees, my dear," the old woman said slyly from inside the thicket. But the boy leapt forward.

"I think someone's dancing now, too," he said. "Hey, let's go on back."

And the two of them went. The old woman stood absolutely still in the middle of the road and watched them.

They tried as usual to peek through the windows first — the curtains were drawn. But inside, shadows were hopping around. And so they went to the door and reached for the latch, but it was bolted.

"Let us in," cried the boy and pounded with his knuckles, "We aren't many — there's room for us."

"No, there won't be anything tonight," was the curt reply.

"But I saw someone dancing."

"Did you? No one is here."

The old woman was still standing motionless on the path when the couple came trudging back; she sniggered and had an evil look about her. "*You* go alone," she proposed to the girl, "and see how it goes then."

No, if there wasn't any dance, then there *wasn't* any dance! And they couldn't deny feeling a little spooked by what they didn't understand, and they went their way.

Shortly afterward a solitary girl scurried along toward the music and the light, and she was let in, just as the old woman had hinted.

A third Saturday evening there was again fiddle music in the meadow. Lilting tunes — *polskdans* and hornpipe. The notes turned somersaults across the crusty snow and there was a teasing laughter in them, a plunking like the popping of corks in bottles and sleigh bells on a horse's harness. And the meadow lay still and white, and it shimmered in the moonlight.

A flock in fluttering clothes, white and black, swarmed like mosquitos right toward the hut. They knocked on the wall, on the windowpanes, and on the door.

"Hans Peddler!" they called. "Hans Peddler! Why don't you open up? Why do you play when we don't get to dance?"

"Dance outside!" rasped a hoarse voice from inside. The *julebukkene* didn't need to be asked twice; they grabbed onto each other's waists and shoulders and stomped and kicked around in a circle so the snow flew. Ola Vold, Karsten Skillet and Jens Asen were there with long beards and white sheets. And there were five heavily-padded girls with masks. They had been greeted with home-brew at many of the places they'd been to before and now the spirited fiddle

---

polskdans: a folk dance in which the couples whirl around in ¾ time music set them off — they became crazed with their revelry.

Mari Hauen burst into the room of another girl in the worker's barracks, her face chalk white. "Oh — God help me, I saw a vision, Bergitte."

"Are you mad?" Bergitte gave such a start that her sewing tumbled onto the floor. "What'd you see?"

Mari Hauen sat down and it took a while before she was able to speak; when she spoke, she spoke fitfully, breathlessly, as one who had been running hard. "I saw it lit up and heard the fiddle—thought there was a dance, you know—and well, yes there *was* a dance—the dead dancing with the *hulder*—you should've seen 'em swing around and carry on—and inside the peddler was playing!"

Bergitte Flabråten was small, sly and extremely curious.

"I want to see, too," she said and put a knitted scarf on. And she stopped by and told two other girls who weren't afraid of the dark and who were just as curious and game as she was.

"I've never seen ghosts before — neither the dead nor the *hulder*." The girls chattered away as they hurried expectantly arm in arm. "There have always been stories about the meadow and the peddler — once I thought I saw something too — he lures you with his fiddle and with a light in the window — and now he's lured the ghosts the same way."

While the girls were coming up toward the hut, the *julebukkene* were dancing on toward huts farther up the hillside, unseen and unnoticed. And the girls came closer and closer to the meadow. Everything was hushed and peaceful there, no fiddling and no dead — not even a light in the window. Cautiously the girls snuck all the way up, and then, of course, they saw how the area all around the hut had been trampled by people. Just then the light appeared again, and they jumped to the side and hid. Once again there was fiddle music from inside the hut and at the same time someone began to dance in there —a shadow flickered past the windows. The girls nudged each other.

"There is a dance after all but something's strange. Some of the ghosts must have gotten inside. Well, we have to see it." And two of the girls helped the lightest of the three up high enough to see over the curtain.

Inside, lanky Hans Peddler hopped around by himself, while bowing a *reinlender* on the fiddle he held under his chin. But

---

reinlender: dance in ²/₄ time similar to schottische.

occasionally he stopped dancing and played and listened; his beady eyes, set close to the hooked nose, blinked, and his sunken mouth trembled with excitement.

Then Bergitte Flabråten had a flash and she couldn't help herself from screeching out: "Oh, stop dancing with yourself, Hans — we're not fooled, you'll never get us inside!" Then the others let her down and all three broke into a run as if a whole party of ghosts were on their heels.

Original title: *Felelåten i engen.* Translated by Katherine Hanson

Gro Holm

(1878-1949)

Gro Holm grew up on a farm on an inner arm of the Hardangerfjord, in the western part of Norway. She had no brothers and, being the oldest child, should have inherited the family farm, but it was bought out by industry soon after the turn of the century. In 1920, however, a small farm in Hardanger was left to her by an uncle, and that was to become her home and her livelihood. Twelve years later, at age fifty-four, she published her first novel, *Sut*, the initial volume of a trilogy depicting life on the Løstøl farm from the time Brita arrives as a newly-wed until, as an old woman who has survived the deaths of her husband and oldest daughter, she leaves to join her other daughters now living in America. (The second and third volumes were published in 1933 and 1934 and in 1951 the entire trilogy came out under the title *Løstølsfolket*.)

"Life on the Løstøl Farm" consists of four excerpts from *Løstølsfolket*. The novel is set during the second half of the nineteenth century, a time of social unrest in rural Norway. Roads and improved communication introduced an urban culture to small communities tucked away in the mountains and valleys, undermining the traditional way of life and luring young people away to an easier and more lucrative existence. Beyond the city lay the promise of America which, more than anything, represented a break between the old and the new. The narrator is Brita and her account of daily events on the farm and in the community at large is factual and unemotional, yet at the same time there is clear social criticism in her observations of a farm woman's traditional role. The narrative opens at the time of Brita's return from America; she had been living in Iowa with her aunt and uncle for two years when a letter proposing marriage came from Lars, her friend from childhood who would one day take over the farm at Løstøl ...

Life on the Løstøl Farm

Oh, how unhappy I was the first year we were married! Everything was fine as long as the wedding celebration lasted; for the first eight days we slept in the storehouse. My mother-in-law did the cooking and other chores; no one expected me to do any work yet. I was free to walk around and become acquainted with everything on the farm. The cows were out to pasture, the sheep were in the mountains. It was just between planting and harvest so there wasn't much to do besides general upkeep.

Løstøl was a fine farm. Just enough incline so water didn't remain standing, and good soil. You could see the entire fjord, the farms on the other side, Bø, Hauge and Tveit and all the others, lined up along the shore.

The days are longer on the mountain farms and they get more sunshine—that's what makes them habitable. We could put our potatoes in the ground just as early in the spring as those down by the sea. In that respect we were better off than Skår, which faces north and is at least fourteen days later with spring planting.

The farmyard ran like a corridor with buildings above and below. On the upper side the dwelling houses and storehouses, cookhouses and smithies were lined up one after the other. On the lower side were the barns. Hay was stored on the top level and animals were stalled below. It was a better layout than I've seen in many other places, because we didn't have the problem of water seeping from the floor of the cow barn down into the farmyard. The dwelling houses were old log cabins, but they were tall enough so that most of them had lofts. Some of the farmers had their storehouse with loft right next to the house, so one could go from one into the other. Gjøa Teigane was the only one who had a new house.

They must have done a lot of clearing at Løstøl in the old days before they'd built it up the way it was when I arrived. You could see that from the huge rock piles. A lot of rocks had been dumped right over the cliff. Farther south, where there weren't any cliffs, the rocks were piled up and the fields and meadows were enclosed in rock fences.

One morning I heard a terrible racket out in the farmyard. My mother- and father-in-law came out of the hay barn pulling and dragging a blue bed. They were heading toward the house. I went back into the storehouse and asked Lars if we were really going to sleep in the house with the old folks.

"Is that so strange? We certainly can't heat up both places," Lars said.

I hadn't thought about that. I had of course heard that people lived this way at some of the farms. I remember how we used to laugh about the people at Rødna. The old folks and the young ones shared the same house and each had a cradle in front of their bed. If there wasn't screaming from one cradle, there was screaming from the other. There was no need to worry that Lars's parents would be having any more babies and that was some comfort. But I no longer thought it was anything to laugh about.

I couldn't bring myself to go into the house because I knew how things would go. One thing was clear to me: My mother-in-law was in charge—she didn't have to ask anyone.

So I walked out to the pasture where the cows were and busied myself with them. My mother-in-law was extremely capable as I had already observed. She would soon find fault with what I did and there would be no use setting myself up against her. It would be difficult for me.

"Come on in now, lunch is ready." My father-in-law was standing out on the steps and I could tell by looking at him that he had something he hoped would please me. When I came in, the blue bed stood against the far wall behind the other bed. Mother-in-law was walking back and forth setting the table and my father-in-law, taking me by the hand, led me over to the bed, patted the new coverlet and said:

"Here's where the young bride shall sleep."

I wasn't able to say anything. I glanced over at Lars but he wasn't looking at me. No, I would have to give in, there was nothing else to do. All three of them were against me and would have thought I were crazy had I objected. Let them have it their way, I thought, I'm not going to cause any trouble.

"You can do the cooking for the time being, Brita," my mother-in-law said after we'd eaten a while in silence. "I'll take the milking until the cows go to the higher pastures for the summer—no sense in you milking strange cows. When we start the haying you can work in the fields and I'll take over the cooking again."

I nodded. I had never really enjoyed cooking, had always preferred outdoor work. But it probably wouldn't be long before I'd have to be both indoors and out. I nodded. Lars hadn't taken over the farm; his parents weren't more than sixty or thereabouts. They didn't want to hand over the farm yet, so I'd just have to go around like a hired girl for a few years.

Well, there was an end to that day too. We undressed—I took most of my clothes off after I was in bed. Father-in-law wandered around in his underpants for the longest time. I couldn't imagine what he was doing.

"Come on, Hans, stop fooling around and come to bed."

He got in bed and soon there was a terrible yawning and wheezing. Sleep was the farthest thing from my mind. Then it was quiet for a while.

"Hans."

There was no answer.

"Hans, take off your underpants."

No answer.

"Do you hear, Hans? You're to take off your underpants, I'm telling you."

Mother-in-law was angry now.

"You know very well we can't afford to wear out our clothes at night."

I had to laugh then; I laughed so hard I had to bite the covers. Lars couldn't contain himself either and there we lay like two kids, hidden way beneath the blankets, hiccuping and laughing. After a while Lars stuck his head out.

"Brita," he whispered in my ear. "The old folks are asleep now."

Gjøa Teigane was looking at me.

"I see that you're pale. You're probably pregnant, so you ought to get whatever food you have a taste for. I've just made some rennet cheese and I'll give you a piece of it."

I was so sick and uninterested in food; nothing tasted good. Mother-in-law soon understood my condition and said one day:

"Go down to the store, Hans, and get some dried fish. We are going to have a little change in our diet for Brita."

They were all caring and attentive toward me. Lars was in the barn with me every day and lifted the wooden tubs with mash-fodder up to the cows. He carried water and wood, wanted to protect me as much as possible. Father-in-law ran around like a youngster, smiling and happy, always with a friendly word for me. He was looking for the cradle now and ran up and down the steps of all the buildings on the farm. He finally found it in the hayloft above the smithy, clumsily carried it out to the farmyard and got himself set up with blue paint and paintbrush. The children tagged along behind him asking all kinds of questions:

"Is it America-Brita who's having a baby?"

I suffered more pain than anyone knew when I thought about the little one who was coming. At night Lars moved way over to the wall saying, "I want you to have lots of room. I don't want to bump into the little boy."

Father-in-law winked at me and asked: "Well, how is it going with my little namesake?"

Each day went as the day before. Mother-in-law didn't say much. Not about that, whether it would be a boy or girl. She never said a word about that. But when I had found a bundle of rickrack in the tray of the clothes chest and sewn it on some little shirts, she praised me, saying it was nicely stitched.

The midwife came.

They made the necessary preparations of water, linen, a sharp knife. It was terrible to watch.

"Endure with patience," the midwife said when the contractions were at their worst. "You'll see it will be a boy, so you'll be repaid for your efforts."

It wasn't a boy.

When it was over and the midwife saw what it was she whispered to me:

"It's a little girl; but she's well-formed and really very pretty."

When I had the child in my arms and looked at her, it didn't matter one whit what it was, it was just as dear to me. But that was obviously not so for Lars and the old folks. They shuffled around the room, didn't say much. There was a terrible silence. Even the midwife was quiet; this wasn't the first time she'd been in this situation. It wasn't long before she was finished and, being tired from lack of sleep and all the activity, she went to the storehouse to lie down. After a while the others slowly walked out, one by one, without so much as a word and there I lay, alone with my thoughts.

"Don't you want to see my little girl, Grandpa? Isn't she pretty?"

We were taking her to her christening. I had sewn a christening dress from some flowery fabric I'd brought with me from America. I had just dressed the little thing and held her up toward Father-in-law.

"Hmph," he said, "she looks like any other baby girl, I expect."

Mother-in-law was touched, for the baby had been named after her.

"It is a gift," she said. "We must be thankful no matter how small it is."

I wasn't any less sick each subsequent time I was with child, but no one asked me how I was or showed concern, no one lifted the wooden tubs up to the cows for me. I had only girls, something they all regarded as insignificant.

A short while after I had recovered from the birth, Mother-in-law wanted me to go through the ritual of churching. I answered evasively, thinking there was no great hurry; surely that could be done anytime. There were some clothes for little Torbjørg I wanted to make first.

"You must walk to church and be churched," Mother-in-law said.

"You know it is God's commandment which you cannot ignore. Monse-Marta couldn't be bothered with it, said it was rubbish. She always has to be different from other folks. The minister sent her one message after the other and the people on the farm thought it was shameful. Her sister said that she'd have to submit to the law just like other women, and that's what you'll have to do too, Brita."

"Well," Father-in-law said, "our neighbor Nils's grandmother was killed while she was on her way to be churched. That was a long time ago, I was just a boy then. I went along and helped pull her up. The baby was killed immediately, but there was still a little life in her when we came. It was in the wintertime, not exactly stormy weather, but a lot of snow. She had lost her footing in Røynelia and went over the cliff, Jostupet. There were several in the group and one of the hired girls tried to help her and slid down after her. If she hadn't managed to grab onto a juniper root, she probably would have gone over the cliff too."

"It's summer now," Mother-in-law retorted.

Those of us who lived so far from the church had to take our children with us and pack food for the whole day. Lars took a small tub of butter so he could get money to pay the minister.

I thought about Nils's old grandmother as I walked down Røynelia where she had gone over the cliff. Now there is a full grown forest above the cliff and that would catch anyone who slipped and fell. But in the old days they chopped more trees and fed the cattle leaves.

Several women were sitting in front of the church door that day. Line Leite was there with her fourteenth child. She was in her fifties and I saw that she wore glasses when she read the hymnal.

We weren't allowed into the church before the minister held a little sermon for each of us. He came out to where we sat and led us in one by one. To me he said: "Women are unclean because of their fleshly infirmity." Then he read a nice prayer and said in conclusion: "Now you are no longer unclean, but are once again accepted into the Christian Church."

That was the only time I went to be churched. It was later abolished, word has it, because the ministers didn't earn enough from it. But how could they justify that? When it was so important that Nils's grandmother had to risk her life for it! If women were in need of it before, then surely they're in need of it now as well.

I don't know why it was that there began to be so many old maids in the community. There weren't so many when I was growing up. There was always one or two who went from farm to farm, but not such a crowd as there later was.

I think it resulted from the fact that so many of those who took off for America were boys. The men weren't so generous with money for a ticket when it was for the girls. So they were stuck at home, poor wretches. They worked hard and received little for their toil. I'm sure they wanted to go, just like their brothers, and many did leave. But for every girl who left, there were two boys.

Ingeleiv, Åse-Knut's sister, was one of those old maids. She came home to the farm to die.

She had made the rounds, been on almost every farm in the community. She did all kinds of heavy work, from cleaning to washing clothes. Every spring she came home to her family for spring cleaning and whenever she wasn't engaged elsewhere she helped me too. She demanded very little, came quietly and peacefully and left the same way. You had the feeling there was something she was ashamed of. Jeers and taunts were heaped upon her. "Servant girl" and "old maid" were the most common.

Her mother had struggled to get her married, but as homely as she was, it was to no avail. You couldn't say that she was really ugly, but the fact remained that she stayed single.

Her earnings were modest: two dalar per year, homespun with which to make clothes, and a pair of shoes during her first year of service. Later they increased her wages to sixteen kroner and gave her a sheep that was kept and fed at the farm. She stayed on at the Mo farm longer than any other place.

The homespun clothes she had from home lasted almost her entire life. She put the money she earned in the bank. Every little bit helps, and what with her having good luck with her sheep, she was able to save.

When the work became too heavy at one farm she moved to another, but there was heavy work everywhere. No one spared her. She moved back home then; her brother was kind as he always was and took her in. As long as she was able, she took what work she could get.

One evening she dragged herself home; she had been weaving that day. She went to bed and lay there only a few days before she passed away.

"Ingeleiv has had a heavy and thankless fate," Knut said.

He saw to it that she had a proper funeral complete with food and drink. But when it came time to put the corpse on the sled, there weren't many who wanted to join in the procession. The north wind was blowing and it was cold and nasty. Nils in particular came with all kinds of excuses. I stood in the farmyard and watched them as they walked down beyond the fence and I thought about what kind of life she had had. She had suffered a long workday and much ridicule and received little joy. Life could be fraught with misery and drudgery for us married women as well, but still it wasn't the same. Marriage brings a woman honor; that is something everyone knows.

I hurried in to help with the meal that would be served when they returned from the churchyard. I had to go home to fetch some cups and on my way I met Nils.

"There weren't many who accompanied Ingeleiv to the churchyard," I said.

"Should there have been many? I'm sure they'll manage to get that old maid scarecrow into the ground."

We had just eaten our afternoon meal when my brother Jens came with an America letter from our father's brother. It was Sunday and Lars was at home. Jens came in dejectedly and he sat down before he said anything.

"I have a letter from Uncle with me. It is very sad, but there's also good news. He writes that Anna has died—here's the letter, you can read it yourself."

Lars took the letter and read it out loud. Uncle wrote most about how Anna had been toward the end and that he missed her. Ah yes, they had been very happy together when I was there. When Lars came to the end of the letter, both the children and I cried. Uncle asked Jens to persuade us to let Madli come over to him; she had been named after my grandmother who lived on the farm at Halvgjenge.

"Seems to me that Uncle is making you a good offer," Jens said. "Torbjørg is the only one who can have the farm here. As I understand it, Uncle is not a poor man, and when one has gone over and assumed some responsibility, it will be easier for the others to follow."

I looked over at Madli, "What do you think about this?"

"I don't know," Madli said. She was sobbing as could be expected and I didn't have an answer to that question either.

"Well," Lars said, "we can't decide anything today; we must consider this very carefully. Force Madli we most certainly cannot. She is big enough to know what she wants and she can speak for herself. But I will say that Uncle has made us a fine offer."

"You can see," Jens said, "from what he writes that his health is not good, and it would be a terrible shame if he were to die before Madli gets there. And if I might state my opinion, I think you should write to him as soon as you've reached a decision." Jens was all fired up; he saw this as a tremendous opportunity, which of course it was. We saw this too, but for us there was something that wouldn't be easy, and that was to part with Madli.

Mother-in-law had been listening to all of this and I saw her drying her eyes. She didn't say anything. She knew what it was like—most of her children were in America and she had no hope of ever seeing them again. She had given them life, been totally occupied with them in their early years, scraped together money for their passage to America, but that marked the end of her involvement with them. She didn't know what to say.

"Sit down and stay awhile, Jens. A pity the others didn't come with you. I've baked for the weekend and now I'll put the coffee on." Jens was a cheerful soul, full of fun and merriment. Soon all of us were in good spirits and it was late in the evening before he headed home.

The news brought disquiet to all of us. In the days to come we cried and we worked. Of course we were pleased and grateful to Uncle, but it was the parting. In my toil and struggle at Løstøl I had not often thought about Mother, but now she was in my thoughts. I knew that this was how she had felt at the time I left for America, and I understood that there was nothing else to do but to let Madli go. I made myself hard and strong in front of the children and boasted about everything over there. I think the fact that her sisters could follow her over, when the time came, was what counted most. And I made it very clear to them that if they weren't happy, they could come straight home. I painted a bright picture, brighter than it was, but I knew that I had to do something. I didn't want to see my girls living on small farms in the community here and I knew that it was difficult to marry into the large farms. Those who have much receive more; many's the time I've experienced that.

I gave myself plenty of time and wrote a long letter to America.

Original title: *Løstølsfolket.* Translated by Katherine Hanson

Nini Roll Anker

(1873-1942)
At the time Nini Roll Anker was beginning her career as an author,
Norwegian women were campaigning for the right to vote. The time had
come for women to expand their sphere of activity to include social concerns, a challenge Anker took up in her many novels and short stories.
She exposed injustice and urged reform. In *Det svake kjønn* (1915) the
Church was criticized for oppressing a healthy development of the
feminine psyche with its pietistic preaching on the virtue of sexual
morality and submission to authority. The plight of working women was
depicted in several stories, and most successfully in the novel *Den som
henger i en tråd* (1935), an intimate portrayal of garment workers and
their struggle to improve labor conditions. Her last novel, *Kvinnen og den
svarte fuglen* (1945), is a plea for pacifism in which Anker admonishes
women to reaffirm traditional feminine values and bring them to bear
on world peace.

The main character in "A Crime" is a woman who appears only as a
memory; in characteristic fashion, the author's criticism is indirect, but
her indignation unmistakable.

A Crime

I stopped by the day after the funeral. I felt it was my duty. We've
known each other since childhood, Torvald Landsrud and I, and soon
we'll have worked in the same office for twenty-five years. I was also
Elise's godfather—though I paid little enough attention to her while
she lived, I'm ashamed to admit. Landsrud has a way of keeping people at a distance—not obviously, but at a distance all the same. I've
often wondered exactly what it is that keeps us at arm's length from
him. He's just a little fellow, not much to look at, unremarkable, you
might say, but there's something about him, just the same. Frankly,
the people in the office are afraid of him. What is there about him?
There he sits in his glass cage, taking in money, paying out money,
orderly in the extreme. He'll return an account for the least error in
spelling. "One small letter has toppled greater men than I," he says.

And it's true, isn't it? We have to give him credit, don't we? A precise and conscientious man, starched collar in place, well-groomed white beard, polite, kind to everyone. Yes, but just the same! I don't know if it's the soft voice, or the nose that is clearly too small—I've actually brooded over it many times. I think it must be the eyes. Clear, blue, unblinking, expressionless eyes. I've tried to meet that gaze. I have nothing to hide, but I can never look him straight in the eye. I break out in a sweat, I just can't do it...

He's so *damned spotless*, Landsrud is, you see, and he knows it. There's never been any talk about him or his wife or their two daughters—there's never been any gossip about them before this thing happened to Elise. So you can imagine—I'm a callous old bachelor, but the day I heard about Elise I felt sorry for Landsrud and his family and his Free Church flock. You know how people are—bank teller Landsrud doesn't belong to the State Church. He's been an elder in his Free Church for many years. For my part, I prefer to listen to the Bishop when I need bolstering. To my way of thinking, if it's going to be, let it be straight from the top, and surely the Bishop is closest to Our Lord. But Landsrud has gone his own way, and people have the gall to remember that, too, when misfortune strikes a man.

Well, I put on my mourning gloves, and went over the day after the funeral. I felt it was my duty to show Landsrud that I was his comrade in sorrow. The Landsruds have a nice home. I'd been there two or three times before—there aren't many who can say *that*. The Landsruds keep to themselves; they're self-sufficient folk—rare enough in our day. Anna once went to the sanatorium for her lungs, but that's a great many years ago, it must be almost twenty years now; she's never been anywhere else that I know of. And there was never anything wrong with Elise; Elise had been at home with her parents her entire life. When she spoke it was like listening to Landsrud himself, though for the most part she didn't have much to say. A nice, quiet girl, you know. Earned her two hundred kroner a month at Hjortdals. I've bought ties and such from her many times. She clerked exactly like a machine—never any foolishness there. No glances and curls and head tilted at an angle. It was clerk and customer to everyone—prim and proper. She wasn't Torvald Landsrud's daughter for nothing. Both she and Anna lived at home, and paid for their room and board. Everything was up to snuff in that household—regular household help, it could even be called ample under the circumstances—but with the accounts in order, you can be sure. Landsrud is not one to hand out pennies before he has squeezed them. What can I say?

What can I say? A nice home, nice furniture, clean and tidy.

Embroidery wherever one looked and three women to look after it all. Well, there *were* three, before Elise died.

I'll never forget that morning, two weeks ago today, when I opened the office door and the bookkeeper came rushing up to me asking, "Have you heard the news, Jensen?"

What could I have heard? I sat at home all evening, went to bed at ten o'clock and slept tolerably well, shaved and ate breakfast in the morning, and went to the office without speaking to a soul.

"Elise Landsrud has disappeared," said the bookkeeper.

"Disappeared?" I asked.

"She was going for a walk in the storm yesterday, that's what she *said,* at any rate. And no one has seen her since. Now they're out searching for her, Landsrud and a group of others. A minute ago my wife called and said they found her hat on Kropstad's dock."

I was speechless. Elise—Elise—I thought. I could see her as clearly as I had seen her the last time I bought some small item at Hjortdals— the small, thin mouth that never curved upward in a smile, the sharp nose and the black eyes—her mother has black eyes. She wasn't pretty, beauty doesn't run in the family, but she was a nice, quiet girl. From that home, too! It was inconceivable.

Well, they found her later on in the day, as you know. Her body lay in shallow water; there was an on-shore breeze and the tide had done its work. She lay smiling. Inconceivable—or? Or?

As I said, I went to Landsrud's after the funeral. The deceased's godfather—it was my duty.

The three of them were sitting in that lovely parlor. It must have been around six o'clock. They stood up when I came in. Black mourning clothes in a nice room. It was a sad sight.

Both Landsrud and his wife thanked me for coming. Anna sat locked within herself. Anna might well have thought she would go first, she who was the eldest—but no one knows what she thought. She and Elise had shared a room since they were little girls, and though there were ten years between them, they had grown more and more alike. Elise celebrated her thirtieth birthday the day before she disappeared.

Landsrud appeared the same as always. And I couldn't look him in the eye now either, when he looked at me.

"You've heard what they're saying?" he asked before I had a chance to sit down. I had heard so many things, people can't say enough on such an occasion.

"I never listen to loose talk, you know that," I answered.

"No, not you," he said. "But there is an abundance of those who do. An occurrence such as this is a good mouthful and a real treat for the mob. Then they can fall upon a decent man and a happy home for their own pleasure, Jensen. Their imagination knows no bounds."

Landsrud talks this way—pedantically—he is an elder in his church. My chair began suddenly to feel hard and uncomfortable. I had come to bring condolences and had intended to leave again right away.

Landsrud began to pace around the table. His head was thrown back, as was his custom, as if to make him appear taller; his hands were clasped behind his back. His whiskers were freshly trimmed so you could see the skin underneath; it was as white as his beard.

Mrs. Landsrud had obviously failed; she sat wringing her hands. Anna crocheted...

"The police have been here," Landsrud said. "Are we to be spared nothing? We have been questioned; the rumors have done their work. We were asked if there was a man in Elise's life. In *Elise's* life, Jensen! In my daughter's life! They questioned Anna, too."

Anna immediately bent her head. She mumbled something; I couldn't hear what it was.

Landsrud asked if I could imagine a man in Elise's life?

I had to answer as I saw it—I couldn't imagine it. I was satisfied that I could truthfully say that—to his comfort. Landsrud didn't raise his voice. He never raises his voice, but I could see that he was shaken and upset. I could see it by the trembling in his beard.

"There you hear it, Anna. You hear what Elise's godfather says. So should you have answered, also," he said in his customary mild tone.

"I said the truth. I answered, 'Not as far as I know.'" Anna also spoke softly.

Landsrud knocked on the table with his ring. "*But we do know it,*" he said. "And you shouldn't exaggerate your truthfulness, Anna. A man? Where would he come from? Elise went to the store at ten minutes to nine; at precisely two o'clock she hurried home by way of Storgaten and ate her dinner. And you sat with her, Mother."

"Every day," mumbled Mrs. Landsrud.

"She took Storgaten back and worked until closing time. After supper she took a walk around the hospital for her headache—on well-lighted streets—when we weren't in church. Where would a man come from? I've kept my little girls close to home, and the whole town knows it."

I had to agree to that.

"Do you know of any reason your daughter would take her own life?" they asked me. "She didn't commit suicide, Jensen! Why ever would Lisa want to do away with herself?"

He didn't shout, but his voice shook. "We're happy and well-contented," he said. "We've always been happy. Between these walls fall no hard words; here rules peace and harmony. Here is a *home*. Our Lord and I have provided for that."

Mrs. Landsrud looked up.

It was the first time she had looked up since I came into the room. I have brooded over this visit, you see. I have recalled every moment. I am not mistaken; she looked up for the first time. She did not look at her husband, she looked at me. She has dark eyes, dark and small, and not easy to read. It seemed to me that her eyes begged for forgiveness, begged my forgiveness for something. But that is an impossible idea. It was a strange look...

"A crime has been committed," said Landsrud quietly and slowly. "It will probably never be solved. Jensen, our police chief is a drunkard."

"Come now, 'drunkard'? That's a strong word, Landsrud," I said.

"I've seen for myself how much beer is carried into that house," he answered. "We see it from our window every day, as you well know."

Yes, naturally, I've seen the beer wagon from the office window as well. But I'm very near-sighted and, unfortunately, there's a lot that I miss.

Landsrud told me that Anna had seen the police chief come staggering from the club many times. "You remember we've talked about it, Anna?" he said.

"Yes, Papa," Anna answered.

"You remember you saw it?" he asked.

"He wasn't steady," Anna said.

There was nothing I could say. I'm an old sinner myself.

"The police chief won't investigate," said Landsrud. "Elise has been the victim of a criminal. But now she is with God. He has taken her to Him, and He alone knows how she came to Him."

Mrs. Landsrud folded her hands. Her tears fell on them.

I wanted to get up. I didn't feel well. But Landsrud laid his hand on my shoulder and said, "If you had only been here that last evening, Jensen. If you had heard Elise say, 'Now I'm thirty years and one day old.' If you could have smelled the sweet fragrant spices from the stove, and cast an eye over our little circle, you would understand that no one would desert this home of their own free will."

Anna laid down her crochet work. She got up, crossed the room, and opened the stove door to put a piece of wood in the stove. The red light from the glowing coals reflected on her face; a closed-in face, as I said before.

Suddenly Mrs. Landsrud spoke. Or possibly she was just thinking out loud. It seemed a feeble cry from one long silent. It took me by surprise.

"We sat, all three of us, around the table," she said. "Papa wandered around with his pipe. We talked about the Olsens down below who are never at peace."

"I've reported him, Mother," Landsrud said. "It's the last time he'll use our garbage cans."

I don't believe she heard a word of it. She sat and rocked, her hands had become still.. She recalled that last evening just as I have gone through this visit in my mind—I could see it in her eyes. She just went on:

"And you remember, Anna, you said you had seen Netta Olsen come home with a fellow again, and you remember you said they turned the phonograph on in the middle of the night, and Elise cried because she couldn't get to sleep. And then Elise said, 'I wasn't crying,' and then you said you must have heard wrong, and then Papa said that a person ought to be able to weep over their sins without witnesses, and he asked Elise to fill his pipe and she got up and filled his pipe. And I said, 'You should stuff cotton in your ears at night, little girls, then you would sleep as well as ever,' do you remember, Anna?"

Anna didn't answer. She was about to begin her crochet work again, but Landsrud pointed to the tongs she had forgotten to hang up, and she got up and hung the tongs back on the rack. Her mother continued:

"And then for tea we ate the rest of the cake that Elise had for her birthday, and we lit as many of the thirty candles as were left and watched them burn one by one, and Lisa snuffed out the ends one by one with her spoon."

Landsrud stood and looked at me. When I looked at him, he nodded. His head sat straight on his shoulders, his eyes were filled with tears.

Mrs. Landsrud continued:

"So then Papa sat down in the rocking chair and read through the newspaper page by page, and we sat with our embroidery and listened to the rain on the windowpane. We didn't talk then because he was reading. When the church clock struck nine Anna took out the deck of cards."

"We play double solitaire in the evenings, Anna and I," said Landsrud. "I'm no card player, Jensen. It's just a harmless pastime."

"No, I know you don't play cards," I answered.

Then his wife chimed in again:

"And when Anna took the tablecloth off the table, Elise said, 'roll it up the other way just for once.'"

Anna looked up. She turned red. But why should she blush? Her mother said:

"But surely, Anna had to roll up the tablecloth wrong side out, just as she's always done, didn't she, Jensen? It was just a whim on Lisa's part. Then Papa sat down at the table and they began to lay out the cards, and I sprinkled a few more spices on top of the stove and Lisa said she wanted to go for a walk. Then I asked if she really wanted to go out in this awful weather, and she said she wasn't afraid of the rain, and I followed her out into the entry and saw to it that she put on her galoshes and raincoat, but I couldn't persuade her to take an umbrella. And then she left."

When the poor woman finished talking, it was as if she died. It was awful to see. I stood up.

"Well, Jensen, now you've heard about our last evening with Elise," said Landsrud. "Can you imagine anything in this peaceful night that would make a young girl want to abandon this life?"

I couldn't meet his eye; I bowed my head and said good-by.

Anna followed me to the door. When she had opened it for me, she came with me down the stairs past the Olsen's apartment and out the front steps to the street. There she took me by the arm and said, "For my part, I stopped crying at night a long time ago. And Elise would have too, if only she had been patient. But when people say that Lisa was pregnant, then you can tell them from me, Mr. Jensen, that it is a dirty lie. For she drowned nobody but herself."

I came down here to the club and had a good stiff whiskey and soda. I'm just telling what happened. But thoughts, they are strange things. I—I, too, have come to the conclusion that there was a criminal. And drinking doesn't shake that idea from my head. A good home—irreproachable, one might say. But—but when they found her, Elise was actually smiling. A mystery, yes, but one is free to ponder.

Original title: Gåten. Translated by Torild Homstad

Sigrid Undset

(1882-1949)

A novelist of international acclaim, Nobel Prize recipient (1928) Sigrid Undset is best remembered for *Kristin Lavransdatter* (1920-22), a trilogy set in the Middle Ages. She wrote yet another monumental work about medieval Norway, *Olav Audunsson* (1925-28), so it is with good reason her name is associated with the historical novel. But she also authored many novels and short stories with a contemporary setting, including the present story "The Charity Ball" from the volume *Fattige Skjaebner* (1912).

Whether she writes about the distant past or the people and places of her own day, Undset displays the same keen eye for detail, resulting in vivid re-creations of milieu and everyday activity. Characters are drawn with warmth and insight and through conflict they are confronted with moral, ethical and, in her later works, religious questions. For her female characters, these conflicts almost invariably revolve around love, sex and marriage. In a period marked by social transition, Undset retained a traditional view of women and woman's role: the Undset heroine experiences true fulfillment only when she has met the man she can love and respect and with whom she can create a home and family.

"The Charity Ball" gives us a close-up view of life in Norway's capital city during the early part of this century. Like other stories in the collection, it reveals the strained circumstances, both economic and social, of unmarried, middle-class women.

The Charity Ball

"You know, it really is a cause that everyone ought to support," she said. "Hans, darling!" He was sitting behind the morning paper, but she knocked it out of the way with her napkin. "Oh, you are awful to me—can't you listen to what I'm saying?"

"I am listening, Missi my sweet—just glancing at the paper—"

"You dreadful boy! I'm far too nice to you—you shouldn't be allowed to read the paper at the breakfast table. Darling,"—she slipped her hand inside his cuff and let her fingers crawl upwards until her soft bare arm lay over his hand. "I really do think it's our duty—we who are happily married and have lovely homes and gorgeous little babies and such—who live on the sunny side of life—it's simply our duty—"

"Yes, my love."

"Just think of our little baby, Hans darling. Just think that all those poor girls were once innocent little cherubs like that. I think it's so dreadful—I can't bear the thought of it. Don't you think we should go?"

"Of course, my love."

"Oh Hans, you're so cold and stiff and horrible in the morning. Don't you agree, it's our duty, plain and simple?"

"Thy will be done—plain and simple, I agree."

"Shame on you! You know I can't bear it when you say things like that. Blasphemy is so vulgar. But darling, I must have a new dress—"

"But sweetheart, you've only worn that green one a couple of times."

"That one! Good heavens—I got that a year ago—and that idiot Miss Hansen ruined it completely when she was altering it. Though actually it's not really her fault, poor thing—the way fashions are at the moment. It was just too full in the skirt and too narrow at the waist. Besides, you must remember, my love, that you've had a whole little cherub from me since I got that dress from you. You can't expect a little mother to be the same as she was before the cherub was on the way, really you can't!"

"Missi-mamma looks every bit as beautiful to me now as she did before—"

"You silly boy! What you mean is she's much more beautiful than before!" She stood up and smoothed down her robe of yellow-grey shantung over her supple young body.

Officially she answered to the name of Mrs. Hjelm-Hansen, wife of Director Hjelm-Hansen. But she didn't look at all like a director's wife. At home she was called little Missi-mamma, and that name suited her much better. She had chestnut-brown hair that framed her finely-freckled childish face with bouncy curls, and the smile never quite disappeared from her eyes and the corners of her mouth.

"Ooh! Little angel has woken up!" She trilled the words joyfully and ran towards the door of the nursery. "Sofie, Sofie, is baby awake, Sofie—"

The mother took the little white flannel bundle from the nursemaid and walked over to her husband, with her cheek nestled tenderly against the little child's downy head. Her face shone with happiness.

"Here's my ickle tweetie—now say dudmornin' to dadda—kiss for mamma!

"Just fancy, you don't think little Missi-mamma is more beautiful than little Missi-girl was—"

"Much, much more beautiful." He embraced his wife with the child in her arms. "Lovely, lovely—my blessed madonna. No, for shame, I musn't blaspheme, must I."

"No, for shame," said Missi, but she said it softly and gently.

"You know," she said to her friend Mrs. Schiørn, the solicitor's wife, "I have a good idea! You know that green silk dress I got for the dance at your place last year? I'm going to get some dark blue chiffon to go over it—you know, that lovely rich color—and then a bit of guipure lace or something. I'll get Miss Granum to do it. I'm sure she won't charge more than fifteen."

"Oh, don't mention that woman's name to me!" said Mrs. Schiørn. "I've been owing her fifty-two kroner for nearly a year now. Oh Missi, I owe money to so many people—I have no idea how I'm ever going to pay half of it. After all, I only have fifty kroner a month to spend on myself; Oluf, poor dear, can't give me any more than that with all the children we have. I'm really at my wits' end."

"Oh, I know." Missi's face assumed a serious expression. "And you can't go running to your husband all the time either. Oh, they had some white crepe de chine with dark green embroidery on it at Simonsen and Dahl's—you know what *gorgeous* trimmings they have there. What I would have given for some of that! But I daren't even think about it.

"But don't you think I can ask Granum to do this for me, though? She's much cheaper than the bigger places, and when it's just a question of making a few alterations, it's maddening to have to pay such exorbitant prices."

"Certainly I do. There is that about Granum, she's fairly new, so she goes to *so* much trouble, and does it *so* well—and so frightfully chic. And she *never* lets you down. If she says it'll be ready for a fitting, then it'll be ready. You know she wants to attract a good class of client, so she goes to such a lot of trouble. Yes, I certainly think you should ask Miss Granum."

Mrs. Schiørn stood in front of the mirror at Miss Granum's being measured. Mrs. Hjelm-Hansen was sitting at the table, sorting through heaps of fashion magazines and snippets of tulle and trimmings.

"Yes," said Missi, "you know, I think I'm going to have this one after all." She held up a piece of peacock-blue embroidered silk. "I wasn't really thinking of having anything as expensive as this. I was thinking of having ivory-colored lace. But this will look prettier, won't it, Lullik?"

"It would certainly look more sophisticated," said Miss Granum. Miss Granum was tall and slim and wore black. Her sandy blond hair was scraped severely back from her pale face, and billowed out from the restraining combs in a luxurious mass of curls. She had a wobbling pincushion pinned on the left of her high and shapely bust, and some scissors hanging from a belt around her slender waist.

"So we'll both come along for a fitting on Thursday at half-past one, then," said Missi.

"But it *must* be ready by then," said Lullik, "I have *so* little time to come into town—as I told you, my parents-in-law are coming to town, and I have *so* much to do."

Miss Granum assured them. And the ladies repeated: it must be absolutely certain! Miss Granum assured them.

"It's really marvellous," said Missi as they walked along the street, "that she's started to keep a stock of trimmings and such. Because I couldn't really afford to pay for that edging at Ellingsen's. And it's a bit embarrassing to ask them to let me have it on credit, when I never buy things there normally. I am really pleased—it must mean that business is going well for her, don't you think? What beautiful things she has—I must say she has taste. I like her so much. It would really make me happy if she made a go of it."

"Yes, it is lovely," said Mrs. Schiørn. And as if thinking aloud: "Now I'll be able to pay off a little of what I owe her. I'm glad I decided to have the brown dress made. It's splendid when Father-in-law comes—I always get fifty kroner from him when he leaves, and Oluf has to give me a little bit extra, too, of course. So I can pay off a few bills here and there...Oh Missi, it's so dreadful to be in debt."

"Oh, I know. Just think, Caro Werner is getting her to sew *her* ballgown too. I must say Granum is doing well for herself!"

"Yes—just imagine! Caro Werner at a charity ball for unmarried mothers!"

"Yes. Why, Mr. and Mrs. Werner are among the organizers." They both laughed long and heartily. "That takes the cake..."

"No, but honestly! Can you understand how Caro has managed it? Because it's been common knowledge right from the start that old Poulsen didn't leave anything but debts. And yet she and her sister carried on going to absolutely everything—just as if nothing had happened. Went absolutely everywhere—in spite of all the things people were always saying about Caro.''

''Well, she is an adorable little thing,'' said Missi. ''People are such terrible gossips.''

''Yes, but even so—she was as they say 'engaged' to that painter, what's his name now, and Jacobsen the store-owner, and that son of General Damm's who went to the Congo—I mean, absolutely everybody knows that. And then that trip she made to London that time—''

''Well, after all,'' said Missi, ''if Werner doesn't mind, why should we others?''

''But have you heard that story about when she came back from England?''

''No—do tell!''

''Well, what happened was—but let's go up and have a cup of tea, shall we?''

''Yes,'' said Missi. ''But listen, Lul—I'm going to pay!''

''No, I insist,'' replied her friend. ''Now that my parents-in-law are coming to visit and I shall have some money for once! Anyway, about Caro...''

It was dark in the fitting room; Miss Granum was sitting in the sewing room, making small roses of chiffon, when the doorbell rang. Little Oddlaug, who was both maid and errand girl, came in and said there was a gentleman asking for Magnussen.

''Say that he's moved.''

The gentleman put his head round the door of the sewing room: ''Evenin', evenin'.''

''Oh, it's you, Egelien, how are you?''

''Oh, not too badly, thank you. So Magnus has moved, has he? Do you know where he's holed up now?''

''I've got his address somewhere—just a minute, I'll have a look.'' She took the lamp and went into the fitting room, moved Missi's ball-gown to one side, then picked it up and held it out: ''Just look how elegant this is! This is really something special—don't you think it's *sweet?*''

''Yes, it's a sweet dress, as you say. Redfern! Paquet?''

Miss Granum looked uncomprehendingly at him. ''Translated from the French, I mean.'' Egelien smiled and screwed up his eyes behind his pince-nez.

''Oh, that. Yes, they're all French ones, the magazines I get. You can't deny it, there's something about the French ones that the others haven't got. There's a certain style—"

"Naturally. But of course they use the same clichés as the other ones. But they're in French, right? Which you don't understand—and I'm sure your ladies don't either. That makes it all so much posher."

"Get along with you! You don't know what you're talking about, old boy. Weldon's catalogue and *Sewing Weekly* and such are all well and good, if you want to sit up in Homansbyen or out at Grønnerløkka and sew for shop assistants and traders' wives and secretaries and teachers and the like. But if you're trying to set up an establishment that aims at catering for the smart set, then—"

"In any case, I should have thought that both wives and secretaries—and serving maids and factory girls as well, come to that—that they would all want things translated from the French anyway." He laughed. "Across the yard from where I live in Wessel Street there's a poor little office girl who sits and stitches together her own clothes on a sewing machine in the evenings. But she was wearing some cotton dresses this summer that were so tightly pulled in—just like the French—that you could see everything she had. Her bottom stood out like a delicious little peach—and when she walked—"

"Really, Egelien, the things you say!"

"I'm only telling you what I've seen. But seriously, don't you think it's peculiar? Fashions like that, which have been invented for the richest whores and duchesses in Paris, who have ladies' maids to change them more often than you change a baby. And then an outfit like that, which is dreamed up for the sort of lady of leisure who drives out into the Bois de Boulogne, is helped out of her carriage and trips a couple of hundred steps and then is driven home again and changed—an outfit like that is translated by a little Norwegian seamstress into woollen or cotton material for a little Norwegian housewife who has lost her shape, like a worn-out shoe, as a result of constant childbirth and toil—that's not French either, you know—or for a secretary who sits out the backs of her skirts, just like office workers and teachers ruin the knees of their trousers—or at least, that's what they did in books twenty years ago."

Miss Granum pursed her lips, offended:

"Well, I dare say there are seamstresses who live in the back streets of Paris as well. And for your information, the young woman who is going to wear this dress is every bit as smart and stylish as any Parisian lady. The way she's made, it's a real pleasure sewing for her. What a figure that girl has! Just like a doll. You should see her bust and her arms—"

"I'd love to. Who is she, anyway?"

"The wife of Director Hjelm-Hansen. And she is so sweet, it's a sheer pleasure dealing with her. She's a real little charmer." She moved around, tidying up the room as she spoke.

"Is that French lyricism as well?" asked Egelien, as Miss Granum hung up Mrs. Schiørn's reddish-brown woollen dress.

"No, not exactly. Poor thing, that's more what you would call a peasant costume." She smoothed it down a little contemptuously. "When a woman has had six or seven children like that, then it's not easy to sew a skirt for her without it looking like a barrel."

"Hmm." Egelien had sat down in the armchair with his cane between his knees and his chin resting on it. "You know, Miss Granum—you know, you really are a remarkably interesting person."

She looked suspiciously at him. Egelien had furnished his small, ruddy-complexioned, narrow face with a black-pointed beard below and a large soft felt hat on top, pulled down to his eyebrows. When he smiled, as he did now, he half-closed his eyes behind his pince-nez.

"Up to a certain point of course. Up to a certain point you are quite an original woman, I believe. Up to a certain point, yes—for example, if I had said that you are an unusually attractive girl, then you wouldn't have stood there and looked at me like that, would you? You would have liked that better, wouldn't you? Even though a great many men have said it to you before, of course. But when I tell you that you are a remarkably interesting person—a completely new kind of woman—then you stand there and look at me like that."

Miss Granum smiled a little confusedly. Then she laughed:

"Pooh! I think you're the original one, Egelien. What is it that's so strange about me?"

"I really do believe that you like sewing. Right? Love your work, as the good old saying goes?"

"One has to do something," she replied evasively.

"So they say. And there is some truth in it, unfortunately. But you—when you talk about Mrs. Holm-Jensen, or whatever her name is, and her ballgown—almost with an artist's enthusiasm—"

"Well it's always more fun sewing something fine than something ordinary," said Miss Granum after a while. She sat down in the other armchair. "I lived up in Dahlsberg Road for a year or so," she said after a moment. "Oh no, I would much rather have the smart set to sew for and live down here, than sit up there sewing plain, ugly light blue or strawberry-red woollen dresses with cream-colored jabots of cheap tulle and dreadful braid, for these common ordinary shop ladies and the like, who would come for fittings in grubby underwear which smelled of sweat if it was the middle of the week—and wearing the sort of corsets that make it just impossible to get clothes to sit properly.''

"Listen, Miss Granum.'' Egelien stood up with a resolute expression. He pulled a bottle wrapped in blue tissue paper out of his coat pocket. "This is brandy. I'd brought it along for Magnus and me. Listen, why don't we have a drop, while we're sitting and talking? It's so pleasant sitting here—''

She sat and thought for a moment. "You're a strange one,'' she said, not really knowing what else to say. "Perhaps we'd better have a cup of coffee with it, then.''

He was walking up and down in the room when she returned from the kitchen.

"Well, this is the only sitting room I have,'' said Miss Granum, laughing. She tidied the magazines away onto a little cupboard in the corner.

"Should we not call it your study—or atelier?'' Egelien helped her to collect the magazines. There was a little stand on the cupboard with a few knick-knacks and photographs—a couple of portraits of men, a light-colored farmhouse with dark outbuildings in the background and a little four-year-old girl in a lacy dress. Egelien looked at the pictures:

"Well, if it isn't Magnus—in full uniform as a reserve, the idiot!''

"Yes, he gave me that without my asking,'' she said laughing.

"And this?''

"That's where I come from—Granum, in Rakkestad. Though it's other people who own it now, my parents are dead, you see.''

"And this one?'' He looked at the picture of the little girl.

"My sister's child.'' She took the photo from him and looked at it for a moment. "Wasn't she a pretty little girl? She's dead now.''

"That's probably the most sensible thing she could do. Pretty little girls avoid a lot of problems that way. She looks like you.''

"Perhaps she does. She was called Margit Evelyn—isn't that a pretty name?'' She pronounced each syllable separately.

"Yes. By the way, what's your first name, Miss Granum?''

She hesitated a moment:

"Elina. Do you think it's an attractive name?''

He nodded. "Yes—for someone who can carry it off. It's like something out of Ibsen. It suits you. You know, it makes the devil of a difference—just one letter, and it becomes Oline—''

She turned bright red: "That was a mean trick. Who was it who told you—was it Magnusen?''

Egelien burst out laughing:

"No, on my honor—I really had no idea! My dear girl, don't be cross—''

The little girl came in with the coffee tray. Miss Granum threw the cloth onto the table and banged cups and glasses down with an irritated rattle. Egelien settled down comfortably in the chair again and poured brandy into the glasses.

"No really, my dear, I had no idea that you had been christened Oline. Well, well. But it really is remarkable—as I said, you are a remarkable woman. There you are, handicapped ever since your christening with an impossible name like that. And then with a single little—how shall I put it—just as when you with your fine artistic talent adapt an impossible dress, so that it sits properly, obediently follows the lines of the female body which it reveals and conceals—just by changing a letter like that you make your name sit properly on you. For Elina was absolutely the only title Our Lord could give His work when He had created you. Skål Elina!"

"If you're not as peculiar as porridge in a bottle and water on a fork." She laughed, appeased.

"My dear lady, we are all peculiar. It just depends whether anyone notices. You yourself, for example—you've probably never discovered how odd you are yourself."

"No, Lord knows I haven't. Anyway, skål. I don't see how you can think that it is odd that I am trying to get on in the world. I mean, just sitting there in that shabby district with one or two seamstresses and sewing for the likes of those who live there, there's no future in that. No, just let me get a footing in the smart set, and you'll soon see. It's not as boring as all that, either, sewing—like for Mrs. Hjelm-Hansen, that's really enjoyable. . .Do you think that your work is as dreadful as all that, you poor thing?"

"Well, I will admit that I think most things in life are more enjoyable than work. . .Do you mind if I smoke? And you—no, you don't smoke."

"Aren't you going to be a medical student?"

"Am, am, dear lady. I will admit that I have not made any very great inroads into the study as yet. But nevertheless I must be allowed to call myself a medical student."

"Oh, all right, excuse me. So you're going to be a doctor. I should think that ought to be most enjoyable."

"Hm. Well, when your choice is limited to one or other of the branches of science taught at our venerable university. You see, I am the son of a village teacher and *kirkesanger.* And people there were so kind (the minister and the doctor, etc.) as to decide that I was a clever

---

kirkesanger: see earlier note p. 38

boy, and they wanted to help me to make a good start in life. That means of course attending the said venerable institution. Well, since I had, for the time being, used all the energy I could muster to avoid becoming a minister, the study of medicine was my only option.''

''Yes, but surely, it seems to me that you should be pleased that you've been helped like that. It must be fun to be a student, anyway. I would much rather be a doctor in any case than something like—''

''—a farmer or a *klokker* or a stationmaster—yes, that's true. Oh well, if I don't manage to become what I really want, then in time and with God's help I shall finish up as a fat and contented general practitioner out in the country—or a fashionable ladies' doctor here in town, doing some sewing for your fine ladies as well—'' he laughed.

''Oh, you do say such dreadful things! But Egelien—'' she leaned towards him. ''Tell me what it is that you really want to be.''

''Some other time perhaps.'' He emptied his glass and poured them both some more. ''Over a different glass. Then I shall confide in you all my secret hopes, my little Elina.''

''My dear sir, it really doesn't matter to me,'' she said indifferently.

''Very well, very well. But listen, Miss Granum, how about if we went out together one evening? It's really so pleasant talking to you.''

''Well thank you—but I really haven't much time for that sort of thing. I have so much to do that I can hardly keep up. Often I have to make my girls stay until it is ten or eleven o'clock, or even later. And this week I have three gowns for this ball at the Rococco Room, and another two which have to be ready by Sunday, and then there's a lot of other things I've promised to do. So I don't think I can, thank you.''

''Oh, surely you can? You must be able to take a bit of a break on Saturday evening, just like other people do.''

''Saturday—are you mad? I'm afraid I'll be terribly busy then.''

''But the ball gowns will have to be delivered, surely, before that dance for the protection of morality begins?''

''Oh, but there's always so much to do afterwards.''

''But then you really will need to get a bit of fresh air. If I dropped by let's say around half past nine—''

''You know, I really would enjoy that.'' She paused a moment. ''Yes, if you come around that time, then—I should like to.''

''Oh, by the way, while I'm thinking about it—have you got Magnussen's address? Why did he move out, anyway?''

She shrugged her shoulders as she went over and began looking in a

---

klokker: see earlier note p. 24

drawer.

"He no doubt owed you some rent?" Egelien laughed.

"That too, yes."

"Well...*So machen wir's alle.* Or perhaps you belong to that class of people who have the bad habit of paying their debts?"

"Sometimes you have to." She laughed a little. "*I* can't owe four months' rent for this place, you know. And things like those—"she pointed to the shelf of trimmings—"you have to pay for them after three months—if you don't have to pay on delivery, they even insist on that sometimes. And my seamstresses must have their wages promptly on the right day. And then coal and coke and paraffin and gas—you wouldn't believe how much gas I use for all those irons—there's always something you need money for. But collecting it isn't always as easy as all that, believe me."

"Can't you send a bill?"

"I do that sometimes, you know. But I just get them back again. And you can't pester people, not when you want the sort of clients I'm aiming at. They want to pay when and how it suits them. And you have to be *so* extremely careful, otherwise you risk ruining your whole business. There are many people I never send a bill to, because I know they wouldn't like it. Oh, there are some people who owe me for a whole year, or even two—and there are some that I know quite well will never pay. It isn't always easy, you know." She sighed. "I should really be glad if I could get a new lodger for Magnussen's room."

"I have a friend—"

"No," said Miss Granum in a determined voice. "No, I'm not going to take young gentlemen as lodgers any more. Ugh, no, Magnussen was so disgusting! When he first came to town, he was so clean and tidy, it was lovely—paid his rent and everything. But then it started. Yes, he's even gone so far as to bring girls home, just think! Ugh, and then he came home late in the morning as drunk as a skunk and threw up on the stairs and in the entrance and in his room too. His room often looked just like a pigsty. I felt quite sorry for Oddlaug who had to clean there. I really had a bad conscience about her—she's only a child, and the sort of things he used to leave lying about his room—"

Egelien laughed.

"Oh yes, you can laugh! No, I'm going to see if I can find a nice quiet middle-aged lady. It's not as easy as all that, because women like that prefer to have their meals included, or at least breakfast, and I can't be taking that on as well. I'm sleeping in that room myself at present, so that Oddlaug has the maid's room. But I shall have to see about getting a lodger. If only I could find some old teacher or office secretary or something like that—"

"Who doesn't change her underwear all week—"

"I'd have to put up with that!" She laughed. "No, I think I'd prefer them anyway—they pay when they're supposed to. And then there's the fact that they have to be at work in the morning, so that you can get the room cleaned at a reasonable hour. Men like Magnussen laze around in bed till three or four in the afternoon."

"You know, it seems to me that people like that are a much better proposition altogether when it comes to business dealings!"

"That's true enough. I do have quite a lot of ladies like that too, you know, who come to me for sewing when they want something a bit special. And they usually pay more promptly."

"So you wouldn't say no to a schoolteacher or a butcher's wife?" She laughed:

"You must be joking! Of course I don't—though I'm not particularly keen on butchers' wives—or dry old biddies. No, it's not that I'm a snob. Just let me tell you about one particular case. A few days ago I had a young girl in here, she's just become a teacher—not more than eighteen as far as I can see. Lovely, she was, with blond curly hair and blue eyes—buxom, and so pretty. Well, she needed a ballgown, and it was so important to her to look nice; and then she showed me the sample material she'd brought—some dreadfully creased, thin, pale blue silk and some white pearly fringing and such-like. So I said to her, I wouldn't wear that, Miss, I said, it'll make you look like a milkmaid in a lampshade, but if you'll just let me explain what I would do, if I were you and had your looks, and it won't cost you any extra, I said, and so I managed to talk her into it. So now I'm making her a sheer white dress with gathers in it here and there, and I'm making roses of white chiffon and three shades of pink and a few leaves of green silk, and putting them in a garland around the neck with a corsage of small fluffy buds hanging down, and a few on the sleeves and the skirt. I've been sitting here in the evenings making roses until I couldn't see straight, you know, and I've promised to make it for her for fourteen kroner, because I could see that she hadn't much money. But now I'll get her looking just like I want her. You should see her, she'll be just like a Christmas angel, and that's exactly how she should look.

"No, while I was working as a seamstress up in Dahlsberg Road, I collected in the little bits owing to me fairly easily. But even so! I don't like putting work into something that I can't possibly make attractive, however much I should like to because, you see, the clients *want* it to be ugly. Ugh! You see, it's quite possible to make a dress which is smart and graceful even out of cheap material—just think of cotton or muslin dresses, how elegant they can be. But the trouble is that the less taste a woman has, the more obstinate she is. What do you think of sky-blue silk against gravy-brown cloth? It made me feel sick to sit and sew that dress. And pink or pale blue silk blouses with yellow ruffles—and fat old wives who want thick woollen tweed made up in styles that were designed for muslin or voile. . .No thank you! Now I'm beginning to be reckoned as one of the finer dressmakers, so I can express an opinion now and then: I think this would suit you, and I don't think that would suit you. . .I made several gowns for the castle ball this year.

"So there will be money coming in, you see. And I can get more credit as time goes on. Pooh, you wait, I'll manage all right. Just wait until spring. Then some of the money will come in. Do you know what I'm going to get then? A new suit of thick, soft, pearly-grey silk. The same style as one I saw recently in *Chic Parisien*...

"Then I won't have a lodger in that room, I'll use it myself and let Oddlaug have the maid's room. It is a bit unpleasant having her sleeping in the kitchen—although she's very clean and orderly, that girl. Oh, I do like fine, pretty clothes, Egelien—more than anything. Look!"

Humming gently, she pulled an enormous cardboard box out from under the sofa: "My winter hat!" She lifted it out almost tenderly and put it with great care on her head.

"What do you think? Large? Pooh, it's not at all too big for this year's fashions. You should just see Mrs. Hjelm-Hansen's hat, for example. But don't you think it looks as if it was made just for me? It looks quite simple, doesn't it? Guess what it cost! Twenty? You're joking!

"Forty-three was what I paid—it had been sixty-five, but I know the manager from the time I worked at Simonsen and Dahl's. It's a Paris model."

She laughed:

"Actually, I haven't even paid for it yet."

When Egelien arrived at Miss Granum's on Saturday evening, her seamstresses were just getting ready to go. She herself was sitting at the table, wearing a soft, lilac-grey evening dress with black trimmings.

"Good evening, Egelien! Would you mind sitting down a few minutes? I'm waiting for Oddlaug to return. You'd better wait a few minutes, Jensen."

Jensen, a little seamstress with dark curls, went into the sewing room.

"Oh, Egelien, so many things have gone wrong today,. you wouldn't believe it. Really, I hardly feel like going out any more."

"Really? What's the matter, then?"

"Oh...But how fine you look!"

"Fortunately." He was wearing a top hat and a borrowed fur overcoat. "Since you overwhelm me completely—my God, you look stunning, Miss Granum!"

She laughed, a little tired. She took out the black velvet hat and fastened it lovingly on to her blond hair. Then she draped a dark, wine-red evening cape around herself.

"Where in heaven's name is that girl anyway?"

At last Oddlaug returned.

"Well?"

"I got thirty kroner from Mrs. Schiørn, and she asked if you would send a receipt on Monday. And that Mrs. Hansen said she hadn't the time to look at the bill now, it was so late—she'd been waiting over an hour for her dress, she said."

Miss Granum put the bills in a drawer:

"Can you change ten kroner, Egelien—here you are Jensen, there's nine kroner—good night. Just try and see that you get here in good time on Monday. Shall we go then, Egelien?"

He saw that she was out of sorts and in low spirits.

"Money troubles?" he asked, after they had walked a while.

"Oh yes. I know it's stupid of me to take it so much to heart. After all, it shouldn't be any worse for me to owe money than it is for the others. Heavens! I don't know how some people can do it. Just think, there were a couple of my clients sitting here recently, young ladies, just girls they were, and one of them was telling the other that she owed over fifty kroner at the confectioner's just for cakes and port and so on. Yes, I can remember from the time I worked in the dressmaking department of Simonsen and Dahl—there were society ladies who owed a thousand kroner and more and the bills went back several years. They knew they would never recover the money from some of them. Sometimes it makes me so cross when I think about it. Is it refined to act that way, do you think?"

"Well, isn't it precisely the fine folk who do that sort of thing most?"

"Yes, of course it is. Other people can't get that sort of credit. But that's what's so annoying. Because they have to make up for the losses, you see. So it all falls on those who can't get credit—on all the little people. Oh, don't let's talk about it any more—I get so worked up these days..."

Egelien suddenly realized that she was close to tears. She stopped for a moment near a gaslight, but not too close to the light, and rummaged around in her handbag until she found a small tin box.

"Isn't it clever that they can get a whole silk veil—four meters long—into such a tiny box? I got it from the French manufacturer's agent—it's a kind of advertisement. Oh, they know how to do things in Paris! What I would give for a trip down there." She tried to laugh as she fastened the veil in place.

Damned good-looking, thought Egelien, as she advanced at his side through the restaurant. And when she let the waiter take her cape, raised the heavy black silk veil from her pale, fair face and slowly drew off her black gloves—

"Shall we begin with Briand then—and wine? What sort would you like—red wine? Sauterne? That's perhaps a little sweet—"

"My dear, are we really going to have wine?"

"Of course we'll have wine...You know, Elina Granum, I really think you should travel to Paris."

She laughed out loud:

"And just how should I manage that, Egelien?"

"Hmm!" He threw up his hands and smiled behind his pince-nez. "Couldn't you get some kind of grant? Get someone to take an interest in you—so that you could go down there to study. With a letter of introduction to one of the world-famous firms—the ateliers—down there. Don't you think there might be a chance?"

"Oh, no, that's surely impossible."

"If you believe a thing is impossible, then it becomes so, you know. But think about it. I am sure you can do it if you want to. And once you were down there...The bon viveurs of Paris come to those big shops with their wives and mistresses. You would have opportunities there. There are those great palaces of entertainment—and the boulevards—there are thousands of chances for a woman like you."

"Egelien, if you intend to carry on talking like this, I shall leave!"

"No, you won't do that. There's no need to be a goose and get cross just because I'm talking to you as if you were a sensible and unprejudiced person. You know, you really are damned interesting; I think it's a downright shame that you should have to slave away like you do—when I think what you could become if you got into the circles where you really belong."

"Well really! If that's why you've asked me to come out with you! Well, Egelien, you think that I am best suited to being a kept woman, do you?"

"Kept woman—" he laughed. "My dear Elina, what do you think that most of your finest clients are in actual fact? What do you think is the difference between the vast majority of those women who are dancing at the Rococco Room tonight and the women for whose benefit they are dancing? That the former have traded themselves once and for all, and the sale is officially sanctioned by a minister in a church, while the latter—poor girls—have to struggle and toil again and again every evening to find customers, and conclude the deal under gaslights and in entryways. But both kinds make a living by exploiting men's sexual drive—and sometimes his love, especially the former. Which is the reason why I rate the streetwalkers higher from a moral point of view. Is it not a dirtier trick to make a man's most sacred feelings into the object of cold-blooded speculation to earn a living than it is just to traffic in the so-called basest instincts?"

"Really, Egelien, the things you say. Of course there are quite a number of women who only marry in order to be taken care of. And I wouldn't exactly defend that. But there is a difference—"

"That's just what I'm saying. There's a devil of a difference. The more expensive a commodity is, the more the buyer prizes it. An expensive lady is honored and respected—but a cheap tart...One of them is borne aloft by the whole of society; the other is trodden underfoot by the whole of society. The former has secured herself respect and protection. She can afford to preserve her virtue from all other men except her husband—if it doesn't amuse her to be unfaithful. If it does amuse her—very well. If she is unlucky and is found out, then she can arrange a new and advantageous deal, if she hasn't been entirely stupid and made an idiotic choice of a lover. She can make a big thing of everything she has sacrificed for his sake—husband, home, children, virtue and reputation—so that he is forced to enter into the contract, take over her maintenance, marry her. In other words, a married kept woman from higher society has arranged things so that she is always safe. She can have it just how she likes. If she is cold, and doesn't really enjoy what she is paid for—well, if she likes it like that, she can put her husband on a reduced diet and get her payment for a minimum of service.

"A poor prostitute is kicked and scorned just because she can be bought so cheaply. She becomes coarse and foul-mouthed because she is treated in a coarse and foul-mouthed way; she becomes an outsider, shies away from work, one of those persecuted by the whole of decent society. She drinks—has to drink as a rule in order to carry out her chosen trade.

"But it is the same thing, Elina Granum, for which the former receives house and home and invitations to palace balls and respect and peace and villas and rest cures and sweet little children to caress and play with—and for which the latter gets curses and poorhouse and hospital."

"Oh Egelien, the things you say. The way you put things, it makes me feel quite dizzy." She sat still, almost frightened. And her eyes, glistening from the wine, became dimmed. "But it's true enough— the dreadful, dreadful life that those girls have. No, anything must be better than that. Oh no—if you don't watch out for yourself, then you can finish up in the gutter in no time at all."

"Exactly. If you don't watch out for yourself. You know, there are ladies in Paris, demi-mondaines, who have retired from the business—sucked hordes of men dry and thrown them aside like squeezed lemons. Then they take their leave one day and have nothing more to do with the male sex—live comfortably and respectably, following their own interests, whether it be art, religion or charity.

"You would be able to watch out for yourself. Use men, and not let yourself be used. I can just see how you would be, so pale and cold and unfathomable—distant and cool and clever. Living only for what you love—beauty, refinement, exquisite delights—in a little villa, a dream and a poem in colors and forms—sheer silk and soft velvet—old furniture redolent of the past glory of vanished queens.

"And then you yourself. All that beauty which you compose for other women, those lovely outfits that you create for others who go out and conquer men, furnished by your own pale, tired, busy hands. While you yourself make do with a few scraps which can come your way now and again—a dress like that one for the autumn, a hat for winter and a silk suit for spring. Wouldn't you rather create, compose, dream for yourself alone? Hundreds of poems, one for each day and night of the year, one for each shifting mood of your heart: plaintive songs of mourning in midnight blue and deathly black velvet—white idylls like the one you described to me—exuberant ritornellos in light rustling silk—baracolles in sea-green covered with sunlit gold—"

She was sitting there staring into space, entranced. Now she tried to laugh, but it was a feeble attempt:

"I honestly think you're not in your right mind!"

"No." He tossed his head proudly. "No, I'm certainly not. Waiter! Coffee and cognac...Oh hell, I'd forgotten, we're still in Norway. Well, let's have a wine list them." Egelien studied it carefully. "That one!" he finally indicated to the waiter.

"Then I shall come down to Paris and visit you. For you shall come to live this life! By God! Not the way you're sitting here, looking so frightened at me. *I* shall give you this life. In my poem. I shall write a book—so violently truthful, so consumed with passion, so daring, that it will terrify them all—so brimming with beauty...Now you know."

The waiter arrived with the coffee and port. Egelien poured it into the glasses so that they overflowed.

"Skål, Elina!"

Miss Granum sat still, looking at him.

"Well. So it's a writer you're going to be, Egelien."

"Ah, yes," she said a little later. "It can all sound very fine and attractive in a novel. There's no doubt a lot of truth in what you say too—"

"Truth! Do you know what the truth is, Elina Granum? There are only two kinds of women. Those who are useful, whom we call respectable because they are useful. They are housewives in woollen dresses and corsets which don't fit properly, and silk blouses in the theatre; secretaries and teachers with worn and shiny skirt seats and tired eyes—those you yourself spoke so scornfully about, who smell of sweat; the sweat of honest toil, in which God has so tastefully said we shall eat our bread. And who are so repulsive to you, for your soul longs for what is not useful, for what is beautiful. But you cannot worship beauty in the sweat of your face—it must be gathered from another's field. Beauty is a parasite, Elina. The high priestesses of beauty are parasites one and all—married or unmarried, duchesses or streetwalkers, in the depths of their being they are all what society castigates as whores, for they are useless and infertile. But literature, the most useless and most beautiful thing of all, it glorifies them, Elina!"

He nodded, staring ahead, lost in thought.

"Now you understand me, don't you? Why I say that you are so remarkable and new? You are yearning with all the strength of your being for beauty—for the refined and the superfluous. It shines like a dream, a mirage, over the grey toil of your days. And yet you are trapped by prejudices which prevent you from entering into your kingdom and conquering it."

Miss Granum sat with her hands folded under her chin.

"Well one thing I do know," she said suddenly, in a determined fashion. "And it's what I have always thought—to stoop so low as to take money for *that*—they should be ashamed!"

"That's a fine thought, Elina. But a foolish one. After all, why should you give yourselves to us for nothing? Because you're in love? What do you get in return? Either he loves you faithfully in return, and then you get a house and work and children and sleepless nights and grow old and ugly in no time. Or he doesn't love faithfully, and then it's so long sweetheart and thanks a lot—"

"Ha! Yes, that's true enough." She stared into space. "I say Egelien, how old are you really? You must be older than Magnussen, I suppose."

Egelien studied his cigar:

"Some of us seem to be born old, Miss Granum. My parents were old when I was made—years of struggle and hardship had made them old. I suppose they couldn't give me any other soul than the one I got. Actually I'm twenty-three—going on twenty-four."

"Just think, I'm thirty-one. Would you have thought so?" she took out a handbag mirror—her face had become somewhat flushed—and a powder compact.

"When I was your age I got engaged. I was working in a shop then. I earned thirty kroner a month and slept in a bathtub at my lodgings. He was a salesman, my fiancé. Handsome he was too—and God knows I loved him. I have never been in love with anyone else—never been near anyone else either. I can swear to that. Well—his family arranged for him to be sent to Germany, and then he wrote and broke it off."

She was silent. Her whole face trembled.

"He was from a good family, you see. His mother came along and offered me some money. You mustn't think that I accepted it, Egelien—not one penny. Oh, how hungry I was then. You can't imagine what it's like to go hungry when you're in the state I was in at that time. I lived up in the poor district at Grønnerløkka, and I managed to rent a sewing machine and made boys' clothes for a firm when I couldn't keep my job in the shop any more. Dear God, what a dreadful time it was—and not a single person to help me. And what shame I felt! My father was still alive at that time. I'm sure that he would have killed me at the very least if he had found out about it.

"She was mine, you see, that little girl whose picture you saw up in my room a few days ago."

"Poor little Elina." He whispered it gently and took her hand under the table. "Poor brave, proud little Elina.

"And then you became so very fond of your little girl, didn't you—your little Evelyn?"

Miss Granum blew her nose:

"Oh yes, I did. Especially after I'd brought her to live with me. But then she died. I had to let her be fostered, you see, when I came out of the home. Then I started working in a sewing workshop. But the people she was living with left and went to America, and then I took her to live with me because I couldn't find anywhere that wasn't too expensive. And the people I was living with were so kind to her; they were such a nice elderly couple, real Christians they were—he was a foreman at Nyland's and they didn't have any children themselves, and the wife thought that it was fun to have a little girl to talk to during the day—to look after and take care of. And she was such a lovely little thing—so pretty and clever and sweet. . .And then she died of diphtheria at Ullevold hospital."

The lights were dimmed for a moment and then came on again. People started to leave from the surrounding tables. Egelien beckoned to the waiter.

They walked slowly along through the park. The tree-tops stood pale with frost against the dark sky, which was blotchy with clumps of cloud. The palace courtyard lay deserted and cold in the frosty night—the gravel hurt through her thin shoes, and she shivered with cold. The palace stood there heavy and grey with black windows—only a couple were lit up—but below the slope with its few scattered gaslights there hung two long chains of arc lamps over Carl Johan Street.

"There is a ring of women around our lives," said Egelien in a deep and mysterious voice. "A ring woven from gold and platinum. Do you know what platinum is? It is the most precious metal in the world—even though it is grey and dark and cold and barren. Yes, it is woven from cold platinum and from warm, soft, pure gold. They are woven together in a clasp around a clear diamond, and that is called Elina.

"I can't say Miss Granum any more," he said drily and ironically. "I should have to laugh at myself. Will you allow me to say Elina? And won't you call me Arnljot? That's my name."

"That's a nice name. Oh, I don't know what to think any more, Egelien," she burst out. "It's all just talk. I think you end up being just as miserable whether you work hard and keep yourself respectable or you don't.

"But one thing I do know: those who are well off ought to pay us properly, those of us who slave for them—instead of flitting off and dancing to raise money for charitable homes for prostitutes in gowns that they haven't paid for—

"No, what I don't understand is how any woman can stoop so low as to take money for—

"But that one thing can lead to another for the sake of a bit of enjoyment and warmth, when there is someone who behaves as if he cares and is prepared to make a bit of a fuss of a poor girl who has no one in the whole world to be fond of and has nothing but toil and worry from morning to night—*that* I can understand, I can tell you that—

"Oh, I'm so tired, so sick of everything—Oh God, I'm so

miserable," she sobbed.

"Elina," he put his arm around her. "Elina—I don't understand anything either," he said darkly and broodingly. "It's only something I write and dream about. A proud and carefree and defiant world of beauty—"

He lifted her hands and kissed them:

"They are holy, your hands. I drink from them—they are a white alabaster chalice, full of bitterness and pain.

"You see, life is a grim farce for those of us who are poor and full of longing. How I love you—"

"Arnljot," she said softly and came into his arms. And they kissed for a long time. He was vaguely aware of the fact that they both smelled of wine, and was distracted by the memory of the hole in his finances made by the Park Cafe's cheapest port. Ah me, and it should have been dark blood-red burgundy or extravagant champagne. But he said merely:

"Two poor birds we are—in fine feathers which we haven't quite paid for. But your red cloak is dark tonight, Elina—it runs over your shoulders like the dried blood of martyrs."

"Baby's been asleep for a long time now," said Missi in the carriage. "Hans—I've never been away from my little girl for such a long time as this."

"Our little angel is sleeping soundly." He put his arm around her. "Sofie will look after her all right. Now little Missi's going beddy-bye too—isn't she?"

"Yes." She yawned. "My darling Hans will look after his little Missi, won't he?

"—It was fun, wasn't it? Aren't you glad we went?"

With that she lay her head on her husband's steadfast breast and went sweetly to sleep in the carriage.

By then Miss Granum had already been asleep for several hours in her student's arms.

Original title: *Omkring saedelighetsballet.* Translated by Janet Garton

Cora Sandel

(1880-1974)
When Sara Fabricius left her parents' home in Tromsø in 1905 bound for
Paris, her aspirations were not to become a writer but a painter. She spent
the next fifteen years there, often with barely enough to get by, and when
she returned to Scandinavia in 1921, it was not to Norway but to Sweden,
where she settled. In 1926, forty six years old, she published her first novel,
Alberte og Jakob, under the pseudonym Cora Sandel. This was only the
beginning of Alberte's story and in 1931 and 1939 the second and third
volumes appeared, *Alberte og friheten* and *Bare Alberte*. The *Alberte* trilogy, a
classic in Norwegian literature, is a moving portrayal of a young woman's
struggle to become a writer.

In the years between the publication of the first and third volumes of her
trilogy, Cora Sandel completed three collections of short stories. Here, as in
her novels, she demonstrates a strong empathy with society's defenseless
and vulnerable individuals, women and children in particular. With subtle
irony she conveys the narrow-mindedness that flourishes in small groups
and communities. Sandel depicts the traditional woman's role as stifling
and isolating, as illustrated in the two stories below. The protagonists rebel
against society's expectations and demands—they choose the liberating,
'masculine' activity of wandering on roads and forest paths over the
confining, 'feminine' activity of sitting in the parlor—but they each
discover that independence is not without sacrifice. "A Mystery" is taken
from *Carmen og Maja* (1932); "The Child Who Loved Roads" was first
published in the magazine *Kvinnen og Tiden* (1947) and was later included in
the collection *Barnet som elsket veier* (1973).

The Child Who Loved Roads

Most of all she loved roads with the solitary track of a horse down the
middle and with grass between the wheel ruts. Narrow old roads
with lots of bends and nobody else around and here and there
perhaps a piece of straw, fallen from a load of hay. The child turned
light as air on them, turned springy and filled with happiness at
breaking free, at existing. Behind every bend waited unknown

possibilities, however many times you'd gone down the road. You could make them up yourself if nothing else.

Down the highway she walked, dragging her feet in dust and gravel. Dust and gravel were among the bad things in life. You got tired, hot, heavy, longed to be picked up and carried.

Then suddenly the narrow old road was there, and the child began to run, leaping high with happiness.

She hadn't been so tired after all, the grown-ups said. There's a lot grown-ups don't understand. You have to give up on explaining anything to them and take them as they are, an inconvenience, for the most part. No one should grow up. No, children should stay children and rule the whole world. Everything would be more fun and better then.

Early on the child learned that it was best to be alone on the road. A good ways in front of the others anyway. Only then did you come to know the road as it really was, with its marks of wheels and horses hooves, its small, stubborn stones sticking up, its shifting lights and shadows. Only then did you come to know the fringes of the road, warm from sun and greenness, plump and furry with chervil and lady's mantle—altogether a strange and wonderful world unto itself, where you could wander free as you pleased, and everything was good, safe, and just the way you wanted it.

At least it was in the summer. In winter the road was something else entirely. In the twilight of a snow-gray day your legs could turn to lead, everything was so sad. You never seemed to get any further; there was always a long ways to go. The middle of the road was brown and ugly, like rice pudding with cinnamon on it, a dish that grew in her mouth and that she couldn't stand. People and trees stood out black and sorrowful against the white. You did have the sledding hill, the field with deep snow for rolling on, the courtyard for building forts and caves, the skis without real bindings. For small children shouldn't have real bindings, the grown-ups said; they could break their legs falling. In the twilight everything was merely sad, and nothing about it could compare to the roads in summer.

To be let loose on them, without a jacket, without a hat, *bare*, that was life the way it should be. Only one thing compared to it, the hills at the big farm, where she was often a guest.

There were paths bordered with heather and crowberry leading up to views over the blue fjord and to a light, never-still breeze that tickled your scalp. White stone protruded from the heather and the path. At the bottom of the hill you found wild strawberries, higher up blueberries, not just a few either, and bilberries. On top lay the crowberries in patches like large carpets.

The child could pass hours lying on her stomach near a bush, stuffing herself, and at the same time thinking of all sorts of things. She possessed an active imagination, seldom longed for company and could sometimes fly into a rage if she got it.

"You're so contrary," said the grown-ups. "Can't you be nice and sweet like the others, just a little? You should be thankful anyone wants to be with you," they said.

"It won't be easy for you when you're older," they also said.

The child forgot it as soon as it was said. She ran off to the road or the paths and remembered nothing of anything so unreasonable, so completely ridiculous.

One road went from the house on the big farm, went along the garden where huge old red currant bushes hung over the picket fence, casually offering their magnificence; the road went across the fields, bordered by thin young trees, made a leap over a hill and swung two times like an S before it wandered out in the world and became one with the boring highway.

The child's own road, newly taken possession of summer after summer. Here no one came running after you, here you could wander without company. Nothing could happen but the right things. If anyone came driving or riding it was uncles, aunts or the farmboy. They saw you from a long distance, they stopped; if they came by wagon you got a ride to the farm.

Here and on the hills were where the stories came into being, short ones and long ones. If it didn't look like they were living up to their promise, you just stopped and started a new one.

A place in life where freedom had no boundaries. Very different from what the grown-ups meant when they said, "in this life," or "in this world," and sighed. They also said, "in this difficult life." As if to make things as nasty as possible.

Being together with someone—that was sometimes fun and sometimes not at all. You couldn't explain why or why not; it was all tied up with everything you were pretending, things you'd never think of talking to grown-ups about. On the contrary, you held tightly to it, like someone insisting on something wrong they've done. Maybe it was "wrong"; maybe it was one of those things that ought to be "rooted out of you." Or at best to laugh about a little, to whisper over your head.

"Constructive" it wasn't, in any case. They were always talking about the necessity of doing "constructive things."

It could be fun, when Alette came, Letta. She was a redhead, freckled, full of laughter, easy to get along with. At her house, on the neighboring farm, was a chest in the loft, full of old-fashioned clothes. Dresses in wonderful light colors, flounce after flounce on the wide tarlatan skirts, a name that was far prettier than, for example, blue cotton cambric. A man's suit, yellow knee breeches and a green coat with gold buttons, an unbelievable costume that didn't look like anything the uncles wore. A folding parasol, a whole collection of odd hats. To dress up in all that, strut around in it, stumble in the long skirts, mimic the grown-ups and make them laugh where they sat on the garden steps, was fun enough for a while. But it was nothing to base a life on.

For that you could only use the roads, the paths and the hills.

Grown-up, well, you probably had to turn into one. Everyone did; you couldn't avoid it.

But like some of them? Definitely not.

In the first place the child was going to run her whole life, never do anything so boring as walk slowly and deliberately. In the second and third place. . .

The grown-ups didn't have much that was worthwhile. It was true they got everything they wanted, could buy themselves things they wanted and go to bed when they felt like it, eat things at the table that children didn't get—all the best things, in short. They could command and destroy, give canings and presents. But they got long skirts or trousers to wear and then they *walked. Just* walked. You had to wonder if it had something to do with what was called Confirmation, if there wasn't something about it that injured their legs. There probably was, since they hid them and walked. They *couldn't* run any longer. Even though—you saw them dance; you saw them play "Bachelor Seeks a Mate" and "Last Pair Out."

Maybe it was their minds something was wrong with?

Everything truly fun disappeared from their lives, and they let it happen. None of them rebelled. On the contrary, they grew conceited about their sad transformation. Was there anything so conceited as the big girls when they got long skirts and put up their hair!

They walked, they sat and embroidered, sat and wrote, sat and chatted, knitted, crocheted. Walked and sat, sat and walked. Stupid, they were so stupid!

Trailing skirts were dangerous. She'd have to watch out, when the time came. Run away maybe.

At home, in the city street, were the mean boys.

Really big boys, the kind that were practically uncles, were often nice. They were the ones who organized the big circus in the empty lot, with trapeze artists, clowns and tickets that the grown-ups bought in complete seriousness: parquet circle, first class, second class. A ringmaster in a tuxedo went around the circus ring and cracked his long whip at the horses doing tricks. A true circus, so to speak, except that the horses consisted of two boys under a blanket that sometimes sagged in the middle. But that was easy to overlook.

The big boys arranged competition races in the winter, saw to it that you got new skis and real bindings; they were pillars of support. One of them once got up and lambasted his sister, who had tattled on him. A bunch of lies, made-up, shameful, that you just had to sit there and take, for you didn't get anywhere saying it wasn't true.

They were pillars all the same.

But there was a half-grown kind, a mean kind, that made such a racket. They ran back and forth with wooden bats in their hands and the balls shot between them like bullets. In the winter they threw hard snowballs, and if anyone had put up an especially fine fort anywhere, they came rushing down in a crowd and stormed it, left it destroyed. Sometimes they threatened you with a beating. For no reason, just to threaten. The child was deathly afraid of them, took any roundabout way she could to avoid them; she would rather be too late for dinner.

Sometimes she *had* to come through enemy lines to get home. With her heart in her throat, with her head bowed as if in a storm, she sneaked sideways along the walls of the houses. The taunts rained down.

One day a boy of that sort came after the child, grabbed her arm, squeezed it hard and said, "You know what you are? Do you?"

No answer.

"You're just a girl. Go home where you belong."

Hard as a whip the words struck the child. Just a girl—*just*. From that moment she had a heavy burden to bear, one of the heaviest, the feeling of being something inferior, of being born that way, beyond help.

With such a burden on your back the world becomes a different place for you. Your sense of yourself begins to change.

But the roads remained an even bigger consolation than before. On them even "just a girl" felt easy, free and secure.

The child was one of those who feels sorry. For skinny horses and horses who got the whip, for cats who looked homeless, for children who were smaller than she was and who didn't have mittens in winter, for people who just looked poor, and for drunken men.

Why she was so sorry for drunken men was never clear. They'd drunk hard liquor; they could have left it alone: They were their own worst enemies, the grown-ups explained; if things went so badly for them it was their own fault.

In the child's eyes they were nothing but helpless. They tumbled here and there; sometimes they fell down and remained lying there—the constable came and roughly dragged them off. Sorry for them, she was sorry for them; they couldn't help it, they couldn't help it for anything, however they'd come to be that way. They were like little children who can't walk on their own and do things wrong because they don't know any better.

The child cried herself to sleep at times on account of the drunkards. And on account of the horses, cats and poor people. Once you're like that, you don't have it easy. The cats she could have taken home if it hadn't been for the grown-ups. She wasn't allowed. As if one cat more or less mattered. You were powerless, in this as in everything.

On the summertime roads you forgot your troubles. If you met a poorly clad person you usually knew who they were, where they lived, that they had nicer clothes at home that they saved for Sundays. The horses you met were rounded, comfortable, easy-going. They waved their long tails up over thick haunches and grazed by the road-side as soon as they got a chance. The cats rubbed against your legs, purring loudly. Farmcats who belonged somewhere and were just out for a walk.

However, you hardly ever met anyone, neither people nor animals. That was wonderful; it became more and more wonderful as the child grew older. She had a steadily stronger desire to keep making up stories in her head. There was no place that they came so readily as along a two-wheeled track with grass in between. Or up on the hill where the breeze brushed your scalp.

Time passed. The child ran, long braid flapping, on the roads.

If she was overtaken by the grown-ups, she heard, "You're too old now to be running like that. Soon you'll be wearing long skirts, remember. A young lady *walks*, she holds herself nicely, thinks about how she places her feet. Then she can't rush away like you do."

The child ran even faster than before. To get out of earshot, out of range as much as possible. Her legs had grown long; they were an advantage when she took to her heels. The braid swung, the lengthened skirt swung. The child thought—one day I won't turn around when they call, I won't wait for anyone. That might be sooner than they suspect. The roads lead much farther than I realized; they lead out into the world, away from all of them.

When she stopped, she looked around with new eyes, seeing not only the roadsides any longer, but the horizons. Behind them lay what she longed for, craved: freedom.

But one of the big boys, the kind that were practically uncles, suddenly popped out of nowhere. He was Letta's cousin, had passed exams, was called a university student.

You didn't see much of him. Letta said he was stupid and conceited, a self-important fellow who kept to his room or with the grown-ups. He himself was definitely not that old, said Letta, who remembered him in short pants, remembered that he stole apples at someone's and got a caning for it at home. That wasn't so very long ago; she'd been ten years old, on a visit to his parents. Now she was thirteen, almost fourteen.

He had a strange effect on the child; he upset her from the first moment in a way that was both painful and good. It was impossible to think of him when he was nearby and could turn up; you can't think when you're blushing in confusion. But out on the roads he crept into her thoughts to the extent that she couldn't get him out again; he took up residence there, inserted himself in the middle of an on-going story, which had to be completely changed. There was no other recourse.

The story came to be about him. He became the main character, along with herself. In spite of the fact that she didn't really know how he looked; she never quite risked looking at him. And in spite of the fact that he wore long trousers, *walked*, and consequently belonged to the poor fool category.

It was inexplicable, and she felt it as slightly shameful, a defeat. The child grew fiery red with embarrassment if he so much as made an appearance. As the misfortune was written on her face, it was necessary to avoid Letta and her family, to keep to the roads as never before.

You could be in Letta's garden and still be unseen.

Letta followed, full of suggestions; she wanted them to get dressed up like summers before, make fun of the cousin, who was sitting on the steps with the grown-ups—mimic him.

"He doesn't interest me."

"You think he interests me? That's why we can tease him a little, can't we?"

"I'm not interested in teasing such a disgusting person," announced the child, marvelling at her own words.

"Come anyway, though."

"No."

"Why not?"

"Because I don't want to, that's why."

But it was a terribly empty feeling, when Letta gave up and walked away. Just to talk about him was a new and remarkable experience, was something she yearned for, wanted and had to do.

The child was beginning to *walk* on the roads. Slowly even. She stood still for long moments at a time. For nothing, to fuss with the tie on her braid, to curl the end of the braid around her fingers, to scrape her toe in the gravel, stare out in space. She sat down in the grass by the roadside, trailed her hand searchingly around between the lady's mantle and avens, did it over and over.

Finally her hand had found something, a four-leafed clover. Thoughtfully the child walked on with it, holding it carefully between two fingers.

"Well now, finally you're acting like a big girl," said one of the aunts, pleased. "Not a minute too soon. Good thing we don't have to nag you anymore. Good thing there's still a little hem to let out in your dress. Next week we'll get Johanna the seamstress."

Hardly was it said than the child set off at full speed, in defiance, in panic.

Without her having noticed or understood it, she had allowed something to happen, something frightening, something detestable. Something that made *them* happy. But nothing should make them happy. For then they'd be getting you where they wanted you, a prisoner, some kind of invalid.

The child didn't hear the despairing sigh of a deeply worried grownup. That would have made her relieved and calm. Instead she only felt torn by life's contradictions, bewildered and confused by them.

One day the cousin left; he was simply gone. Letta said, "Who cares, he was conceited and engaged." Secretly, of course, but it had come out that he went around with a photograph and a pressed flower in his wallet, and that he used to meet the postman far down the highway. Letta's father had taken him into the office, talked with him for a long time, pointed out what a serious thing an engagement is, nothing for a green new graduate. Green, that was probably a good description of him. Anyway, his fiancée's father was nothing but a shoemaker, said Letta. She thought the cousin's parents had been alerted.

"Imagine, engaged. Him!"

The child stood there and felt something strange in her face, felt herself grow pale. Not red at any rate, because then you got hot. This was a cold feeling.

"Well, good-bye," she said.

"Didn't you come to stay?"

The child had already gone, was out on the road, the good old road with the two curves like an S, with thin young trees along it and grass between the wheel tracks. Here was the same sense of escape as always; here you could run, not only in fantasy, but also free from all shame, everything deceitful that was out after you. And that was over now.

For it was over right away. In a short, painful moment—as when a tooth is pulled out.

Follow the road, never become what they call grown-up, never what they call old, two degrading conditions that made people stupid, ugly, boring. Stay how you are now, light as a feather, never tired, never out of breath. It came down to being careful, not just for lengthened skirts, but also for anything like this.

For a moment the child stopped, fished out of her pocket a dried four-leaf clover, tore it in pieces and let the wind take the bits.

And then she ran on, over the farmyard, right up the path to the hill, where the fresh breeze blew.

Original title: *Barnet som elsket veier.* Translated by Barbara Wilson

A Mystery

She arrived in a terrible storm. It didn't look odd in the least not to go onboard, so Mrs. Isaksen didn't, but kept in the lee of merchant Flaten's warehouse on the wharf; she stood there wearing Isaksen's sou'wester and raincoat and looked on, while a solitary passenger came up on deck and fought her way down the gangway. There was no doubt who the passenger was.

Mrs. Isaksen didn't go to meet her, but turned in the opposite direction toward Kaia, who sat in Ola Galterud's cart under the maples by the telegraph station, called out something about the horse, about being sure to hold him well, in case the steamer should blow. The words were carried off in the gale, and Mrs. Isaksen added loudly to herself that she had misgivings and that she was annoyed Kaia hadn't heard her.

In this way the stranger came unnoticed right up behind the warehouse. There she stopped and said, "Is this Mrs. Isaksen?" And the wind bore it along, so you couldn't possibly avoid hearing it. Mrs. Isaksen started in surprise, turned and shouted with all her might—she had both the headwind and something else to overcome—"Hello, hello, welcome. This must be Mrs. Arnold."

"Yes, I am. I'm so grateful to you that I could come."

"Oh, my dear—"

Mrs. Isaksen stopped. It was only right that Mrs. Arnold be grateful. She certainly had reason to be. On the other hand there was no need for effusiveness. That kind of thing could easily get out of hand. It was just as well that Mrs. Isaksen made her own position clear, now as later, by shouting, "It's for Uncle's sake. . ."

"Of course, I understand that," said Mrs. Arnold, growing red. She turned to the man with the baggage. And Mrs. Isaksen, who saw her now from the back, ascertained in silence: Beautiful coat, good shoes, pretty hat—looks anything but needy—I can't offer her my old gray coat after all. . .

The gale put a temporary stop to all conversation. It was all she could do to shout that, yes, it was that cart up there. None the less Mrs. Isaksen shouted an additional, "Horrible weather." To be friendly and to make it clear she was a kind, courteous, easy-to-get-along-with person. Up by the cart she shouted, in addition, "My daughter, Kaia," pointing up at the seat. Kaia raised herself slightly, producing with bent knees something between a nod and curtsey, neither one nor the other and a little of both.

They drove off. Out on the main road the gale winds increased, swept howling over them, allowing no conversation. All the same, in her role of hostess, Mrs. Isaksen shouted one thing or another with all her strength: "The minister lives there!" "There's the farm where we get our milk!" "This cart is rented from there!" "Summer visitors are everywhere!" "We live around that bend over there!"

Mrs. Arnold nodded in appreciative surprise at every announcement and said, "Really?" She looked frozen and worn-out, and it was difficult to imagine how her pale blue face would look under normal conditions. Her teeth were chattering. Mrs. Isaksen thought, Do I have to offer her anything before supper? She could easily get the idea that we're well off. I think I'll leave it be. Hmmm, no, I've got to offer her a cup of tea, anyway.

"I hope you'll be content with how we live," she shouted then. "We rent out one floor in the summer, as you know. We have to, unfortunately. A folding cot in the dining room is all I have to offer you."

"Thank you very much," shouted Mrs. Arnold. "Just your taking me in is so kind."

"For Uncle's sake!" emphasized Mrs. Isaksen once more so that she definitely couldn't be accused of contributing to any misunderstanding herself. Then they rolled up to the house.

On the porch Isaksen stood with a pipe and in slippers. He looked almost animated and, in spite of his slippers, descended a few steps to greet the guest.

"A hearty welcome!" he called, but got a look from his wife, and welcomed her again in a way that was correct, nothing more.

In the doorway off the entry hall Mrs. Isaksen stopped and turned to her husband. Inside the room she saw a table set with cups and saucers and a few things to eat.

"I thought you might be cold after the drive so I asked Andrine to make some coffee," Isaksen explained.

"Coffee?" Mrs. Isaksen's face went stiff. The price of cream went up yesterday, she thought. If Yngve comes home before supper we'll be five besides Andrine. We live like every day were our last. Aloud she said, "A cup of tea would have suited us better."

But Isaksen was silently examining Mrs. Arnold, who had taken off her outer garments now and stood there smoothing her hair, slender and neat and with something about her that you didn't see among the women in his house. A bit the worse for wear, all right. But not too bad really, all things considered. Frankly he'd imagined her differently, with a little more of a—well, frivolous—character. But now, watching her, he was interested and not unsympathetic. Married and divorced and married again down in Germany. And now escaping from husband number two. Good god, yes, that could naturally mean, as his wife maintained, that Mrs. Arnold was probably quite an impossible person. From the beginning he'd agreed that there was no reason in the world to make changes in the daily routine for the sake of this unknown and slightly obscure woman, whom he'd met on the steps in his slippers. Now he felt uncomfortable and regretted the slippers; he was almost inclined to believe that it was the gentlemen something was wrong with. She really did look like a pretty, refined lady.

He engaged the guest in conversation. Isaksen had been in Berlin a couple of years ago; he could talk about lots of things—about his hotel, streetlife, prices, the joys and discomforts of travel; Danish, German, Swedish and Norwegian customs officials. If he were going to be honest he himself had tried a little smuggling too, had a good many more cigarettes than was allowed on his return, besides other small things. And there'd been no problem. Apropos of cigarettes, however—did Mrs. Arnold smoke? He himself valued a good pipe far more, but he did have a few on hand. He got up and brought them out.

Mrs. Arnold warmed up and got some color in her face, whether it was because of the coffee or because of Isaksen, she answered cheerfully, lit a cigarette, blew a ring—

Under the circumstances Mrs. Isaksen found it best to bring the pair back to earth again. She said, "I'll unfortunately have to ask you to be on your feet a little early in the morning, Mrs. Arnold, so the maid can come in to air the room and so on before breakfast—"

Mrs. Arnold reddened again. Lord only knew if she weren't a little touchy and easily wounded, one of those you can't say a word to. But she answered politely that she hoped she wouldn't oversleep; she didn't, as a rule. For that matter she slept by an open window and she'd naturally make the cot and fold it up herself—

"Yes, thank you very much for doing it," came coldly from Mrs. Isaksen. "We'll put in a wash basin, then, on a chair. As I've mentioned, it's a little primitive at our house in summer." She thought, Aha, maybe you're one of those terribly modest and helpful people, who think they acquit themselves so well that they can just stay and stay. This is where one should be on one's guard, all right. . . .

The next morning Mrs. Arnold got coffee in bed. That wasn't being on one's guard; it was far beyond what one was obliged to do. But it was part of the family tradition and it was impossible to disregard the guest, especially since she slept next to the kitchen. Andrine had orders to put *one* slice of white bread, no more, on the *saucer* next to the cup and spoon. And two lumps of sugar. So it was completely clear that this was an incentive to get up, nothing else; certainly it was no meal to lie there lingering over. Andrine did as she was told. And Mrs. Arnold got up.

And the days began to pass. Already in the course of the first day, Yngve, who had been polite and respectful the evening before, listening to the adults' conversation, had become totally himself again, interrupting them, snorting at what they said, slurping loudly, reaching over the table for food, helping himself so that Mrs. Isaksen felt herself forced to clear her throat. Under other circumstances she would have tried to hold him in check a bit in front of company, given him a little kick under the table anyway. Now she let it pass, true to her plan: no changes in their daily life, no extra arrangements.

In many ways Mrs. Arnold was irreproachable. She got up early, offered to help with one thing or another, took modest helpings at the table, wrote and also received letters, remained in contact with the outside world. There was hope that something was happening, that not everything rested solely on the Isaksens.

Otherwise she looked after herself, took long walks in the woods and didn't demand to be entertained.

But—

Could reserve be carried too far? Mrs. Isaksen wouldn't ask, not for anything in the world. It would be so easy to get too familiar; it would be easy for this person to feel far too much at home.

On the other hand, you'd think it wasn't totally unreasonable to expect Mrs. Arnold herself to have something to say about the situation, her prospects. So you'd have *something* to go by.

"For a short while," Uncle wrote. Could his deceased friend's only daughter stay with them for a while? Until she could get herself straightened out and get on her feet again? She'd been living in unhappy circumstances down in Germany, but had left now and for the moment was poverty-stricken and alone in the world. Mrs. Isaksen, as a woman, could understand and help her better than he could. She would do her old uncle a great favor.

Mrs. Isaksen definitely wanted to do her uncle a great favor. He was a widower, childless, well-off and close to eighty. He could have taken Mrs. Arnold in himself, but he probably didn't dare because of his housekeeper. Lina wouldn't allow it, so he seized on this idea.

Mrs. Isaksen opened her home, was willing to do it, yes, to even share her wardrobe if it came down to it. She wasn't inhuman. But she liked a situation to be clear and straightforward. And the one she found herself in was not only unclear, it was oppressive. A short while, what did that mean? Was it a week or was it a year? And what was Mrs. Arnold doing about finding herself a livelihood? Was she doing anything at all about it? She hadn't inquired, at any rate, about possibilities in the neighborhood or in the nearest town. There could be something right nearby. She sent and received letters. And Lord knows what *they* had in them. If it weren't that you could see her sitting and writing at the dining table, with slashed-open envelopes bearing Norwegian and German stamps in front of her, you'd wonder about· the whole correspondance. For Mrs. Arnold didn't collect her letters at merchant Flaten's like everyone else; she went to meet the postman—every single day, Isaksen, *every* day, long trips—talk about suspicious natures.

And that Mr. Arnold—was he brutal? Did he drink? Had he been unfaithful? Surely there had to be serious grounds for a person just to up and leave a husband and throw herself on strangers. Unless the party concerned was exceptionally pushy and demanding. One or the other, admit it, Isaksen.

Isaksen admitted a great deal, little by little. His sympathy was decreasing; it had been put to the test.

Under the pretext that otherwise the guest could easily get the notion they were well-off, Mrs. Isaksen had from the first moment introduced fare that, without exaggeration, could be called spartan. All the cheese and cold cuts vanished, with the exception of brown cheese. That remained as always by Mrs. Isaksen's place, and as always she cut thin slices of it, easing it on to the plates. But she didn't offer seconds even to her husband. And she remained completely oblivious to signs from any other quarter.

Isaksen's pint of beer had disappeared. Coffee after dinner had disappeared. If anyone alluded to the fact that these were major changes in the daily routine, Mrs. Isaksen said, "Shhhh!"

On the eighth day Yngve said, out in the hall, so loudly that it was heard clearly inside, "If she doesn't move on soon, I'll do something or other, put itching powder in her bed or something—"

The steamer wasn't the only thing that went to the nearest town; there was a bus too. Isaksen took the bus every morning, disappearing for the rest of the day. He had an office there and business affairs, wholesaling something indeterminate.

Mrs. Arnold didn't sit down then with needlework, like Mrs. Isaksen and Kaia and the summer guests upstairs, an older woman and two daughters who were used to calling "Good morning" from the balcony and liked coming down and sitting on the steps with their sewing things. They had been summer guests at the Isaksens for many years—they took good care of the furniture and properly replaced anything that got broken. The relationship was the best possible.

Mrs. Arnold didn't have any sewing things; she didn't even have any clothes that needed mending or putting in order—only new, whole things. A poverty-stricken woman! Understand that if you could.

She helped out with the daily chores, dusting and watering flowers; she was glad to take a dish of peas out of Andrine's hands and start shelling them. She asked if there were errands to run and ran them. But if it involved putting a new patch on Yngve's trousers, just to take a small example, she never offered her help. She vanished into the woods.

The day she sat down and darned some of her stockings, Mrs. Isaksen actually breathed a sigh of relief and almost fell into spontaneous amiability. Now Mrs. Arnold was showing a normal side, a sort of justification for living. But when the stockings were darned, they were darned. Mrs. Arnold rushed off to the woods again and compromised the Isaksens as much as before.

Compromising—that was it precisely. It wasn't possible to ignore it any longer; that was what she was, this lady who wandered around on roads where no one else went, hoarding her letters to herself instead of crowding with the rest around the postman outside Flaten's at one o'clock, calling: "Anything for me, Karlsen?" Who swam when the beach was empty and deserted and, in other words, kept herself apart. People were wondering. Mrs. Isaksen and Kaia were well aware of it. Little by little they were closely questioned both by the ladies upstairs and as they stood waiting their turn in the shop. "You have a guest, I see? A relative? Oh, isn't she? A married woman, I hear? Can she just be away from home like this? Maybe she needed to be away a while to rest—that's what a lot of people need to do, though of course not everyone can, unfortunately. No children? Well now, that's a different story."

And so forth—

Most people would have probably ignored it, thought up something or other, but Mrs. Isaksen wasn't talented that way; she wasn't the sort that *can* lie, she didn't have that gift. When she said briefly that it was a daughter of one of her uncle's old friends, people looked as if they imagined all sorts of things. If only she could have expanded upon the sufferings Mrs. Arnold had been through—but there she stood. And Mrs. Arnold went around well-dressed, polite and correct, didn't look destitute nor weighed down with grief, and didn't even sit sewing.

Mrs. Isaksen couldn't get any of it to add up. She was turning into a nervous wreck from it, beginning to lie awake at night.

Lord knew what Mrs. Arnold was doing on her walks. She could be gone for hours on end. Returning home she often brought something or other—edible mushrooms, berries, flowers. Mrs. Isaksen would have appreciated this, if it weren't for the nagging thought that perhaps Mrs. Arnold believed that she was contributing something and that now she could just stay and stay.

Then, one day, Kaia came running in, out of breath. She'd seen Mrs. Arnold sitting on a stump in the woods, crying—

"What are you saying? Where? When?"

"A little while ago. In the north woods."

"And she didn't see you?"

"Oh no." Kaia had walked on just the moss and had stood hiding behind the trees.

"Are you sure she was crying?"

"*Crying!* She was bawling."

Mrs. Isaksen sat silent awhile, thinking intently. "Hmmm," she said. "So now we're going to have scenes, on top of everything else. How did we get involved in this! But thank you very much, Kaia. I'm glad you came and told me about it, dear."

When Mrs. Arnold arrived for dinner an hour later a certain excitement manifested itself in the Isaksen family. Yet she didn't look either red-eyed or sorrowful; on the contrary, she was livelier and more communicative than ever before.

Then she disappeared again for an evening walk. Mrs. Isaksen sat there, with her hands in her lap, sighing again over what she had sighed over many times before: "She's a mystery to me. A complete mystery."

One day Kaia came to report that Mrs. Arnold was sitting on a stone now, wiping her eyes and eating *pâté de foie gras.*

"*Pâté!*" Mrs. Isaksen bounded from her chair. "Are you completely crazy?"

Kaia wasn't one bit crazy; she'd seen it on the tin, one of the oval ones with gold print like Flaten had in his window. It was on the ground along with a package of biscuits. And as she was saying, Mrs.

Arnold sat on a stone, spreading *pâté* on the biscuits with a little pocketknife and eating amazingly fast, either because she was so hungry or because she had to eat it up right away. Sometimes she took her handkerchief out and wiped her eyes.

"I'm totally at sea," said Mrs. Isaksen. "It's shameful. Instead of coming and asking for a sandwich. If anyone sees her, they'll think she doesn't get fed here. But of course, *pâté* isn't served in this house. . ."

"No, that's for sure," said Kaia. "But that's nothing to her; she goes and buys it herself. . . ."

After that, with lips pressed together, Mrs. Isaksen went inside to bring out the snack of white bread and juice that she had recently, when the family was alone, been offering as a sacrifice to domestic opinion.

That afternoon Mrs. Arnold even wanted to tell a story. But she didn't get very far with that.

Yngve was digging in a flowerpot when she came in. And see if she didn't light into him and jerk his hand out of the pot, saying, "But you've got an open cut there. . ."

"Yeah, so what?" snorted Yngve.

"There can be dangerous bacteria in the earth," said Mrs. Arnold. "Tetanus," she said. "You should go put some iodine on it right away."

Yngve snorted even more. "That's stupid, iodine on a scratch."

"Small wound, needy friends," said Mrs. Arnold. And she began to tell her story, began eagerly and rather quickly.

She knew of a case down in Germany: It was a singer, in fact, who was going to sing at a funeral. He'd looked a little peculiar right before, had admitted that he didn't feel well. But he didn't want to cancel. And so—in the middle of the song—he suddenly couldn't move his lower jaw—his mouth stayed open, paralyzed. He died a few hours later in great suffering—and it came out, it came out—that it was that same day—he'd been planting roses—he was a flower lover—he'd had a tiny cut no one would bother about—a barely visible cut on his finger.

Mrs. Arnold couldn't go on from here. It was as if her own lower jaw also stiffened up in a cramp. There's something tragic about an audience that doesn't give a single sign it's listening and taking it in. That, on the contrary, suddenly exchanges loud remarks on quite different subjects, in this case, a spool of white thread.

"Oh, hand me that white spool, Kaia, I see I have to fasten those buttons better," was what Mrs. Isaksen said.

"Here you go," said Kaia.

"Thanks very much, dear; and here you go. Don't forget to buy another number forty when you go to Flaten's," said Mrs. Isaksen. After that it was completely quiet for a while.

"I'm sorry. Weren't you telling us something or other, Mrs. Arnold?" Mrs. Isaksen looked up distractedly from her sewing.

"Me? Oh, no."

"Imagine, I thought you were. . . ."

Right afterwards Mrs. Arnold disappeared. She probably went out again.

Mrs. Isaksen shrugged her shoulders. "Good Lord, we're really able to deal with our scratches ourselves," she said. "Come here, boy, let me have a look at you. . . ."

It became known that Mrs. Arnold consumed, in turn, crab, chocolate and cheese in the woods. The Isaksen family, which for her sake had imposed privation and self-denial on itself, became bitter. It smouldered dangerously in a couple of quarters. Both Yngve and Kaia made remarks frequently under their breath. Isaksen took it more calmly. He wasn't in town for nothing every single day; he knew where to find the best hot sandwiches. One day—it was the thirteenth—fish balls were reported. The way they came, out of the can, cold. But Mrs. Arnold couldn't handle them. After she'd eaten three, she shuddered as if nauseated, sighed and buried the can and its contents in the moss. Kaia could point out the place where it happened, was ready to do it right away if necessary. Mrs. Arnold was sure not to return for a long time; she'd disappeared into the forest paths. Yngve could come along.

Yngve came along.

A couple of hours later when Mrs. Arnold opened the gate, the can of fish balls stood in the middle of the yard. The widow upstairs opened her window at the same time and called down in surprise: "Look, there's practically a full can of fish balls right in the middle of the yard. You think Andrine's forgotten them? Well, I only want to warn you—there are cats around—humph—I almost think it looks like they've been here already."

Mrs. Arnold stopped, turned blood red. But it passed quickly and she said calmly, yes, even with a little smile: "Maybe Yngve and Kaia know something about it. They're standing in back of the door, both of them."

She walked past the can, past them and past Mrs. Isaksen, who, uneasy, had appeared in a doorway further inside. She took a book and sat down. With a smile!

But that evening there was fried whiting for supper at the Isaksens, explain it who can. Mrs. Isaksen made an attempt by saying, "Ola Galterud came by with some fresh fish. I felt I had to take it—a little taste of something is good with the bread now and then."

No one contradicted her. Isaksen boldly ordered a bottle of beer and offered the ladies some.

Two days later Mrs. Arnold came in with a letter in her hand and announced that she was leaving on the night boat.

"And now I must thank you sincerely for the wonderful hospitality you've shown me," she said.

It came as a complete surprise to Mrs. Isaksen; she broke out, flabbergasted, "But my dear, you're leaving? Are things working out a bit for you then? I thought..."

Mrs. Arnold interrupted her, lightly and confidently: "Yes, thank you. I can imagine you'll be glad to get rid of me. I've taken advantage of your kindness far too long."

"My dear, it's been a pleasure. When you're willing to take things the way they are here," she said unexpectedly and thoughtlessly. To tell the truth, she lost her composure for a moment. But it came back again; she called out to Andrine to put Mrs. Arnold's bedclothes out to air, immediately, so they'd get the benefit of the sun while it was out—Mrs. Arnold was leaving this very day.

That makes it a little more certain that it will really happen, thought Mrs. Isaksen, with the idea of cutting off her retreat. Within moments Andrine came out dragging the pillows and blankets.

Mrs. Arnold went in to pack.

They drove to the wharf in Ola Galterud's cart. Mrs. Arnold wanted to pay for it herself, but Mr. and Mrs. Isaksen assured her in unison that no, there couldn't be any talk of that. Mrs. Arnold had to give way and say, thank you very much, it was far too much.

She didn't say a word about where she was going. She talked quickly and animatedly about anything and everything, about weather and wind, but also withdrew into herself for moments at a time and sat looking, preoccupied, out over the landscape. More than once Mrs. Isaksen had a question on her lips, but it wasn't exactly easy to get out, though it was basically a simple thing to ask. Anyway, Mrs. Arnold kept circumventing her by her constant talk of other things. Finally it was Isaksen who asked. And then Mrs. Arnold answered with a wistful smile, a shrug of the shoulders, a gesture that hinted that the wide, but cold world lay open to her: "Traveling on."

And there sat the Isaksens.

"Well, I was actually thinking of the mail; more letters could come that need forwarding," Isaksen mumbled feebly.

"Yes, letters, yes." Mrs. Isaksen entertained new hope.

But Mrs. Arnold assured them calmly and cheerfully that no more letters would come.

It was a still evening, warm and clear with a softly gurgling sea, blue hills, reddening sky. On board it looked inviting and comfortable, with travelers in folding chairs on the deck and the lights on in the salon. Mrs. Arnold tripped over the gangplank in her pretty coat and was a completely different person than when she arrived—a travelwise lady of the continental cut who was traveling in earnest, no one knew how far, a true globetrotter. She commanded respect, no more, no less.

She decidedly declined Isaksen's offer to see to a berth immediately; she wouldn't even hear talk of him carrying her baggage down under. "We'll chat and have a nice time together as long as we can," she said, taking her things out of his hands and setting them down in the smoking cabin. "I'm sure I'll get a berth."

And she chatted. Now, for the first time, it became apparent how winning, lively and amusing Mrs. Arnold could be. She spoke cheerfully and effortlessly on the beauty of the place, the beauty of the evening, the difference between the German and Norwegian landscape, the character of the German and Norwegian peoples. She said one striking thing after another. And the Isaksen family came to feel stranger and stranger, more and more crestfallen. Especially when, in the middle of everything else, she assured them that she couldn't thank them enough.

Good lord, if they'd only known before that she hadn't intended to be a burden on them for the rest of her life, they could have really enjoyed her company. An enormous thankfulness that she hadn't exploited them, hadn't brought them to the brink of poverty, arose in them, mixed with wonderment, yes, even with sadness and loss. The Mrs. Arnold who cried and ate fish balls in the woods and was nothing but a tiresome hanger-on, appeared to be an unfortunate mistake, a kind of optical illusion. Here stood the real one on the deck in traveling dress, not in the least dependent; she had given Andrine a twenty kroner tip. Andrine had sat, overcome, on the woodbox in the kitchen and dried her eyes with an apron corner at departure time. You couldn't deny it. Mrs. Arnold had played the winning card.

The bell rang for departure. Trembling a little, Mrs. Isaksen managed, "I hope we'll hear from you when you have the opportunity—a few lines, I mean—you understand, it will interest us how it goes with you..."

Mrs. Arnold wasn't made of stone either; she gave her a firm handshake and said, "That..."

But she pulled back her hand a little quickly perhaps, and her voice faltered as she continued, "you'll certainly get." For a moment it looked as if she wanted to say more, but nothing came of it. There was only good-bye and renewed expressions of thanks.

When the steamer sailed from the dock, the Isaksens waved, one and all, as if to a beloved family member off to America. And Mrs. Arnold waved back, walking along the railing and waving with her handkerchief until the steamer went around the point and she could neither see nor be seen any longer. Then she hurried into the smoking cabin after her things, placed them in the lee of one of the benches on the deck and sat down with them. Something windblown and tired and subdued came over her; her face and back collapsed a little. After an hour had gone by and the call for the first sitting for dinner had come, she took out a packet of biscuits from Flaten's and ate some of them. And when she was certain no one was looking she smuggled out bits of sausage for the biscuits from a piece of wrapped paper. Mrs. Arnold was traveling deck class and wasn't really going anywhere. She sat there, growing smaller and smaller in the blanket she'd tucked around her against the evening cold. The hours went by and she became a nodding dark silhouette against the white enameled wall behind her.

During the night, when the sky had begun to lighten over the hills in the east, she got off, as if on impulse, at one of the landing places, went ashore and stood like a shadow in the gray light on the wharf, while the steamer departed and went on. She stood looking around and shivering; she took a few stumbling steps in the direction of a low rural building with HOTEL in large letters on it. The man on duty, yawning and in rubber boots, came down and took her bags...

On the way home the Isaksens were silent. Not until they swung into the yard did Mrs. Isaksen say, as if finishing a train of thought, "Well, anyway—we were probably of some help to her..."

But on the dining table lay an opened letter. Andrine had found it on the window sill. It was addressed to Mrs. E. Arnold, care of Mr. Isaksen, Merchant.

"There, you see—if only we had her address." Mrs. Isaksen turned and twisted the letter. "Well, I'll just have to take care of it in the meantime."

Inspired by the mood of the wharf and by the most honorable intentions, Mrs. Isaksen wandered into the bedroom letter in hand, in the direction of the chest of drawers. This kind of thing should be locked up, not left to lie around. Naturally it wasn't her intention to read it. But there was no indiscretion in looking at the postmark.

It was from the nearest post office, a few kilometers away. Who in the world was Mrs. Arnold in correspondence with there? And whose handwriting was it? Mrs. Isaksen was suddenly certain she'd seen it before.

The letter came out of the envelope. Oh God, it wasn't really right, but. . .

Mrs. Isaksen's face grew blank in wonder. Grew blanker and blanker...

The letter was nothing more than a piece of white paper. There wasn't one word on it. And the writing on the envelope—that was certainly Mrs. Arnold's own! Mrs. Isaksen had stolen past her, peeking over her shoulder, all too often as she'd sat writing, to be in doubt of *that* any longer.

On one of her wanderings Mrs. Arnold sent herself a piece of white paper folded together in an envelope. The postmark was two days old.

Mrs. Isaksen sat on her bed. She stared into space, stared at the letter, stared into space again, tried to understand.

"My mind is blank," she mumbled. "Is she crazy or am I?"

While a blush rose slowly on her face.

Original title: *En gåte.* Translated by Barbara Wilson

Ingeborg Refling Hagen

(1895-1989)

Eerie moods, motifs from old legends and folk ballads and a realism verging on the grotesque characterize many of the short stories by Ingeborg Refling Hagen. But there is also religious conviction and a deeply felt concern for the poor and afflicted in much of her writing, which includes numerous novels, poetry collections and children's books. She takes her material from her native Hedmark, a district of rich farmland and vast forests in eastern Norway, and her subjects are generally the common folk such as the family in "Borrowing Fire." During her childhood she experienced a poverty that drove friends and family to America, and in a series of poems, *Jeg vil hem att* (1932), she depicts the emigrants' sorrow at leaving their homeland and the hardships and homesickness they experienced in the New World.

"Borrowing Fire" was included in Hagen's first book *Naar elv skifter leie* (1920). Superstition and ominous threats from the forest pervade the narrative, but the author offsets these elements with humor and warmth and the forces of darkness are kept at bay.

Borrowing Fire

It was during that time when wolves and bears resided in the forests. When trolls lived in the mountains, elves in barns and stables, and hillfolk in every self-respecting mound. When enemy haunted enemy and ghosts appeared nightly in every single old house. This happened at the time Old Marte was a little girl. The oldest of four siblings at Klypstua—a cotter's farm below Lundgar.

The cottage was situated on bedrock, with a narrow strip of earth in front and a desolate expanse of wilderness behind. A dark grove of spruce cast its shadow over the house. A narrow road with deep wheel ruts led to Lundgar and another led on up to the north village and the neighboring village. And the nearest farm was a good half hour away: Boat-Ola at Slagstua, to the west.

Both husband and wife at Klypstua had to work in the fields every day, and at home the children had to manage things as best they could. Marte was already ten years old and a good and capable girl. After her came Jon, a wild and unruly boy of eight. And then there was Sigrid and baby brother.

Klypstua was not a prosperous farm; but most of the time they had a couple of cows, a pig and a sheep and a goat, so for Marte, who had to take care of everything by herself, it was quite enough. In the winter when all the animals were in stalls it was a struggle just to get everything done. But in the summertime it was easier; then she sent them out to pasture and let Jon herd; still, it was anything but safe, for wolves and foxes were never far away.

One day Jon was feeding the sheep and the pig on the rock outside the barn, and inside Marte sat lulling baby brother to sleep—he was cutting teeth, so he cried and was fussy. Sigrid knelt in the window sill and amused herself by spitting on the pane and drawing with her fingers. But just as the baby was falling off to sleep, Sigrid began to scream and jumped down from the sill. "Marte, look!" she cried. "There's a big dog outside the window."

Marte stood up quietly, softly humming in the baby's ear and shaking her head at Sigrid, that she should be quiet. But suddenly she started. "Yes, there's a dog all right," she said and throwing the child on the bed she ran to the kitchen door and shouted out to Jon: "Put the sheep and pig in at once! There's a wolf outside the window!"

Jon threw himself across the bell sheep, grabbed it by the collar and pulled for all he was worth toward the barn door. The old ewe wouldn't budge and all the sheep bleated. The pig wanted to go in the opposite direction and Jon howled with fright. Somehow—he didn't really know how—the animals got into the barn. And Marte hurried back to the baby, who was gasping, nearly choking, from crying and blue in the face from anger, while Sigrid stood next to him, asking him sweetly to be quiet.

Crunch, crunch...Outside the window the wolf slunk back and forth, scratching against the sill with long, sharp claws. Marte tucked the baby under her arm, grabbed a firebrand from the fire and shouted out the kitchen door. "Jon! Hurry. Hurry!"

A little pale face peeked out through the barn window. Like a lightening bolt Jon streaked across the farmyard to his sister, who handed him the firebrand. "There—take this and scare him. But hurry. You have to!" she cried out when she saw how terrified he was.

Jon tiptoed, his entire body shaking, around the house toward the wolf, who turned and bared his teeth at him.

"Turn around, you bloodthirsty swine," Jon threatened

imploringly.

The wolf took a step toward him, his eyes and mouth glistening against the firebrand.

Then Jon let out a piercing scream and swung the firebrand so the sparks flew. Jumped up and down. Swung and screamed. He shook with fright and the tears streamed down his cheeks.

The wolf reflected a moment, then turned around and ambled away. Down the hill, in precisely that direction where the goat stood tied to the fence.

For a second Jon saw nothing, only black. He circled around and came up right in front of the wolf. Swung the firebrand in its face and shrieked like one who's lost his wits. The wolf did an about-face and trotted up the hill and Jon chased after it, swinging the firebrand, shouting and crying. The farther away the wolf got, the more he scolded. And when it disappeared in the forest, he jumped straight into the air, stomped on the ground and screamed: "Get out of here, you roguish wolf! You sneering swine!"

Then a long howl came out of the forest and Jon was suddenly silent; he bounded down to the house, slipped in, huddled in the darkest corner and didn't say peep for the rest of the evening.

But as a rule Jon was downright reckless. He was impetuous, mad as a hornet and mean-tempered. If he didn't get his way, he used his fists and then it was a good thing that Marte had come into the world two years before him and was a match for him in a scuffle.

One autumn day a little before dusk Jon was standing out by the chopping block, hewing an axe handle. The axe was dull and the birch wood hard and Jon sweated, hacked and groaned and scarcely got a sliver off. And up on the knoll, the highest point in the enclosed field, in an old fir tree sat an eagle owl and hooted. Hoo-oo! The sound carried far in the autumn evening so the hooting was continuous and pervasive. Hoo-oo!

Jon straightened himself abruptly and looked upwards. Dried the sweat under his cap and started in again. Harder, angrier and more heedlessly he hacked away and suddenly the axe slipped out of his hand and the back side of it flew against his knee.

He angrily stomped his feet, hurled the axe handle, kicked the axe so it whirled and hooted up at the eagle owl: "Hoo-oo!"

"Hoo-oo!" replied the eagle owl.

"Hoo-oo!" mimicked Jon, jumping up and down in anger. "Shut up, you beast. You idiotic owl!"

"Hoo-oo!" was the monotonous and foreboding reply from the mountain.

"Hoo-oo!" retorted Jon, hopping mad, but suddenly he fell silent and darted into the barn. Immediately something flew against the barn door and scratched with its claws. It flew about, flapping its wings and beating the air, and hooting with an angry voice. "Hoo-oo!"

Jon was quiet for a minute and caught his breath; but then he jumped up, kicked the door and pounded on it with his fist and yelled back: "Hoo-oo!"

"Hoo-oo!" The eagle owl clawed splinters off of the door with dangerous, sharp claws.

"Cut it out, Jon. The eagle owl is ruining the door, and you're carrying on so they can hear you all the way to Lundgar." Marte had to shout to be heard above the hooting.

"Go inside and keep your mouth shut," Jon shouted back. "Hoo-oo!"

Marte looked around for something to defend herself with and took a pole that was leaning against the house, timidly went over to the barn door and whacked the eagle owl so that it sank with a long hoot toward the ground, but immediately flapped its wings again, flew up over the barn and toward the forest.

Then Jon tore after Marte, grabbed hold of her braid and pulled and tugged and ground his teeth in anger. And Marte bit her lips which were white and twisted herself around and around until her fingers could reach his ear which she held with her sharp nails.

They stood there a minute, rigid and quiet. Didn't dare pull, for then the other pulled harder.

"Let go of my ear, little girl," Jon hissed.

"Let go yourself," Marte snapped back.

"If you don't let go, I'll throw you so high that the swallow will build a nest in your ear before you come back down to the meadow," Jon exclaimed.

"You let go first, or I'll rip your ear right out of your head. Scaredy cat," teased Marte.

Then Jon yanked her braid so Marte nearly broke her neck. She in turned pulled Jon's ear so he screamed bloody murder. Then they stood still again. Bickered and threatened and wouldn't let go, didn't dare let go for fear of the other one.

Then a piercing scream from inside the house gave Marte a start.

"Let go, Jon. The baby's crying. Do you hear? Let go!"

"You let go first."

The baby's crying got worse and worse and Marte wriggled and writhed.

"You've got to let go, Jon. He'll cry himself to death."

"You let go first."

Sigrid stood in the kitchen door and called to Marte. "The baby fell out of his cradle and got an awful nosebleed. Hurry!" And she rushed back in.

"Let go! Let go!" sobbed Marte.

"Shut up and let go yourself," snapped Jon and neither of them let go.

Then Marte inched herself, step by step, across the farmyard toward the kitchen door, all the while holding Jon's ear so tightly that he had to follow. She managed to back herself up on to the stone step, quickly let go of his ear, grabbed both his wrists and worked her braid free. She kicked his legs out from underneath him so he tumbled, slipped inside and bolted the door.

It was about time she came. The baby's nose was swollen and his face was covered with blood and both he and Sigrid were screaming.

Marte tended to the baby, bathed him and calmed him down, while she kept an anxious eye on the window where Jon stood making faces and hooting like the eagle owl, threatening to break the window to bits if she didn't open the door that instant. And when Marte pretended that she didn't hear anything, he hit the pane with his fist as hard as he dared and screamed "Hoo-oo!"

It began to get dark; Mother would soon be there and Marte was about to put the coffeepot on, when suddenly she was ice cold all over and felt tiny prickles on her neck—the fire had gone out. There was only the faint glow from a hot bed of ashes. She threw open the kitchen door and shouted: "Jon, help me! The fire is out. It's black as pitch in the fireplace."

"You must be crazy." Jon's voice was good-natured and helpless.

Marte sobbed and stirred the ashes. "What should I do? Soon Mother will be here. Help me, Jon." And Marte raked so the hot ashes flew and a tiny little ember appeared. Both knelt and blew on the ember and Jon put a splinter of birch next to the coal and blew again; the ashes swirled, his mouth became dry, the ember went out and Marte dried her eyes with sooty fists.

"Will you look after the baby, Jon, while I run to Slagstua and borrow a flame?" Marte asked anxiously.

"Reckon I'd better. But by George you'd better hurry then—it's already pitch black, girl." Jon thrust his fists deep into his pants pockets as he looked out the kitchen window. Marte snatched a kettle from the fireplace and flew out the door. Scared out of her wits she tore down the path to Slagstua and though she thought a host of two-legged and four-legged creatures were after her, she looked neither to the side nor behind her.

She ran and ran so her sides ached and her heart hammered like an anvil. But when she'd crossed the field and was on the road, she slowed down. Tried to walk like a normal person and not be frightened. Said to herself again and again that nothing was wrong. Nothing at all. But it didn't help. It was as if her whole body was listening for danger. The autumn evening was still and clear as if it too was listening in lifeless expectancy. And Marte breathed heavily and unevenly and hurried along on tiptoe even though she was barefoot.

Then she heard the sharp, angry baying of dogs from up on the field. And immediately afterwards the long, deep howl of a wolf. Once again angry barking which, blending with the howl, rose up to the stars, drew a reply from the mountains and, quivering, sank down over the forest where it was succeeded by new howls and new baying.

Marte stood perfectly still, staring at the forest. The howls pierced her like sharp iron pokers and stung her eyes which, wide-open and listening, stared into the darkness.

Creak! Through the split rail fence in front of her bounded a fox, across the road and down into the field. In the same instant the mean dog from Dal tumbled over the fence like a huge, black tuft of wool and disappeared in the same direction. Before Marte could catch her breath, a deafening howl came from very close by. The fence creaked and groaned, claws scratched and the air was saturated with the wailing sounds.

A snapping sound, the fence collapsed and a huge wolf bounded forth. Eyes flashing and teeth glistening, the wolf trotted after the others, its jaw opened wide and ready to devour. Marte broke into a run as if she had all the beasts on her heels, while the baying and the howls moved farther and farther away down toward the fjord. And before she knew what had happened she was at Slagstua; she fetched the fire and rushed off for home.

She hurled herself forward with such long strides that her skirt gathered up above her knees and her bare feet hit the road with dull thumps. Her hair was streaming behind her and her eyes stared right into the darkness, listening more than seeing.

Suddenly she stopped short and, trembling, held her breath.

A strange and eerie sound pierced the black silence. It sounded like shrill drumbeats and came closer and closer.

Marte stood nailed to the spot; her face shone pale and the whites of her eyes glistened out of sheer fright.

Then it was as if the whole road came to life in front of her. Something indistinctly large and long, flashing white and brightly gleaming and drumming, rounded the bend and glided toward her.

She whirled around, braced herself and leapt over the fence, lay down flat behind a bush and peered out between the branches. This was clearly a ghost and of the very worst sort; for the drummer was only heard when misfortune was about to occur, grandfather had said.

The long, weird beast came closer and closer and inched its way by. It was as if it were walking on hundreds of white legs, which twinkled and shone in the darkness, while the drumbeats came from the front. Lying there behind the bush, Marte was out of her senses; her entire body was cold from the terror and suspense. But when the last vestige of the white beast disappeared around the bend in the road, she crept out, climbed over the fence and started out again, her teeth chattering in her mouth. Mean dogs and wolves were nothing compared to that huge blinking beast who filled the air with ugly, black misfortune.

Marte lurched into the kitchen at Klypstua and slammed the door behind her so the windowpane rattled, dumped the fire into the fireplace and fed it with birch bark and wood chips.

"You're in quite a hurry, Marte," her mother said slowly. She stood in the doorway, the baby on her arm, looking white and tired.

At that Marte began to sob. "I've run as fast as I could the whole way, Mother. And still I met a fox and a wolf and that mean old dog from Dal. And on the way home I met a terrible ghost—it had white legs and beat a drum."

"Dear me," Mother Klypstua said uneasily. "Who will misfortune strike now, I wonder. Heaven help the afflicted soul." She pressed the baby close to her and glanced anxiously at Sigrid who lay sleeping on the bed, fully clothed. And at Jon who stood with his mouth open, staring at Marte, who had stopped crying and, while she wiped off the table and brought out the supper, told about the ghost in greater and greater detail.

"Where's Father?" she asked suddenly.

"At the gristmill. He won't be home until late tonight, so we'd better eat," answered Mother as she sat down with the baby on her lap and Jon and Marte right across from her. The pine splinters flickered and flamed and the spruce logs crackled and snapped, so it looked like a wedding procession was moving across the underside of the kettle. In a hushed voice Marte described the ghost and, frightened, they sat listening, with an occasional glance at the black window pane. Jon tucked his legs underneath himself and was full of questions.

"Hoo-oo!" it cried from the forest, deep and penetrating.

The woman started and looked at the window. "If only Father were safely home. That eagle owl is screaming so frightfully," she said rocking the baby, as Jon and Marte crept closer to her.

She shoved her coffee cup away and moved over to the stool by the fire. Jon and Marte followed and huddled together on a bench; petrified, they stared at the window and over in the corners where the fire cast restless shadows.

Silently they sat there, not wanting to go to bed before Father came and not able to occupy themselves with anything, either.

Mother hushed and lulled the baby. Every now and then Jon threw logs on the fire and Marte sat and drew pictures on the fireplace with a piece of coal. And nothing broke the silence but the monotonous and ominous hoo-oo of the eagle owl from up on the mountain ridge.

But farther up the road through the forest marched a company of the "King's Men."

They were to make camp in the neighboring village and they had to get there that night. So they marched, as tired and exhausted as they were, without resting or stopping. They kept step to the drum and their white leather leggings glistened and gleamed in the darkness as they moved forward like a single long and continuous body. While the drumbeats, short and sharp, sounded through the night stillness.

Original title: *Laane varme.* Translated by Katherine Hanson

Magnhild Haalke

(1895–1984)
Magnhild Haalke is from North Trøndelag, the district north of Trondheim, and she writes about the people who live along that sparsely
populated coast and on the many small islands there. Her first novel,
Allis sønn (1935), was published when she was fifty years old and it was
enthusiastically received by the public as well as the critics. It is the
tragic story of a mother and her son, both victims of a hostile and insen-
sitive environment. The weak and defenseless individual, tyrannized
and mistreated, is a motif that goes throughout her extensive production. Her portrayals of women and children, in particular, show keen
psychological insight.

Haalke seems to favor the longer format of the novel (her works include three trilogies), but she has also published three volumes of short
stories. The present story, taken from the collection *Dragspell* (1958),
evokes a vivid sense of that coastal region, far to the north, and of a time
long past. It is reminiscent of a legend and, indeed, is not without an element of Norwegian folklore: the *hulder* is a beautiful female being who
resides in the underworld; she is especially dangerous to young men
whom she tries to lure with music and song.

Stormarja and Lillmarja

Sisters as different as night and day, people said. But they had the
same name. As it happened, Stormarja (so-called because she was
oldest) was sickly when she was a baby; no one believed she would
live. But she hung on and made it to her second birthday, and then a
new wave of illness set in and everything looked very uncertain. So
when another little girl was born, they gave her the same name, only
adding Lill (little). That is how there came to be two daughters in
Sanna and Edevart's cottage named Marja. They wanted to use that
name, you see, because it had been in the family for generations:
Mother's Aunt Marja and Father's Aunt Marja, Old Marja and Marja
herself, all along the narrow spit of land where they made their home.

And their name served them well, word has it, for they lived long lives and were old when they went to the grave. One carried dried brushwood into the kitchen the day she left her earthly home. Another sat spinning yarn for mittens, and still another stood stirring porridge for the evening meal. So none of them came empty-handed to Paradise, as witnessed by Him who watched them on their journey and who, in all likelihood, welcomed them at its completion. They married young and had many children, so one could say they used their talents in the best way possible.

Stormarja survived and grew to be big and strong as time went on. Her hair was dark, her complexion white. And her eyes were blue, an uncommon feature in that family. But there was something peculiar about her. Maybe they had spoiled her when she was sickly or maybe there was some other reason. She was brusque. There was no point in tangling with her, people said. Didn't pay to step on the toes of that girl, her father said with pride.

But how she could work! And what she wouldn't laugh at when she was in the mood. Perhaps it was because she was the way she was that the young men on the beach were so taken with her. The one she favored was a fellow named Herlof. But he was not a working man, neither at sea nor on land, so it must have been because he was the only one on the beach who had a coat, people figured. Otherwise he was downright lazy. Just wanted to walk along the road and act important—as if he were a bishop or a bailiff, they said.

Her father was used to hard work, and when he saw Stormarja keeping company with that boy outside the cottage, he looked at her askance: "Do you see anything in that fellow?" he said softly.

"He hasn't asked me about that," Stormarja's laughter was strangely derisive.

"Let them be," her mother said gently when she saw that Edevart was disheartened.

Herlof took to idling outside the door of Sanna's cottage from morning to night. Black coat and derby and white scarf. He looked remarkably like a raven. And Stormarja went around with eyes so bright and shining that you wouldn't have believed it—not Stormarja, who had always been so serious. She wore her white pinafore in the middle of the week and acted like she thought every day was Sunday. She was so happy that she sang, though she wasn't one who had a pretty voice.

It is strange indeed how foolish one can be in one's youth...

"You'd better watch out, Stormarja," Mother Sanna said when he came too often.

"That guy is nothing but a flighty bird, Stormarja," Father Edevart said.

But then she gave them a look that frightened them, for in her eyes they saw that to her this was a matter of life and death.

So they just had to keep still, though it wasn't easy. Because it can scare you when a young man has no ambition beyond wearing a black coat on a weekday.

In the meantime, Lillmarja grew up and was no longer a child. She was an exceedingly curious and inquisitive girl who was not frightened by her sister, so she spoke to Stormarja about things no one else dared mention.

"What do you want with Herlof anyway?"

"He's really fine," Stormarja said.

"Surely not *that* fine."

"He's an important man," Stormarja said.

"He's no big shot—just an ordinary guy," Lillmarja replied.

Stormarja laughed then at all the ignorance engulfing Lillmarja. "Step across the threshold some evening and listen to his talk. Who knows, perhaps Lillmarja would become wiser than wise..."

"So you really like it then," Lillmarja said in amazement.

"Since you are my sister, you can come, but otherwise not a soul," Stormarja said. And her voice was so strange that it silenced Lillmarja for a long time.

"Sometimes I think you are a complete stranger," Lillmarja said with a shudder. "There's something weird about you. You frighten people with your looks."

Stormarja laughed so that it gurgled in her throat. And then she sang a melody as strange as anyone has heard.

After that Stormarja seldom met her sweetheart alone. Lillmarja was always there, listening and laughing. Her hair was as light as the other's was dark. And her complexion as dark as the other's was light. They were as night and day, those two girls, not a trace of family resemblance. Herlof was no longer sure, wasn't able to decide whom he should favor. There stood Stormarja, so bewitchingly beautiful that you'd think she were from the land of the *hulder*. And there stood Lillmarja, so radiantly lovely that you'd swear she were from a land far above the earth. It wasn't easy to keep a straight course. He had made no promises, no banns had been read, no rings exchanged. No, it wasn't that. Just that when he looked at Stormarja, there was an aura about her that bound him to her like a rope. And when he looked at Lillmarja it was as if she thrust him so far away that he wanted to soar.

One evening he came and found only Lillmarja, for Stormarja was in bed with a cold.

"You look like a conceited fool walking around in that coat of yours," she said.

Never before in his life had he felt so deflated. He wasn't even able to answer, just stood there. She walked right up to him and stared.

"Poor fool," she said with a voice full of mirth.

He unbuttoned his coat and threw it far across the field. She let out a cry, ran and brushed the dirt off and hung it across her arm.

"Good grief man, what a heavy garment. How can you move in it?" He snatched it away from her and threw it again as far as he could. She ran and fetched it.

"For shame, what a terrible, stupid way to treat such a fine coat," she said angrily.

"I'm going away," he said suddenly.

"Do that, Herlof. Then people will be spared saying that you're a loafer."

"Do you care about that, Lillmarja?"

"I care about all the people on the earth," Lillmarja said, and knew that she had never in her life thought that thought before.

Herlof left.

Now a flood came and took Sanna and Edevart's cottage. They moved to another beach on the other side of the sound. And it sometimes happened that Herlof returned and that his boat was seen over by Sanna and Edevart's beach. They no longer minded so much, because now there was more to Herlof than a coat. He had earned money and bought himself a boat that was larger than the one Edevart had had to manage with for a lifetime. He tacked across the fjord in all kinds of weather—but never came ashore. They would hear his cry, though, and see the spray whipping across the bow of the boat when he streaked by.

"Marja, I can't come up on land, I have to stay in the wind..."

Stormarja and Lillmarja looked at each other but understood nothing. Mother Sanna said that the one who was oldest should go down and find out what he wanted.

Stormarja walked down to the beach, alluring and beautiful as a *hulder*, sat down on the rocks and looked at him. He spoke to her each time he tacked by, but it was Lillmarja he spoke of. And there was a hint of anger in his voice because two hadn't come.

When Stormarja came back to the cottage not a word crossed her lips. She sat down at the spinning wheel, looking darker than a winter's day. And the neat little balls of wool Lillmarja carded were never good enough. She was curt and snappish and was a torment to Lillmarja. Her cheeks turned white from anguish.

Mother Sanna wanted to put an end to this. She had a serious talk with them.

"Take our boat when he comes again, Stormarja, row out to meet him and find out what this is all about. There has to be a reason for his coming here."

Stormarja did as she was told, set the sail on the boat, tacked and chased him. She was wild and reckless, valued neither life nor death. For this was the hour of truth. Now there would be settled justice and and injustice between two sisters. All the while she listened to a voice in her heart: "The lot falls to the oldest. The youngest can wait." And she was wild and furious when another voice made itself heard: "But what about Lillmarja...think about Lillmarja...there are some things in life that aren't governed by age."

At first Herlof laughed when he saw her tiny little sailboat. Wasn't a bit scared by her approach...wasn't afraid of her speed...a large boat is a large boat...and a small one is too slow...

This time, it wasn't so. Stormarja set her sail directly at him, circled round and round. If he slipped away she was there again, emerging like a whale right in front of his bow. No getting around her, no escaping. She shrieked and laughed. She sailed insanely, defying all rules, all custom.

"Stormarja, what are you doing?" he shouted across the sea.

"I want to know what *you're* doing, that's all," Stormarja answered. Her voice was seething and the words were tossed at him like yellow phosphor in the breaking waves.

"Why didn't you bring Lillmarja with you?"

"She's afraid of boats!"

Then he saw her face and was scared. He tried to bring his large boat alongside her smaller one so that, by seeing how vastly superior his was, she would come to her senses and give up.

But it didn't work. She headed right for his bow, gnashing her teeth—he was sure he saw lightening flash from the corners of her eyes. Give in to him—oh no, she wouldn't do that.

His face was more white than red. He let out a cry, so harsh that it must have scared all that could hear.

"Don't you see where you're heading, woman!"

"I see only you, as long as you're above water. I dare say we'll have a closer look at each other later, perhaps when there's no boat between us," she cried. It was as if he saw her now as he never had before. She looked gigantic on the seat of the little boat. He screamed as loud as he could: "Are you *standing* on that seat, Stormarja!"

"Maybe I am," she laughed. "You just sit there as long as you can. I'm doing fine."

He dropped his sails. His hands were shaking. He would have to talk with her. No getting around it, the way she was right now. He turned to her and called in a small coaxing voice: "Let's talk to each other for a few minutes, Stormarja..."

"Are you teasing now, Herlof?"

"No, absolutely not. I'm serious, Stormarja."

"Dead serious, Herlof?"

"Yes, I'm telling you, now sit down in the boat, you cursed woman!"

She sailed in and brought her gunnel next to his and stared at him for a long time.

He was both hot and cold. Nowhere in the world had he seen such eyes in a human being. He held her boat and stared back at her.

"You should be happy there wasn't a storm today," he said quietly.

"You should wish there had been," she answered with a snarl. "Because then we would have been finished with everything."

Then he understood that this was graver than he had thought, and that he would have to say what he had never before dared to think when he saw her.

"Stormarja, it is no longer you I wish to speak with."

"He who calls to me must state his errand. I have come to hear it. And you won't be allowed ashore until you have said it."

He shrank and was smaller than he'd ever been. He wept. Didn't she understand that seeing Lillmarja, so bright and beautiful, so sweet and mild, was like seeing an angel of light? Didn't she understand that for him there was no other way? He couldn't forget how good it was when Lillmarja smiled. He couldn't live without her.

Stormarja's smile was as white as the winter sun when it sinks behind snow-white mountains.

"Then you had better go as far from here as you can. Then you had better not sail along this coast any longer. Because Lillmarja will never come outdoors to listen to your talk—remember that I'm the one who said this...if you value your life you'd better get going right now. Hurry before I have a chance to decide what I'd like to do with you. Hoist your sail I said!"

All day long Stormarja sat in the boat close to the shore. The sea was so calm when he was gone that she thought she heard his footsteps on the other side of the fjord. Couldn't she just set sail and find him, just today, just this once...come as one who wants to come...and then she could leave and sail where no one is seen again.

But Mother Sanna came and said: "Come in now, my Stormarja. There's no one like you. And there are so many young men in the world who will kiss your fingers when they see you...that's the truth, Stormarja."

As it turned out Father Edevart had to bring her ashore. Stormarja had lost her will. She just sat wherever they put her from that day on. She only repeated what they said to her. She ate the food they put in her mouth. It was an illness no one understood. Absolutely impossible to cure, the doctor said.

But as the years passed, it sometimes happened that she expressed a wish, called to Lillmarja and gently murmured: "Want to go out walking, Lillmarja. Come, Lillmarja."

She knew the way herself. It went down to the beach. They sat there for hours until Mother Sanna came and fetched them, brushed them off and brought them back to the cottage.

No one ever heard mention of Herlof again. He sailed far away with a foreign ship. But there was a saying there on the coast, when a young girl was heartsick.

"Don't catch Marja-sickness, girl!"

Stormarja and Lillmarja never left home and their many gifts and talents were locked away.

Stormarja spun when they sat her at the spinning wheel. Lillmarja carded. Their handiwork was of the very finest. A more peaceful life than theirs did not exist on this earth, people said. And no one felt the slightest bit of fear when someone cried: "Here comes Stormarja and Lillmarja."

Original title: *Stormarja og Lillmarja.* Translated by Katherine Hanson

Åsta Holth

(b. 1904)

Åsta Holth is from Finnskog, a forested area northeast of Oslo along the Swedish border that was settled by immigrants from Finland. She has been actively writing since the late 1920s: plays for a local theatre group; some fifty short stories for *Arbeidermagasinet* (magazine for the workers); poems and children's books. Since 1955 she has completed two trilogies, one a history of her mother's family, the other of her father's. Her account of life in the Finnish settlements is realistic and colorful; she relates their traditions, their struggle to make a living in the great forest, their conflicts with an encroaching capitalism—themes which are echoed in "Salt," taken from the short story collection entitled *Gamle bygdevegen: Finnskogfortellinger* (1944).

Salt

"I had imagined that she would be a mean old witch, but she was a gentle, sweet and sensible woman."
—C.A. Gottlund

Heikki Karhinen stood sniffing the air like an animal. Surely there wouldn't be a thaw now? It had been cold all fall, the rimy trees looked mangy and unkempt. But when such long rime fringes hung from the birches, it was never long before the cold broke. Oh well—just as long as the thaw didn't last too long.

"You'd better come in and eat," his wife said quietly. In a tone as if she were asking him to do something unpleasant, but necessary.

He sat down at the table, his face dark. Unsalted porridge with unsalted pork. They didn't look forward to meals at Honkamäk. Marit looked pained, but as always her mouth was firm. They were in a bad way these days. There was something missing, their mouths watered when they thought the word, their bodies cried for it, it felt like a kind of hunger or thirst—yes, they actually thirsted for *salt*. Marit had scrimped and saved as well as she could, but the bottom of the salt box was now empty.

"There's going to be a thaw," Heikki said. Marit offered no reply; her mouth was drawn even tighter. It sounded as if it was her fault, the mild weather too. Every morning when they awoke, they anxiously looked at the window and were glad when the frost lay thick on the windowpane. Because if it thawed, the meat would spoil. The brine was so thin that there may as well not have been any.

Heikki ate slowly; the food grew in his mouth.

"Couldn't you have signed?" he said after a while.

"No." It sounded curt and hard. And afterwards a threatening question mark hung in the air: Is there anything else you'd like to say?

Marit Karhinen had gone to Grue to trade this fall instead of Heikki. He had cut his foot. She rode the long journey to Grue Parish with four or five men from Finnskogen. They made these trips every fall, sold meat and hides and wrought iron and bought seed, salt, sugar and other things. This time they were met at Gruset by a stranger. He was a refined and distinguished man who said he was Mr. Anker's secretary as he spread out huge documents that they were to sign. They were informed that Anker owned Finnskogen, the land and the forest, and that he was a good and understanding man who took their interests to heart and gave them good terms. The folk from Finnskogen looked long and hard at the white documents but didn't understand a thing. They could understand and speak both Norwegian and Swedish after a fashion, but this was a convoluted, legal Danish—they couldn't make anything out of it.

"I can't sign something when I don't know what it is," Marit Karhinen said.

But when she went to trade, she was told that, unfortunately, they didn't have any more seed and salt. She ought to speak with Mr. Anker's secretary, however. Maybe he could help her. So she had to go back to the secretary who smiled and bowed and put the paper in front of her once again. She understood very little of the document and very little of what he said. Her eyes, questioning and alert, were on the secretary. All the others had signed. But they were men. And it's the feminine instinct that is always on the alert, always smells danger. She shook her head. Wasn't it true that she wanted seed and salt? Yes, could he please help her buy those things? Once again he tried to get her to sign. But Marit was stubborn as a mule. His face grew taut and he said that he was sorry, but he could not get her the goods she wanted. Marit began to feel confused. But she wasn't stupid and gradually she understood how everything fit together. If she signed, there would probably be a way for her to buy seed and salt, but she understood that putting her name there could be dangerous. She fixed her gaze on the elegant man. There was a faint, yet unmistakable glint in the Finnish woman's good-natured eyes. She turned her back to him—a fine, stubborn woman's back—and left.

And that is how there came to be a salt shortage at Honkamäk. Her father had given them a little rye seed, enough that they could do some planting in the spring, though less than usual. But with the salt it was worse. She could borrow from the neighbors, but perhaps they would say: "Why didn't you sign? What if we had been as obstinate as you?" Besides, salt was a precious commodity at Finnskogen; it was thirty to forty kilometers to the merchant, on roads that were not always passable. And no one was so rich that they could buy as much as they wanted at any one time.

The sky was grey and mangy; it ran together with the scruffy forest. No doubt about it, it was going to thaw. Heikki took his gun and headed for the forest. Not because they needed meat, but because he was unhappy with himself and everything else and was in no mood to talk with people. It was the lack of salt that was to blame. Now it had come between him and Marit. They were peevish and mean toward each other. He knew so well that Marit had done what was right and even so he had to rebuke her by asking: Couldn't you have signed? And Marit turned a stubborn back—it was her back he saw most often these days—and her mouth, which could be so soft, was firm, showing clearly that she fully realized what she had done.

Marit fed the animals and then put on her kerchief and shawl and walked to Revholt to listen to the visitor who had come. The student from Finland, who spoke to the people at Finnskogen in their own language and who worked for their rights.

A delicate shower of hoarfrost needles drifted down from the forest. Grouse wings flapped in among the spruce trees. Strange— until now people at Finnskogen had believed they owned both the spruce and the bird. Most of them had bought and paid for the ground they built on. Before their forefathers came a couple hundred years ago, no human foot had trodden here. The gigantic spruce trees had stood until they rotted. Large herds of moose grazed in the vast marsh. They roamed at will. Now when the wind rustled through rye fields and cows shared the pasture with the moose, now fancy gentlemen came and said, "This is ours!"

Heikki's parents came by foot to Honkamäk when it was covered with forest. With them they had a cow, an ox and a little pouch of rye. They tied the cow to a tree and started to clear! Now Honkamäk was a farm, with luxuriant fields of rye and cows and a horse. And here came that swell gentleman Anker saying it was his.

Poverty grew and many Finnskogen folk had no choice but to become cotters for Anker and others just like him. Actually, they were worse off than cotters, for they had no rights; they could neither clear land nor fell trees to build their homes.

Marit Karhinen had a heavy heart. Life at Finnskogen had become so dark and difficult. Everyone kept to himself. Though it had always been that way since the distance between neighbors was great. The young people were growing restless and longed to leave the forest. Here they found no answers to the thousand questions that torment youth. Here they had only the forest and the animals and the Bible—and their own inexpressible longing.

For that reason they inhaled every word the visiting fellow said. For that reason the boys flocked around him and the girls blushed and gave him their trust. Carl Aksel Gottlund was his name.

Marit and Heikki came home at the same time at dusk. Both of them were happier than when they left. Heikki had shot a hare and sucked the blood from the warm animal throat—*salt* blood. And Marit's cheeks were warm from everything she had heard.

"We can't be sure the thaw will last long," Heikki said. Then the two of them went out to taste the brine.

"It *does* quench our thirst," Heikki said and licked his index finger. Marit did the same. Two times they tasted. Good, very good.

Marit had many things to tell about. They'd better sit down a while on the couch. She took his arm and put it around her waist. And then she told about the wonderful visions, dreams of the future, Gottlund had unveiled. A church here in the forest, with a Finnish minister and Finnish songs, teachers who taught the children in the cherished, soft and trilling language of their native country. A little Suomi for themselves in the midst of this foreign land.

"I did the right thing by not signing, Heikki. They have signed away the right to their land; Anker can force them to leave their farms any time he wishes! Gottlund explained to us what it said in those papers."

"Of course you did the right thing."

Later they read the little book Gottlund had given her, *Pienä Runoja.* It awakened a new hunger in them. They could feel that they had been living in spiritual darkness. But Gottlund had said he would help them get Finnish magazines and books—for spiritual nourishment, the salt of life.

The next day four neighboring Finnish women came to Honkamäk. After they had chatted a good, long while about the weather, about encroachment from Grue parish, about the wolf that had torn apart Lehomoinen's goat over in Revholt—right outside the barn!—and, most particularly, about Carl Gottlund, they got around to the real reason for their visit: A small bag of salt from each of them—they hoped she didn't think it too modest a gift. It occurred to them that Marit might be without salt, not having been able to trade this fall. They knew what a shortage of salt meant at Finnskogen.

"You did the right thing by not signing. If we all held together, it wouldn't be so easy for these bigwigs to do as they please with us."

"Monda kosti Jumala!" Marit's eyes filled with tears as she thanked them.

Outdoors the mangy sky was falling in a drizzle. Salt-white snow covered forest and field. But the winter solstice was not far off...

As she stood grinding the salt with a round stone, Marit had to taste it. She smiled warmly at Heikki, like in the old days.

"Better times are coming, you'll see."

"We certainly don't need to worry about a thaw now."

Heikki kissed a tiny grain of salt from her lips.

Original title: *Salt.* Translated by Katherine Hanson

Monda kosti Jumala!: God bless you!

Inger Hagerup

(1905–1985)

Inger Hagerup's medium is poetry first and foremost and she is regarded as one of Norway's finest lyric poets. She writes openly about erotic love, from the woman's point of view. In her voice there is defiance, a cry of protest against the conventional love relationship in which the woman is the dependent and therefore manipulated partner.

In addition to her many poetry collections, Inger Hagerup has written radio plays and prose fiction. In the 1930s and '40s she submitted a number of short stories to magazines, among these "The Woman at Klepp" (first published in *Arbeidermagasinet* in 1938, later included in *Noveller fra Arbeidermagasinet*, 1974). In this story, as in much of her love poetry, woman's warmth and longing for fulfillment through love is met with cold rebuff.

The Woman at Klepp

When Eli first married the farmer at Klepp, she was young and beautiful and lively. Everyone in the parish wondered how long she would stay that way. The men from Klepp had a reputation for wearing out their women faster than most, and what Trond didn't manage to do, Old Mattis, her father-in-law, would surely take care of.

It would be a lie to say that Mattis liked his daughter-in-law. She was too young for him, she was too lively for him, and she was far too beautiful for him. Mattis liked his women ugly and hard; that kind made the best workers. And women weren't brought to Klepp just for fun, but to work. His own three wives had learned that lesson all too well—they were all now laid to rest in the churchyard—the only rest Mattis had not begrudged them, people said.

Eli was light-skinned and dark-eyed and she pinned her heavy, glossy braids around her head like a bridal crown. She was lissome and straight-backed as a young boy, and had a warm mouth made for laughing. Mattis disliked her intensely. She wasn't even from

Øvrebygda Parish. Trond had, in an extraordinarily rash moment, brought her up from one of the big valleys down south. Even her name didn't fit. The women at Klepp had since time immemorial had names like Berte and Marit and Mattea, and other proper women's names. Eli was a foolish name, and Eli was a fool herself when she came to Klepp.

She tried to bring new practices with her when she came to the farm, but after Mattis had looked at her a few times with those ice-gray old eyes of his she lost the inclination. She quit running to the front steps when Trond came in from the fields in the evening, and stopped waving to him from the kitchen window when he left in the morning. Maybe she grew tired of waving to his broad back as well. For Trond showed clearly that he was ashamed of his wife because she was not like any of the other people from Klepp.

Little by little Eli did become more like the others, at least to look at. She didn't sing anymore, her eyes no longer smiled, and she stopped disturbing Trond with foolish talk as they sat around the big kitchen table in the evening. In reality she had no time to hang around the table either, for Eli soon realized that she alone was in charge of the housework at Klepp.

Otherwise, Mattis had to admit that where work was concerned Eli was as good as any of the previous women of the household, in her own way. But even when she worked there was something about her that wasn't right. When she swung her thick braids around her head in the morning, it was as if she plunged into her work at the same time. It seemed as if chores finished themselves between her fingers. She had time to rest in between, too, to sit on the steps and look out over the countryside when the weather was good. And her face didn't become gray, or her back crooked, as had happened to the Klepp women before her. The tough, young body bent and straightened up like a willow branch. The sin in her must be strong, thought Mattis. It actually helped her to *like* the work at Klepp. Yes, sin was strong in Eli. It could even make Trond's sluggish heart hammer faster in the spring nights. But afterwards he was still more ashamed of his wife. Even at night she wasn't like other people. She could almost frighten him with her shining face and her hot mouth. He began to wonder what kind of a wife he had found for himself.

When the first baby arrived it got better. Moreover, Trond taught her not to behave so indecently at night.

After two years had passed, Eli had become taciturn and obedient, as a woman should be. Now and then a strange light might flare up in her eyes, but it was quickly extinguished when Mattis or Trond came near, so neither of them suspected that the flame burned steadily inside her, and was about to consume her.

How did it come about?

The new substitute pastor stayed overnight at Klepp one Saturday. He was riding the circuit, and was to go over the mountain early the next morning. New and young as he was, he could scarcely be called a pastor. He didn't even look like a clergyman, he was so thin and famished.

Eli came into his room that evening with a wash basin and towel. He had thrown himself down on the bed and sprang up, a little confused by the young woman standing there. Stillness sang in the room; the strange light flared in Eli's eyes. When the pastor took the wash basin from her, he noticed that her fingers trembled. He slept poorly that night. He couldn't forget those eyes.

It became customary for the pastor to stay overnight at Klepp on his way over the mountain. The farm was located so conveniently. The light in Eli's eyes blazed stronger and stronger every time he came, and the bridal crown around her head shone as it had never done before. Eli began to glow once again.

Mattis looked at his daughter-in-law and at the pastor. He said nothing, but he read in Eli's bright shining eyes that now sin had come to Klepp in earnest.

To be sure, sin had probably ruled for a long time over Klepp before that evening when Mattis was lucky enough to catch Eli and the pastor together. They stood in the dark entryway, believing that Trond and Mattis were in the barn.

Mattis shone the stable lantern directly on them. There was nothing to be done. They didn't even try to move. Eli's mouth was still red, but otherwise her face had little color. The pastor's face was nothing to brag about either.

"Well," said Mattis. He set the light down on a stool. "Well," he said again in an almost friendly tone.

The pastor tried to find something to say.

"We—We—"

But Mattis took his light out to the barn again, closing the door firmly behind him.

The men at Klepp never struck anyone. They were Christian folk. But that evening Trond locked his wife out of their room.

"You can sleep there," he said, pointing to the pastor's room.

Eli sat on the kitchen floor all night long with her forehead against the door. In his room the pastor paced back and forth thinking about the salvation of his soul and the pastoral call he would now never receive.

That Sunday Mattis finally managed to break his daughter-in-law's spirit, if she hadn't already done it herself against the locked door that night.

He drove the pastor and Eli the twenty kilometers over the mountain to the country church. After the pale, bewildered young pastor had stammered through his sermon, Mattis came forward. His ice-gray eyes blazed with the zeal of the Lord.

"Today a sinner will appear before Our Lord and confess," he said. Eli came slowly out of the pew. Women and men stretched their necks to see. Nothing like this had ever happened in this country church before. Eli stood for a moment beside the pew, clinging fast to the edge. But Mattis went down to her and loosened her fingers and led her up the two steps to the choir.

"Confess," said Mattis.

Eli opened her dark eyes. For one helpless moment she looked down over the staring faces. Her lips moved, but no words came forth.

"Confess your sins," said Mattis.

And so Eli confessed. She confessed with the words Mattis had taught her on the trip over the mountain. In a high, sharp voice she confessed that she had lived together with the Lord's servant under her husband's roof, that she had sinned against God and man, and that she repented her sins.

Then she sank down at Mattis's feet. The ushers had to help him carry her out to the wagon again.

Out in the sacristy the young pastor sat with his hands over his ears. He had escaped making a public confession. Mattis thought that one would do. But he had to promise to write to the Bishop.

When Eli got home that evening, she tried to drown herself in the well. But Mattis came after her with the milk pail, so it turned out that she went into the stable to do the chores instead. On the whole, everything went the way Mattis wanted it after that. Eli had finally become like all the other women at Klepp had been: submissive, quiet, and obedient. And no one could blame her if she never came down into the parish any more, or if she usually hid when people came to the farm. Strictly speaking, she had nothing to say to anyone either; she no doubt thought she had said it all that Sunday when she stood in front of the congregation and confessed her sins.

Original title: *Kjaerring på Klepp*. Translated by Torild Homstad

Torborg Nedreaas

(1906-1987)

In 1945, the year of Norway's liberation from Nazi occupation, Torborg
Nedreaas published two collections of short stories, one of them entitled
Bak skapet står øksen. The stories in this volume depict everyday life in an
occupied country. At a time when patriotic feelings ran high and
collaborators were condemned, Nedreaas wrote with sympathy and
understanding about young Norwegian women who associated with
German soldiers, as in "Achtung, Gnädiges Fräulein." Her compassion and
sense of solidarity with weak, lower class women are stronger yet in her
next work, *Av måneskinn gror det ingenting* (1947). This is the story of a
woman who in effect became an emotional prisoner to a man who wouldn't
marry her, and who was forced, by economic circumstances, to twice
undergo the trauma of illegal abortion.

Torborg Nedreaas is best remembered, however, for her stories and
novels about Herdis. In the earliest stories from *Trylleglasset* (1950), Herdis is
a little girl, and in the novels *Musikk fra en blå brønn* (1960) and *Ved neste
nymåne* (1971) she develops through adolescence to womanhood. Nedreaas
shows an amazing capacity to intuit the thoughts and feelings of
children—not the least those that are only vaguely perceived. Through
Herdis's observant eyes we view the environment and people that are
forming her: the Great War was being waged in Europe and though Norway
was a neutral nation, its effects were felt there nonetheless.

"Music from a Blue Well" is the first chapter in *Musikk fra en blå brønn*.
This episode takes place far away from the busy city—Herdis and her
mother have been spending the summer at a cottage by the fjord. In the
peaceful quiet of the evening, Herdis yields to all those strange and
wonderful songs only she can hear. . .

Achtung, Gnädiges Fräulein

. . .*Herein!*. . .*Ja ja ja,* just walk in. Oh! Darling! Wonderful girl! Good
heavens, you came all the same, my darling. Wonderful little girl, my
goddess! Yes, yes, I'll smother you, I'll crush you, I could kill you with
my love. But what's the matter, darling? Oh, oh! You've been crying,

ja, mein Gott, you've been crying again. Has anyone hurt you? Who
has been hurting my little girl? I'll kill him. Oh yes, God knows I'll kill
anyone who hurts you and makes you cry. My passion! My fate! I
worship you, worship you, do you hear? Oh yes, I'll kill him, who is
it? Tell me! . . . What is this you say, they will drive you out, drive out
their own daughter? That's shocking. Criminal! *Ach, du lieber Gott!* So
you come to me. To me. God bless you. But listen, no more crying,
no more crying ever again with me. Confound it – I'd almost forgotten – look here! Look what I've got for you. Now, my pet, what do
you say to that? Eh? Chocolates. All little girls like chocolates, don't
they? Ha ha ha. "King Haakon" chocolates. None of them left in the
shops, and the whole box is for you. Come along, eat. It was terribly
expensive. That doesn't matter. No, no chocolate box is too expensive
for you, money doesn't matter to me if I can make you happy. I swear
to God, it's true. There, there, look a little bit pleased, we want to be
happy now. Just happy. Look, I'm choosing the best one for you. I do
believe it's marzipan with strawberry inside. What? Delicious? Ha ha
ha. Now I'm not going to let you think about anything upsetting.
Nonsense, you don't want to bother about those stupid little girls. If
they don't want to talk to you, they needn't bother. They're not worth
talking to. Now now, does it really hurt you so much? They're only a
bunch of stupid schoolgirls. They don't know what love is. You didn't
know either; don't you remember, none of them was more stuck-up
than you. Ha ha ha, how you pointed your little nose in the air! Your
display of patriotism was more vehement than anyone's, and I
thought you really ought to have had a smack on your little botty – oh,
what a little high school prima donna! No one is easier to catch. No
one falls so easily as the ones who are most demonstrative. They'd
better be careful, those little bitches who are tossing their heads at
you. It took me a week. I kept on the look-out for you, and you flashed
your eyes at me. Oh, you were lovely, I fell more and more in love, ha
ha ha. You didn't even thank me, the evening I saved you from those
drunk sailors. Imagine, you didn't even thank me! What if I hadn't
been there then, just behind you in the dark? I can't imagine what
might have happened to you if I hadn't saved you. Good God, I
daren't even think about it! Those fellows in the Navy are a pack of
Godforsaken rascals, bloody riff-raff the lot of them! And you didn't
even thank me. You said nothing, you didn't answer me when I introduced myself and told you I lived here. Went on your way without a
word, I was about to give up, I can tell you. . . And then you came to
me. Quite of your own accord you came to me. . . Oh, my God, how
frightened you were, how you trembled. Only a few days later you
came, do you remember? Never before had I felt so victorious, so

happy. I knew that now you were mine, I knew it as soon as I saw you standing in that doorway, looking as if you were going to run away if I so much as moved. You were beautiful then. Beautiful! And you didn't run away. You didn't move, not even when I locked the door. But you trembled, God, how you trembled! You were like a flame, you trembled and burnt yourself into me, by God I've never met anyone like you. No, take those hands away, you mustn't hide your sweet face. Bless me if you aren't unhappy still! My sweet, my dear, what are you going to do with yourself? *Aber Mensch,* little love, you're going to stay here with me. At least tonight. Heh heh heh. Listen, I think you need a glass of wine. That'll make you feel better. This one isn't at all bad, and it was quite expensive. There now! *Skål,* goddess! My goddess. *Ach,* but you are sweet. And how much you must love me, my little lambkin. Yes of course, I love you too. I swear to God. This is serious, this time it's the great, divine love. You do believe me? You are the only woman – yes, you're a proper woman now, aren't you glad about that? You belong to me. Do you understand, you belong to me? You have given me your innocence, I thank God for it. Do you know, I pray to God for you and thank Him because you gave me your innocence. You have given me something that you can never, never give anyone else. *Ach, du lieber Gott,* how you must love me! And all this you are suffering for my sake, only for my sake. All your friends you have sacrificed for me, ha ha ha – no, I'm not laughing, it's just that I'm happy in spite of everything. I have unique power over you, have you noticed? I've always had fantastic power over women. *Ach, mein Gott,* it's shocking that they have driven you away. But don't think about it any more. Just think that it's for my sake, for the sake of your love. Imagine, an innocent little girl, driven away from home for my sake, just for my sake, a proud, Norwegian girl. Fabulous really. No, drink up now, drink, do you hear? It'll do you good. We'll come to some arrangement, trust me. Oh, but what a fool I am! I'd quite forgotten that I had some supper for you. You must be hungry. Not hungry? Oh, surely? Look here, I've buttered them myself, here's one with excellent sausage. Not that one? Not cheese either? But later? Oh, yes – I expect you'll be hungry later, ha ha ha, I'll take care of it. But I'm hungry. I'll order a wienerschnitzel. I don't suppose you feel like a wienerschnitzel, poor thing, since you're not hungry? It's terrible that they're so unkind to you that you lose your appetite. Oh, people are wicked. People ought to be kind to each other, yes indeed. Then there'd be no war. My God, I'm hungry, isn't that bitch coming soon? Oh, *herein!* Now then, Miss, you will please to bring me a wienerschnitzel. No no no, only one. One wienerschnitzel, understand? This little lady here is not hungry, she doesn't want it. Thank you, and plenty of gravy and potatoes. *A-a-achhh,* it'll be good to eat. You certainly know how to make gravy in this country. You haven't emptied your glass yet, come on, drink it up. Yes, you must – oh dear, I've spilled it on your dress, dear me, dear me, such a pretty dress, *ach* what a shame! What a big oaf I am, oh, I'm so unhappy. But don't be upset, I'll buy you another. But look, I think I'll manage to get the stain out. My wife ought to be here, she's so good at getting out stains – no, don't cry, I'm *going* to get it out, the dress will be like new, no one will notice...*Herein!* Thank you, Miss, put it here. Ahhh, smells marvelous. This is going to taste good. Don't you really feel like a sandwich? My own little girl. My God, how I love you. And cauliflower – not bad for this time of year! Done to a turn, my wife couldn't have cooked it better. *Skål,* little love! No, give me a smile! I'm a happy man, you love me, you, you! I can't understand how your father can be so cruel. Yes, all right, I can well believe it, I'm sure he's a good Norwegian. We might have been the best friends in the world, isn't it strange that he should hate me so? We're all human, aren't we? Yes, don't you see, that's the solution, we're all human, we ought to love one another. This really is a senseless war. For my part I love everybody. Those damned Englishmen! They're the ones who want war, you know. Mmm, what wonderfully tender meat! Yes, because they're a nation of Jews and capitalists. The Jews are the filthiest invention of the Almighty. No, we won't talk about it, you don't understand these things. One day you'll see it from my point of view. When we have won, then you'll understand Germany's struggle. I think it's wonderful you're so Norwegian. I value your love even more. How should that charming little head of yours have room in it for things like politics? You have not thought out your so-called opinions for yourself, you have learned them, they reek of English propaganda. When would such a young girl have had the time to find out what she thinks about international affairs? You beautiful, wonderful creature! We shall find you an apartment. A nice, cozy little apartment, where nobody else shall come but us two. Where there are no Norwegians or Germans, just two people, ha ha...Don't worry, I'll give you money so you can eat dinner every single day. You don't eat much, do you? Of *course* I would not abandon you for anything in the world, you must trust me, pussy cat. I would sacrifice everything for you, you know that. You won't be expelled from school, just let them try. Well, if you want to stay away that's a different matter. In that case, perhaps you could find a job. I can get you a job if you want. Yes, of course you'd be working for the *Wehrmacht.* But they pay well, remember that. Then we might be able to afford a really comfortable little apartment. Then you would be just like a real wife for me.

Nonsense, I'd like to marry you. I love you, I have never loved anyone else. Well – er, um. I was so young, I thought I really did love her. It has been a mistake. On my honor, it is no longer a marriage. Well yes, she's a good woman, but I do not love her. I love only you. For you I can sacrifice everything. I am thinking seriously of getting a divorce, we'll have to see when the war's over. I wouldn't do that for anyone but you. *Mein Gott,* how wonderful it would be to be married to you! I love you, not just because you're a wonderful girl, but because you have a celestial *soul.* I love you with a holy, a spiritual love. That can never die. Good God, what a gravy, won't you taste it? Come on, my dear, just a little taste? I really can't manage any more, there were too many potatoes and gravy. Here's a little bit of cauliflower, too. It would be a pity to have to send it out again, wouldn't it? I have to pay for it just the same. No, damn me if it's going to be thrown away, I'll have to loosen my belt a little. You really don't want any?. . . Bless me, my own treasure, my little pussy cat, whatever is it now? Are you not well today? Oh, my sweet little woman, I understand, you are unwell. . . But what is it, then? . . . Surely you're not—it can't be that – no, that couldn't be possible, I'm almost certain. But you must tell me immediately if you suspect anything of the sort, do you hear? Because we would have to inform the authorities at once. They take the responsibility in such cases when – well, you understand, it would be somewhat embarrassing for me as an officer. Uhhh, I'm really full now. Hey, where are you going? Stop! What do you want with your coat? Oh no, that won't work, ha ha ha, I've got you now. I see you're teasing me – oh, how lovely you are when you struggle – no, look here, what sort of nonsense is this? Do I have to fight you? Oh, what a tease you are! There, come now, my love, I shall not neglect you any longer. So, so. No, listen to me, for goodness sake. What's the point of all this tearful drama? I've had enough of it. Anyone would think you were unhappy because you were with me, with me! . . . Very well. There's your coat. *Bitte.*You are at liberty. All I wish for is an explanation. Well, well. You don't like my uniform? Ha ha ha ha! But I'm taking it off. No, stop! This was interesting, *gnädiges Fräulein.* Enormously interesting. Because it occurs to me that you have had nothing against this uniform before. Not when I was inside it, at least, ha ha ha ha! My apologies, young lady, but the door is locked. *Ja,* and the key I have here, I permitted myself to take it when you started to fight with me. Because I haven't finished yet, I do not accept this nonsense about my uniform. That was quite funny actually, ha ha ha!... Well, so you've only just discovered that I am a German? Somewhat strange, Your Ladyship, since I have not for an instant pretended to be an Englishman. *Mein Gott,* I can't take you seriously, you're so sweet when you look scared. Well, well, so I have suddenly become a German bogeyman! Was it the chocolate that didn't agree with you? Those chocolates I sacrificed for you, that I gave you to make you happy, even though I bought them for my wife in the first place... No, you needn't try to open the door until it suits me. I shall of course let you go, but I demand an explanation; I won't put up with women's whims. I do not intend to tolerate your insults any longer. Many times you have insulted my nation. I have not taken it seriously, you were only a sweet, stupid little goose. But now you have offended me personally, you have *offended my honor* as an officer and a German. *Achtung, gnädiges Fräulein!* This I will not tolerate. After all that I have sacrificed for you, it would be reasonable if I reported you, reported your provocative attitude. In the midst of your ecstacy, of your falling in love, you have retained your hostility towards my nation. *Achtung!* You should not forget that I *am* German, body and soul. And I have had an enemy in bed. Nevertheless I am generous enough to give you your liberty, you are too harmless, too insignificant, to be punished. But after your shameless behavior towards me of course I have finished with you. Oh, that doesn't mean I do not desire you, here and now. I could easily take you, against your will... I cannot be bothered. Take note of that: I cannot be bothered. Here are your gloves, young lady, do not forget them. You may go wherever you wish, you may go home to your parents and ask their forgiveness. They are unlikely to take you back. Quite reasonable, they will not acknowledge a daughter who sleeps with the enemy. I would not have done so either. At home in Germany we call it treachery. It would be interesting to know what *will* become of you. Do you think the friends who no longer talk to you will receive you with open arms? Ha ha ha! Perhaps you have a Norwegian boyfriend who will receive you with gratitude straight from your German lover? My God, how miserable you are now. This is the most amusing thing I've ever experienced. Don't cry so hysterically, you'll look dreadful when you get out on the street. Here's the key. I'll unlock the door with pleasure. *Bitte? Bitte,* my lady, the way is clear. Well? You hesitate? Make up your mind *gnädiges Fräulein,* I no longer desire your company. May I request you to control your tears a fraction? There are others besides myself who live in this hotel. Meant? Meant! What you did or did not mean is not of the slightest interest, God knows. I am mortally insulted. Go away, no, you must let go! I find all this extremely boring. You've lost your glove. I bend down in the dust and hand it to you, as a final compliment. I offer you a wide open door and take my leave of you with the utmost respect. What did you say? Certainly not. Hush, not so loud, let go of me. Don't talk so loud, woman! Certainly not – love? Ha ha ha, what do you know about love, Your Ladyship? You have killed my love. Murdered it. But I am not vindictive, I wish you well and give you my advice: watch out for the Navy. Whoever gets the honor of protecting you in the future, don't let those fellows from the Navy get hold of you, they're bad types, you'll risk disease and worse. No. No! After such an insult – very well, I'll shut the door, they might think I was ill-treating you. Now get up, let go of my leg. Good heavens, you're nothing but a contemptible chit of a girl who falls to her knees. That's it, up you get, oh my God how lovely you are, I forgive you, I have to forgive you, my lovely one, my beauty. . . I knew it, I knew it. You're not going to leave me, you'll never leave me again. . .of course I love you, my pussy cat. . . oh ho ho, of course there are others who care about you. That sergeant in the press office is crazy about you, he's only waiting for me to be finished with you to get a chance. . . there, there, don't cry any more. I'll kiss, kiss. . . kiss all your tears away. God how lovely you are, yes come, come. . . .

Original title: *Achtung, Gnädiges Fräulein.* Translated by
Elizabeth Rokkan

Music from a Blue Well

Only the name was blue. The well itself was black, or silver-grey, or bottle-green or bog-brown. Once it had a blue-painted cover. That was why they called it the blue well. "You mustn't go to the blue well," they said. "Little-Lars fell into it once." Herdis's mother said, "If you ever go near the blue well again, you'll get a spanking."

For Herdis, the old well was as alluring as an unknown adventure. In the evening there were stars down there. She had seen them herself. But Judith and Esther and Peter and Little-Lars's mother said the Evil One was down there. She used to believe them. She was afraid of the Evil One, though she feared Jesus at least as much. But that was a long time ago, certainly more than a year ago, when she was little.

There was music down in the well. She once told Esther and Judith about it, but she blushed as she said it. It was much too hard to explain what she meant by that music. And that was the way it was with so many things, they were hard to talk about. When they came out of your mouth they turned into lies. Then they said, "Herdis is lying." Judith and Esther looked at each other, and then they looked at Herdis, and Judith said, "You're lying. I know it." Then Herdis shouted, anxiously, "But the brook sings. After it rains, a lady sings in the brook."

They were allowed to go there. Herdis took the two girls who didn't believe her to the brook, to the place where it tumbled down a slope into a small pool. "Shhhh," she said. And then they listened for a while, all three of them. Herdis explained in a whisper that you always had to be quiet for a while before you could hear the song. And when she finally heard the voice above the brook, rising and falling in a gentle murmer, she felt very happy.

"Now you can hear it for yourselves!" she whispered.

As soon as she said it, she felt miserable in the pit of her stomach, for the other two heard nothing but the rushing of the brook.

She walked away from them, saying, "I don't want to be with you. I might catch fleas." With these words they became enemies. She was really very sorry about that.

When they did not say anything, she turned back with a tight feeling in her throat and said, "Because you have warts on your hands."

Afterwards she cried a little. The tears were thin and sour, the way they are when you have to cry all alone.

That had been a long time ago, sometime in the middle of the summer. Now the sky was brighter. Everything had grown cooler and more spacious. There was a distant scent of jam in the air. The evenings were darker, and there were stars in the sky. The land in the fjord seemed even farther away yet at the same time more distinct. All summer long it had been lying in a blue distance or hidden in mist. Now she could see houses there, with red roofs, and amber-yellow fields and bright green meadows and shade-green trees. The small island where they set out the fishing nets when her father came to visit had moved farther out into the fjord. Its crags stood clearly with their light and shadow, and moss and stones, and knolls and gullies.

These days were filled with a bitter tone of longing. Dusk fell quickly, ending the cozy times when the kitchen side of the house was red in the late afternoon sun and there was milk and buttered bread on the table outside.

This was the best part of the summer. She had known it before and recognized it as she would a girlfriend she had not seen for a while.

Everything was fine this evening, calm and orderly. Her mother had gone back to town with the black currants and gooseberries she was going to preserve, and she had kissed Herdis and roughhoused with her, and played with her hair and blown in her ears and laughed and carried on with her before she left. Herdis could still feel the effervescent warmth of her mother's caresses, like laughter inside her. Still, she was happy her mother had left. She would be allowed to stay up later. Jenny was not so particular. The feeling of freedom made her dizzy. She owned herself and could do just as she pleased.

She could have gone to the summer pasture if she had wanted to. Judith and Esther and Peter had gone there with their mother to milk the cows in the barn far up the field. She could hear the solitary cowbell from up there all the way down here at the water, where she sat watching the dusk spreading seaward from the land. Down in the stones that mark the tide the sea was spitting in the seaweed and licking its lips. There was a fine jingle of bells in the sound, a peaceful little music.

She began to listen for something she had hidden inside her, something that was her secret.

Her songs, songs that were not like any other songs she had ever learned. Songs that had come to her through an open window of a white mansion sometime that spring.

She remembered every little detail, and now she relived them all and felt how good the moment had tasted. But her songs would not come. She heard only the sea strumming on the stones. A slow humming in the treetops behind her passed like a small shiver across the shining surface of the water.

She closed her eyes.

She had been happy even before they came to that white mansion. It had been one of the good days. She had gone to town with her mother and had bought new sandals, which she was allowed to wear right away, and fabric for a new middy dress her mother was going to sew for her. Her mother had bought herself new gloves and a fluffy white lace affair to wear inside her jacket. It was terribly exciting to have so many new things. Her new sandals danced on the sunbleached sidewalks with a happy clapping noise that sounded like her mother's castanets. Herdis scurried along with her hand in her mother's. They walked toward home through the park, and her mother talked about the trip they were going to take to the country and about all the nice things they were going to do. She was really, truly with Herdis and answered everything she said, not just saying ''mmmm'' or walking along wrapped up in her own thoughts, as she so often did.

It was then that her mother stopped in front of the fine white mansion and listened. Notes from a piano were rushing out of an open window. It was not a song you could sing but a rippling stream of notes that frothed out into the flower-scented air of the park. Notes, notes, many at once, a thousand notes. But there was a song far inside the thousand notes, a sad song. Terribly lovely and terribly sad. But mostly lovely. Lovelier and more beautiful than you could understand just with your mind. It was not the kind of music Herdis's teachers played to reward her for doing well. It was strange and unsettling, quite different from anything her mother played.

The music rose and fell inside her, giving her a feeling of happiness that was almost more than she could stand. Silent and a little afraid, almost, Herdis looked up at her mother. It seemed as if her mother's face had fallen apart, feature by feature. Her eyes were closed and she was far away. But the hand in the smooth glove squeezed Herdis's own. Its warmth ran up through her arm in sweet little spurts. She twisted her hand out of her mother's, for she wanted to be alone. She had to be completely alone to touch all this beauty that was streaming through the open window. Quite slowly, her mother began to walk. A slight scent of perfume rose from her purse when she opened it to find her small handkerchief. She lifted her veil and carefully dried the tears under her eyes. But she was smiling!

Herdis hung back a little. She heard the music getting fainter as they walked. But even after it had completely disappeared, she still heard it.

She could not talk and did not know whether or not she wanted to cry. But it was alright.

Since then she had searched for the music inside herself. Sometimes it came, but it was no longer the same. There were new notes, new songs inside a rush of notes. Sometimes the songs were sad and sometimes they were happy, but the feeling was always strong and joyful. Still, she could not find them again whenever she wanted. Often other songs came and disturbed them, hymns or songs she had learned at school, or the kind of tunes her mother played.

This summer she had heard the music only once.

The well. The blue well.

Not that she planned on going to the dangerous blue well. She had gotten up and was standing with a small round rock in her hand. When she threw it into the sea, the shining surface broke with the faint sound of breaking crystal. There was a sigh along the shore, then everything was quiet again.

Her sandals crunched slowly in the gravel as she walked up the slope.

Jenny had lit the lamp in the kitchen. It glowed orange and made the evening dark blue around the kitchen windows. The sky glowed, as transparent as aquamarine. It was not dark yet.

Perhaps she could find some leftover blackcurrants. She was allowed to pick them now. The blackcurrant bushes stood behind the small potato patch on the hill. They smelled bitter and a little rancid. The blue well lay close by, but she was not planning to go there.

She closed her eyes and sucked in the fresh, raw smell of the potato tops that lay in rags across the torn up field. It was a good smell.

But among the bushes it was too dark to see any blackcurrants. And she could not see the large nettles that were there, either. To avoid the nettles, she took the path around the blue well.

A cover had been placed over the well, an ugly, rusty piece of tin or something, and rocks had been put around the edges to hold it down. .It was as if somebody wanted to hold a hand over the well's mouth so it could not breathe.

The cover gave an ugly creaking sound as she took it off. But she thought a gentle glimmer came from the well, like a grateful glance. Otherwise it was just dark. It had gotten darker everywhere. That was good.

Herdis had never been afraid of the dark. Mostly it brought sleep or good thoughts, and sometimes sweet music. She thought of the dark as something snug and cozy that cloaked her like soft velvet and let her be at peace with herself.

She sat sideways on the stone edge and stared down into the well. It was like staring down into a large, black eye. She listened and felt ever so slightly cold. For a moment she heard Jenny's laughter from the kitchen window. She had a girlfriend with her, and there was a good chance she had forgotten that Herdis ought to be in bed.

Herdis listened until she no longer heard the strange little drips far down in the well, but only the music it gave to her.

It came and stayed inside her. The music came out of the silence and the twilight and began to glow. She sat with half-open mouth and empty eyes, sunk in a sweetness beyond all measure.

The fine silence was torn by three stupid, insistent cries of a crow. The echo swept heavily across the treetops.

The music was broken, scattered into the twilight like a torn string of pearls.

Forlorn, she stared after it, down into the well, and she became aware of sitting uncomfortably, even painfully. She swung her feet around and supported them on a small bump in the wall of the well. She shuddered a little as she felt how slippery the bump was. A chill rose up to her from the unknown depth, and the music that was no longer there left an emptiness inside her. She wanted to swing her feet up onto the other side. As she moved, she noticed that the stone supporting her hand was loose.

It all happened so quickly. Because she was frightened, she probably did something stupid, and her feet slid away from the bump too soon. Her arms grabbed the wrong side of the well, crookedly and clumsily.

Her body slid down slowly while she hung by her arms. Terror flapped like black birds' wings before her eyes. She gasped for breath and pressed her knees and feet against the slimy rock. A scream for help turned into a useless growl. Her body did not dare give away any of its power to her voice.

All her consciousness was concentrated in the trembling body nailed to the wall of the well like a terrified animal. Her fingers were skewered over the edge like two dead hooks of bone. She could no longer feel them. Only with her shoulders did she know that her hands had seized hold with skin and nails. Her shoulders had become one with the stone and soil and nettles above her. Her mouth was torn into a grimace from the scream that did not dare to come out. Even her tears did not dare to let go. Only her stone-dead hands held her, with weak support from the splayed knees that lay skinned against the slimy stone.

One knee had found a perch of sorts in a sharp hollow. Blood ran in a warm streak down her shin, out she had no feeling of pain. She did not know how long she hung there, cramped, unable to move. It could have been a year.

Then one of her feet began to move. Cold and clinging like a snail it crept inch by inch, searching the sharp edges in deadly terror, as if it had nothing to do with her.

It came up against sharp resistance. Herdis held her breath. Her heart was not beating. It just quivered and roared, a grey noise in her ears. She pushed her shin bone against the object in the wall and felt it drive viciously into her calf. The pain seemed to carry a message. The icy waves of pain flickered through her body like a small flame of hope. Her heartbeats stumbled into life again. She released her breath and it came back from the rock wall like a warm cobweb against her face. Clinging like a horsefly, she forced her leg to move. It cut itself as it inched slowly, slowly along the sharp object, which could have been a large nail. She had to push her thigh completely sideways to lift her foot high enough without slipping from the wall. It took a thousand hours in a blind madness of fear and defiance before her foot had the solid object beneath it.

And then it had found a hold.

And her heart began to beat again. It beat in her neck like a small hammer. It beat in the scratches and bleeding wounds. It hammered in her throat and in her deadened fingers that had turned to stone on the edge. It finally beat with a little piping sound, as if bursting with every blow.

The terror that had fluttered blindly inside her had sunk down into her stomach and come to rest there, like a heavy sorrow. Only now did she dare to bend her head back and look up.

She looked straight into a pale green star. A strange warmth trickled down through her body and then something hot and humiliating burned down her lacerated legs. It dripped and fell far down into the well for a long time.

Then she bent her head toward the stone wall again. The cold, moldy smell rose inside her like nausea.

Across her shoulders she was carrying an iron weight that was beginning to hurt her like a toothache. She noticed it with a certain numbness. She felt no other pain besides this aching weight of life and death in her thin shoulders. And it was her foot on the nail that she ought to be thinking with now. It should push her weight upward. Up into the green starlight. Up into the world.

She did not move.

An empty drowsiness was seeping into her, into her thoughts and her body. She could think only in images. She thought of the clock that ticked on the wall at home in town, and the glossy pictures they were given when they bought new school books, and the balcony flower box at home, with its rich scent of nasturtiums. They were good thoughts, but no matter what she thought about, she became more and more nauseous.

Time stood still. From up in the World she heard a gentle rustling, like silk skirts. The scent of the late summer evening swept coolly across her forehead, but it was only the evening letting out a sigh. Once again it was quiet.

She should be pushing down on her foot now, but the very thought made her nauseous. She did not move.

From down in the well an eye was staring at her. An icy vertigo swirled through her stomach. From the soundless vortex something breathed up at her. It whispered sweetly and seductively across her exhausted limbs and into her ears. Something down there touched her and made her weak. She closed her eyes and felt what it would be like to let herself slide down and down to meet a black velvet darkness and let herself be sucked into a dizzy abyss of sweet music, of rest and warmth.

It lasted perhaps only for a moment. She opened her eyes wide and gritted her teeth in sudden anger and defiance.

Her terror came alive again. It summoned power to her powerless limbs. With a furious growl, she wrenched her thigh so that her foot could get a better grip on the nail and felt herself messing her pants like an infant. Her thigh and calf trembled like a taut wire for a whole night and for many nights, and lifted her up, up.

Up. Back into the World.

The evening air felt lukewarm after the raw chill in the well. The air in the World was full of living scents, and she sucked them in with a trembling mouth. And the World welcomed her with the petulant stinging of nettles. Legs splayed like a toad, she crawled on knees and elbows some distance away from the well, which was still reaching for her with its sucking blackness.

Then she heard her name. Jenny was walking around the house calling her. She wanted to answer. She got up with difficulty and wanted to run. But she could not shout and she could not run. Then nausea, vile and relentless, overcame her, and suddenly the air was full of black birds that blinded her and blocked her path. The nettles rose and whipped her arm.

And a thousand notes and the sweetest music came rippling up from the well's blue artesian water and lifted her and carried her and rocked her in a rush of happy waltz music and flung her out across the world so that her stomach tickled, and she lived nine lives and a hundred years and then someone was hitting her, wanting to break off her legs, whipping her throat and arms with nettles.

It woke her up. She was lying near the blackcurrant thicket with one arm in the nettles, with burning wounds and aching limbs, miserably filthy as an infant in her torn clothes, and she heard with blissful joy that Jenny was calling her.

Original title: *Musikk fra en blå brønn.* Translated by Bibbi Lee

Solveig Christov

(1918–1984)
In Solveig Christov's earliest novels, from the late 1940s and early '50s, the
dehumanizing effects of war and the anxiety brought on by uneasy peace
are recurrent motifs. Several of these novels are allegorical, but most of her
fiction is decidedly realistic. Characters, portrayed with psychological
depth and insight, often experience erotic longing and conflicts center
around sexual tension. Her first collection of short stories, *Jegeren og viltet*,
appeared in 1962. There are many familiar themes in the stories in this
volume, which includes "The Paradise Fish." But in addition to Christov's
previous concern with violence and war and her interest in love
relationships, an emphasis on ethical questions emerges regarding the
problems of guilt and individual responsibility.

The Paradise Fish

We lived under threat of being "condamned," as Goggen called it.
That was distressing, of course, but also understandable, because
nowhere in the city or the surrounding area was there another place
like Repen. A cluster of old, tumbledown houses camped by the
bridge. The bridge itself was so old that no motor-vehicle traffic was
allowed on it; originally it had been built to support a man and a
horse. But it arched beautifully toward heaven, and bore no
resemblance to new flat, sensible bridges. Things were difficult for us
in many ways, but we didn't mind that. We had the river's sedate
distance between us and the turbulent life of the big city; we had the
scent of the sparse woodlot of fir trees growing in the old ropewalk,
we had larkspur, lupine and peonies in our gardens during the
summer. We felt exclusive and privileged. It was sad to know that the
city over there stood poised to gobble us up, but before that
happened, we would all have moved to other places. Not that any of
us had dreamed about those other places. No place in the world could
begin to compare with what we had.

The strange thing happened that last summer. We didn't know

then that it was the last. When the strange thing happened, perhaps we didn't know either that it would change us, make us cautious. So cautious that, from that day on, we set our feet only hesitantly upon the unkempt fields of life.

But before it happened. . .

There sit Goggen and the Philosopher, fishing on the river bank. They sit there constantly, morning, noon, evening. Rather absentmindedly, they watch the bobber floating on the yellow river water; no one has ever seen them catch a fish. Goggen is jovial and loquacious, the Philosopher is a man of few words. On the other hand, he has what Goggen calls schoolling, that is to say, schooling. We had the habit of doubling the number of consonants whenever possible. That made the vowels juicier, and gave our words a bubbling clarity. The Philosopher used words in a different way; he used them to create wonder and conjecture. But on those few occasions when he said something distinct and definite, his words were in the same class as the Almighty's.

There was our Erna, twenty-summers-old. She worked in a bakery on the other side. She wasn't pretty, but she was neat and healthy and generous with leftover buns from the bakery. We put the buns in the oven for a while, and they tasted as good as new. Moreover, she took good care of her old father. His clothes looked so fine that we dubbed him the Consul.

There was the apprentice, Anton, who lived at the home of Amanda, the mother of the madcap twins. Anton loved Anni. All of us knew that, including Anni. And she challenged this shy and cautious love with all the shamelessness of which only a fifteen-year-old is capable.

At dusk, when the neon advertisements begin to lick the sky with yellow and red tongues on the other side of the river, Amanda trudges slowly across the bridge. She has finished work for the day, and her hands are red and sore from soapy water. She sits down beside Goggen and massages her legs.

"If I could just be sick for a while," she says. "I could go t'the hospital and rest for a coupla days. I've got my health insurance, give 'em money ev'ry single Friday. . ."

"Y'should be ashamed of y'rself, talkin' that way," says Goggen.

"Just a little bit sick," says Amanda pleadingly, "just for a coupla days."

"Thank the Creator y've got your health," says Goggen sternly.

Amanda merely sighs. The worst part of the day is yet to come. She has to go home to the twins, and to new bills. How many light bulbs, window panes and mailboxes she has scraped together money for over the years nobody knows. One thing is sure though, the twins are worse than whirlwinds, hurricanes and cyclones. We don't dare say anything to them. But we advise Amanda to give them both a good thrashing. A recommendation which she apparently follows once in a while. There is never any sign of improvement, however.

Then Frida happens to come along, walking stiffly across the bridge in high-heeled patent-leather shoes that are worn down on one side. She is on her way to her working day, or rather, working night. But it must be said to her credit that she never brings her traffic over to our side. And she often has cigarettes to give away.

Frida stops, gives yet another jaunty tug to her hat, and calls out: "Y'look tired, Amanda."

"That's what comes of honest work," replies Amanda. "Y'maybe wouldn't know 'bout that. . . ."

And this gives Amanda the little injection she needs in order to get up and go home.

"Fuck you," says Frida indifferently.

Amongst us also lives a person whom we call the "Artlerist." When he arrived, he took down the old sign outside the blacksmith shop and put up a placard bearing the word "Atelier." From that he got his name. He paints pictures on sacking and pieces of cardboard. Once in a while he wraps up a painting and takes it into town. In the evenings he comes back with it. But there have been times when he has come back without the painting. He may have sold it, or he could also have left it somewhere in order to impress us on his return. We don't know him, perhaps we're a little afraid of him. He walks by, stares at us with his wild, dark eyes, looks as though he wants to say something, but doesn't. Not until he gets on the bridge is he able to speak.

"The river flows!" he shouts. "The river is like life, it flows, flows. Life is like the river, a rotten sewer full of dead rats and used condoms. The source was pure, the great sea is pure. But the river. . . Do you think anything can live down there? A fish? Never. . . You'll never catch any fish."

And he pounds his fist on the railing.

Somewhat to our surprise, Goggen makes no retort, but merely spits. Perhaps the Philosopher restrains him, for the Philosopher seems to have a secret knowledge about this vile desecrator of our river.

The spring preceeding this summer began so well. Erna found a boyfriend; she was so happy that she often took the wrong buns, bringing us completely fresh ones. We finally had to point this out to her. But no, she had intended that we should have fresh ones. The cost was deducted from her salary.

"I want to be good," she said, giving us a long look of overwhelming happiness.

They met on the bridge. They came from opposite directions and met in the center. It was lovely. Afterwards they walked into the city with their arms tight around each other.

Her boyfriend was handsome. "Like a god in the mornin'," said Amanda. He had a helmet of very curly blond hair, dark skin, and a shirt that was white as snow. The shirt was open at the neck besides. In fact, it was probably this white shirt open at the neck which made the hearts of both young and old women in Repen beat so strangely.

All of this had a most unfortunate effect on Anni. She found herself a boyfriend too, a young fellow from the other side who had a delivery bicycle. She became boisterous and boastful, and claimed the fellow also had a mandolin. Of course, we didn't begrudge Anni a boyfriend with a mandolin, but the sad part of it was Anton. Anton went to pieces with sorrow before our eyes. We tried to comfort him. It did no good. But Frida took him to task with a good scolding. "That's what happens," she said angrily. "That's what happens when y'just go aroun' dreamin'. A woman ain't made so a man can go aroun' dreamin' of her, a woman wants a man t'touch her, t'hold her tight. An' whaddya do 'bout the other part of it, I wanna know, where d'ya smuggle away the desire? So y'can go aroun' dreamin' of poor Anni. An' what's she s'posed t'do? Go aroun' starin' at this dream y've got? Well, serves y'right."

Anton locked himself in. The summer became one great gasp of flowers, heat and flies. And Erna came to Repen with fresh coffee-cakes; she would be spending her summer vacation at the seaside, where she was going to meet Alf's parents. She was nervous about his parents, but the sea. . . She had dreamed of the sea—the big, refreshing, heavily salted sea. In fact, a radiance came over all of us because of that love affair.

It was Goggen who first warned us what would happen.

"She's too much on the dot. She shouldn't come right on the dot. It's the man who should wait."

Was our Erna too much on the dot?

"Way too much on the dot. . ."

"Tell 'er that," we said uneasily.

"Have told 'er. But she don't hear nothin', see nothin'."

After that we watched the bridge carefully. And it was as Goggen had said, Erna often stood waiting for him a long time. Longer and longer. But he came. And weren't they soon going on a trip to the seaside?

One day he didn't come. A heavy, painful silence settled over

Repen.

He never came again. Erna stood on the bridge for many days, but no young man in a white shirt appeared. Our memories of that white shirt were so vivid that we thought we should be able to conjure it up. But no.

All we could do was leave her alone. Or rather, Anni did something else; she broke up with her bicycling boyfriend. Out of a feeling of solidarity with Erna, out of loyalty toward Repen? We didn't know for sure, but Anni grew dear to us again.

So surely things would at least improve for Anton? Not that either. He turned his face away when he walked past Anni. He had lost his faith.

The summer grew old and sluggish. One such sluggish day, the Artlerist crossed the bridge with a painting. About sunset, he returned with it. He stopped on the bridge; we saw his silhouette against the flaming sky.

"The river flows," he shouted, "flows and flows. The river is like life, poisoned like life. I can't live among dead fish any longer. I want to go to the sea. . ."

With that he climbed over the railing, and threw himself into the river. The whole thing happened so fast we could scarcely believe our eyes. But Goggen and the Philosopher acted, they acted with such speed and purpose one might think they had practiced for a long time. They propped up their fishing poles between stones on the river bank so that the bobbers still floated. They practically slid into the small flat-bottomed row boat. The Philosopher took the oars and Goggen a long, black boat hook. We saw the Artlerist's head rise to the surface of the water a few times, but by the time Goggen and the Philosopher reached him, he was gone. The Philosopher rowed around a little, while Goggen thrust the boat hook into the yellow river water. After a few tries, they found him and got him up into the boat. Frida had enough presence of mind to send Anton for an ambulance. Anton returned just as the boat jolted against the shore. Goggen made a thumbs-down gesture.

"Dead," he said quietly.

They carried him onto the river bank; we could see for ourselves that he was dead. Anni sobbed loudly and threw herself on Anton's breast. And Anton was no stronger, he put his arms around her and told her not to look.

The Artlerist lay there on the river bank, looking so alone and forlorn. He had lost his ragged scarf, and we could see right in to his thin chest under the velvet jacket. But still, the worst thing was seeing the underside of his shoes. There were no soles left, and the dead, dirty bottoms of his feet were an accusation against us.

We hadn't seen this abject poverty.

Perhaps he had tried to hide it from us with that strange intensity he had when he was alive. But now the wild, dark look was no more, and he was surrendered to us, surrendered to the truth. We stood on the river bank filled with shame.

The ambulance arrived. Two men with a stretcher, a doctor and a policeman ran across the bridge. The doctor leaned over the dead man, shook his head, and gave a sign to the men with the stretcher. They eased the body carefully onto the stretcher and covered it with a blanket.

This was what kindness looked like.

The policeman said, "Are any of his relatives here?"

More shame. We didn't know anything about the dead man, much less about his relatives. And wasn't it we who should have been his relatives? Shame. . .

Then Erna took a step forward and said, "Sir, I was engaged t'im."

"Then you can come along with us," said the policeman.

"Thank you," said Erna in a firm voice. And they started off, the two men carrying the stretcher, Erna on one side, and the policeman and the doctor on the other side. They walked across the bridge, and we heard a vehicle start up.

"But she ain't never been engaged t'im," said Anni.

"That's sure nice of Erna t'do," said Frida, "so he got company the last little ways."

Yes, it was nice of her, Erna was good. She knew better than any of the rest of us what pain and sorrow are.

"An' remember," Frida continued, "both of 'em wanted t'go t'the sea."

Yes, just think there was a bond between those two after all.

"An' now she's got a father for her baby," said Amanda.

Her baby? We were stung by the words. But we looked at Amanda's mouth, and suddenly knew that Erna was going to have a baby. We should have known it before, from many indications. And it became very clear that a dead fiancé was a far better father for the baby than a living traitor. Now it wasn't certain that Erna had considered this fact, because Erna was good. But if she had, we would make sure that not one seed of doubt was allowed to grow in Repen's soil.

Dusk fell on the river.

"We never talked t'im," said Goggen sadly. We were moved to realize that even Goggen felt guilty. But Anni was too young to be willing to bear such a burden.

"He said himself that the river flowed," she said. "An' that's true. He said y'd never catch a fish, an' that's true too. There wasn't nothin' for us to say, when he said himself how ev'rythin' was."

There was something insidiously liberating about this logic. It made the Artlerist himself to blame for all his loneliness and need. Since he had only said things it was impossible to disagree with.

At that moment, Goggen let out a roar and rushed to the edge of the river. His fishing pole formed a graceful arc over the water, and something had pulled the bobber down. Goggen snatched his fishing pole loose and threw the fish on the ground.

Because it was a fish.

A silver-shining fish with clear, blue fins, a blue-black head and yellow-rimmed eyes. None of us had ever seen such a beautiful fish. That such a marvel had swum in the filthy, stinking river water had to be regarded as nothing less than a miracle. It was not a mackerel.

Nor a trout nor a perch. . .

Then Anton said that he thought it was a Paradise fish, for since there were birds of paradise, surely there were fish of paradise as well. Anton still stood with his arms around Anni; his voice had acquired a new note of authority, and there was something to what he said. The fish flopped its blue tail cheerfully.

"I think y'should make a good broth with him," said Frida.

Amanda laughed furiously, and said she had never heard of anyone making a broth out of a fish like that. A fish like that should be fried. In pure butter. . .

"No," said Anton, "y'oughta stuff him, an' hang him on the wall. They ain't got fish like that, for sure, even in the zoo."

This was an idea, of course, but Goggen looked undecided.

Then the Philosopher spoke.

"It's y'r fish," he said, turning to Goggen. "Now y'do what y'want with y'r own fish. But I wouldn't advise makin' no broth out of him, an' I wouldn't fry him or get him stuffed. Y'don't do things like that y'see. . . with a soul. . ."

A soul?

The word grew wings and whirred among us.

A soul. . . A soul. . .

"The fish is the Artlerist's soul," continued the Philosopher. "We've got his own word that he wanted t'go t'the sea. Besides, what other explanation could there be?"

When we stopped to think of it, there wasn't one. And it was the Philosopher who had spoken. We nodded silently to one another.

"He stuck himself on Goggen's hook t'say goodbye t'us," said the Philosopher in a loud voice. "We're reconciled with him now."

Reconciled? That was certainly well and good.

But couldn't we more easily bear a little lack of reconciliation, a little ordinary shame and guilt, rather than this awful knowledge of strange happenings between heaven and earth?

Goggen held out the fish and looked questioningly at the Philosopher, who smiled and said, "It's y'r fish."

Then a decisive expression came over Goggen's face. He turned toward the river, and threw the fish back in. The fish traced a wriggling silver arc toward heaven, and then glided gently down into the river.

"He's wavin'," said Anni solemnly.

We stood there on the river bank for a long time. And for a long time, it seemed, we could follow the Artlerist's soul on its journey to the sea.

Original title: *Paradisfisken.* Translated by Nadia Christensen

Ebba Haslund

(b. 1917)
Ebba Haslund is one of the leading feminist writers in Norway today. In novels, short stories, plays, radio plays and children's books, all set in her own time and milieu, she has sought to depict attitudes and trends in a society dominated by men. The goals and values of the "ideal" family in the modern welfare state are questioned in several works including *Krise i august* (1954) and *Det trange hjerte* (1965). In *Syndebukkens krets* (1968) she focuses on a woman who for twenty years has nurtured a bitterness and hatred toward the man who informed the Gestapo of her husband's underground activities. In each of these novels the protagonist has rejected her Christian faith. Failure to replace religious attitudes and beliefs has resulted in a spiritual void, thereby rendering her incapable of accepting personal loss and defeat.

The expectations women try to fulfill is a recurrent theme, but it is most clearly formulated in *Bare et lite sammenbrudd* (1975). Concerning the impetus of this novel, Haslund has said: "Above all I wanted to torpedo the myth of the good mother. Because it is such a mighty weapon to keep women at heel and give even the most conscientious of us an eternally guilty conscience."

For many years Ebba Haslund has held informal talks on the radio, witty and thought-provoking causeries about current issues and events. A selection of these commentaries plus other articles by her was published to commemorate her sixtieth birthday and its popularity has resulted in two subsequent collections.

"Santa Simplicitas" is taken from the short story collection *Hver i sin verden* (1976).

Santa Simplicitas

Ellen Andersen was her name. Could anything be more ordinary? As a child she had experienced "Ellen" as something round and friendly—a basket she lay in, a soft, fur-lined nest. She was surrounded by friendliness. Her parents were older, quiet people; her sisters were teenagers when Ellen was born. "Our little sister," they said with tender pride. She had been something to show, something to push along in the baby buggy: "Look at her. Isn't she good"—because she was so little and they were so big. When they got to be even bigger, they had other things to think about. They married early and moved to other parts of the country. Ellen remained in that middle-sized town in Eastern Norway. Her parents were newcomers and kept to themselves. Her father worked at a warehouse; her mother did piecework for a clothing factory. Ellen was always nicely dressed. But she had to be careful with her clothes, not get spots on what her mother had toiled over, first sewing and then washing and ironing. She stood on the periphery of the games and watched carefully. She saw what was scribbled on the walls in the stairway, knew all the rules for hopscotch and ball, had memorized all the songs they bawled out when they danced up and down the street and chose partners. But if anyone asked: "Do you want to play?" she shook her head and moved away from the group, quietly and attentively.

At school she was aware of how ordinary she was. She was neither smart nor dumb but something in between. She was good in Religion, but that didn't really count very much at school. She was a little smarter than average in history and Norwegian, a little dumber in arithmetic, dumbest in handwork. She clutched her knitting needles with stiff, sweaty fingers and knitted so hard that the stitches stayed right on the needles.

"Oh, but Ellen," the teacher said mildly and went on to the next table.

Nobody ever scolded her. Nor was she teased, even when she told them that at home they always said a prayer before meals and that she wasn't allowed to go to the movies. "Poor thing," they said and continued talking about something else.

Before she started school she had on several occasions done something wrong. One time when she had been given pencil and paper so she would sit still and draw, she drew a picture of herself the way she looked down below: beautiful, soft curves. When her sisters asked what she was drawing she answered truthfully: "My bottom, front and back." But that was both sinful and ugly she was told, and she had to promise to never, never do it again. No one told her why she shouldn't do it, but she figured it must have something to do with the first commandment: Thou shalt not create false images.

When the first snowfall came, they made snowmen in the street and one of the girls made a snowlady—it was to be the Sunday school teacher. Ellen remembered that the teacher had two pointed bumps in front under her glistening green sweater. So she put two snowballs on the snowlady so that it would really look like a lady. The other girls began to snicker and the one who had made the head on the snow-man said:

"You're crazy!"

But Ellen didn't understand then either, what she had done wrong. Later on she thought it was probably the same thing about creating false images.

One Sunday the teacher told about Abraham who bargained with God over the city of Sodom which was to be destroyed because the people there were so evil. Finally he got God to agree to save it if there were only ten righteous people in the city. But there weren't even so many as ten righteous souls. Ellen put her hand up, because the teacher had said they should just ask if there was something they didn't understand.

"But then Abraham was lying!"

The teacher explained that she musn't say such a thing. Abraham was a man of God. He wanted to help the people in the evil city and so he prayed for them.

Ellen understood it like this: It was all right to lie in the Old Testament but not in the New, because then Jesus came and said Thy speech shall be yes, yes and no, no, and that meant that one shouldn't lie.

She gradually learned that there were rules everywhere, various sets of rules for how one should behave. Just like hopscotch on the sidewalk—you couldn't step on the lines. The same was true for numbers. She wanted to write the number 5 and the number 7 next to each other, since they had the same bright blue color. But at school there was something called number sequence and the number 6 had to come in between, even though 6 was light brown like the walls in the hallway. The number 3 she wanted to put up above by itself, because it was so fancy, but at school it had to go right on the line between 2 and 4. It wasn't difficult to learn. But she never quite got used to working with the numbers the way they did at school and she often made mistakes when she had to go up and write on the black-board. In junior high school it sometimes happened she stood with the chalk in her hand and didn't know up from down.

"Oh, Santa Simplicitas," the teacher said once when she stood staring at him helplessly like a kitten. "Oh, sacred simplicity!"

He said it with a thick "l" the way they talked here in town, the way she herself normally talked. But when she came home, she said it to herself in her bedroom, said it with a thin "l" and a whistling "s," like the minister's wife, and she drew the "i" out after the "l." Santa Simplicitas.

Sacred simplicity—that was she, Ellen Andersen. And hadn't He, her bosom friend, said blessed are the innocent!

"You're just an Ellen Andersen," one of the girls in the class said. Ellen happened to hear it, though that had not been intended. The girl blushed and said:

"I only meant that Lita is shy and quiet like you are."

But that wasn't what the girl meant. Ordinary was what she wanted to say. After that Lita did everything to draw attention to herself—answered the teacher during class, painted her lips with lipstick, smoked during recess in the girl's lavatory.

That was because she wasn't close to Jesus.

Ellen's father always said that it was a pity about those who weren't close to Jesus. The men he worked with weren't—they smoked and drank and swore. Those who weren't close to Jesus, they were the unfortunate ones.

At Ellen's home they were close to Him and read every day of His works.

When she was little she played with the baby Jesus. When her mother asked her what she was doing, even though it was obvious that Ellen wasn't doing anything, she was sitting quietly with her hands in her lap, she answered:

"I'm playing with the baby Jesus."

"My little one," her mother said then, and stroked her thin, wispy hair. The bow wouldn't stay put. It slid down over her ear even when it was secured with a bobby pin.

But when she got a little older, she noticed that her mother became uneasy when she gave that answer.

"You should go outdoors on such a nice day," she might say.

Or, "Why don't you come to the store with me?"

As if it weren't quite right to play with Jesus. Even though both the Sunday school teacher and the minister said that Jesus was the children's best friend, their bosom friend who longed to come into their hearts.

For a while she thought of Him as her brother. An older brother who was always with her and helped her. When she started school, He had turned twelve and came to the temple with His parents. They were simple, ordinary people just like Ellen's parents, and He became a carpenter like His father. Even though He was wiser than everyone else and was to be the savior of the world. And those He loved the most were the poor in spirit, the simple, all those who the extraordinary people called "poor things."

Sacred simplicity, Santa Simplicitas. Sacred commonplace. Just like the bread—the daily bread—and the wine. They didn't have wine in Ellen's home, of course, but in Palestine wine was as common as water. Christ manifested Himself in bread and wine. He loved the commonplace.

When she was thirteen she had such strange thoughts. Colors flickered incessantly behind her eyelids. At times it felt as if she were walking beside herself, her voice sounding as when a stranger speaks. For a time she thought she was going crazy, but she didn't dare share her anxiety with her parents who were themselves tried by illness; they both had bad hearts. Once when Ellen was in bed with the flu, she had such a high fever that the doctor was sent for. He was the family doctor, a friendly old man. While her mother went out to the kitchen to get a spoon, Ellen confided in him. With his dry, old hand on her feverishly warm forehead, he told her that this was nothing to worry about. It was completely normal for young people to have unusual thoughts when they entered puberty. They would go away.

She was fifteen, childishly thin and undeveloped, when Jesus came to her for the first time, as a groom comes to his bride. That morning at church she had sung "My faith I bestow unto you, my bridegroom, I am the bride" and "all that a heart can grow rich and rejoice in, is Jesus to own, to love, to embrace." In the Epistle lesson it was written that one should present one's body as a living, holy sacrifice. The minister explained that one must open oneself to Christ and his words were: "When He touches your breast." At that instant she felt His hand, how it tenderly closed itself around her one little breast. It was so small, lying nestled like a baby bird in His secure hand. A sweet tremor ran through her: He who had been her older brother had now come even closer; He was now her sweetheart.

After she had gone to bed that night, He came to her and she exploded in ecstasy. The next morning her eyes shone in such a way that her mother anxiously asked if she had a fever. Later on that day she began to bleed. It was what they called "the usual excuse" which allowed girls to skip P.E. It made a girl grownup; more than confirmation, it made her a woman. But she felt that it had happened in such a way that He had consecrated her. In the hymns there was so much talk about blood: the Bridegroom's, the Lamb's holy blood. Menstrual blood, on the other hand, was unclean. Woman was unclean. But in union with Him, the holiest, the cleanest, she was cleansed and made holy.

The following year she was confirmed. Her parents went to communion with her; her mother was moved to tears. She herself experienced nothing as she knelt there between them. Eating His body and drinking His blood was a poor substitute for her experience of Him. She thought that communion was for men who couldn't be

His bride and for those women who had an earthly sweetheart. After a while she stopped going to communion almost completely, going only now and then to keep her parents from being unhappy.

Throughout her childhood she wrote what one would have to call poems. Still, her writing didn't resemble those poems which were in her reader. They seemed to be formed within her, one by one, and when she got them down on paper she experienced it as a relief, as if her mind were somehow cleansed. She hid them in her dresser drawer under the clean clothes, just as one hides keepsakes from a loved one.

Her parents died, first her father and then her mother a few months later. Her grief was heartfelt for them who had now passed into eternal bliss. Where the Lord sat on His throne of heavenly gold, enveloped in a mantle of clouds with stardust in His hair. Seraphim stood round about and the train of His cloak filled the temple. She knew that her good and pious parents, ordinary, little human beings who were His children, would be well received by Him. But she herself did not have the same intimate relationship to Him as to the Son.

Her sisters came to the funeral with their husbands, cried profusely and worried about their little sister. But Ellen, who was by now twenty-four, assured them that she was just fine, the rent was reasonable and she was happy with her work at the post office. So they went home, each to her own and as the years went by, it was longer and longer between letters.

She sat behind the window at the post office weekdays from eight to five, Saturdays until three. The routine work provided her with a livelihood and a generous one at that. Every Sunday she dropped a ten-crown note in the alms box. The rest of her savings she divided into envelopes with different inscriptions. The contents were later sent together with those forms she received from charity organizations—Save the Children, Home missions, the Salvation Army—but she always kept one envelope in reserve for crises such as earthquakes, flood disaster and other natural catastrophes.

From the time she was a child she had been taught to look upon what they called *adiaphora* as a sin. But she couldn't bring herself to look at the pleasant people who came to the post office with their postal banking books and checks as sinners. Nor could she regard her co-workers in that way, even though she knew that the people at the post office went to the movies, smoked, drank and danced. And she assumed that most of the customers did the same. She told herself that they needed that kind of superficial diversion because they were not holy, commonplace people like herself, but rather poor, wayward souls who wandered about in a cold and drab world.

She herself lived in beauty and abundance. She was in the world, but not of the world. When she had closed the window and put away her work, she began to open her mind and heart. She always stood for a few minutes outside the post office and inhaled the evening air while she opened herself more and more. In this way she prepared herself to receive His gifts: rain which cooled her face, gentle breezes which moved quietly and stealthily, bands of sunshine on a summer evening, the fresh breath of frost in January. She felt His presence in everything, but sought it particularly in the little things: the glitter in a drop of dew, a blanket of new fallen snow, the sparrows in the field—His sparrows. The brilliant sunset on a February sky was almost too much for her. Tears of ecstasy came to her eyes. But He said to her: you shall love me in all things, not only that which is beautiful. Then she began to notice that He was also present in the smoke which was emitted from the sooty smokestacks of the factory, in the mud puddles on the worn-down sidewalks, in the autumn fog and the winter cold.

She spent her vacations at the pension where she and her parents had vacationed the last years they had lived. It was located a few miles from her own town, in a peaceful, green landscape surrounded by ridges. But that was almost too much—just seeing so much sky everyday from morning to night. Most often she went into the forest behind the house and found herself a rock or a stump. She could sit there for hours, breathing in the smell of damp moss, listening to the birds, following with her eyes the ants as they darted back and forth on the brown path.

She was actually happiest at home in her apartment where she had always lived. Everything there was within her perspective and she could take pleasure in each and every thing, take it into herself, sing its praises. Praise was an important part of her existence. It was the means by which she kept herself prepared.

It wasn't always that He came to her. She lay awake and prayed. She fasted. One time she tried to whip herself with a leather strap, but she was unsuccessful and cried tears of shame over her own inadequacy. Then He said to her that it was unnecessary, unworthy in fact. It was fine that she fasted, because then she saved money and there was more to apportion to the various envelopes. But she must not fast for too long, for she then weakened the body which His heavenly father had created and in which He himself found pleasure.

When He had been with her, she awakened early and felt the joy surging upward, like the sap in a tree, until it burst forth in a poem. She kept her poems in a chest which had belonged to her mother's family. In this chest she had a treasury of memories from which to nourish herself. It was to be kept as her most precious secret and follow her to the grave. This is what she had thought and had, in fact, written in a little letter addressed "to my family." It would probably be one of her cousins who would open it. Even though they scarcely knew her, they would surely respect the wishes of the deceased, that the chest should be laid unopened in her coffin. She couldn't bear the thought that anyone should read these candid depictions of the secret which was for her life itself. It must never happen.

Great was her consternation one morning when He told her that this should be made known to everyone. She should step forth with her treasure so that others could see it, turn away from their pitiful diversions and gather around the Essential. At first she couldn't believe that He really meant this—that her precious secret should be put on display. She felt indignant, that she had been violated. For the first time she dared to upbraid Him. She knew of course that she couldn't own Him alone, He was for everyone. Nevertheless this felt like a betrayal, that He now turned from her, the one and only, to all the others. At times the temptation was so strong that she came close to destroying the poems—burn them or tear them into a thousand pieces and scatter them from the window. But when it came to doing it, she didn't dare. Night after night she lay awake, filled with a troubled longing, but He didn't come. Then she understood that this was His will and that she must submit, so she made clean copies of the poems—over the years it had become quite a thick stack. She wrote in her most elegant handwriting, but still it went much too quickly. One evening the last poem was written down. She placed the stack in a large, yellow envelope and sent it to a Christian publishing house.

It did not bother her that she had to wait a long time for an answer. As long as it didn't come, she could pretend that the envelope hadn't been sent and each day that passed raised her hopes that it would be returned. He was the one who had wanted this and perhaps He had only wanted to try her obedience.

Finally one quiet, grey-white day in early March she received an answer. It came in the form of a strangely ambiguous letter; she read it several times unable to grasp the intent of the letter. As far as she could understand, they didn't want to publish her "manuscript," as it was now called. But she still couldn't feel completely safe, because the person who wrote wanted to talk with her about it.

Talk with her about her secret treasure, she flushed at the mere thought and was filled with mortification. So she was to be tried even further!

It was not difficult to get the day off. In all the many years she had worked for the same post office she had seldom missed work and never without a valid excuse. So she went into Oslo and appeared at the publisher's at the appointed time. She was shown to the office of a young man who was visibly confused when he saw her. He couldn't get started with what he had intended to say, but ran his fingers through his hair and moved things about on his desk, while he talked about trivial, irrelevant topics: the weather, the city she came from, his own position in the publishing house. It appeared as if he had prepared a speech which he now found to be inappropriate for the situation and so he was forced to improvise. Like the minister when he paid a visit to wish her mother a quick recovery and found her dying.

"Yes, and now to your manuscript," he said at last in a cordial tone of voice as if he were finally coming to the matter at hand. Whereupon he became very serious and said that the head of the publishing house had wanted to return the poems and let it go at that. But he himself felt his responsibility as a reader and since the poems were undoubtedly of literary quality...

He looked at her questioningly, but when she gave no sign that she wanted to say anything, he continued to explain that at this publishing house there was so much to take into consideration. He elaborated on those many and various considerations for a while and then recommended that she go to another publisher, the name of which he gave her. There she should refer her manuscript to a certain reader. At that point he politely showed her to the door. He was on all accounts impeccably polite. But she felt embarrassed nonetheless. Even though his eyes were moving in all directions, she felt as if he was staring at her the whole time. She wasn't used to being looked upon as anything noteworthy. At home in her own town no one ever noticed her. She made an effort to dress as inconspicuously as possible. Her dark grey winter coat had, for a time, been a bit too long, but now they were wearing skirts in the middle of the calf again. Her hat was an ordinary grey felt hat; her gloves didn't have any holes, her low-heeled shoes were polished.

She took the big, yellow envelope home and wondered if this wasn't good enough. But He said to her that she had to send it in again to the other publisher, addressed to the person whose name she had received.

Two weeks later she received a letter from this name. He wrote that he had read her poems with great interest—the word made her wince—and he would like to meet with her on thus and such day, at thus and such time. "Please inform the publisher if this is not convenient."

She thought that this was something she should and must go

through with. If she could only survive this new meeting, she would be able to return to her old, happy life. Once she had passed this test. For it couldn't be His intention that the envelope should be sent to yet a third publishing house. So she asked to have the day off and arrived on a bright and sunny winter-spring day at the second publishing house, which was larger and fancier than the first. It relieved her that none of the attractive, well dressed women in the outer office seemed to take any special notice of her. She was shown to a little room which seemed crowded because there were books all over the place. On the walls hung pictures in clear, strong colors. Behind the desk a young, dark-haired man stood up, and she once again began to wonder if there were something wrong with her clothes after all.

He introduced himself, and she said her name.

"So you really are Ellen Andersen," he said as he peered at her with narrow, dark eyes. "You are the one who has written this?"

And he held the yellow envelope up in front of her.

She nodded and felt the color spread from her face down to her neck.

"Don't misunderstand me," he said quickly. "These are good poems, some of them exceptionally good. It was therefore difficult for me to believe that an amateur—this is your first effort, isn't it? You haven't previously published anything?"

She shook her head terrified.

"Have a seat, won't you please sit down," he asked and immediately became just as polite as the man at the last publishing house, offered her a cup of coffee, a cigarette, to take her coat.

"No, thank you," she mumbled and just wished that he would come to the point, so that it would go quickly and she could get her envelope and go home. But gradually his friendliness was able to loosen something in her. After the first look of astonishment, he spoke to her as to an old friend.

She realized that he was used to dealing with very different types of people, many of whom were in difficult situations, were poor, nervous, agitated. They weren't like normal people; poets especially were different. What she didn't understand was how this concerned her.

"Poets," he said, "like yourself."

"Because I write poetry, do you mean? But I," she looked straight at him, "am not like that. I am completely ordinary."

"You, ordinary! Your poems," he said with a sudden, warm smile, "are in any event not ordinary."

She answered stiffly that they were religious poems.

He looked at her for a long time as if they shared a secret. But when she gave no indication that she knew this secret, he dropped his eyes and drew lines on the table top with his forefinger.

"They're love poems, aren't they?"

She nodded.

"The poem's speaker is a woman. . ."

"The bride," she said softly.

"Yes, exactly. Everything is depicted from her point of view, her experience of. . . ah, what you're depicting is of course the act of love."

She stared down at her lap, didn't answer.

"It is beautiful," and now he spoke rapidly, stumbling over his words. "I can't remember having read anything recently that has moved me so profoundly. Precisely because it is a woman who experiences this. I read them out loud to my wife—I often ask her advice. And she was—very moved. It was then I began to understand—how a woman feels."

He suddenly became silent. To her amazement she saw that his cheeks had turned red. His face was beautiful with an even golden brown hue. She couldn't help but think of snow-covered mountain plains in the sun. His eyelashes rested on his cheeks, thick and dark, like a woman's.

"I'm afraid that these poems," he said after a bit, "that they might seem—offensive to many people, not because they're so, ah—open and sincere, but because it is so clearly indicated that Christ is the bridegroom."

"But," she said, "that's what it says in the Bible. We sing that in the hymns."

"Yes, but that is understood as purely symbolic. This is so direct, so concrete. It could easily be interpreted as blasphemous."

"Is the Song of Solomon blasphemous?"

"Well, no. But the effect is completely different when it is the male body, ah, and on top of that the masculine genitalia which is described so—ah—explicitly."

"Christ is a man."

"And when you use words like. . . these candid, naked words. . ."

"Is it because"—she felt that she turned deep red—"Is it because I am somewhat advanced in years that it is not fitting for me to use such words? I have read in the newspaper that the young poets do."

"And suffer the consequences."

"Yes," she remembered, "the young man who was stoned for the sake of his words. But wasn't that chiefly because there were so few words on each page?"

"Don't misunderstand me," he said quickly. "Your poems are of considerable literary quality. Don't doubt that for a minute. And they seem so—there is such joy in them! I'm just afraid that—you do want us to publish the collection, don't you?"

She nodded. Even though this truly was not her will. She felt like she was sinking. . .

"I don't suppose you would consider striking out the name of Christ?"

She stared at him horrified: "Strike His name?"

"That would solve the problem." He spoke eagerly like a young boy. "There's no need for the text to reveal who the bridegroom is. And that way the poems will also become more universal. We could give them a nice format and see to it that the book is promoted in such a way that there's no room for speculation."

She wasn't listening. She struggled to find words which could explain but she wasn't used to talking with people about anything other than the most common, everyday trivia.

Haltingly she related that she had depicted everything exactly as she had experienced it without adding or deleting a thing. It had been her feeling that it should be kept secret, but He had enjoined her, quite against her will, to step forth with her praises.

"You perhaps do not believe that one like me can be the bride of Christ," she concluded. "You see only my grey hair, my nondescript appearance, my ordinariness. But he chose me for the very reason that I am one of the small, the simple and weak, precisely because I am this way. I am a sacred commonplace."

She looked at him earnestly, for she seemed to perceive that he was a good person and it became a matter of greatest urgency that she make him understand.

"May I be permitted to ask you," he said seriously after a long silence. "Of course, you must by no means feel obligated to answer. Have you ever been. . . in love with. . . anyone besides. . . the one you now love?"

"No," she answered gravely, without the least bit of hesitation, "I have never known any other man. I have always kept close to Him alone."

The book came out the following autumn, a nondescript grey paperbound book with a plain, printed cover. It had received the simple title "Poems" and underneath in small letters was her own name.

It aroused a storm. It was as if a tidal wave, which rose higher and higher, surged through her, uprooting everything, the entire foundation of her safe and secure existence.

The young man at the publishing house sent her a letter. He wrote that most of the serious reviewers had given her collection of poems extremely favorable mention. Enclosed were xerox copies of reviews, where the most laudatory remarks were underlined in red. She read them dutifully, but didn't understand a thing other than the fact that these critics were of the opinion that her poems had literary quality. Literary quality was all they thought about. That wasn't much compared to everything else in the papers: articles by ministers, teachers, housewives, letters to the editor signed "believer" or "concerned father." She herself read only one newspaper and seldom anything but the headlines. Now she began to read everything that was printed about her poems and about herself. She couldn't keep herself from doing it, even though she became increasingly horrified and unhappy, especially when she thought that everything in the newspapers she didn't read was perhaps just as bad.

Everywhere she appeared, in the store where she usually shopped, in the stairway of the building where she lived, in church on Sunday —everywhere she was talked about. People put their heads together and whispered. It was as if they reached out and took hold of her with their long, sticky glances. In front of her window at the post office they stood in line. On the street where she until now had gone unnoticed, faces turned, fingers pointed. People wrote to her, anonymous letters which threatened and frightened her or suggested the most disgraceful things. The little collection of poems was sold out and had to be reprinted. At the same time a young theologian announced that he intended to report both the author and the publisher for violation of the paragraph on blasphemy.

She withstood the storm as long as she could say to herself that this was His will. She had placed her entire life in His hands and He had held it tenderly and cautiously as one holds a baby bird, just as His hand had held her breast that Sunday in church so many years ago. Now the storm had come and torn down everything around her. And, naked and trembling, like a solitary tree battered by the wind, she told herself that He would save her, if she only withstood.

But one evening the young assistant pastor in the congregation came to her home. She had turned away all the journalists, both those from the newspapers and those from the magazines, had refused to speak on radio and television. The minister, though, she did not think she could turn away. He spoke softly and in a songlike manner; it lulled her into a kind of confidence. Which resulted in her telling him everything, just as she had told it to the young dark-eyed man at the publishing house. When she was finished with her explanation, she felt a wonderful sense of relief. It was the first time she had exchanged more than two words with anyone since the storm had broken loose.

He nodded to himself as if he found her explanation reasonable, then he asked evenly and directly:

"Are you sure that it was Christ?"

And before she was able to answer:

"You don't think it was the Devil?"

The Devil? She almost had to smile. What did the Devil have to do with her? She who ever since her earliest childhood had rested so safely in the bosom of Christ. She had never felt tempted by the Devil and all his works and all his ways. It was rather the rich and powerful who were caught in his net, all those who served Mammon, or those beautiful, overbearing girls who called attention to themselves and tried to be something special.

"I," said the young pastor and looked at her seriously, "think it was the Devil. No, wait a minute, let me explain to you. . ."

He spoke for a long time—he was very eloquent—and with this friendly, singsong voice. At first she thought that what he said sounded absolutely impossible. She even interrupted him—several times. But he patiently explained to her again and again that this was exactly the way the Devil usually acted when he wanted to catch a young woman. He kindled a sinful desire in her and since she had been a pious girl who would not allow herself to be tempted or enticed, he had taken on the appearance of the Savior himself.

After he had admonished her in this way for a while, she put her hands over her ears and rocked back and forth, didn't want to listen to the soft, singsong voice. But he took hold of her hands and held them firmly, away from her head.

"Remember," he said almost sternly, "it is never too late to turn back, to turn to Christ with prayers for forgiveness.'

"How do I know," she said with stiff lips, "that it isn't you who are the Devil."

"You know that," he answered calmly, "because I do not entice you to sin. I show you the truth and it is of God alone."

The next time—a week later—when he came and rang her door bell, it wasn't opened. He knew she was in there, because he heard a padding sound as if an animal paced about in a ring behind the door. He consulted with the other tenants in the building and found out that no one had seen her since his last visit. Then he got the custodian and together they broke down the door.

She lay on the sofa in the living room and turned a white, emaciated face towards them. When she saw the pastor, she stretched out her hand, pointed at him and cried:

"There is the one who is the Devil!"

"You can't imagine how embarrassing it was," he later told his wife.

Several of the building's inhabitants had flocked to the landing outside the broken door and they stood and peeked in, spectators looking through the bars of a cage. A doctor was sent for. When he had examined her, he called for an ambulance.

At the hospital she was very comfortable. When they asked if she wanted to go anywhere for a shorter or longer visit, she answered that she was just fine where she was and that she was happy with her work which, for the most part, consisted of basket-weaving. The money she received was carefully divided and put into different envelopes which they procured for her. There were only a few crowns for each one, for she always had to keep something in reserve for crises such as earthquakes, flood disasters and other natural catastrophes.

Sometimes she wrote poems. Some of them were about the Devil and were black with fear. But most of her poems depicted sparrows, snowflakes and ants on the path. The name of Christ did not appear and there was no joy in them.

Original title: *Santa Simplicitas.* Translated by Katherine Hanson

Margaret Johansen

(b. 1923)

Margaret Johansen is a social critic, but her attack on the discrimination, prejudice and tyranny that invade everyday life is delivered with humor and satire. A collection of short stories in 1971, *Om kvinner,* marked her debut in fiction (she has a career in advertising). With wit and precision she sketches women and men, in a variety of situations, who are trapped by outdated attitudes and role patterns. The assumption that women will take on the role of nurse should the need arise is of particular concern to Johansen, and in the novel *Damenes vals* (1978) she focuses on the burden of responsibility that is put upon women to care for sick and aging family members, a sacrifice that often claims their own health. "The Office Party" is taken from ... *men mannen ler* (1973).

The Office Party

The company's annual dinner-dance was launched as usual one week before Christmas, and as usual the Director whispered to the organizing committee that he must be excused from sitting next to Miss Mikkelsen at the dinner table, even though she was the woman with the most seniority in the company. He was sure they would find something appropriately, hmm . . . young and pretty. God knows, he too was entitled to a little fun, wasn't he?

Miss Mikkelsen had graduated from the same school as the Director, two years after him. But he was a man in the best years of his life. Well-preserved, as men generally are. And the sweet young things in the secretarial pool never minded paying attention to him at the Christmas party. It was, "Oh, Jacob," all evening long ... But the next day he was "Mr." again, of course. Anything else would be out of the question.

No indeed. These Christmas parties were not pure pleasure. As usual, Smith, the bookkeeper, would probably get a little sloshed and offer him some words of truth, only to sit worrying about it the next day as he bent over his adding machine. Oh well. One could put up with that, because Smith was a good, accurate worker. It was a little harder in the case of their top salesman, Harm. He was something of a lady's man, that fellow. If the Director were to give his honest opinion, he'd say Harm was a conceited dandy. But a good salesman, God knows.

At the Christmas party the previous year Harm had torn little Miss Sparr's dress, and had spilled a cocktail down Miss Mikkelsen's decolletage. But that sort of thing can happen to the best of us, after all. A man must be allowed to let go once in a while. Relax in the midst of responsibilities and stress. To tell the truth, the Director did not remember a great deal about that Christmas party himself.

He chuckled a little at himself and his delightfully poor memory afterwards. It had certainly been quite a bash, that post-party gathering they had at his home.

It musn't be so late this year.

Or rather, "so early" ... hrrmm.

The Director stood greeting people at the doorway of the hotel's red banquet room, which they usually rented for their festivities.

An excellent fellow, the Director. A little stout perhaps, but no more than was suitable at his age. He drew in his stomach when Miss Mikkelsen arrived. Quite an attractive woman as a matter of fact, but much too old for him. Women aged so much faster than men. Whatever the reason for that could be.

"Hello, hello, Miss Mikkelsen. Welcome."

He clasped her hand in both of his, and had thereby done his duty by her for the evening, so to speak.

Miss Mikkelsen helped herself to a cocktail from a tray, and stood sipping it while she studied the actors at this annual company performance. She worked there for eighteen years now. A good job, but not one she wanted to continue in the future. She had tried, in vain, to explain to Jacob—who was a friend from school after all, even though he was older—that she deserved a promotion. She had both the education and the practical experience necessary. But Jacob had held her off in his charming way, feeding her with false promises.

Now, in fact this very day, she had signed the final papers for ownership of her own company. And it was a fantastic feeling, something that should be celebrated. And Miss Mikkelsen knew how.

She drained her glass and walked over toward the young office manager named Boye, who had received a quick promotion due to his qualification as a male. She sucked in her cheeks, and looked up at him obliquely from under mascaraed eyelashes.

"Skål," said Boye, raising his glass a little nervously and wondering what had happened to Miss Mikkelsen. Very lovely woman actually. How old could she be? Well-preserved, that woman.

"So?" said Miss Mikkelsen. "Did you see something you liked, Mr. Boye?"

"Hmm ... yes. You're looking very lovely tonight, Miss Mikkelsen."

"Thank you," said Miss Mikkelsen, and went and got another cocktail.

From where he was greeting people at the door, the Director had witnessed the little intermezzo. Goodness, what was wrong with Mona today? Gliding around with swaying hips and flirting with Boye, who must be at least ten years younger than she.

He politely nodded a welcome to the pretty eighteen-year-old switchboard operator, Miss Evensen, and kissed her hand, while anxiously keeping an eye on Mona Mikkelsen. Surely, she hadn't already had something to drink before she arrived? That wasn't like her, but one could never tell what a woman might do at *that* age ...

During the dinner, the Director gave, as usual, an excellent speech in which he explained "the state of the empire," as he so humorously called it. This explanation generally resulted in the meat course growing cold, but the company had a party only once a year, and this way at least dessert wasn't ruined. He liked to close with a toast to Woman: "Our inspiration, our conscience, our beauty, our children's mother." Deeply moved, he sat down and placed a fatherly kiss on little Miss Evensen's convenient hand. The hand which slid over her thigh didn't seem quite so fatherly and reassuring, but she had only been working there two months, so she let it pass. The last time she'd had to resign from her job after six months. It was bad for one's reputation to change jobs so often. One had to choose. Fat old pig, she thought, smiling coquettishly at him over her wine glass.

Look at that, thought the Director dizzily. This little one here and Old Adam at a late-night party . . .

But good Lord, Mona Mikkelsen was rising to her feet.

Lissome as a goddess, she held one hand on her hip and raised her glass with the other.

"A toast!" she cried. "A toast to Man, our protector, our source of inspiration, our children's father, our dubious lover and tyrannical employer."

Her smile was radiant, and managed in a strange way to take the sting from her words. Mona Mikkelsen sat down and gently kissed the hand of the man sitting next to her—whoever that was.

Had the woman gone mad?

The recipient of the kiss looked at her in considerable amazement.

"Equal rights," nodded Miss Mikkelsen. "Skål!"

I just hope that woman isn't going to ruin the whole evening for me, thought the Director. I'd better get my dance with her out of the way, and give her a little warning advice!

"Why Jacob," said Mona Mikkelsen. "Do you want your obligatory dance with me already?"

And she stretched out her arms and pressed herself gently against him as they moved out onto the dance floor; the Director stiff and unpleasantly affected. Now she was beginning to make a spectacle of herself. Good heavens.

"Surely you don't mind that I let myself go a bit tonight, dear Jacobsen?" she said. (He hated that name from his school days.) "Because, you see, this is the last of the company's Christmas parties that I'll be attending."

"Last. . .? What do you mean. . .?"

"I'm going to quit," she said sweetly. "At long last, I'm going to quit."

"You're not serious," said the Director, calculating coldly and soberly what a loss that would be for the company. And for the first time, all her fine qualifications and abilities struck him with alarming force.

"Hmmm. . . Miss. . . I mean, Mona. . . You don't mean what you're saying. How about if you and I have dinner one of these days, and we'll talk things over?"

"Dinner? You must be out of your mind. What do you think the others would say? Treat an older woman like me to dinner? What were you thinking of offering me if I would stay?"

"Hmmm. Well, we could talk about that."

"We can talk about that now. Maybe I could become an administrative assistant?"

"Assist . . . ? Are you completely mad?"

"I'm not capable enough?"

"Hmmm. . . we-ell, yes. . . but. . ."

"Don't I have enough education? Enough knowledge of the business? Enough strength?"

"Yes, but listen here now, Mona. You must know that becoming an administrative assistant is out of the question. After all, you're over forty already, and besides you are. . ."

"I am. . .?"

"Well, you're a woman, after all. Maybe going through menopause —a difficult stage, menopause is. And. . ."

"What about *you*, Jacobsen? Are you going to start drawing your pension soon?"

"Am I. . .?"

"After all, you're older than I am, aren't you?"

"That's beside the point, Mona, as you well know. A man like me is in the best years of his life. At the height of his career."

"A prime candidate for heart attacks and excessive stress, I read in the newspaper recently. It strikes men in particular. Perhaps we ought to step in soon—we who aren't so susceptible? How do you suppose Indira Gandhi ever manages, Jacobsen? Or Golda Meir? But, of course, you're right. The important things you and I are dealing with are of a very different nature. Wholesale paper. . ."

"If you'll excuse me, Mona dear, I really must dance with Miss Evensen now. It's only polite, you know, since I was sitting next to her at the dinner table. Let's talk together tomorrow. Don't make such a hasty decision, please."

She smiled after him, then turned toward Harm, the top salesman, with an inviting gesture. Cocked her head, and said:

"Shall we dance?"

"Delighted," said Harm stiffly. What kind of a person was she? God knows, a woman wasn't supposed to ask for a dance. . .?

"A woman isn't supposed to ask for a dance, Harm—or wasn't that what you were thinking? I just thought, since you're always talking so much about equal rights and that sort of thing. . . and you being so young?"

"My dear lady, it would simply be a pleasure. That way, I don't have to wait for my turn."

"That was nicely put, Harm, after the way you've been waiting for me all these years. Well, here I am!"

Mona Mikkelsen helped herself liberally to drinks during the evening, and had a marvelous time. Not everyone did.

As, for example, when the Director made his little joke that always went over so well, saying he was seriously thinking of trading in his forty-year-old wife for two twenty-year-olds. Mona Mikkelsen responded immediately by wondering how he expected to manage that? "According to statistics, a man of your age barely manages to satisfy *one* woman of the same age," she said amiably.

"What would happen, then, with two twenty-year-olds? Think of your heart, now, Jacobsen, think of your heart!"

The situation was most unpleasant. But the thought of cutting her off with a reproof didn't appeal to him either. He'd had quite a lot to drink. His tongue wasn't functioning quite properly, and Miss switchboard operator Evensen was sitting on his lap. He felt he'd been made to look a little ridiculous. For the first time in his life, he felt old and stupid. And it was Mona's fault. Damn woman.

Before the party was over she had smashed a couple of glasses, spilled a couple of drinks down Boye's collar, set young Harm on her lap and made herself utterly impossible.

When it was getting close to midnight, he took her aside and said as sternly as was possible in his condition:

"Don't you think you've gone far enough, Mona? Isn't it time we get you a taxi? You must indeed have reached that difficult age."

"Taxi? Me?" said Mona. "No thank you. I'm invited to a late party now with Boye. You see, I'm not as drunk as you think. I just wanted to see what it's like to be a man. Because I've become an administrator myself as of today. I'm starting my own business, dear Jacob, and so I guess it's time I act accordingly. Don't you agree?"

The Director turned on his heel a bit too quickly and got his bearings on the bar stool next to little Miss Evensen. He didn't think Mona deserved an answer.

Goddamn woman!

The following day was not as marvelous for the inexperienced Miss Mikkelsen. She surveyed herself in the mirror.

Well, well, Mona! she said to herself. You pay a price to be a man!

Original title: *Firmafest.* Translated by Nadia Christensen

Vigdis Stokkelien

(b. 1934)
Vigdis Stokkelien grew up on Norway's southern coast where shipping is a
major industry, and at an early age she went to sea as a radio operator with
the merchant marine. In her first short stories and novels she drew from her
experience at sea. The political consciousness that would come to be
characteristic of her entire production manifested itself here as a protest
against the use of Norwegian ships to transport materials to South Vietnam
during the war. She has written on a variety of issues ranging from pollution
and the environment to manipulation by the mass media, but her strongest
commitment has been to pacifism. "A Vietnamese Doll" is taken from the
short story collection *I speilet* (1973).

A Vietnamese Doll

Every morning, until she heard Esther squeaking like a rat in the
bedroom, Gøril hoped that it was just a bad dream. The child hadn't
arrived yet — in a while she'd go to town, choose some pretty dresses,
small shoes, cuddly teddy bears, soft dolls, building bricks, eat lunch
with Leif and plan everything for the new child: a musical
kindergarten, trips to the zoo .....

Esther lay on her back in the yellow crib. She stared at the ceiling;
her eyes were expressionless.

The cheerful curtains with Donald Duck figures stirred in the light
sea breeze. Gøril could hear the waves smack the shore. It smelled of
warm earth and cherry trees.

Everything she'd bought during the long waiting period stood
untouched on the long, low shelf: a white doll and a Black doll, a red-
painted dollhouse with tiny furniture, a candy-striped ball, alphabet
blocks, a flute, a drum, a bucket and spade.

Each thing was chosen with care. She'd even tried to find a
Vietnamese doll, but there weren't any. So she'd bought a Black doll
with curly hair, thinking it was more "homey" than a white one. But
Esther's skin wasn't dark, it was very light. The dresses in the closet

were also unused; the four-year-old could only wear baby clothes.

Lifting the child out of bed, Gøril took in her strange smell, an acridness that reminded her of bark, and for a moment she felt complete aversion. Esther's hair was thin on the crown; little drops of sweat sprang out on her forehead. The narrow brown eyes stared past her, but the child stopped squeaking.

At the airport, when she and Leif stood there together with eight other adoptive parents, she knew immediately that something was wrong. The local paper took pictures: Leif lifting the child up, Gøril giving her the Black doll, the child stiff as an Oriental ivory figure.

In the evening the family came to see "the new child." Esther sat where they'd placed her, on the blue sofa, and stared straight ahead; the pile of gifts in cheerful wrappings was left untouched.

"Take her right to the hospital before you get attached to her," said her mother-in-law. "It's sad, but I've had years of experience with children, and this child isn't normal."

"Get attached to." Gøril felt only confusion when she picked up the child; feelings came over her almost too strongly—disgust, fear, compassion.

One of her friends had put it brutally: "You should have a right to a refund on a kid like that. When you're nice enough to take one, they shouldn't send an idiot."

But she was certain that the child wasn't an idiot. Inside she had the strange feeling that Esther was somehow sleeping; if she could only reach her, she would wake up.

"Maybe we should look for a child psychiatrist," Leif had said last night. He tried to talk to Esther, pointed at himself, said, "Papa," pointed at the doll and said, "Baby."

When he straightened up, she saw that his face was damp with perspiration, that he tried to hide his aversion.

She poured water in the bassinet, set the child in it. Unclad, Esther was a pitiful thing, with a swollen stomach and small baby limbs. She had bad balance, too; her head wobbled, her body moved in little jerks. It was like a weird dance.

Gøril was afraid to soap the small limbs, felt a disgust that crept through her whole body; her fingers twitched away when they came in contact with the tense skin.

One morning when Esther lay there unmoving in a blue towel and she was drying her, a feeling of hopelessness rose in Gøril.

She called the nurse who'd brought the children to this country, expecting to get good advice, sympathy—or maybe she'd really been wishing that the nurse would come and fetch the child, that the days with Esther would lose themselves in memory like a bad dream.

The nurse had said angrily, "I thought you were mature people. Did you believe you'd get a doll baby when you got a child from a country that's been in a war so long?" She'd called forth terrors Gøril could hardly grasp, talked about napalm and death.

It was too awful to listen to.

"She doesn't even understand the language," the nurse had said. "Don't go dragging her around to specialists, give her time, have enough love ..."

Gøril put the little boat she'd bought a few days ago down in the bathwater, pushed it back and forth while she cried, "Tututututut."

For a moment it was as if Esther followed the boat with her eyes — didn't she see the signs of a glimmer of joy in the slanted Asian eyes? No, she stared straight ahead, without expression.

Gøril dressed her, carried her out to the kitchen, brought out vitamins and cornflakes, boiled an egg.

Esther ate a couple of mouthfuls.

"Shall we go to the beach and swim, Esther? Swim?"

Did happiness glint in the dark eyes? Did Esther understand? How should she understand? The child hadn't uttered a sound in the three weeks that she'd been with them, not even in her own language.

To go to the beach took all Gøril's willpower. They were stared at on the road, chattered about in the gardens: "That's the Vietnamese child they took in when they couldn't have one themselves — she's the one who can't have children — and then they got an idiot. Imagine."

Esther could walk, if she wanted; she took a few steps, then sank down on her bottom. Her head wobbled back and forth, her body stiffened when Gøril pulled on her leg.

She'd bought a stroller for the four-year-old, and now Esther was sitting in it, stiff as a stick, staring straight ahead.

On the way to the beach Gøril prattled along automatically — "See the tree — the car's driving fast — see the kitty — the dog — the flower."

Everyone they met stared at them, stared curiously at the foreign child. Gøril was ready to cry.

She'd dreamed in the months before the adoption came through how it would be, how they would run to the beach, play in the garden.

Had thought of how the child would rejoice with happiness to come to a home like this — live in a big house with a garden, have good food, real toys, her own room.

They'd called her Esther after Leif's grandmother. Now it went coldly through Gøril—she couldn't even keep her real name—everything had to be alarmingly foreign.

Down at the beach she lifted Esther high in the air. A gull came towards them on wide wings; the child's fragile body shook.

"Bird—bird," said Gøril and pointed, but Esther didn't follow it with her eyes.

She set the child on a blanket, brought out the colorful buckets and shovels, built a castle, decorated it with shells and seaweed, made ramparts around it.

Far away down the beach some children laughed; they were playing with a polka-dot beach ball.

Suddenly Gøril wept.

"Mama's going swimming."

A sort of longing arose in her to swim far far out, to swim and swim until the water soothed this feeling of helplessness.

The water washed coolingly up towards her thighs. Esther sat there on the blanket and Gøril imagined that Esther was following her with her eyes, wanting to wave.

Gøril lay in the sea, floating. The sun was hot just over the sea and the shore. In the west, dark clouds floated in over the skerries.

On the beach Esther sat like a statue, only her hair lifting in the slight breeze.

Water sprinkled the child as Gøril went ashore, knelt on the sand, filled the colorful buckets, turned them over, saying, "Sandcakes, sandcakes."

It was like talking to a stone.

Then a little finger came as if by accident near the sandcakes; Gøril took the thin hand in hers, led it over the bucket, the sandcakes.

A trembling went through the hand.

Esther slept and Gøril rigged up a kind of sunscreen, lay down and peered up at the drifting clouds. As a child she'd made up fairytales about such clouds, had seen how they took wonderful forms; elves, trolls, fairies from the stories. Now and then a complete pirate ship floated across the sky with filled sails and Captain Kidd at the helm.

She herself must have slept as well, for when she looked up the sky was dark. Esther squeaked.

"Home, shall we go home?"

Gøril felt a numb tiredness, barely managed to push the stroller over the beach.

It would be that way at home, too. She would pace back and forth, looking at Esther while her dejection grew. Dust settled on bookshelves, the dishes piled up in the sink; she threw together pre-cooked food for dinner, no longer had morning coffee with her friends.

Lightning flashed across the sky.

Esther stirred, and suddenly Gøril's nerves crept to the fingertips of her shaking hands.

Esther got up, holding fast to the stroller frame, and stood there looking at her.

It was eerie, like a dead person waking. Gøril let go of her grip, took a step backwards.

Esther just looked at her, and Gøril thought there was hate in her eyes.

Then the thunder sounded over the beach; the lightning zigzagged towards the waves.

Esther threw herself forward and Gøril caught her in the air, falling to the sand with the child. Esther had gone crazy, was trying to bury herself.

The lightning was so near that Gøril saw it strike; the sand scorched.

And suddenly she clasped the child, covered her completely with her own body, whispered consoling words in her ear, heard herself sob.

Ashamed, Gøril brushed them off, hoped no one had seen it all.

Esther was still sobbing.

And suddenly she understood that Esther believed it was a bombing attack, that she must have dug like that in the earth before, trying to hide herself.

Gøril felt a burning tenderness, held the child close to her, kissed her hair, her cheeks, her nose, whispered meaningless words, "My Esther, no bombs here—they're gulls, not planes—it's thunder and lightning."

For a moment Esther was a tense, shrieking bundle, then she looked right at Gøril.

A little hand stroked Gøril's chin cautiously; tiny fingers caressed her.

They sat there, both of them, and sobbed aloud.

Original title: *En vietnamesisk dukke.* Translated by Barbara Wilson

Bjørg Vik

(b. 1935)

With seven collections of short stories and a number of dramatic works to her credit, Bjørg Vik has won wide recognition for her penetrating portrayals of men, women and children searching for happiness and fulfillment in an impersonal society. Her subjects range from marriage and the dynamics of the nuclear family, to the interaction of schoolgirls and the companionship of elderly widows. Her characters are sometimes working class people, sometimes professionals or artists and she observes their frustrations and anger, their longings and dreams.

Vik's concerns are more specifically feminist in her fourth collection, *Kvinneakvariet* (1972). She reflects on the societal pressures and restrictions women contend with in stories depicting girls during childhood and adolescence (including "The Entryways"), working wives and mothers, and 'liberated' women. In *Fortellinger om frihet* (1975) and *En håndfull lengsel* (1979) Vik continues to explore, again from a woman's point of view, the problem of freedom and personal development within marriage. The women in these stories seem to mature as they realize that freedom is more than the loosening of external bonds. The confrontation in "The Breakup" (taken from *En håndfull lengsel*) does not end conclusively, but in fact deepens the characters' understanding of the complexities of their ties.

The Entryways

If her street is long and gray, Tora's is short and steep and dark gray. Tora has to cross through an entryway and walk up an old stairs, while Lillian has a stairway from the sidewalk and stone steps. Tora's stairs are creaking and dark, there are boots and milk bottles outside the doors; smells of fried herring, wardrobes and wet shoes fill the stairway like a gloomy grayish-brown color. Lillian feels as though she has been walking in these streets forever, as if she is imprisoned and can never leave. In class she hears about Tokyo and New York and London, but they don't exist — they are just sounds, stories. The world is these streets and the streets nearby just like them, it is stairways and cellar shops, store windows, streetcar tracks, churches, people on the sidewalk, the playground and the entryways.

At Lillian's there is a radio console and carpeting, but Tora has a dog, a huge German shepherd that sleeps under the table, that has a tin dish with breadcrusts and table scraps, that wags his tail and licks Tora's hands when she comes home from school—his name is Taggen. All the children are scared when Tora goes walking with her dog—it looks splendid. Tora lies on the floor and rolls around and scuffles with him, Taggen growls and has sharp yellow fangs and could bite her throat.

When they visit each other they must sit at the kitchen table or the coffee table and draw, read or cut out things. Many weeks they cut out movie stars and paste them in notebooks. The table overflows with paper and newspapers and magazines, their fingers are stiff with glue, Lillian presses the clippings flat against the notebook paper, she merges with the pictures, drawn toward the smooth pale skin, shining eyes, moist lips, drooping eyelids, streaming hair. They debate intensely who is prettiest. Tora is loyal to Elizabeth Taylor but Lillian holds out for Jennifer Jones and Veronica Lake. Tora might go along with Jennifer Jones, but Veronica Lake is not a bit pretty. Lillian understands why, because she herself looks a little like Veronica Lake. When she stands by the bathroom mirror and just one light bulb is on and she sucks in her cheeks and half closes her eyes, she looks like her.

If they are alone they get out lipsticks and powder and brush their hair and stand in front of the mirror, or they dig through their parents' drawers to find something exciting. Sometimes they take off their clothes and are naked. Most often they are at Tora's, her mother has a job at a store, Tora has a key. She runs errands and peels potatoes and takes Taggen out, afterward Lillian can visit her. Tora's brother delivers flowers on his bike. Their mother is always worn out when she comes home; when she takes a nap, they have to whisper.

Lillian's mother stays home, she straightens up and vacuums and bakes and makes clothes for Lillian or alters those that arrive from America. She wishes her clothes looked like Benedikte's. Mother makes dinner and watches the clock and looks out the window. When she starts to look out the window, something is wrong. If the sun is shining, the light seems to grow harsh and poisonous, it makes the kitchen threatening and too distinct. Father often comes late; when he has been drinking, Mother doesn't say a word while they eat. Lillian wants to rush out but she can't—she must be careful, so careful that nothing happens. Father lies down, she tiptoes around, pretending she has something to do, just to be there. Or she dries dishes with Mother, tries to tell something. Mother's face is pinched, she isn't listening.

Benedikte. Just the name: Benedikte Schøning. She's not like the others in the class, she talks differently. The teacher often lets her read aloud and is sweet to her. Benedikte's mother is a violinist, she has played concerts. There is something about Benedikte, something none of the others has—a kind of radiance.

The autumn is long and tedious. They peel potatoes and take Taggen for walks, the notebooks are full of movie stars. They go skating at the playground which has been sprayed, there are too many tiny children. A couple of times she and Tora have been with some boys in the bushes around the playground or in one of the courtyards when it got dark in the afternoon. They took off their clothes and looked at each other and stood close. They have done something bad, something no one must find out about; afterward they have never mentioned it. Lillian wishes the boys would move away from the street, often she pretends she doesn't see them or crosses the street when one of them shows up.

When they get money they go to the public baths. They jump in from the slippery tile edge and swim in the pool. Mostly they are in the shower room looking at the grown-up ladies. They have strange heavy breasts and hair under their arms and hair under their stomachs. Afterward they giggle in the changing booth and describe the big disgusting bodies with ugly words, choking with laughter. They look at their own smooth young bodies, they cannot imagine that their bodies will change and betray them in this way. They walk home with wet hair, excited and noisy, they begin to quarrel and aren't friends by the time they get home.

Since then they have stood in Tora's entryway with bigger boys, they shove, grab each other's caps and run through the entryway and into the courtyard or out on the street. Their faces are hot, their backs sweaty, and restlessness tears through their bodies; they run, laugh, stand out of breath in the entryway, won't let the boys touch them. Soon the boys stop coming. Mother asks why she is always with Tora, why she can't be with Ellen in the new building? Ellen, who is younger than she is, who goes to the Methodist church and doesn't have a dog or a key. Tora has gotten small lumps in her breasts that she wants Lillian to feel, when she touches them she says ouch.

Lillian sits by the kitchen table drawing, she is the best in her class at drawing. She wishes she had her own room with curtains and a desk with drawers she could lock. On Sunday mornings while Mother makes breakfast, she usually crawls in bed with Father, crawls close to his warmth, nuzzles him; Mother says she is too big for that.

She runs errands, walking along the long gray street which has trapped her with its brick buildings and sidewalks on both sides, small shops, stairs, entryways. Lillian thinks about how it is going to be: she will get married and live in a beautiful house and have many children. Perhaps she will become a painter. She watches the children playing on the sidewalk, dirty kids in thick clothes and mittens hanging by safety pins on their sweaters. Her children won't look like that. She will have four girls, they will dress alike and have long hair and play piano and violin. In magazines she has seen famous people and royal families — the governess of Elizabeth and Margaret Rose of England told about the princesses from the time they were tiny in a serial she has read in its entirety. They almost always dress alike, in white dresses and white stockings. Margaret Rose is prettier, for once she and Tora agree. She has seen pictures of beautiful rooms with huge furniture and lamps, she walks from room to room on soft carpets and puts roses in crystal vases, she lies in front of the fireplace on a bearskin, she has several small dogs, she receives her guests in a black or yellow dress, she has a string of pearls and rings on her fingers.

Mother has been to the customs house and picked up a package from America with clothes that are almost like new, chewing gum, compacts and magazines and nylon shirts. And colored pencils, wonderful thick pencils which cannot be bought here. The next day she is wearing a striped sweater and has the colored pencils and chewing gum in her knapsack. She divides the flat pieces in two—only Benedikte gets a whole one. Benedikte minces along ahead of her, flinging her long dark hair over her shoulder. The classroom smells like peppermint, they chew slowly, pushing the wad behind their molars when they have to answer. During the geography lesson Benedikte sends a note: Do you want to go home with me today? She writes yes on the back. She should go home and let her mother know, but then Benedikte would have to go out of her way. As they walk out of the school gate together she feels Tora's eyes on her back — Tora, who knows about the entryways and everything else, Tora, who has been naked with her. She feels a knot inside, a cold scared knot. They walk around the park and along the streetcar tracks and come to the street with the old wooden houses and gray or white brick villas. Benedikte lives in a gray brick house with a pointed roof and garden and fence and garden gate. They stand in a big hall with stairs to the second floor, there is carpet on the stairs and music coming from a room. Lillian takes off her boots, her heart is pounding, she looks at the umbrella stand, at the woman's head on a pedestal, the wide doors, the plants. Mrs. Schøning is standing in the living room, in a red sweater and black velvet slacks, playing the violin. She has long dark hair and a face like an Indian. She nods, the long soft tones continue, she looks at the music stand, moves the bow — it is beautiful. The velvet slacks, the violin, the dark hair. Lillian takes a deep breath, breathing it all in — the soft chairs, the book shelves, the paintings, the drapes, the light through the big windows with trees outside. Mrs. Schøning puts down her bow. Hello, dear, she says and asks her name. So your name is Lilli-Ann. She doesn't say Lillyun like everyone else does. Let's go up and draw, Benedikte says. They go up the stairs, past several doors. Benedikte's room has a slanting ceiling and pale wallpaper, she has movie stars on the walls and water colors in frames. Lillian asks what all the rooms are used for. One is my older brother's room, the other is my little brother's room, then there's Mama and Papa's bedroom and the bathroom, Benedikte says. My little brother is out with Marit. Marit? Our nursemaid — she does housework and such too. Lillian is trembling — a garden gate, her own room and desk, the mother with velvet slacks and violin, little brother and maid. But surely they don't have a dog?

Benedikte finds paper and sits down with the colors. Lillian looks out the window at the trees, the picket fence and hedges. The desk is cluttered, clothes and slippers are flung around the room. She asks if they can straighten up. You can straighten up, Benedikte says, I can't stand to. Lillian puts all the clothes on a chair, she straightens the desk and the drawers, maybe Mrs. Schøning will praise her. Pretty colors, Benedikte says. She draws ladies with long curls. Lillian thinks of what Benedikte would say if she came home with her, maybe she has never been in such small apartments. Lillian draws a skating rink full of children. How pretty, Benedikte says. Mrs. Schøning calls to them. Benedikte takes the drawings along. They have rolls and juice with ice cubes in the big kitchen. Mrs. Schøning drinks tea and looks at the drawings. You're really talented, Lilli-Ann, she says. What does your mother do? Do? Oh, nothing, she just stays home. And your father? He's a plumber. Really, is he a plumber, Mrs. Schøning says and laughs a little. Lillian's face feels hot, she spills juice on her sweater. Mrs. Schøning has smooth, fresh hands you want to touch. Do you have a refrigerator, Lillian asks, we ain't got one. You mean we *don't have* one, dear, Mrs. Schøning says. Benedikte takes her upstairs again. Benedikte is tired of drawing, she sits on the windowsill and looks sad. Several times Lillian talks to her without her hearing. She twists her dark hair over her shoulder, Lillian wishes she could touch it, feel how thick and soft it is, hug

Benedikte, tell her to smile. She cannot, she who has played in the entryway and done terrible things, she cannot touch Benedikte. So she acts funny, imitating the teacher and Tora and others in their class, the way they walk and talk—she's good at imitations. Benedikte laughs, she does imitations too, they bend over and laugh and press their knees together.

Walking along Benedikte's street, past trees and hedges and garden gates and mailboxes. It is still too bad that Mrs. Schøning laughed, that she said "ain't," but she can correct that, she can correct everything.

She is sitting in the kitchen with her lessons when she hears footsteps on the stairs. She hears that it is Tora and she hears Taggen's paws clicking against the stone steps. She sits quiet as a mouse, doesn't open the door, chews on her pencil. She feels a gnawing sensation in her stomach. She stands behind the kitchen curtain and peeks down at the street, at Tora coming out the entry with Taggen on a leash. The gnawing does not stop, she feels it all afternoon and evening. She can go over to Tora's, ask about homework. She doesn't do it, she has decided now.

Before school lets out that year, right before summer vacation — she and Benedikte have been best friends for a long time — they are wearing summer dresses and knee socks and suddenly she notices how fat Tora has become, her breasts have grown too. And Tora has gotten worse in several subjects, the teacher has said. She is just a fat, dumb girl who cannot do her any harm. Has she been afraid of Tora? Or really cared about her? Taggen has gotten fat too, the children on the street shout Taggen and Fattie when Tora takes her dog for a walk.

Once outside the dairy store she sees that Tora is about to cry when the children start shouting. Lillian stands on the steps, watching all the children with their scrapes and bruises and dirty sneakers, watching Tora's back. She pretends she does not hear the shouts and opens the door and goes in.

Original title: *Portrommene.* Translated by Carla Waal

The Breakup

He was completely calm when she told him.

Her words hovered somewhere above the desk and twisted in the air, they quivered and glittered like rare insects. He moved the cups of instant coffee, his face was smooth and vacant—nothing revealed that he felt like crying.

She had practiced several variations. One went all the way back to the day they met sixteen years ago, she had several speeches on how fond of him she still was, but it was all unnecessary. This morning, an ordinary morning in February, she had felt that she could stand it no longer, despite all the joy she had lived with for weeks, she could not bear the burden of dread and guilt any longer. There were already too many who knew or thought they knew, it was just a question of time before others would tell him. She phoned him at the second-hand bookshop—that was not unusual. She said she had to talk with him—that *was* a little unusual. She usually said that she would stop by, they often had a cup of instant coffee together in the little office behind the shop. She had left the library where she worked with an unsteady feeling, she wasn't completely sure of what she was doing. Nothing had come of the long explanations. He had seen it on her face, she sank down on the chair with her coat on. She looked at him and thought this must be the way sleepwalkers look at people they meet in corridors by night. Then the words dropped—very few, clear as glass, impossible to misunderstand.

He nodded, as though confirming thoughts he had already formed, finalizing familiar trains of thought. He sat with his back to the window, his body hid most of the surface of the window, she could see a little bit of the walls in the back courtyard, old snow lay on the cornices. The weak winter sun drew squares of light on the brick walls, the small cracks in the stucco were like veins.

"Won't you take off your coat?" he asked.

She stood, he stood too and helped her off with the dingy gray sheepskin coat, an old ritual, he must have helped her off and on with the coat hundreds of times. Now she sensed a stiffness in her movements, as though her skin was watchful, as though her muscles were cold and scared. She sat strange and tense. She had expected to feel great relief after it was said. She felt only emptiness. Thank God, she thought, now it's been said. She felt no joy at the thought. He sat and turned his cup. His hands were lifeless, he still looked calm, but his face had turned paler. Chills ran through her body, she shivered as though from a sudden frost. She felt tears fill her throat and chest, she cleared her throat hard several times, drank coffee, put both hands around the cup—still it trembled.

"I've realized," he said dully. "You had changed so."

"I can't help it," she said—she had already spoken those words. "That's just the way it is. I've become so terribly fond of him." Her voice sounded almost complaining.

He nodded again. He lifted his head and looked at her, his gaze like a great empty stretch of sea swept clean of all flashes of light from lanterns and lighthouses.

"Do you think it's worth it?" he asked.

She did not answer right away, she was still shivering. She did not want to get up for her coat now.

"Once in a while you must follow your feelings," she said. "It feels as if I have no choice."

She thought of Matias. That quiet strength which swelled within her each time she thought of him—for a few seconds it seemed weak, exhausted, a light bulb flickering several times before it decided to go on shining calmly.

"Then there isn't much more to talk about," he said quietly. She felt that he straightened up in his chair. "Other than practical matters," he added. His voice sounded firmer.

He asked how far ahead she had thought. She had not thought especially far, it was enough just to feel. The thinking stopped when it reached practical matters. The children, the house, daily life. Sixteen years of their life to be cleared away. Two families breaking up, two marriages coming to an end, four children . . . So that she and Matias . . .

They tried to talk about practical details. He stayed calm the whole time. He repeated a couple of times that they had to make the best of it, that they must be sensible. Did she want to move? She nodded uncertainly. He mentioned that it would perhaps be as well if he moved.

They had a big old-fashioned apartment into which they had put many years of work. They had fixed up room after room, modernized the kitchen and bath, put down new flooring, repaired the plaster of Paris decorations on the ceiling, searched for nice old-fashioned wallpaper, re-upholstered old furniture, collected apothecary jars and brass. She tried to picture Matias with her and the children in the old apartment. Matias at the kitchen table, Matias in the worn easy chair by the window, Matias in the double bed, Matias in the bathroom. Something shrunk within her, and she denied it. Conventions, she thought, habits, guilt-feelings. This is just a transition, then everything will be right and natural. Surely *things* could not trap them in that way. Or could they?

"Are you angry with me?" she asked. She thought it sounded pitiful.

He looked at her again. It was as though he gazed over the battlefield their life had suddenly become.

"Were we really so unhappy?" he asked.

"Something must have been wrong," she said quickly and with a messy feeling of avoiding something. Her voice was suddenly intense: "Something must have been wrong, since this could happen. Since I could be so captivated by another man."

He sat still. He seemed to be struggling with a thought.

"Things have changed around us," he said. "The children have grown up, we've gotten everything we need. Perhaps there isn't so much to struggle for any more."

She had no answer. Her gaze drifted out the window behind him, the spots of sunlight were duller on the stucco.

"We seem to have a new freedom," he said.

She nodded out the window.

"Or emptiness," he said. "Perhaps we haven't known how to fill the empty spaces."

The word hurt when it struck her. He had also felt the empty spaces. Perhaps after all he was happy about this, relieved? Free? She could not distinguish among the feelings slithering within her, she tried to cling to the one that resembled relief, that he was not going to take it so hard. A pain tore at her, she had not been enough for him, perhaps she had not tried earnestly to reach out. She was about to lose something different from what she expected. Somewhere there was something important and untried, things could have been otherwise.

She thought over what he had said about the new freedom. He had said it without sarcasm, she sensed a shadow behind the words. She knew that he looked with compassion and a kind of quiet sorrow at all the marriages breaking up around them. Was he reproaching her for trying to explore and use the new freedom? Perhaps not reproaching. Despising? He felt sorry for her because she had to do it. She felt he considered it a weakness, like a weak link in a chain, a crack in a foundation.

She felt she must defend herself.

"People can also stay together from cowardice," she said. "Or from laziness."

He looked at her with a desolate calm in his eyes. Now something was flashing deep within, the beam from a lighthouse, a distant storm warning.

"Was that why we lived together?"

She looked down, ran her hand over the smooth surface of the desk.

"No," she said. "That wasn't it."

They were standing on a tiny island, it was growing colder and colder around them, the tide rose. She did not believe that his calm would last, she did not believe in her own control. Soon everything would be different.

She had put on her coat, he had helped her as usual. They always used to caress when they parted, for a few seconds she felt herself drawn to touch him, to throw herself at him, to let out her despair. Or at least stroke his cheek. But that would release too much of what she was holding back. He made no effort to touch her. As he opened the door, he said slowly:

"Don't forget it's possible to turn back."

The winter morning waited outside, about as it had been when she was on her way to him. She had felt the day shining and vibrating, had felt life pulsating close to her, the weak winter sun shining on her joy and expectations and courage. Now the streets seemed a little more lifeless, the light was flatter, and she felt colder inside.

Matias!

She clung to being in love. The wave of warmth which would carry her through all this, the love which would justify everything. Was it strong enough? They would just have to live it, they would get the answer along the way.

It was several blocks back to the library. She took a detour to gain a little time, there were many thoughts and feelings to clear up. She thought of the apartment, that they both had been willing to move out. Perhaps they had been too occupied with things, perhaps they had both grown tired. Perhaps I am just as tired of the man as of the things, she thought bitterly. Again she tried to see Matias in the old high-ceilinged rooms and the children around them, her children, sometimes his too. She couldn't. All that she managed to see clearly was herself and Matias alone, and those images were radiant. They could meet openly, eat together, sleep together, listen to music, read books, meet people. Where were the children? Could she leave them? She couldn't visualize that.

There must be a solution. Other people had managed this before.

She felt tired and dizzy, something contracted inside her head. She must find a place to sit down. Here were only streets and sidewalks, offices and show windows and cars parked along the curbs. She stopped by a station wagon and leaned against the hood. She noticed dully that the car was dirty and thought that her sheepskin coat needed to be cleaned anyway. As she stood in the chilly February light and tried to rest against the car, she saw with stinging clarity that one day being in love would end and ordinary daily life awaited Matias and her. After the powerful feelings faded away, there would be quiet insight.

She stood shivering at the clear thought.

There is some happiness. You can be content with what you have. You can search for a little more and pay what it costs. There is some happiness. That is all.

The winter sun fell on the sidewalk, surrounding the bowed figure with a merciless stream of light.

Original title: *Oppbruddet.* Translated by Carla Waal

Karin Sveen

(b. 1949)

Karin Sveen had already won recognition for herself as a poet (with three collections of poetry in the mid-1970s), when a book of short-stories, *Døtre*, appeared in 1980. The stories in this volume are about daughters and about their mothers, sometimes about the daughter-mother relationship, as in "A Good Heart," always about women—working class women living in post-war Norway. Karin Sveen grew up in a working class family and is very conscious of class discrimination and its effects on the individual, not only social and economic, but also psychological. Her perceptive, often touching character portrayals in *Døtre* draw attention to the psychological implications of class barriers. In 1982 she published another prose work, *Utbryterdronninga,* a modern fairytale about a girl who challenges her oppressors and masters the art of breaking out of cages.

A Good Heart

Out from a black chimney on a little brown house with white window frames on the outskirts of a green pine forest and a flat quiet city float little clouds of cobalt blue smoke and silently they cling to the trees.

As if someone were smoking in there, puffing and smoking and blowing! Outside it's raining, a fine drizzle upon the city, the forest and the roof and in the grass which glistens with moisture. And up from the walls of the house rises the heavy smell of logs and pine tar. Stacked in the yard are a couple of cords of gleaming birch; the split wood is the color of cream, almost golden against the black stained wall of the wood shed, the grey sawhorse and the grey axe and the grey saw.

There is no fence around the house and no wood thief in sight, nor is there anyone who expects there to be, even though the times are more grey than golden and more and more are having trouble making ends meet while others do better and better and speak louder and louder.

Some get together with friends and talk quietly. They sit in their little houses and puff on their pipes, formulate thoughts and think them out loud.

Standing next to the fire wall, the wood stove sends its scant warmth out into the room and its blue smoke up through the chimney and out into the cold.

Sitting around the round table, Olaf and five or six other men are reading pamphlets out loud, passing books across the tablecloth and leafing through papers; smoke is pouring out of the kerosene lamp that's hanging by a chain between their heads and the voices rumble through the body of the fifteen-year-old Synnøve, who is sitting on the divan under the window, listening and watching. Out in the kitchen her mother is watching the coffee pot and sitting on the wood box in her brown Sunday skirt, chewing on granules of coffee. She has a little silver cross in the throat of her blouse and is religious in her own way and a good singer—everyone asks her and she expects that to happen any minute now.

And the men call to her and beg; she stands in the doorway between the living room and the kitchen, gives in to them and folds her arms behind her back. Sitting over in the pale light under the window, Synnøve listens to her mother's deliberate, billowing voice, like an emerging dawn, or steam that rises from the earth after chilly nights:

Wealthy folk are often feasting at home and with their friends
and rarely do they give a thought to the working men!
They should take the crofter's place, if only for a year,
so they might understand his lot, the life he has to bear!

When she has sung all the verses and her face is red and glowing, one of Olaf's friends, who has spent several years logging in the Soviet Union, walks over to her and kisses her on both cheeks and whispers "comrade" in her ear. The mother's eyes fill with tears, she looks down and over at her husband and at Synnøve and says:

"Terrible manners he's picked up in the woods!"

Because people might just as well appear stark naked as kiss each other while someone's watching!

But the men just holler and clap their fists, suck on their pipes and pack up their papers; and the mother puts on a clean tablecloth and brings out the coffee.

Olga Berg has faith in common folk and in a people's God and she sings at all kinds of meetings; everyone always wants her to sing and she enjoys it and likes to be asked. At the prayer house and the community hall and even at a strike meeting at the market place one time. That was when the seamstresses in the town were threatened with dismissal because they had organized. She had stood in the picket line and sung; why shouldn't she?

Olaf Berg says the same, and even though he's not exactly religious, he'll go so far as to say that there's more deviltry between heaven and earth than the Lord could have dreamt up—damned if it isn't other lords who have done it, he'll say. And Olga Berg is pleased that he says that. And is satisfied.

The two of them have agreed that every other child should be baptized and since Synnøve is the eldest and therefore baptized, she shall also be confirmed. Today is the Sunday before catechism; Berg and the men are going off to a meeting across town and Synnøve and her mother clear the table, open a window to air out the room and wash the dishes.

Synnøve dries. The cups scrape against the bottom of the zinc wash tub. The water is steaming and condensation forms on the little kitchen window.

It's quiet after the men. Synnøve likes to listen to them. One time one of them had asked what she was going to be when she grew up, and she burst out that she was going to be a communist and she would have twelve kids and all of them would be communists and loggers just like the man who'd been in the Soviet Union.

And the men had slapped their knees and laughed and asked: "And what if you have girls?" It was quiet for a minute, because at the time that hadn't occurred to her, but she found her tongue and said that that made no difference! Loggers they'd be, the whole pack of them! And while the laughter pounded against her and her face reached the boiling point, she decided that she would rather have strange ideas than be taken for being shortsighted.

Her mother draws her breath a couple times as if she intended to say something and then she says it: "I wish I were in better shape."

"How's that?"

"So I could earn a little more money and you could get a decent confirmation dress."

"It doesn't matter," Synnøve says. There's nothing more she can say and nothing more she does say.

"But I did get some nice bleached sugar sacks from the store which I'll try to use. If all else fails."

"I'm sure that'll be fine," Synnøve says and tries to imagine what she'll look like.

Outside it's raining and the loggers are at a meeting and inside the living room it's chilly and the kerosene lamp casts a yellow reflection against the low ceiling.

It's raining the following day as well, all day long, a wet, watery rain that splashes and washes everything it comes in contact with. In the late afternoon when the ground is squishingly soft and soggy and the grass can be peeled loose from the earth, along comes Mother's aunt, puffing down the road.

No one really knows if she is the sister or half-sister or foster sister of Olga Berg's mother or if they have simply grown up under the same roof. However it is, she's so old that no one can remember her as a child, and so spry that it's inconceivable she'll ever pass away. She has lived forever, and since Olga Berg's mother is dead, she regards herself as her successor and everyone's mother for all eternity.

She has a crimson silk dress, a brooch and white hair and she's so round and stout that she doesn't fit in the armchair but has to sit on the divan.

With fervent motherliness she calls the mother Bitsy and Synnøve Little Bitsy. She always looks like she's come straight from the prayer house; her heart mild—yes, truly!—and her eyes tender from sacred songs and the soul's sincere prayers for life and nourishment for friend and stranger alike and for itself.

She always has good ideas and now she's brought one of them with her. In her strong matronly hand and bulging out from underneath her snug, light-grey rain cape is a large handbag. She walks right into the living room beaming her hearty smile; mother helps her out of her wraps and boots and into a shawl and ragsocks. They hug each other and look so wonderful that Synnøve almost feels ill at ease because she doesn't have Jesus in her heart too! She's almost at the point of wishing that she had Him there!

Then Synnøve gets a hug as well and it's exactly like having a whole clothesline of warm rustling clothes fall on her head.

"To think you wanted to go out in this weather," mother says.

"Nothing can stop me when I have a mission," Auntie (everybody calls her that) replies mysteriously and lowers herself onto the divan with a contented grunt. Tiny raindrops glitter in her little curls and her eyes shine grey; she folds her hands across the ample crimson silk stomach and gazes at Synnøve with friendly, almost loving eyes and says, "Well, well," with a long, cheerful breath.

"My, but you're getting big, Little Bitsy!"

And when Mother comes in with coffee and a plate of cakes, and the convivial aroma seeps out from the spout, she again sighs her cheerful sigh and says:

"Oh, but you are a blessing, Bitsy; first you clean and cook and sew for others and then you do the same at home, and He (that's Olaf) is always at work or out running around. Yes, it is true what is written:

He who will eat must work in the name of the Lord."

Mother just smiles with her big lips and her big melancholy eyes. In the grey light of this rainy day she looks like a narrow shadow of the rotund aunt.

And now, leaning over the cake platter so that the silk ripples, Auntie grabs a *krumkake*, crumbles it in her round paws and puts the crumbs in her tiny mouth, just like a squirrel munching on a pine cone.

Synnøve chooses a piece of *julekake*, saturated with the fragrance of fresh yeast, and when the clatter of coffee cups has stopped and the raindrops have disappeared from Auntie's hair, her full voice floats through the room as if she spoke for the congregation and for God:

"To think that I, an old sinner, should live to see you, Little Bitsy, stand before Jesus and confess your childlike faith. He who has saved us from damnation and death. Stand forth like a white-clad angel among your loved ones. Oh, how happy I am! Can I be anything but thankful that I shall experience such a glorious day!"

Auntie takes a deep breath and continues with a fervor that makes Synnøve's ears burn. Her voice low and almost intimate, she says: "I have prayed to Jesus about this!"

Then she takes a new *krumkake*, crumbles it between her hands and blissfully eats like the squirrel munching the seeds in a cone.

It's steaming on the inside and pouring on the outside of the windows. Synnøve picks out the raisins from her piece of cake, looking at no one but knowing she is looked at. Her tongue presses against her mouth and she feels the words growing inside her until she becomes quite speechless.

"And then I hear Bitsy say that she doesn't know how in the world she'll ever get you a dress, and that's when I decided that you could have my wedding gown. She doesn't think she can take it, but I said 'yes, indeed,' Little Bitsy is going to have the finest dress I have and be every bit as good as the other girls in the church. A better looking confirmand no one has seen, you can be sure of that!"

Synnøve feels her heart beginning to move inside her. Auntie stops to take a breath and then she pulls from her bag a huge lace thing, as big as a pile of curtains, as big as an entire laundry, with the unmistakable smell of mothballs. With gathers and pleats and scallops, embroidery and lace, and a train, swishing like bird feathers

---

krumkake: a delicate, cone-shaped cookie
julekake: a sweet yeast bread, containing raisins and citron, flavored with cardamom.

and wind through the trees. Before she gets the whole thing out of the shopping bag, Synnøve bursts out: "I don't want it."

The bridal rustle stops momentarily.

Everyone stares at the dress. And Auntie says, her voice suddenly metallic: "Nonsense, of course you do! Get up now so we can try it on."

"Aren't you happy," Mother says. "You'll be so pretty. Of course it has to be altered, but I can do that and no one will be able to see it was Auntie's wedding dress."

Synnøve stands up and screams with a fury and an astounding desperation that don't come from her head or her thoughts and that she didn't know she had:

"I don't want it! It *is* Auntie's wedding dress! I don't want to wear it! I'd rather run away, I will run away if I have to wear it!"

Auntie stares at her as if she'd fallen off the roof, her mouth is open, her eyes the color of pewter. Suddenly mother begins to cry, a terrible, sad sobbing and Synnøve feels the rain and grey weather eating into her and she stomps on the floor and shouts, "No! I don't want it!"

Now Auntie takes control and gets angry. She hoists herself up from the divan, holding the bridal finery in her hands.

"You ungrateful child! Now you listen here: Bitsy can't afford to get you a new dress, can't you see she's crying! She can't *afford* to, I'm telling you, and you can't appear naked at your own confirmation. Use a little common sense, girl, this is going to be a big and joyous day for all of us—let's not have any nonsense."

"Not for Father!" Synnøve holds her arms in front of her face, waiting for a slap. But it doesn't come.

"No, not for Father, the heathen, but for us and for you and everyone else."

"Besides, I didn't ask for a new dress. Mother said she was going to make a dress from sugar sacks and that's good enough. Isn't that good enough!"

All of a sudden Auntie has started to pull the dress down over Synnøve's head and gasping she tries to fight herself loose. Mother sits straight up in the chair crying and Synnøve screams and Auntie scolds like one not yet saved. And Synnøve, Synnøve doesn't have one good reason to say no, but her whole self says no, her toes and her arms and her body, everything in her cries out. And it's pouring rain and you can't see out through the mist and steam and smoke. She jerks and tugs at the fancy dress and Auntie lets go, horrified, and says, almost snarls:

"Are you out of your mind, girl! You mustn't rip to pieces the most precious garment I own!"

Synnøve hears from her voice that that's enough. Twisting and turning she yanks the big white net off and scurries out before anyone manages to stop her. And she runs, runs down the road until she is sure no one can see her and find her and get her.

And she cries over her mother and she cries over herself and curses those wretched kroner that are forcing her to be confirmed in a wedding dress.

And she hates herself because she's alone with herself in that eternal rain, among the dripping trees, in the empty streets and the muddy gravel and the soggy earth. She can't go to anyone and tell them and she knows she has to go back, always and forever back.

Later on when she again stands outside the house and her face is streaked with the stinging rain and she's sure that Auntie must have gone and Mother is alone, then she feels compelled, by despondency and defiance, to silence, and she feels sorry for her own mother.

When she comes in neither of them say anything. The table has been cleared. The dress is gone. Mother doesn't look at her and she doesn't look at Mother. She changes into dry clothes. She goes over and stands in front of the window by the divan.

After a while she has to say something.

"Look at this weather, every day."

The air is oppressive.

Olga Berg is looking out through the other window and replies:

"If you'd like, I can try to make something with the sugar sacks."

"Yes," Synnøve speaks to the windowsill.

She should have done something or said something.

"I've been thinking you should get my sewing machine as a present," Mother says.

Synnøve wanted to hug her.

Original title: *Det gode hjertet.* Translated by Katherine Hanson

Kari Bøge

(b. 1950)

About her writing Kari Bøge has said: "I write because there is something in society and in our way of looking at things that I want to change. I want to point at things that have all too often been skipped over. Look at things from an angle one usually doesn't see them from." In three novels about Viviann (*Viviann, hvit*, 1974, *Lyset er så hvitt om sommeren*, 1975 and *Viviann og Lin*, 1980), Bøge writes about a woman's life, not in terms of the expectations and demands society makes on her, or in the way she is seen by men, but as she perceives herself, in terms of her own reality. During pregnancy, Viviann discovers the distance that exists between herself and her husband. She reflects over her situation, attempts to re-establish contact and warmth, and when this fails, pulls away and slowly constructs a reality in harmony with her needs and demands. "Viviann, White" is excerpted from the beginning of *Viviann, hvit*.

Viviann, White

3

I am 27 years old. My name is Viviann. I am married. My husband is named Marius. We've been married for 7 years. So much for that.

I am pregnant.

I woke up one morning and my mouth was full of cotton, and I was "filled with a strange whiteness." My entire body was soft. Not weak, not soft in the sense of supple (delightful), but perhaps something on the order of flabby. Since then, I've had a curious need to put everything I really mean in quotation marks. Since then, everything "from me and inward" has been dead and all the outward things have increased to a deluge. Somewhere between laughter and tears.

Do I mind having a baby?   No.

Did I want to have a baby?	Yes. I got married because I wanted to start a life together. Wanted the relationship to develop, "become enlightened." Become fruitful in more than one way.
Am I happy?	Content perhaps. "Happy in a preoccupied way." And at times a sort of spasm, happy beyond all reason, "as though I would burst."
Do I love Marius?	What is love? I'm with him, isn't that enough? A mo. ago I'd have answered yes, a week ago no. I don't know. Don't really think it matters anymore.
Does Marius love me?	I'm not Marius. He "binds me with all bonds." (Do you love me, Marius? Don't ask such a foolish question—you know that I do.)

Why did I drown when the embryo of a new human being took hold of me?

My name is Viviann.

I have hands, feet and a body, like most people, and I've been mirror-blind long enough for me to forget how I "look."

When I look in the mirror I don't see anything. It's not just that I don't see anything I can connect with myself; I see absolutely nothing. Blank. I have my own theory about that.

I suppose I resemble most women of twenty-seven (27). Sometimes I'm reflected in other people, but the effect varies. People love me. Because they take stock of my white power. Bouillon extract.

My head must be different, however (oh dear, it's going to be the familiar picture), since I haven't met anyone I can recognize myself in. Men are different, and women become mere surface. No, it's not just that. It often seems that at the very core of human beings is the desire to not be alone. Not just that either. The desire to overlap each other, DEPEND on each other, bind each other, be alike, be one. But no matter how deeply I look into myself, I see only the desire for freedom. Desire to live alone, together with another person, who does likewise. Is that how it is?

No, there's more to it. Many people want to be understood in order to be utterly and completely un-alone. I only want to understand. I know I'm alone, that anything else is impossible. I live, and so I'm alone. I wouldn't trade my life for anything. When I want to be close to a person, I want to be close enough to see that person. See that person move, independent, unconstrained. I don't want to become part of that person in order to gain control.

Marius and I, for example.

We were attracted to each other, as they say, and we grew close. We were very different. He was completely himself, and I enjoyed seeing him. He said that he loved me. We talked a lot about a life together, and finally we got married. After a while, I realized that I controlled Marius, and that he was happy. Not that I directed him, etc., but he enfolded his beloved Viviann so wholly and completely that his innermost life revolved around me in a kind of shadow dance. This discovery gave me a strange feeling. But I realized that's how he was and that, after all, it was his right to live that way. The outward aspects of myself were enfolded, and that suited me fine. Inwardly, I was freer than ever, and more alone than ever. I was also happy.

I'll probably come back to Marius and me later.

4

I've read it all through.

From what I've written, it sounds as though I went "away" because I got pregnant. That's not what happened. My life circled me in to a tiny dot. When I stood still, I no longer *was.*

And when I woke up, I'd been loved with a sort of welcoming feeling and I found myself with child.

Two things that have long been in motion, and finally meet in a mild collision.

What I don't understand is, why did I become pregnant only after my life had slipped away from me and I'd become truly impenetrable.

Perhaps these things have more to do with one another than I think, after all.

If you throw a stone on the surface of the water, aren't two movements started simultaneously? The stone descending toward the surface of the water, and in the mirror image: the stone rising from the deep. What happens at the instant the two images meet? Or if you walk toward a mirror and know you are moving toward the glass, see the movement reversed simultaneously, are suddenly so close you can't go further. Stare in at something brought to a standstill?

I don't know.
Something happened once, and when it happened I knew it would affect me.

Are such images possible?

5
My life begins here, and stretches out across the fields. My life is that life which lives in the soil and makes the grass yellow. My life is that which places me behind the window and makes the house quiet.

None of those things.
At times I came closest to reality that way.

Which reality?

There is not one reality, but many. I am not one, but many. My life is essentially something to do with silence.

"Our" living-room window faces a field. The window fills the entire wall.
I've never liked the living room, the window nor the view.
It's windy.
If the field hadn't been covered with snow, I'd have stood looking at the grass "swaying" in the wind.
(Now I must stop using those damned quotation marks.)
The grass nearly always reminds me of water. It can appear as though the whole field is flowing up toward the edge of the forest on an escalator. At the top, the whole field glides in under the forest floor, and I'll never see it again.
I've seen many fields leave.

Perhaps I sort of like the view after all.

I'm "at home." (I think it will be more difficult to get rid of the quotation marks than to accept them. I'll deal with that later.)

I'm at home.

The house where Marius and I have lived for three years.

Living room kitchen hallway carpets "parlor" and bathroom and storeroom on the first floor; bedroom closet and built-in shelves on the second. Garage and accessories.

I'm not happy here.

The double bed is precisely as narrow as propriety demands. Precisely narrow enough so that my sleep seems more like compulsion than enjoyment, and our love more like genetics than freedom. And yet wide enough to sleep with our arms away from our bodies and to turn over if we wish. Within reasonable limits. Clean sheets every Saturday. Perhaps it's not the bed there's something wrong with after all. And yet—it's too NARROW. Even if I can't specifically prove it with a tape measure it doesn't matter.

I'm neither more nor less happy on account of it. "The bed is all right." YES, it's all right, everything is all right. Why should we go to the trouble of making things better?

At times it's impossible to reach Marius. I get the feeling that he's forcing me, even though I can't put my finger on anything. Specific. I'm just slowly turning grey. As if I were standing in rainwater up to my ankles and couldn't care less that the water was rising up my legs.

It's the sort of greyness one doesn't see until it's too late. When one becomes indifferent to one's "peculiarities," one ought to stop everything and take a look. Indifference is a slow and dangerous form of perfidy.

I'm the one who changes the sheets, does the shopping, and that sort of thing. I did so before, too.

Marius left in the morning while I was "lying as if asleep." (His lunch lay in a plastic bag in the refrigerator on the lowest shelf.) I woke up slowly. Got up. Looked out the windows, got dressed. Drank a cup of tea in front of the large window.

Then "looked around reluctantly." Sometimes I wept. I did the housework as quickly as possible. Made the bed (did the worst task first), cleared up, moved objects from one room to another and back again. Then I washed, and vacuumed, and all that sort of thing, and finally I took the car and bought detergent bread butter milk food for dinner and all the usual items. I put the things in cupboards and closets and crannies and some in the storeroom (toilet paper apple crates beer cases and things that took space).

Then the day began.

I locked the door got into the car and drove. It is 20 kilometers from Marius's house to my life. With each kilometer, I came closer to reality and to myself. Once I'd reached my house, it often seemed to me that the skin on my hands had disappeared. That's perhaps not a good image, but that's how it seemed. The things I touched filled me. I could create with those hands.

To open the door to the room—
Always the same excitement before I saw the painting. Always the slow, sure happiness afterwards.

And from that moment until four o'clock, nothing else. Just light, distance and life.

Wasn't that enough?

Yes, that was enough, and no, it wasn't enough.

It was enough when I was there and was alive, but when I was back with Marius and what we had together (or didn't have together) it often felt like the opposite, a demand. No, not a demand, perhaps, but something immense. Something impossible to suppress. I often wondered whether it was right, responsible, to stifle creative abilities solely out of consideration for a person. Who could not, and did not wish to, create. I often thought that anything whatsoever could be justified if it helped in the liberation of a life. My life.

No, I didn't think that.

Not always. Never in the beginning. I was rich, I gladly shared my time with Marius.

It could have been so good.

6

Marius took more than my time, and now we're going to have a child together.

Marius is glad.

Marius is glad, but not as happy as I thought he'd be after all he's told me about his longings. This lack of happiness is what convinces me to go through with the birth in spite of everything. A kind of loyalty toward the child. Perhaps something that will develop further in time.

Not quite yet.

When I sit quietly and try to imagine the fetus, I'm overcome with disgust. An intense yellow nausea that puts me on the verge of being driven to anything whatsoever. On the verge of.

Nothing is more than almost now, and that's what is truly terrifying. I'm absolutely powerless when it comes right down to it, and everything that's still me is heavy, even though the child isn't noticeable yet.

Our marriage has been so blocked that I can't imagine how a child can possibly be created in it. Thus, it's not a child I'm waiting for, but something I'm "impregnated with" and must empty out of me when that time comes.

I hate, hate, and yet that's only words. I'm not in touch with what I'm feeling, am not in touch with what I'm aiming toward. Am nevertheless alive. No, not alive—living.

Marius will arrive soon. Because I can't bring myself to explain to him why I think it's meaningless to eat, I prepare dinner. Because I don't want to hear him talk about night-time and sleep, I change the sheets. Because I don't want him to learn to know me now, I fix my hair and rub my cheeks so he won't have to ask how I am.

Things haven't always been the way they are now.

7

One night I woke up with pain in my shoulders. A tight grip at the back of my neck and down my spine. I sat up in bed.

I wept.

I asked Marius to bring me some pills, but he refused, because now I am responsible for another life besides my own. I sat awake for the rest of the night while he slept. Each time I took a breath it hurt; if I touched myself, the pain got worse. If I'd been able to, I'd have gotten up and gone into the bathroom, found the bottle of pills, and kept swallowing them until I couldn't feel anything anymore. That night the child became something more than whiteness. Something on the order of total paralysis.

8

I was nauseated and had swollen legs and headaches and a sore back and discharge and feelings of disgust. Occasionally I thought about the baby. I often had a sense of panic—because the baby was hidden, because I felt heavy and only wished everything dead. Occasionally I wanted to talk to Marius about this. I somehow thought that it ought to concern him.

He didn't like to talk about such things. All women have babies. The next day he bought a book for me, *Hygiene for Pregnant Women and Mothers.* There I'd find answers to everything that was bothering me.

Saliva. I looked it up in the book, page 17: "Some women have a profuse flow of saliva, etc. More than 1 liter of saliva per day may be excreted. When they (the women) lie down, saliva runs out of the corners of their mouths, making the skin around the mouth sore."

I looked under "aversion to smell":

"The husband must be considerate of her aversion toward certain types of smells, even when the aversion applies to his favorite pipe (page 80). And he must try to lead her thoughts away from what's bothering her. Bring her along to visit other people, or take walks with her (like a dog)." I can't stand the smell of Marius. If I say "skin" to myself, nausea rises like a haze around me.

On page 87: "Birth is connected with pain. This is true not only in the case of women, animals also experience pain during birth." On page 115: "Some concluding hints and advice. Even though the birth has been conducted according to all the rules of the art, the vagina may be so wide afterwards that it allows air in and out, to the great concern of the woman. It goes without saying that such a wide vagina does not satisfactorily fulfill the task it has in marriage either. Since it is easy to correct such a defect, etc..."

Now I'm completely reassured, and no longer expect understanding from anyone. I approach my 9 mos. isolation calmly, and withdraw from humanity as is befitting a person in my situation.

But when I see Marius, something happens to my blood, and if I could, I'd wring his entire slimy progeny out of me and throw him away.

9

I went for a check-up today.

Everything looked fine. As may also be said.

I was told to lubricate and massage my nipples. They were introverted. Like the rest of me. But no mention was made of *that.*

I told Marius I wanted to visit my sister.

A lie.

I wanted to be alone a bit. Sleep and wake up without Marius for a while.

10.

When I arrived at my house, it was after five o'clock.

It was dark.

I shoveled the snow from the driveway and parked the car.

Then I shoveled around the oil drum.

The sounds are different in weather like this. It's like digging your way into something. I shoveled a path to the door.

I found the green oil can in the shed and filled it with oil from the drum. The shiny tap was smooth and cold to the touch. By the light of my flashlight I saw that I'd gotten oil on my hands. A strange smell. Thinner to the touch than water.

It was quiet in the house.

White snow lay in the window sills—the windows became friendly ovals toward the outside world. I brushed the snow off my outer clothing, hung it up in the entry, and went inside. I walked carefully to prevent spilling oil on the floor. The "pot-burning" stove is in the kitchen. I filled up the stove's oil tank, opened the valve all the way, allowing oil to flow into the pot until the bottom was completely covered, then closed the valve. To ignite the oil more easily, I lit a match and held it under a plastic bottle from which I poured distilled alcohol. Blazing drops fell into the dark pot. The oil caught fire, began to puff. I opened the valve slightly, and watched how the flame found its rhythm on the surface of the oil, burning in somersaults. I warmed my hands. While the coffee brewed, I cleared things away. The house was no longer quiet. I heard the crackling of the fire. Over by the sink stood the sacks of food; the bedclothes were spread out in the living room and gave off a slight chilliness. The books already lay on the table. I was at home. I started a fire in the fireplace in the living room, and sat there the rest of the evening. I didn't touch the books.

The smell of coffee pervaded the house.

If I didn't feel like it, I didn't have to go to bed tonight. My sleep was my own.

11

The ice, the snow in front of the window.

I am standing in a white picture, and am at peace with myself.

Original title: *Viviann, hvit.* Translated by Nadia Christensen

Tove Nilsen

(b. 1952)
Tove Nilsen grew up in a working class milieu on Oslo's eastside and in several works she has depicted this area and the people living there. The dialect spoken by these people has traditionally been regarded as inferior by the establishment and part of Nilsen's development as a writer has been to return to the language she learned as a child. The best example of this to date is *Skyskraperengler* (1982), a novel based on experiences from her own childhood.

Tove Nilsen's novels and short stories are characterized by a concern for the more unfortunate members of society (such as the bag lady in "Scum") and by an involvement in social and political issues. Problems relating to youth unemployment and juvenile delinquency and the controversy surrounding legal abortion are treated in two different novels. In a third, Nilsen describes a woman's decision to leave her friend, Klaus, and enter into a lesbian relationship.

"Scum" first appeared in an anthology of feminist prose fiction, *Ut av det lukkete rommet* (1975), and was later included in *Hendene opp fra fanget* (1977).

"Scum"

I don't know why, but every time I try to picture her, it's her hands I see first—how different they were from the hands of another woman I noticed that same day. Yes, in fact I saw the two women in the space of only a few minutes, but the first barely made an impression on me: I think I hardly even threw a glance at her face. Only one thing caught me as I stood before one of the flower carts at Stortorget, after having capitulated to the fragrant shock of color that attacked me on the way home. The hands that gave back change from a fifty kroner note were large and coarse as a man's, with skin like bark, and black, ingrown streaks along the sides of the fingers and under the nails—the way mine only get from working in the garden during the summer. The stubborn traces of her work certainly didn't disappear from her hands, no matter how hard she scrubbed. And while I took my change and noticed how she packed the flowers with quick, practiced movements, I had to admit to myself, a little absentmindedly and almost dutifully, that yes, indeed, the practical gardener's hands *were* more beautiful than mine with their gold rings and filed nails (though self-criticism forbade nail-polish now).

Though my acknowledgement definitely wasn't free of sentimentality, I feel *now*, in any case, that it has a disgusting tang of the cheap phrase-making I used to fall back on at the time. It was nothing anyway but a fleeting notion, one of the aphorisms that seem to move of their own volition deep in the brain; I'd already forgotten it when I rushed breathlessly down the street, coat flapping and shopping bags bumping against my legs. Out in the impossible traffic circle in front of the churchyard with its jumble of road construction and its threats of sudden cars—down the stairs above the Viking Hotel—impatiently through the ticket gate—and at full speed down a new set of stairs. To see the tail of the Østensjø train disappear like a red snake out of the station into the tunnel.

There was no use swearing; there was nothing to do but wait—I had to have a seat with all these packages, though. And when I turned to the benches along the wall, my gaze fell right on her. On a brown crow's nest of a head, bending over uncertain hands that strove to keep a tobacco pouch steady between her knees. Something that was anything but easy. She had taken the whole bench for herself and sat in the middle of it in an unstable position, apparently completely out of control and ready to tilt over to the side at any moment—she'd had more than a nip. There weren't many people on the platform so early in the day, but the few who hadn't gotten a spot on the other benches stood, one and all. Whether it was a silent protest against sitting next to her, I don't know, but my going over to sit down beside her wasn't, in any case, meant as a quiet declaration of support. On the contrary, I pressed myself as far to the end as possible; I was simply too exhausted to stand for a quarter hour.

Fortunately it didn't seem that she even took any notice of having company; she drooped down, undisturbed, trying without particular success to get the tobacco and paper to come together in something resembling a cigarette. With reluctant curiosity and quick glances to the side I took in the unkempt appearance of the outdoor sleeper—there was no doubt she'd been one for a while. The light-colored pants were rumpled and disgusting, as if mud had been smeared on them, and her shoes (if those worn boats deserved such a name) were well on the way to decomposing to their basic elements. Not to mention her hair, which had probably been permanented once, but which now stuck straight out in a confused shock above her coat collar. All in all, the way she looked, she must be glad she was sitting in the artificial gray light below ground level — outside the mercilessly sharp spring sun poured down, revealing every single speck, exposing one's winterpale skin and shabby clothes in a far from attractive way. It was the sort of glittering April day that had made my own corduroy jeans seem unwearable and that had brushed aside my resistance — instantaneously — to the new fashions. I'd been stupid enough to let myself be lured into the clothes stores; the results were to be found in more than one bag.

There wasn't time to repent my rashness, however, for, with a sudden jerk, my sitting companion straightened herself up, a maneuver that came so unexpectedly that I was barely able to avert my gaze in order to stare, unaffectedly, straight ahead. Something I could surely have spared myself; well-aware of my proximity and without the slightest hint of a turn, she broke out, unclearly but loudly: "Please keep your seat!" The expectant expressions of the bystanders revealed that it wasn't the first time she'd opened her mouth, and almost automatically, I smiled indulgently, an unconscious sign that I understood how it was. A clear indication of distance and belonging at the same time, of a common accord with the others. At the same time my stomach tingled anxiously, as it always does over people who are drunk enough to strike up conversations — but I hoped fervently that she wouldn't continue to address herself to me. For the time being she was just mumbling to herself in that inarticulate, inebriated excitement that is the Norwegian stand-up comic's main act — or last hope, depending — but the irritated outbursts about not finding what she was poking around for in her pockets didn't seem exactly reassuring. From the corner of my eye I followed her agitated movements, and I think it was only when she gave up the search and concentrated on her cigarette again that I first really noticed her hands. And I couldn't avoid comparing them with the gardener's hands I'd paid homage to just before. Those had been black in a healthy way, from pure dirt, while these were a uniform gray, like day-old filth, so that the idea of touching them gave me a shuddering feeling of greasiness.

As if with intentional irony she suddenly held one of them up in front of my face and waved the deformed cigarette she'd finally gotten rolled up — it was matches she wanted. Something I didn't have, I said, with an apologetic, "No, I don't smoke," and met her eyes for the first time — and if I didn't exactly get a little shock, I was startled, to put it mildly. For until then I hadn't dared to examine her profile more closely; by reason of her generally wasted appearance

I'd taken it as a given that she had to be quite old. She was certainly wrinkled and drawn enough, but not the way you get from age and toil. No, what struck me first of all was a stamp of irreparable ruin, something that had gone too far too quickly. On the whole it's difficult to describe her face, for under the skin color that was the alcoholic's muddy red-violet, there was something slack and blurry, almost doughy, that seemed to blot out her features. Between the two swollen folds of skin her eyes were ugly from drink and broken blood vessels. Behind the wrinkles and decay, however, the remains of a soft smoothness were preserved, suggesting that she could have even been pretty once. Though it was difficult to guess her age, she couldn't possibly be older than forty, perhaps she was no more than in her mid-thirties.

For her voice was young; I heard it in the lucid pauses between the times when it collapsed in weepy mumbling. She was luckier when she turned to ask some of the others if she could get a light; her voice sounded high and pure with the round ring of the Sørland dialect. All the same, only an elderly man went out of his way to search through his pockets before he shook his head; the others didn't even bother answering. I remember that in my naiveté I was especially angry that a young guy with the same kind of political buttons as me couldn't lower himself to respond either. And that, of course, annoyed her no less; something brewed up plainly in her ravaged face, and for a moment her expression was dominated by bitter lines around her mouth, lines I thought I'd seen before on other women in her position. On women who walk around in the streets talking loudly to themselves, slandering their surroundings by their mere existence.

Though, from where she sat, wobbling irresolutely with the unlit cigarette between her fingers, she seemed either helpless or incapable of carrying out anything like that. I soon understood that I had to reckon with surprises, however, for when a new subway train was readied for departure by the monotonous, "Watch for the doors, the doors are closing," she straight out uttered a caustic, "Oh, shut up the goddamned nagging." I didn't see if there were others besides me who had to hide a smile, for no sooner were the words slung out than she lurched over in a way that would have sent her headfirst to the stone floor if I hadn't reacted. Without thinking I grabbed her dirty coat sleeve, but it was like coming to grips with some formless material. Weakly but surely she slid over, heavy and loose as a sack, and anything but cooperative. I had to let go of my bags and use both hands so as not to lose her. Probably it was a rather entertaining little scene, for people stood around observing it without so much as lifting a finger. It wasn't until later that it angered me—without forgetting that I myself would have doubtlessly looked the other way and avoided helping if I hadn't accidently been needed. For the time being I had more than enough with holding on to the passive bundle that seemed to get heavier and heavier. It was such a repulsive, unexpected moment that I don't recall much about it—other than that I registered an ugly wound under the unwashed bush of hair, and that the idiocy of the situation, my struggling with an unknown drunk of a woman, more than annoyed me. But finally I got her more or less back in place.

Without doubt she needed time to gather herself, and sat a while swaying with an introspective look and heaving breast before turning a red and devasted face to me; her lower lip was wet with spit as she emitted something that might have meant thank you. And at that moment I recognized the stink—there's honestly no other word. That I hadn't noticed it before seems quite unbelievable; the one explanation must be that I was only focusing on not letting her out of my grip. Anyway, now it gushed towards me in an indescribably queasy blend—a concentration of stenches that included old alcohol and sweat .... And something remarkably familiar that I couldn't manage to identify at first. Not until a picture struck me with unmistakable certainty: warm summer days in the years before I started to use tampons and had gone a few hours too many with the same pad. That was exactly the same smell that wafted up—so acrid that it cried out for soap and water. I couldn't be *completely* certain of course, but from the moment I thought I recognized it, it seemed to grow stronger and stronger, like a disgusting reminder of that embarrassing feeling of sticky, bloodied underwear.

I suppose it was then that my superficial, feel-sorry-for emotion turned into something that contracted painfully and angrily within me: No one should have to go around like this! Maybe she didn't have the means to wash herself or money to use the right thing. And even though the odor almost made me flinch, I was glad there weren't others near enough to also *smell* her degradation. But, just the same, it was as if I sat there mocking her with my prosperous grooming—and with my huge paper cornucopia of flowers: iris and tulips and Easter lilies, a small fortune of irresistible, springlike freshness. . . .

Although she looked far from discouraged. A sneer actually lurked on her lips when she asked again for a match; it flickered like the resigned shadow of old experience. But when she didn't get a response this time either, she let her gaze rest ominously on a woman in a Persian coat in front of us. And sure enough, with devil-may-care abandon she called, "You look like you have a goddamn rabbit face." The observation was followed by a blaring laughter that tweaked the lips of the bystanders, for the party in question did have truly comical protruding front teeth. The possibility of goodwill was immediately spoiled, however; her eyes narrowed with sudden anger as she burst out, "Get me a match, you fucking fur-coated whore!"

And from then on the situation developed quickly and uncomfortably. Screaming and shouting, a whole gang of teenagers came clattering down the steps: seven, eight boys who tore by to catch the train. They didn't let the opportunity go by, however, when they set eyes on her; with unique intolerance of the confirmation-aged, one of them slung out an insolent, "Is that who you're going out with tonight, huh? That old bitch! Have fun!"

To tell the truth, I thought she was so out of it that the remark would go right by her, but the howls of laughter hadn't died down before she shouted back furiously, "Shut your mouth and come back when you've got something besides a snail between your legs!"

I have to admit I couldn't suppress a twinge of malicious delight: a poison jab to their labored toughness—You needed that, young jerks! She got a good one in. But most of those who had been appreciative spectators turned their backs demonstratively—only a few continued to gape, and one man, of the correct, tailored school, measured her up and down, offended. She undoubtedly felt harassed because she waved her index finger at him and barely took enough breath to let a new bomb fall—"Go home and fuck your wife! If you can!" she added scornfully and attempted to get up. The only result was that she remained halfway lying on the bench, while she flailed helplessly with her arms to get a good grip. Then she took up the thread again, threateningly dark of face. "But you don't look like you're worth a whole fucking hell of a lot. You goddamn cuntlicker!"

The words shrilled embarrassingly between the stone walls; they sank into me so brutally that for a moment I couldn't manage to look around. When I allowed my eyes to fall on those nearby, I saw them standing there with the same idiotic, mortified expression I'd felt tighten up around my own mouth. The same unwillingness among them to acknowledge the meaning of the word. Among a few of them there was something else besides: an impatient irritation that showed she wasn't just an element of entertainment to shudder over or smile at. Now she'd crossed a line and had begun to be too provocative. The certainty that she was drunk enough to ignore every convention was getting a firm grip on me, when her voice grated again, "You're not good for much more than that, any of you. Not a fucking thing," she snorted. Unfortunately her eye fell upon the woman in the Persian coat again, "You, you probably get a blister between your legs after a fuck." Her rage gave way to an unexpected and almost cheerful, bubbling laughter, as if she'd said something really good.

If that were the case, she was the only one who thought so. The clamped jaw of the gray-suited man who'd had his potency put in question was less than benevolent. And the woman in the Persian coat, still fighting for control over her red cheeks, steamed with disgust and looked like she wanted to punch someone. Only a young boy grinned good-naturedly and all-forgivingly. I noticed them while my thoughts multiplied. My sitting next to the object of their attention gave me another perspective in a way; I could both watch her and the bystanders and at the same time register my own reactions to both of them. For the moment she was cursing continuously; her all-encompassing anger expressed itself in words all directed below the belt. It seemed she took a real pleasure in sexual talk—though she was missing the shine of greasy laughter and damp glances that might indicate she enjoyed the connotations of the words. She let them fall from her mouth hard and unswerving, with a challenging shamelessness I'd never seen in a woman. This didn't fail to have an effect either; the exchanges around us were no longer limited to rolling eyes or indignant expressions. Even though I didn't hear what was said, it was plainly enough in the air—that it was wrong for someone like that to go around badgering people.

Of course I could understand their indignation. She was disgusting, sitting there screeching until the spit flew. I couldn't deny myself that I was feeling a weak smouldering inside, probably as much over the way she was compromising herself as the way she was abusing people. It was probably the germ cell of that same aggression that makes some people write nasty letters to the editor about scum and dregs and the disgrace of the city and what must the tourists think?

It remained at the germination stage, however. Whatever had been ready to boil up into rage disappeared into a heavy grief, like a dark wing descending weakly and quietly, as I looked at the shabby specimen of humanity next to me. The lackluster skin, the filthy hair, those worn-out clothes—everything combined was proof of a hard gray poverty that is officially a closed chapter here in this country, put behind us after the thirties, once and for all. She had calmed down a little and was muttering angrily to herself now—I caught something about a prescription she wanted to renew, but that it was "used up, they told me!" Only now and then did she rattle off any curses of the same caliber as earlier. Actually, I was ridiculously afraid the whole time of having something or other slung in my face, and sat as still as possible so as not to rouse her attention. My fear was dampened by a painful curiosity about a way of living I knew little about and could barely guess at. Words and phrases whirled annoyingly in my head: tramps, precarious lives, wretched existences—all these people dehumanized, deprived of the essentials. The words arose from what I'd read or heard: about going out and freezing and sleeping in doorways and dumpsters and shelters. Waking with the vinegar-sour belches of the hangover and an iron ring around your forehead, having to stand your own clammy uncleanness for days on end. Standing in unkempt clusters in parks, entryways, drinking from bottles—around the streets of Grønland, behind the emergency room, at Ankertorget, and down by the docks. All that could give me the framework for her misery, but I couldn't know what kind of memories and thoughts she had. I knew nothing of the important details of her life. And I couldn't help the emotion that welled up in me about *this* being her lot in life, this being her piece of eternity right *now*. Unsummoned images crowded up, embarrassingly banal. Not that I was taking refuge in the opposite extreme of sweetness and light, but all I could think of were clean sheets and the smell of soap-scrubbed skin.

Naturally it's hard to distinguish what I thought then and what I've added later. There wasn't that much time for musing in the middle of her spectacle. She sat apathetically only for a short while, moving her lips soundlessly—then she was off again. Her jaw veered uncontrollably between laughter and anger, directed toward everyone and no one. Nervously I caught myself looking at my watch, counting the minutes until I could get away—over four until my train pulled up. The soles of my feet began to itch, and I had an anxious knot in my stomach—it would probably be my turn soon to get to hear something; my mind was full of unreasonable and alarming possibilities. It wasn't without some small relief then that I saw her interest fix on a newly arrived man with a coat and briefcase. Glinting with drunken sharpness she sized him up from his toes to his crown and then turned the volume up again—"You have to put your hat on right! One of your ears is turned out!"

Everyone's eyes went to the innocent, to the ear that really did stand out like a red handle under his hat. "You can't go around like that," she decided, her tone almost meditative. And then an incomparable pantomime began to play itself out—strange signals ran through fragile wires, although they only seemed to go in one direction: she tilted her head and arranged an imaginary hat; she showed with her hands how it should sit. While he stood, stiff and rigid and so strained with the effort of pretending that nothing was happening, anyone could see he was sweating angrily from trying to straighten the unfortunate ear—which was positively growing in its anxiety. And she, so drunk she couldn't sit without swaying, seriously taken up with getting him to place his hat differently.

Oh—for a moment she was priceless, captivating; she had all the aces in her hand and played them out sovereignly in a way that should have won most everyone's respect. The whole time she oscillated as if between two points, as if she were in the lucid borderland between the alcoholic state where the body is dead-drunk, but the gift of observation is intact. It brought no response in the question of the hat, however, so she plainly decided to take matters into her own hands. With a powerful effort and an outburst that she could fix it, she tried to get up, but fell down and remained on her knees in a twisted position, with her torso hanging over the bench.

I didn't react so quickly this time; at any rate a man appeared before I could manage to do much of anything. Fortunately I must say, for when he bent over, intending to haul her up, she burst out anew in unforeseen wrath, as if this were the last straw, "Get away from me, you prick! You goddamn PRICK! See what you've done, you've stepped on my cigarette! Asshole!" Then came the whole rigamarole again, in combinations that sounded like anatomical perversities. A whole little crowd was summoned by her uproar, and more kept coming, letting the last of reticence go by the board, pressing together around her. I remember their faces in disconnected clips: some openly and hungrily curious, with an undisguised appetite for scandal. Others with a stiff air of this all being really below one's dignity, but all the same, just a little peek...And as if it were me they stood staring at, I felt thrust into a corner. For the first time something threatening and nightmarish weighed the situation down: the cold gusts from the tunnel, the wide-eyed looks, and the woman who lay half on the floor swearing like a snarling cat. Her shrieks trembled between the walls with a hollow, unearthly sound that gave me an almost uncontrollable urge to shake her like a rag, to stop the avalanche of obscenities. If only she could topple over into the second stage of intoxication, at least turn a little maudlin. But her anger was raw and unadulterated and it didn't leave us much room for sympathy.

The obscenities had already been repeated so many times that they no longer had their full impact. Now it was the grotesque drunkenness that seemed worst and that gave a word like inebriation a pale innocence. It was as if her blood alcohol level suddenly rose to the point of total lack of control—her arms and legs collapsed weakly, as if they were made out of rubber and had no regulating mechanism. She was in no condition to get up on her own, but there was no one who dared so much as touch her. Her inflammatory vocabulary gave us no reason to suppose that an attempt to help would be met with good will, let alone gratitude. I scrutinized her openly; her coat had slid down over one shoulder; during a pause for breath she pulled it up and brushed her hair from her forehead. Her face hád a strange, faraway expression at that moment; her gaze became stiffly fixed on something beyond us, as if she had suddenly fallen into a reverie about something or other, and the corners of her mouth, where it hung open, were sticky with gray saliva. But then she pulled herself together with a shudder, maybe just a twitch of discomfort—as if something was unfolding, so that her skin turned vulnerably naked. For reasons dim and uncertain I had to think that maybe she was lying there with her period, bleeding—it was as if something inside me was exposed, and I had to turn away. It was only deep, deep inside that the helpless and painful beginnings of something I wish I could call solidarity beat even slightly. What it felt like was falling headlong and grazing the palms of your hands on sandy asphalt—smooth flat patches of damp skinlessness with thin threads of bloody scratches. I had a tight stinging pain somewhere in my chest...

And then there wasn't any more. Not for me. The long quarter hour was over and the train glided up. There was an opening in the ring of bystanders as I rose—I don't know who'd alerted them but two black uniforms were arriving. Maybe it was just my imagination but before the subway door snapped shut I thought I heard her crying out for matches.

Now and again I think of her. Not often or long—there's no reason to exaggerate—she doesn't torment me or cause me sleepless nights. The thought of her, on the contrary, can irritate me because it shows my tendency to a useless and sentimental susceptibility. Even writing this down can seem meaningless, make me want to object: There are so many around in her position, and plenty of them have it worse. What do I have to do with her, a complete stranger I'd probably find totally unlikeable if it came down to it. And anyway, she needs my facile and uncommitted momentary sympathy least of all.

Perhaps that's exactly why her image springs up at regular intervals, whether I wish it or not. It's called forth as if of its own accord, pricking my perfect social consciousness a little and making my fine words grate. It demands something completely different from me. Suddenly her face, or rather, her hands, appear, trembling annoyingly behind my retina, scratching a rough surface on something smooth in me. But as I said, it seldom lasts very long.

Original title: *"Subb"*. Translated by Barbara Wilson

Cecilie Løveid

(b. 1951)

Cecilie Løveid is among the most innovative and imaginative of Norway's young authors. To date she has published six books of prose fiction and a collection of dramatic works for radio and stage (*Måkespisere*, 1983). Her approach is experimental, employing a combination of dramatic dialogue, prose narrative and lyricism. The novels seem disconnected, in part due to the important role imagination and dreams play in Løveid's fictional world, and also because her language is filled with imagery and unexpected, fanciful associations. However, underlying the fragmented text there is a story line, involving the character's development and her relationships.

"Dancefjord (The Sailor)," excerpted from *Sug* (1979), depicts a segment of Kjersti's journey toward greater understanding of her attachment to her sailor father. Typical of Løveid's women, Kjersti is sensuous and eager to love, open to what life has to offer.

Though there is no narrative thread holding the texts from *Captured Wild Rose (Fanget villrose,* 1977) together, there is unity of style and theme. The present selection exemplifies Løveid's humor and fancy and her delight in language.

Dancefjord (The Sailor)

I HAD ALWAYS TOLD THE USUAL STORIES ABOUT FATHER HAVING DROWNED AT SEA IN A STORM HE WAS A PIRATE CAPTAIN BUT AFTER ALL IT'S NOT ABSOLUTELY IMPOSSIBLE PERHAPS HE IS DROWNED I THOUGHT

Something about Mats made me feel secure.
(I have a lover to affirm me. One who fulfills all needs, sexual, my greediness to give and to take. Handclasps, opinions.) But I didn't formulate the question: is this the way it should be, is it really Mats.

I had Mats's hand to hold. Had Mats's hand to hold if I couldn't hold Father's. Old enough and independent enough, courageous. Could even take back my hand from both of them if I wanted, I thought.

FATHER WAS A WHITE SHIRT AND TIE
AND HIS HEAD A GLOBE DIVIDED INTO DEGREES OF LONGITUDE AND LATITUDE

●

LOOKED AT MY FRECKLED ARMS AGAINST THE BLACK SWEATER

Would Father like freckled arms?
I don't like them myself. It's not certain he'll like them. But maybe he has exactly the same kind of arms himself. Probably. Will I like his arms? Probably I won't like freckled arms.

I laughed, didn't for an instant believe what I had decided. Prepared the disappointment in time, to put it more correctly.

ONE WHO WALKS ALONE SEARCHING, SOMETHING ALL
BOOKS DEAL WITH OR ATTEMPT TO
NOT DEAL WITH

My name is Kjersti Gilje.

●

STENCH DESTRUCTION OH UGH OH UGH OH UGH
GIVE ME AN OUNCE OF POTASSIUM BROMIDE
DEAR PHARMACIST
IT DRIVES THE STENCH OUT OF THE IMAGINATION

Father was his name and he cried when he was born.
But when he sat upright in mother's huge scarlet cunt he sunned himself and glistened.

When he grew up he would be a sailor: It was so gloriously dangerous. Travel through salt storms, procure himself children to buy dresses for, collect the faces of his children, his guilty consciences!

He rises and declares that *if* he is going to die, it must be inside a woman!

He rises under the rotating sun, stands there with his legs apart on deck with oranges and filled chocolates in his codpiece and shouts: A sailor must have wide trousers and be geometrically conscious!

•

SO I CAN WALK AROUND AS AN EVEN FREER PERSON
(The Sign of the Frog)

The bus is a cake pan. I sit in it and puff up, see the sun. Expectations rise. Now I've finally decided to visit Father. He lives at a sort of sanitarium for people who are blind or have poor eyesight. There was a fire on his ship. At the bus stop are tall, strong-smelling plants, and a smiling woman, who is not blind and who works in the kitchen, is waiting for me. "Hello, I'm the new cook," I say, shaking her hand. But in the grass down in the ditch, behind the naked legs and the flowers, who is waiting there, blinking, panting?

I have to go down the long cellar stairway to my room. The walls are covered with thick rugs. The seeing-eye dog licks my ear and stops in front of the first step so I won't fall. The animal leads me down. Then it howls down there in the darkness. Who is hopping around on the soft rug? I find a beer glass, catch the frog and let it go back out into the sunshine-grass so that no blind person will trample it.

Upstairs I introduce myself to the Sailor:

"I'm the new cook."

He doesn't see anything. He can't hide. He has taken along a cassette of music from the sea. He doesn't see anything. Out on the terrace the blind people stumble around looking for their seeing-eye dogs.

"What lovely weather." I see him. I see he has become quite stooped because he is constantly groping for actual or imaginary chairs and doors. "I'm the new cook." He hasn't seen me for twenty years. I think he goes according to smells, and must learn to go according to room sounds. "I'm the new cook."

The property is large, the house is a shipowner's palace. The rhododendron are blooming, there is buzzing and humming. The Sailor and I grope our way along metal pipes and rope railings, we're going to the fjord for a swim. We can choose between the fjord and a heated swimming pool. (Support the auction for the blind, buy lottery tickets.) He walks one step behind me, I've never led a blind person before. (Perhaps it is sitting there in the grass with a tiny secret microphone hidden in its jumping foot?) I try to pretend I'm blind by closing my eyes, but get very frightened and have to open them after two seconds. He is attractive. He still has a way about him, stronger. He asks what I look like. A devilish impulse makes me give him completely false information. ("I'm the new cook.") Lie about my hair color and say that my eyes are blue.

The water in the pool is utterly still. I pull my dress over my head, tight against him, rush into the pool, shout that he should come. He is shy, doesn't want to take off his clothes. "Come on," I shout. ("I'm the new cook.")

I put my legs around the warm-water pipe. No one can see. A lovely feeling of playing in water of two different temperatures.

The Sailor advances carefully, steps neatly out of the yellow beach shoes. I swim away, taking him along to show him the fountain carved out of stone, the one that smiles and spews fresh water at us. Grope with my hands like an art historian hunting for unpolished Stone and Bronze Age rock carvings in northern Norway. *(Does the reindeer have an eye? No, the reindeer never has eyes. It mustn't see its hunter!)*

I swim away from the Sailor, he can't tell where I'm swimming. I swim around the careful strokes of his arms in a typical flirtation. ("I'm the new cook.") I do something brutal. My mother has always described the Sailor as an attractive man, a ladies' man, with "a way about him." It's difficult to find rules for this game. We need to have dice with raised dots, not black writing or drawling voices from the Society for the Blind. He suddenly changes into a green frog. Gets hold of my hair. (Which I said was blond, not dark like his.) Puts my hair into his mouth in order to hang on behind me. He tries to be a coupling male frog. I swim a few strokes with the Sailor on my back, teasingly. He starts to tremble. "Why don't we try going for a little swim in the fjord," I, the new cook, suggest.

"Don't go out in it alone," she shouted. "It's slippery." He wanted to try the ocean. He had never swum in the ocean before, even though he had been a sailor for thirty years. He had always wanted a firm bottom beneath him. The swimming pools on shipboard were fine for tropical nights.

He sniffed. He groped with his toes. He held tightly to a large rock before he tremblingly let himself glide out into the water.

She came right behind him. "Don't go out alone," she said. "You might slip."
He smiled with chattering teeth.
But she followed him. The yellow beach shoes stood back at the edge of the pool. No boats on the fjord. No folk, no foes. The wind was working somewhere else. "If anyone screams now, it will be heard all the way into town," she thought. The sun had left them.

She swam around him. She swam round and round him like a seal around her young. The sun had left them. Once again he got hold of her long hair. "Swim!" she shouted. He had never tried swimming in the ocean before. "No, the whole archipelago is clear, there's nothing to be afraid of here." "Swim ahead of me," he said. "Are you there?" "Oh yes," said she, the mermaid. "Come on, Captain."

He took a couple of puffing strokes, then suddenly he lay on top of her, even though they had an entire shining dance fjord of space. She lay on her stomach over a slimy round stone in the water. "I have always. . . I have wondered. . . what color your hair is."
"Blond."
He could not know whether her breasts are round or flat.
"Blond," she said.

(Dark like dried kelp, and eyes like the queen of amber,
she thought.)
His body, naked and near now.
She grew frightened.
Her head exploded.
Her body wild, sweet, furious.
Her strength, his weakness, groping and submissive.
"If anyone screams now, it will be heard all the way into town."

She lay her arms lovingly around his neck. Like a thin
seven-year-old, afraid of the strong shower at school.

The smooth slime on the stones.
His chest covered with gray hair. His teeth.

Her hand slid in toward his throat, took a strangle-hold, wanted
to pull him under.

"I love you," she screamed. It could be heard all the way into town.
"I love you, love you, love you!"

"Hey," called a voice from up on the path.
"Do you have problems down there?"

•

NOW I KNOW WHAT YOU LOOK LIKE

I escape, as I let the frog do. It's just a matter of keeping oneself suffi-
ciently far away, so he can't know whether I see him. When I come
close, I let my dress brush his hand.

I walk down toward the bus. Am going back to town. Have visited
Father. At the bus stop are tall, strong-smelling plants. He wanted to
say good-bye to me. He held me close and said: "Now I know what
you look like!"

But in the grass, behind legs and flowers—who is sitting there? The
frog isn't sitting there. It's lying in the middle of the road in front of us.
Dead and dried by the sun. I say to myself: *It's not a sign, it's not a
warning, phew, phew, it's a dead frog.*

In the bus, the pictures link together. The pictures of the frog form a series: The frog in the grass in the ditch, the frog on the rug, the frog in the water, the frog on the road. *"Now I know what you look like."*

●

HOW COULD SHE BE SUCH A DIVIDED UNHAPPY SISTER

AFTER ALL THE BELOVED FATHER WENT TO TOWN TO BUY ONE WHITE SPOOL OF THREAD JUST FOR HER WHILE SHE CUT UP ALL HER CLOTHING AND THREW IT TO THE DOGS HE QUIETLY STROLLED DOWN FOR A WHITE SPOOL OF THREAD

Not because her mouth was to be sewn up. But so that her life would hold together, he strolled down. Nevertheless she awoke the next morning with her mouth sewn up. The next morning she awoke and was used, split open between the legs and sewn together at the mouth. (If you say anything to anyone you won't be allowed to stay here any longer.)

EVERYTHING COULD SUDDENLY BE TURNED UPSIDE DOWN

Original title: *Dansefjord (Sjømannen)*. Translated by Nadia Christensen ι

Captured Wildrose

AIRSHIP

Can my words be pale blue airships?
Why do you fly them so high, friends ask.
They disappear from us, we don't see them
properly. Especially in June.
In June? I ask.
In June the children wear short sweaters and have bare
bottoms, we get ready to go to jazz festivals.
Wait instead till October. Then I fly the airships so
low you can touch them, laugh at them, see and shoot them.
They fly so low over the clotheslines and playgrounds.
You're always looking for ships to shoot, after all.
So why not wait till October, then my airships streak
over the islands in Sandøy district, blinking to the
rescue boats. And at Christmas they lie, calm and proper,
in the snowdrifts outside Oslo. That's the time to
capture them, fill them with wine and uproar. Inside
you'll still find the dear old wall covering, even on
brand new ships, the motif repeated in all alphabets in
all languages: fiction fiction fiction fiction fiction.

Original title: *Luftskip.* Translated by Nadia Christensen

THE MOUNDS GREW AROUND HER

Liv sat knitting for *Husfliden.*
The mounds grew around her. On an island in Norway
she knit men's sizes all day all night. Smoked
hand-rolled cigarettes, knit, drank coffee hot as hell.
Let the circular knitting needle rest in her lap as
she rubbed her eyes and looked out at the breakwater.
Lovely Norwegian patterns. Rich in tradition, cheap
to produce. Two nervous hands and aching shoulders.
Cheap to operate, that body. A frail female organism.
Around her grew the mounds of clean clothes that never
got ironed and soiled ones that never got washed,
children that grew and small creatures in the walls that
bred and multiplied. Growing mounds of coffee grounds
and fish guts in back of the house where the cat sang,
the hens tripped about and lay eggs, the pig broke out of
the pen one day and dashed into the sea and drowned.
The mounds grew around her. On the mounds grew small
bird's-foot flowers with yellow shoes for elves to wear.

Original title: *Rundt henne vokste haugene.* Translated by
Nadia Christensen

Husfliden: store where handicraft products are sold

MY HEAD HAS A CLEAR PERSPECTIVE

At last, my dearest wish was granted!
At last!
From up here at the window I can watch all that happens.
Cats at night and the repetition and variations in people's
parking habits. When lights are turned on and off in the
row houses across the street.
I've achieved freedom! I'm rid of my body! A transaction
that didn't cost me anything, but what toil and effort it
cost my fiancé! That day my fiancé gave in to the pressure
and chopped off my head, separated my head from my body. He
left with my body one Wednesday afternoon. After long
intense discussions. Put my body in the back seat of his
car and drove away, out Highway E6 toward Trondheim. Arms
and legs sprawling, I don't see how he had the guts for it.
Oh god, I know what he's going to use it for. Nothing
very original or creative you may be sure. And he has
several advantages. He's rid of my nagging. In a way
he's rid of me, but has me, and I'm rid of him, and have
myself and am with him. I know many women envy my situation.
I have a clear perspective, I don't need to go out and
struggle. I don't pursue anything, don't strive. If
I could possibly desire anything more in this world it
would have to be a set of headphones for good music. . .
and or. . . a linguaphone course in Everyday French?

Original title: *Hodet har fritt utsyn.* Translated by Nadia Christensen

KISS

My breasts my belly my fingertips
the grass the trees the water
downy feathers in the grass
the park where the dogs trot.
I am gleaming with water and naked as at the time I got
twenty-five kroner for sitting in a posture of fear—
something the sculptor wanted to capture, so he had me
stiffen in this position, a master.
My husband was in the navy when I became this way.
It was summer uniform, it was winter uniform. He was
always on a cruise to secret destinations, he called me
his Mata Hari, my son was three months old. I was so
lonely. Came to the sculptor each day for as long as he
could afford that. There was a thick lap robe for me and a
stove, glowing red in front of my white, post-pregnant body.
You are so pale, he said. Never touched me. He corrected
my posture with a modeling pin when I shuffled off. One is
still not allowed to touch me, even though I am the only
naked woman in the park. Forbidden to embrace me. Some day
he will come back. As a ninety-year-old man with a cane
strolling in the park where the dogs trot. His kiss on
my thigh will shatter bronze.

Original title: *Kyss.* Translated by Nadia Christensen

INCONVENIENT

Grandfather was dead. It was almost Christmas.
Inconvenient, but then it always is, said Uncle.
Just so we don't spoil Christmas for the children.
There was room for all the relatives in a niche at the
hospital. Picked at the rubber plants, stared at the
death-bare tree outside. All thought they were the only
ones grieving and all hid it. A nurse came and asked if
we had gotten to see him. No, that's what we're waiting
for, said Uncle, we'd like to see him before he's put into
the freezer. Just before he died he had scolded the family
for political tepidness. He himself was red-hot.
A nurse came with two *nisse* costumes. We stood by an
empty coat tree. We hadn't dared to take off our coats.
We were just waiting to say good-bye for the last time.
She hung the two masks on the hat hooks. Dangling there with
the *nisse* suits, they looked like two hanged men. We were
given the undershirt and the underpants and the well-worn
gold ring he was wearing when he died. Then we drove
home without getting to see him. No one really wanted to
anyway.

Original title: *Ubeleilig.* Translated by Nadia Christensen

---

nisse: Christmas elf, similar to Santa Claus

Karin Moe

(b. 1945)
Karin Moe, an active contributor to the ongoing debate about the function of
literature in Norway, has published numerous poems and prose texts in
magazines and journals, in addition to two books, *Kjønnskrift* (1980) and *Fyk*
(1983). Her books cannot be described in terms of any one genre. They
comprise texts, poetry and prose, which are sarcastic, incisive, humorous
and serious, and deal with topics relating to politics, rhetoric and eroticism.
Karin Moe does not fit into any tradition within Norwegian literature—the
impulses for her work have come from France, contemporary French
feminist theory in particular. As the title of her first book indicates
(kjønn = sex, skrift = writing), she believes that language and sex are
interrelated, that just as women and men are biologically different, so too is
their language. Her texts then, represent a conscious effort to use language
in a way that is specifically feminine to convey specifically feminine
experiences. "The Lady in the Coat" is taken from *Kjønnskrift*, "Eagle
Wings" from *Fyk*.

The Lady in the Coat

Begin with the coat.

It is a common ugly coat. Brownish-gray with rabbit fur on the
collar and cut full across the back. The pockets are sewn into the side
seams and have flaps held down by large oval buttons. The same in
front, with large gaping button holes on the other side when the coat
is open. The sleeves are raglan and have cuffs riveted with yet
another oval. The fabric is wool, tightly-woven. It shows signs of
having been through messy movements. Folds along the sleeve and
wrinkles across the hip. The coat just barely stays together, stuffed
with a 200-pound 65-year-old female body.

The coat has no waistline. Beneath the loose hem, rolypoly legs
stick out. In brown tie shoes with broad, crooked heels. The heels'
beat against the sidewalk is carried up under the chin, which bobs
down into the acrylic scarf inside the rabbit collar. The hair across the

forehead is greasy gray with remnants of brown color on the ends, at one time parted down the middle, now a broken line along the scalp. The face is divided into puffy bags. Two on each side under the eyes, two down the jowls, two under the chin in the acrylic fabric. Beneath the drooping lids: the eyes. Beneath the flat nostrils: the lips. Inside: yellow-blue teeth. The skin is the texture of yeast dough. The forehead is slightly furrowed and shines broadly beneath the globs of hair. The skin hangs to one side and down, toward the handbag in the right fist. It is a flight bag of moss-gray plastic and fire-engine red pockets with big handles and room for everything that's brought along. It's brought along and bangs against the thigh that bulges and rubs against the crinoline dress inside the coat every time the weight shifts foot. The shoe lifts up from the asphalt and forward, giving movement to the body. Then the heel tramps and slides down and billows out through the wool. The lady in the coat walks. The lady in the coat is my mother.

Happiness was holding her free hand and looking up, hanging out in the air at an angle in order to see my fill. With fluffy blond hair streaming out in the wind and the tiniest turned-up nose in the whole town in the middle of my face. My mother is the finest princess in all of Bergen. A vision in a cream-caramel suit fitted at the waist. Pink silk blouse with bow, silk stockings that feel like powdered sugar, leather shoes with thin straps across the ankles. The princess. The way she steps through the crowd. And the swarm of smells and people and fish along the wharf. With leaden sea and sky around her. And me. I keep a strong grip on the fist. On the white cotton glove with crocheted pattern drawn together in small wrinkles in the palm of the hand where the skin is warm. I am jumping with joy at being in the fairy tale of Bergen and frightened to death that the princess will go to pieces on me. She has heavy breasts imprisoned in fabric cups with fancy lace around and thin silk ribbons across the shoulders that I've seen cut red stripes in the skin. I can't do anything. My hands don't reach around the narrow waist either. How I guard the swaying hips from other hands! My eyes flash and keep away wet rubber gloves with fish entrails and smooth knuckles around the handles of briefcases. If I let myself fall backwards as far as the arm reaches to a safe place among the shrimp crates, I see the calves behind the silk mesh. No one is allowed to tear open the mesh and make the skin cold. The warmth is mine. The warmth in the lap, too. They'll never get me to leave it! It is my soft corner beneath the skirt. There I find warm laces and nice stomach and smells. When I twirl her curls of hair, the princess shuts her eyes and rides the dewy bay in a white bobbing rowboat. I watch the smile that rocks on the lips. No one may take it. And when she makes the eyes darker and forces the lashes up with a little tong and splits the eyes into two suns! Then I am the nicest troll in the blue mountain. I will never burst in suns like that.

I can't manage to hold the suns captive. They glide out of my pictures. Don't want to be part of the fairy tale. One more than others silences my expression. It is taken with back lighting. The outline of the hair floats in vague coils. The mouth is slightly open. The skin is sheer with shadows for the bone structure. The eyes look straight through me. They are too naked for me. Too naked for the big, hairy hands behind the camera, just as greedy as I for princesses. The expression of coat-and-body in silk blouse. Words disintegrate in the back lighting. The lady in the coat walks away. Free at last. Does not let herself be led. My mother. Your woman. Her own.

Original title: *Dama i kåpa.* Translated by Janet E. Rasmussen

Eagle Wings

I am in the eagle house. Lying on my stomach beneath a giant boulder on a rock-strewn slope dotted with snowdrifts dripped with blood. I came up across the marshes, onto the mountain several hours ago, warmly dressed. Fur coat and boa over the beaded dress with the long slit. Out long before the ravens wakened. Menstrual blood on the snow. A sign, along with the sheep intestines that are fastened as bait to a rope I have in my hand behind the sod piece that covers the opening to the blind. I wait, shorten the waiting with another cigarette in the holder. A weak flicker from the lighter flashes life into the pearls around my wrist, the ruby in my ring, the polished nails. I am lying on my knees now, with the high heels tucked under me, my shoulders just barely touch my kneecaps, my breasts rest on my thighs. All my senses are tuned outward toward the mountain, toward the sea. Tiny drafts sneak across my neck, down the skin on my shoulder. I hear the frail November light being tossed about outside. The last gasp from the rough sea far down below. I am not the only hunter on the mountain this night. I have my methods but still don't know what they will lead me to. Tonight is the first time in this dress, this color. A swish! The beating of wings? Just my own hoarse breath. More eagles have been seen than in a long time this year, this early-frost winter with hard-packed snow masses in the interior. It sends the eagles out here to the coast, farthest out. For hours on the beaches I have followed their drift in circles, in ovals, calmly, calmly, no hunger panic yet. Have followed the White-tailed Eagle in lazy flight on rectangular wings. Her. Larger than the male. Up to two meters, sixty centimeters between the wing tips. At the closest point, at her most curious, she bursts the lenses on my opera glasses. Glides. Glides. But not as playfully as the Golden Eagle, with its sudden pirouettes. The black velvet band at the tip of the tail waves on the young Golden Eagles, chubby with feathers down to their black claws. On the boldest ones I can see between the outer feathers the deep notches that trick the retarding air pockets when the wings flap, the steering strokes. This rests the muscles. Not many sea birds spending the winter, not all are as greedy for fish as the sea eagle, not many sheep to frighten over the cliffs any longer. Rest your muscles. Gaze precisely into the distant goal from a mountain ledge. Gaze. No young ones to feed in November. Long flights! My foot is asleep. I have to get down on my stomach again; it's good I put gunny sacks on the stone floor. A jerk on the rope! I manage a tiny peek; two ravens! Above the bait they peck and peck and flap. More of them hone in, the rope jerks, the bait is alive with greedy pecking, still no one forgets that larger birds of prey may be on the wing nearby. Suddenly the flock disperses, flees at a sharp swish. Her! She is here. Guardedly lowers herself, plants one claw on the bait and snatches it with her predator beak. When she swallows I pull the bait closer, the sod cover is off now, my hand poised to grab the claw, the rope in my mouth, ready to tie around. She is close enough. I don't have time to change position. Grab. My hand squeezes with all its might around the foot, right by the claw. So warm! I hear the wings try to open and flap. Quickly, pull, pull in so the wings have to fold back along the bird's body. Resistance. Resistance. The opening is only twenty-five centimeters wide. I brace my heel in a crack. A sudden kick. She is inside! I know she is frightened, without the advantage of long-distance vision, no light, no confidence in her wings, I know it and lash both the claws together. Then I pull her farther in, into a corner. Hoarse breathing, just a deep kya-kya from her. I let go of the rope. Confront her from the opposite corner, on my knees with my neck stuck out. Project all my senses in one direction, move forward on my knees, slowly. She is completely quiet now, has moved her eyes into position, found a direction for her wings, her beak. I have come so close that I can touch the hooked beak with my tongue. First I cut the rope around the claws. My neck is saturated with perfume. I touch the beak with the tip of my tongue, a faint rotten salt smell. I taste only brandy. I place my cheek against the bristle between the beak and the eyes. She smells of tallow here. I feel that she winks! She lets me place the boa around her feathered neck; shakes herself, afraid of being clipped, of having her neck snapped the way the eagle hunters have taught me? A swift blow and the animal is yours? When I paint the claws red, she leans her body forward slightly, three front toes and a back claw on each foot. She does not touch my brandy, but breathes wetly on me when I stroke her wings and place my hair on her neck. A long time. I have longed so much! Free myself and lift the ceiling slab, stand erect and scream. A hop and she is on my shoulder, gazing far in front of us. Together we walk to where people live. At the boarding house for fishers she sits scraping on the formica and watches me change into sweater and jeans while I gulp scorching hot coffee. It's been long enough. Outdoors she immediately takes wing, circles toward land. Up. Is gone. After this first meeting, we regularly see each other the last week in November, or else she sends a younger sister, one of the snatchers, to the eagle house on the slope. The rest of the year I sometimes have to go to the back of the clothes closet and rub my face in the beaded fabric. When I need lots of air and greater courage!

Original title: *Fyk 17.* Translated by Janet E. Rasmussen

Notes on the New Edition

Returning to *An Everyday Story* ten years later, to update and expand, has been a bit like taking up with an old friend after time spent apart. Lots of catching up to do, lots of stories to tell. And as the hours go by there are discoveries of change—new developments, new interests, new strategies—as well as recognition of the familiar. My task was to find the everyday story of a new generation of writers, to bring the anthology up to date with a half dozen or so stories published during the past decade by authors not included among the original twenty-four.

Norwegian society has undergone change in recent years just like every other in the Western world. One of the more visible developments has been the influx of immigrants and refugees from Africa, Asia and Latin America. Until quite recently the only foreign workers in Norway were from European countries, and they never arrived in large groups. In the early 1970s, however, migrant workers from underdeveloped, non-European countries flocked to Norway where unemployment was nearly nonexistent and wages were relatively high. Though an immigration ban was imposed in 1975, Norway's foreign population continued to grow as refugees, asylum seekers, and families of earlier immigrants came looking for a home. From 1960 to 1990 the percentage of foreign citizens in the total population rose from 0.6 to 3.3, changing Norway from an essentially homogeneous society to one that is multicultural.

Change of this magnitude is unsettling, for those who arrive as well as those who have to make room, and the difficult process of adjustment has been depicted in a number of recent works of fiction. Two of the stories in the original anthology focus on immigrants and refugees: "Salt" by Åsta Holth about a group of Finnish settlers in the forests of eastern Norway, and "A Vietnamese Doll" by Vigdis Stokkelien about a Norwegian couple who adopt a Vietnamese child orphaned by the Vietnam war. Holth is writing about her own ethnic group, but Stokkelien is not. Ten years later I wanted to find a recent immigrant from a non-European country who could tell the story of a newcomer in her own voice.

He Dong, from the People's Republic of China, does not represent the largest group of Asians living in Norway. (Non-

European countries with the greatest populations in Norway are Pakistan, Vietnam, Iran, Sri Lanka, Turkey and Chile.) And "A Dialogue Under the New Moon" does not give us a detailed account of what life in Norway is like for a Chinese woman. It was nonetheless my choice because He Dong has written about an experience common to all people transplanted from their homeland: the expatriate's conflicted relationship with the past. The young woman in the story is struggling to come to terms with her childhood, to integrate past with present, but even as she acknowledges the past through her memories, she realizes she must break with it. Is that not perhaps the reason for the refusal she gives her compatriot at the end of the story?

Another recent development in Norway has been the cultural and artistic renaissance of the Sami, an indigenous people with a history similar to that of the Native Americans of our own country. Written and archeological sources indicate that the Sami have been living in the northern part of the Scandinavian peninsula and on Russia's Kola peninsula for over 1000 years. It is believed that they migrated from the east, from the northern part of Russia, and the language they speak is part of the Finno-Ugric group. Today the largest Sami population, approximately 40,000, resides in Norway. Less than half that number live in Sweden, fewer than 6,000 in Finland, and only about 2,000 Sami are living in Russia. For the Sami, however, their country is *Sapmi*, a word signifying all of Samiland, from Norway in the west to Russia in the east, and all the Sami people.

Traditionally, the Sami have engaged in hunting, fishing, farming and reindeer herding. Although reindeer herding continues to be the Sami people's most important cultural symbol, the number who are herding and leading a semi-nomadic existence today is but a fraction of the total population. One of the reasons for this is limited grazing area—the land cannot support any more herds than it already has—but it is also true that for over a century the Sami people have been under considerable pressure to suppress their own culture and assimilate with the dominant culture. In the Norwegian part of *Sapmi* there are many Sami who still live in Sami settlements and speak the Sami language, but there are perhaps as many who have left their traditional way of life and become integrated members of Norwegian communities.

The most invasive aspect of Norway's policy of cultural assimilation was undoubtedly the requirement that the education of Sami children be conducted entirely in Norwegian. Because of the nomadic lifestyle of their parents, many children were forced to live at boarding schools where Norwegian was the only language spoken. Needless to say, these children were taught nothing at school about the traditions and culture of their own people. For some, the undermining and stigmatization of native language and culture were persuasion enough, and parents came to the decision that they would not speak Sami with their children. As they saw it, teaching them Sami would be a handicap at school—the faster they assimilated, the better.

But there were also Sami who tried to stem the tide and defend their rights as a people, and already at the turn of the century they formed organizations whose activities included the publication of magazines and newspapers in the Sami language. The movement didn't really gain momentum until a half century later, however. In 1956 a Nordic Sami Council was founded and this included all of *Sapmi* except the Soviet Union. Efforts to attain full self-determination culminated in 1988 when a bill was passed in the Norwegian parliament calling for the establishment of a Sami Assembly. In 1989 the King of Norway, the late Olav V, formally inaugurated the first Sami Assembly. This body is meant to represent all Sami living in Norway and its mandate is to preserve and defend Sami language and culture, and to determine further development. The future of Sami culture and society is now in the hands of the Sami.

As the Sami moved toward political autonomy, they also took measures to revive their language and culture. Today there is a thriving arts community dedicated to rejuvenating the cultural heritage of the Sami and instilling in the people a sense of pride and dignity. The Sami's heritage has its origin in an ancient mythology that inspired epic poems which have been transmitted orally over the centuries. Legends and folktales are also a part of their oral tradition and together with the olden poetry form an important source for contemporary Sami authors.

In the story by Kirsti Paltto the fairy tales Sire-Elle is forbidden to tell come to symbolize freedom from the oppression of her husband and his family. As exotic as the elf-woman seems, clad in silk shawl, tassles and reindeer moccasins, the story of her life has the ring of familiarity. The exploitation and insults Sire-Elle suffers bring to mind Gro Holm's "Life on the Løstøl Farm" and Inger Hagerup's "The Woman at Klepp" from the original *An Everyday Story.* There is one major difference, however: Paltto is raising issues of ethnicity as well as gender; Sire-Elle has been stigmatized both as a Sami and as a woman.

These same concerns are present in Inger Haldis Halvari's story even though it has an urban setting and takes place much closer to the present than does Paltto's. In "Little Lake, Hear Me" we see how close the situation of the young Sami woman is to that of an immigrant wife and mother. Cut off from family and friends and the nurturing environment of her homeland, she feels isolated and homesick. Absorbed by his work, her husband largely ignores her and is impatient with her because she is part of a world he left behind and even less assimilated with the new culture than he is.

The stories of He Dong, Kirsti Paltto and Inger Haldis Halvari represent the voices of ethnic minority women living in Norway and *Sapmi* today. Halvari is a Norwegian Sami, but Paltto lives in the Finnish part of *Sapmi*. In keeping with the Sami's disregard for national borders, and impressed by Paltto's contribution to recent Sami literature, I made the choice of including her in this anthology. Fiction by minority authors such as these allows us a glimpse into the culture and experience of their particular groups, and it also shows us Norway and Norwegians from a new perspective. The voices of these women introduce change and differentness to the everyday story of Norway's women, but the stories they tell also have much in common both with those of an earlier generation and, as we shall see, with those of their contemporaries.

The young female protagonist in "Mother Moon" by Merethe Lindstrøm is awash in feelings of loneliness and homelessness as she journeys toward her mother and her childhood home. "I've lived too long in another place," she muses, and it's not clear whether she means this literally or figuratively or both. The homelessness Lindstrøm writes about is experienced by a generation of young people who have grown up in a world that seems to be in a constant state of flux. Loneliness, often their only companion, is deep-rooted, reaching back to the child's longing for a mother's love and approval.

The relationship between mother and child, central to "Mother Moon," is at the heart of several other stories as well. While Lindstrøm views the relationship from the daughter's vantage point, Marit Nicolaysen focuses on the mother's point of view, and Laila Stien shifts perspective from mother to son. The mothers in these stories are all single, another example of the changing Norwegian society—today it is not at all uncommon to find single parent families in Norway. Nicolaysen's subject is a mother, thirty-five years old, who is struggling to be both mother and father to her teen-age son. Earning a living and maintaining a home can be tough, trying to get through to a teen-age son even more so. Nicolaysen's portrayal is frank and realistic, but her tone is lighter than Lindstrøm's, and the mother's anger and frustration are offset by her wry sense of humor.

The mother and child in the two stories by Laila Stien are part of an extended family that lives on a small farm in Northern Norway. Anita and her newborn live with her parents who provide the only real support she has. At some later time, Anita takes a job in the city and makes weekend visits to the farm where her son lives with his grandparents, aunt and uncle, and cousin. What's missing is the boy's father, an absence made especially poignant in the second story told from the little boy's point of view.

Stien writes traditional, realistic prose and there is a strong sense of place and time in her stories. They tell of a way of life in a specific part of the country and recall examples of regional literature in the original *An Everyday Story* by Ragnhild Jølsen, Ingeborg Refling Hagen and Gro Holm. Another author Stien brings to mind is Cora Sandel, who wrote two memorable novels set in Northern Norway, *Krane's Café* and *Alberta and Jacob*. Like Sandel, Stien is a master of the short story, and she also shares Sandel's remarkable ability to experience the world with a child's sensibility.

Though realism is still the dominant trend in Norwegian literature at the end of the twentieth century, experimentation with form and language continues to have many exponents. Experimental fiction can sometimes seem obscure, even confusing, for the text is governed less by external reality than by the author's imagination. The author introduces a sense of playfulness to literature and to language, inviting the reader to open herself to unexpected associations and connections and to see the world in a new context. "My Father's Footsteps in the Room" by Gro Dahle is an example of this kind of text. In a language rich in metaphors and visual imagery, Dahle depicts a confrontation between a father and daughter. With subtle suggestion and measured repetition, Dahle carefully increases the tension until it reaches a peak of emotional and dramatic intensity. It is interesting that the only piece in the original anthology dealing with a daughter's relationship with her father was "Dancefjord (The Sailor)" by Cecilie Løveid, another of Norway's most innovative and experimental writers. And that in both pieces the father-daughter relationship is charged with erotic undertones.

Sissel Lie's writing is so original, both in subject matter and style, that she doesn't seem to resemble anyone else. But her stories are about women, and female identity in particular, and that, of course, connects her with many of Norway's women writers, past and present. Moreover, Lie has the gift of the storyteller, however unconventional her tales may seem, and can take her place alongside all the other storytellers in this volume. Lie is intrigued by the past, by the stories of women who lived their lives two and three centuries ago. She looks back in time so she might better imagine the future, and in her fiction history becomes an example that can offer modern women new perspectives and strategies.

This expanded anthology of Norwegian women's fiction features ten of the everyday stories written in Norway during the past ten years. There are, of course, many more. Another editor might have chosen different stories, perhaps different authors as well. Some of Norway's finest women writers, whose novels have been bestsellers, have not been included here because I chose to limit my selection to short stories and texts, not excerpts. The eight authors represented here are continuing the tradition started by nineteenth century feminist writers such as Camilla Collett and Amalie Skram. They are also moving in new directions, as they explore the challenges women face in a changing society and experiment with narrative forms. Above all, they tell compelling stories about female lives and experiences in a small country on Europe's northern edge.

He Dong

(b.1960)

Until 1985 when she came to Norway for post-graduate study in biology, He Dong's home was Beijing. Her education in China was in the field of sport physiology. She studied at China University of Physical Education and upon completion of her degree in 1982, stayed on at the University, teaching and doing research. Following her post-graduate studies at the University of Oslo, He Dong has taught Tai Chi Chuan and worked at various hospitals and research institutes in Norway. She currently divides her workday between a research position at the University of Oslo and her own acupuncture clinic.

Her spare time is devoted to literature and writing. He Dong has served as editor of two different Chinese publications in Norway, *Nordlys* and *Hua Sheng*, and she has also edited and translated an anthology of contemporary Norwegian poetry for Chinese publication. Her own poems and short stories, translated from the Chinese, have appeared in Norwegian journals and anthologies since 1989. A collection of her poems was published in China in 1990, and her first major publication in Norway was also a book of poetry. *Himmel Innsjø* (1994), with poems in both Chinese and Norwegian translation, speaks of the longing and sense of loss, the search for identity of a person living in exile.

These same themes are echoed in "A Dialogue Under the New Moon." The dialogue is between a young Chinese couple who try to assuage feelings of homelessness by swapping stories. Stories belong to the past, of course—they are memories. And on this occasion memory takes each of the storytellers back to a childhood that is both distant and troubling.

A Dialogue Under the New Moon

"How are things with you?"
"Oh, can't complain. Trying to pass the time."
"How do you pass the time?"
"Day by day."

We glanced at each other. Our smiles were neither bitter nor sweet.

"Well how about today? How shall we pass the time?"

"Let's try telling stories," I said casually.

It was a Friday evening, we were sitting side by side on the wharf. Winter was mild in Norway this year. A couple of boats were crossing back and forth over the fjord. The waves rolled in, soft and silent. Up in the heavens, a multitude of glittering stars circled the new moon.

The moon, only a sliver.

"Hey, look. That's your boat isn't it?"

He pointed to a ferry, which slowly approached the wharf and slowly departed again. "What time of day do you feel happiest?"

"Mornings, on the ferry."

"Why's that?"

"I'm playing a game with somebody." I took a sidelong glance at his eyes, which were gleaming with curiosity, and then went on: "A woman. Every morning we always take the same ferry—the only one that doesn't vibrate so much it wakes me up. I have a set place on board. No, there aren't any reserved seats. You can sit any place you want. But I've picked out a seat for myself. Whenever I have a chance, I take that spot. That's how it all started more than a month ago. Well, there was this one morning. As usual, I took the same seat and turned on my Walkman so I could doze and listen to music. But for some reason I kept having the odd feeling that someone was staring hard at my back. I tried turning my head a little to look. Wow, there was a woman, about forty or fifty years old, in a black fur coat. See, it was snowing out and terribly cold. We looked at each other a second, and then she lowered her head and went back to reading the newspaper in her hands. From that time on, I noticed that she sat in the same seat every day—she seemed to have staked out her territory." I lifted my right hand and drew a small circle—a perfectly round circle—with my index finger. "Since then I've never been able to free myself of this burning sensation coming from behind. Once in a while somebody would get to my seat before me. So I'd have to find a place in the row ahead or behind. And then she would move too. What an amazing feeling! When you know somebody is always staring at you from a certain direction, especially from behind, you always want to try to turn the tables."

"So how did you react?"

"I gave up my favorite seat and started to move toward the back. I decided to take a whole morning to observe her. I moved toward the back. But she did too. I moved two rows back, and she moved two rows back as well. Pretty soon we had moved from the original rows far back in the boat. Finally one day I managed to get on board first, after planning it all out, and found a seat on the very last row. Ha! I can still remember the way I felt then."

"What happened?"

"She wasn't on board that day."

We were quiet for a long moment. He flicked off the long curling ash of his cigarette and asked, with long pauses between each word, "What were you really trying to prove?"

"Oh, I was just amusing myself," I shrugged and tossed the ball to him. "Now it's your turn."

"My turn? You mean me?" He pointed at the space between his eyebrows.

"Well, the most interesting time is the little period just before I go to bed at night, when I listen to pop music and rub a thin razor blade against the tender skin on the underside of my left wrist. Gently, very gently. Just when the razor is about to cut into the skin, but not quite . . . such a strange feeling . . ."

"What kind of feeling?" I asked when he broke off.

He took a new cigarette and lit it. "Homeless."

I asked for a cigarette.

"You said you don't smoke, right?" he said in a pitiless tone.

I lifted my head and looked up at the cool sliver of moon.

"Hey, artist, can you paint the moon, too?"

"I'd rather paint the sun."

"The sun?" At that very moment we felt the cold attack us. We went into a café, sat down face to face, and each ordered a beer.

"Happy New Year! Skål!"

"Skål! Happy New Year!" I calculated the date and realized we must be into February already.

The new year. New Year's Eve I leaned against the window and counted the cars creeping by like snails. It was very strange this year. After counting a hundred, I still didn't feel the slightest bit drunk.

I don't remember when we started wandering back into the past.

"I trained as a swimmer when I was young," he said after a while. "We were all about fourteen or fifteen. Any time there was a competition, we were so nervous that everybody tried to dive into the water first. For a tenth of a second advantage.

There was this guy with long legs on our team, a specialist in the butterfly. I remember one time he got the outermost lane—bad luck. He was so nervous he started his jump before the starter called 'ready.' He didn't hear the starting shot and knew he'd made a false start. So he tried to pull his chest back while he was in midair. It looked like he was trying to hop back onto the platform, but that was impossible, of course. He lost his balance, fell sideways, and hit the side of the pool." He clapped his hands hard, and said "Bang! Four broken ribs."

"A couple of seconds," I was talking to myself. "Time—nobody has managed to define it. That starting shot, according to Pavlov's theory, was a conditioned inhibition of a conditioned reflex." Suddenly I tugged at a long, long silk thread from the past's forgotten memories, and I heard the shot—earsplitting . . .

"One of the comrades on my school team was executed by gunshot. So young. According to the authorities' regulations, the bullet had to be paid for by his parents. It cost the same as an ice cream cone. Before we heard about his death, none of us girls would accept him as a comrade. Because he wasn't smart in school and because he liked to fight."

"You know, I called home to China on New Year's Day and for the first time in my life, I told my parents I love them!" He took a large gulp before I had time to lift my glass.

"You must have been watching one of those American TV series. I bet you shocked your old mom so much you gave her high blood pressure."

"She's already got it," he remarked ironically and shook his head.

"I still haven't been able to break the old commandments. I envy that young girl in the film *Landscape in the Mist*. At least she had a chance to look for her father."

Again it was quiet for a long while. And then our conversation brought us back to an even earlier period in the past.

"When I was six years old I had a best girlfriend. She was four. We were neighbors and played together all day long. I remember one Monday we had a long discussion and decided to use windows instead of doors when we wanted to visit each other. We found a bunch of stones and blocked the door. It caused a lot of trouble for the grownups. One of our neighbors was this big capitalist-lackey. He was a professor, educated at Cambridge. He took the stones away and made me shut the window again. We hated him so much for that. I saw absolutely no reason why people had to go in and out through doors. It was a time for revolutions, after all. Most of the doors in the hall had been torn down and used for huge catapults. We had also organized a Little Red Guard—ten or so kids around six or seven years old. Every day we gathered in front of the professor's room and shouted 'capitalist-lackey, so and so, running dog!' We waved Mao's little red book, proud as peacocks. So he had to go in and out with his head bowed, eat dinner in the canteen with his head bowed, right up to the time he died, quietly and without any fuss, with his head bowed."

I swirled my glass and stared blankly at the foam on the beer. He asked me, "Have you finished your story?" I just nodded.

"So that means it's my turn again." He put out his cigarette, which had burned down to a stub. "I don't remember it very clearly any longer. But I think it was when I was nine or ten years old. Next to our apartment block they built a straw hut and moved a capitalist-lackey in there. He was always being led away by the Red Guard and denounced in public. Even during the few short periods he was at home, he was always in danger of being dragged out and humiliated by the Little Red Guard. One day he came home with a *yin-yang head*. I thought it was so strange and funny. Right after lunch I took a comrade along and ordered the capitalist-lackey to come out. We stood there arrogantly in front of him and followed the usual routine—shouted slogans, read quotations from Chairman Mao, listed the accusations against him, denounced him, and read Chairman Mao's quotations again, and shouted slogans again . . . And finally we demanded to feel the shaved side of his head. I just remember that he bent over, extended his head and said, 'Dear children, I'm already an old man of sixty. What's the point of rubbing my head?' My little comrade and I took turns feeling his head for few minutes. Then we jumped around and laughed, 'Fun, fun! Let us feel it one more time!' He extended his head again and repeated, 'Dear children, I'm already an old man of sixty. What's the point of rubbing my head?' 'Yes, yes, fun! It's fun. Let us feel it one more time.'"

"What happened afterwards?"

"There wasn't any afterwards," he said briskly.

Oh mama, we were just children.

Yin-yang head: One side of the head shaved by the Red Guards.

"Have you asked them? I mean have you seriously asked your parents what really happened?"

"Yes, when I was at university." I decided to change the subject. "How do you like my ring?"

"I couldn't wear a ring. I'd feel like I was locked in a dark room."

"Aren't we in one now?"

He laughed, and I laughed too. With a bitter smile on one side of the face and a sweet one on the other.

"Skål to Ma-year, the Year of the Horse!" In spite of everything we skåled the lunar calendar after the solar calendar, no matter what month it was.

I looked at the beer glass he held up and said, "Ma-year, is a lucky year. 'Ma-dao-cheng-gong,' 'Wan Ma-ben-teng,' 'Sai-weng-shi-Ma,' 'Che-sui-Ma-long,' 'Mang-ren-xia-Ma' . . . Oh no, no, forget the last one. I've gone through the dictionaries, you see— all together there are forty-eight sayings about Ma. Most of them are fairly nice."

"What nonsense! 'Bing-huang-Ma-luan'—The war's noise and chaos!" He put down the glass he had lifted so high. He used only one saying to reject my four.

The night was deep. By chance we both glanced at the leg of the statue outside the window. The leg was extended in a kick. He held my left hand firmly between his two palms. From cold to warm, and from warm to cold again.

"Let's not talk any more," he said.

"You have a girl's hands."

"Let's say a woman's hands."

"No, a girl's hands."

"Let's give it a try."

"No." I pulled my hand out of his warm hands.

"Will not, can not, dare not . . . ?"

"Just not," I said feebly, not looking up at him.

Two "see ya"s and we went our separate ways.

Why?

I tramped on fragments of moonlight shattered by raindrops,

"Ma-dao-cheng-gong": "Success from the very start."

"Wan Ma-ben-teng": "Ten thousand horses galloping away."

"Sai-weng-shi-Ma": "Success in disaster."

"Che-shui-Ma-long": "A constant stream of horses and wagons."

"Mang-ren-xia-Ma": "A blind man on a blind horse: full speed toward disaster."

tramped on fragments of my own shadow shattered by rain-drops. I stamped my foot down and the echo sped away, so clear, so resonant, like a shot just before dawn.

The new moon, that's why.

Original title: *En dialog under nymånen*.   Translated by Judith Messick

Kirsti Paltto

(b. 1947)

In 1971 Kirsti Paltto published a collection of short stories, *Soakŋu*, and became the first woman to publish a book in the Sami language. She has gone on to make a remarkable contribution to the recent blossoming of Sami literature in several capacities: as an author, a teacher, an administrator in the newly formed Sami Authors' Association from 1979-87, and as the head of her own publishing venture, Gielas, founded in 1989. Her literary production includes short stories, novels, poems, radio plays and, not least, books for children.

The daughter of farmers, Kirsti Paltto was born in Outakoski, a village in the larger community of Utsjoki which is located in the Finnish part of Samiland. After a year at a Christian Folk High School, Paltto entered a Teacher Training School from which she earned a certificate in 1971. She has taught in both elementary and secondary schools, but for the most part has been engaged as a full-time author and promoter of Sami literature.

"Looking Back" is taken from the collection titled *Guovtteoaivvat nisu* (*The Two-headed Woman*, 1989). Central to the story is the intolerance of Christianity toward traditional Sami culture and beliefs. Missionaries arrived in Samiland as early as the thirteenth century but their influence was sporadic until much later. In the eighteenth and nineteenth centuries, when pietism swept across Scandinavia, zealous disciples brought their message to the far north, this time with more widespread and lasting results. The songs Sire-Elle sings and the tales she longs to tell her little daughter are part of a rich oral tradition that has been passed down from generation to generation.

The translation below is based on a New Norwegian translation from the original Sami which appeared in the anthology *Våja våja nana nana* (1991).

Looking Back

Today is the official day of mourning. Sunday and sunshine so bright that the snow sparkles. But in my heart sorrow will not awake, does not even stir. When I awoke early this morning, I was calm, and I sensed that nothing bound me here any longer.

It was as if a long imprisonment had ended, as if I finally was a free person who had the right to think as I wanted.

My conscience pricks me, urging me to grieve, but even though I prayed last night for God to let sorrow come, it still didn't come. And it won't come either.

I was just a young girl, barely sixteen years old, when I arrived at the farm as hired help. I sat on the chopping block by the door, lonely and bashful, after Father had cracked the whip over his horse and left me alone on this unfamiliar farm. The mistress poured coffee for me and asked me to come to the table to drink. I went without looking at anyone. The master spoke to me. I answered him quietly and looked down at the table. That's how bashful I was.

But even though I was bashful, I had a cheerful disposition, and had no difficulty talking and laughing once I got to know people. The people on the farm were Christian, and the master himself would travel around the countryside speaking at meetings. The whole clan were known to be religious, God-fearing folk. And some of them lived here at Njáigoguolban, the place I came to on that winter's day forty-two years ago. They needed a girl who was willing to work, and so I was.

Without a peep I did everything they asked me to do. Without a whimper I was both milkmaid and nurserymaid. I had little time to sleep, and the ration of bread for the hired girl was skimpy. Skimpy, though the farm was rich, just like everyone in the clan. I didn't get much in wages either, but after Christmas I had a new pair of reindeer moccasins to show off. At the time, that was a great honor for poor folk's children, almost something to be envied.

There was a handsome bachelor on the farm, the only son. In the winter darkness he began to show up in the cow barn when I was milking; now and then he shoveled the manure out through the barn window and gave the cows water. He joked around and made me laugh, though I almost didn't dare—it wasn't proper to laugh with boys who would one day inherit the farm. Afterwards I was ashamed. But even so, it was nice that someone was interested in me. And he was interested enough that he started putting his arm around me once in a while.

During the winter, when I'd finished everything the master and mistress wanted me to do, I slept on a pelt in the main house. Sometimes I was so tired I couldn't see straight, and at night my arms and legs ached. Still, I folded my hands every night and thanked God for allowing me to work as a hired girl so

I didn't have to fight over the few scraps of food that were put on the table at home.

In the summer I moved out to the storehouse. As I was carrying my bedclothes across the farmyard, Ásllat walked by and winked at me. I didn't understand what he meant, but the very first night he stole into the storehouse and lay down beside me. I pushed him out of my bed. He fell against a chest and swore, and then he pounced on me. Violently he pulled off my pants and stuck that horribly long, thick cudgel of his in my crotch. It didn't bother him that I hit or scolded him, he just laughed. It didn't bother him that I whimpered in pain when he forced himself into my girl-hole. It didn't bother him that I cried. He just did his business, buttoned up his pants and left.

After a week I started throwing up. I tried to hide it as well as I could, but my mother-in-law found me once while I was washing. Her questions were hard and cold, and I told her the truth.

Good Lord, what a ruckus there was! Everyone was convinced it was my fault Ásllat had raped me. The entire clan gathered to figure out what should be done. The next day they'd decided that it was probably best to hide the child away, give it away to someone, or send me down to their relatives on the coast so I could give birth there. They talked as if I didn't even exist. And finally they agreed on the coast, where I wouldn't be able to bring shame onto their family with my bastard. Then in my misery I stood up and said I would rather go home than travel to strangers out on the coast.

"Hold your tongue," my mother-in-law burst out, and announced that in the fall, as soon as there was enough snow for travel, I would go down to the coast; until then I'd better hide my condition.

"That's the way it is," she declared. "We must protect our honor. In our family it simply won't do for the hired girl to start having babies. And don't think you can run away—we have people to keep an eye on you, don't you forget." What could I do? I felt ashamed.

And so the summer days passed and autumn drew near. I don't know what conclusions the family and the other relatives had come to, but one day my father-in-law came to me and ordered me to his room. Ásllat and my mother-in-law were sitting there.

"Sire-Elle," my father-in-law began. "You are a hard-working and willing girl, created to be a man's wife. You know all about farm work and aren't afraid to lend a hand, even though you're

. . . You've made yourself useful on the farm, and we've all seen that you're a blessing for us. You don't ask for too much, but obediently do as you're told. Sire-Elle, you were born to be a wife. And for that reason we want you to marry Ásllat."

"And," my mother-in-law said emphatically, "you should be happy you're marrying into such a prosperous farm, you, the daughter of poor Leastto-Jovnna. We've taken pity on the child you are carrying—it shall be our child, born into our family."

I had no say in the matter, I don't even know if Ásllat had been allowed to speak his mind. But our married life began around the time of Michaelmas with a large wedding. You could hear people saying that the bridal couple were like gold and silver. Adorned and radiant.

In February, during a hard frost, I gave birth. A girl, a skinny little girl, light as a scrap of hide, came into the world. My situation on the farm was no better after I became a daughter-in-law. I worked just as much as before, only now I had my own child who kept me awake at night. I got little sleep and became pale and thin. But life had to go on—there was nothing else to do.

Oh, how I loved this little girl, this tiny little thing, who was named Ánnemuorji. I talked and sang and smiled at her when we were alone. Her brown eyes were my suns, and her little hand my support. She was the only one in the house with whom I felt secure, and she was the only one to whom I spoke. But always in secret, for the others on the farm didn't like laughter and idle talk. Ásllat had often remarked that I spoiled the child when I made her happy. Still, I couldn't bear hearing Ánnemuorji cry, and I insisted that I be allowed to hold her on my lap.

They even forced me to go outside or into another room so the child wouldn't get used to being held. Children weren't created for that. While she's still in the cradle board, a child should learn that suffering is sin's just reward. You shouldn't grow accustomed to the pleasures of the world in your mother's arms. There would be time to rejoice in heaven.

One time I was sitting in the loft above the bedroom, breast-feeding the child. I had my back to the door and thought everyone was outdoors. I sang for my Ánnemuorji, told her a scary story about the spirits of the underworld and smiled at her. We were having a cozy and wonderful time together. It was loveliest when the two of us were alone—everything else vanished and seemed far away. Suddenly there was someone behind me, and before I knew it someone pinched my naked breast—it hurt so much I nearly dropped the baby on the floor.

"Listen here, daughter-in-law, don't bring the child up in sin. Don't tell those old ghost stories—say The Lord's Prayer instead."

I jumped up and turned to face my father-in-law. My God, if I'd only dared, I'd have boxed that hypocrite's ear. I'd have given him such a swat that he'd remember for all eternity whose breast he'd pinched.

But I didn't strike my father-in-law, I just swallowed and felt ashamed. I was on the verge of tears, but managed to hold them back. I buttoned my sweater and started getting the bed ready for Ánnemuorji. My father-in-law stood behind me reciting God's word, what the Holy Scriptures said about frivolity, and what the punishment was.

Fortunately the old goat died that year. My mother-in-law wasn't so bad—she didn't pinch my breast at least—but she too could grumble and scold, order me around, and hold forth about how the wife of her only son ought to act.

Oh, how happy I was the day we put my mother-in-law to rest in the churchyard. I thought that now Ásllat and I could finally have a decent life together.

But dammit all!

Ásllat held his father's and mother's life up as an example for us, and he changed and became just like them. Day after day he nagged about how his mother used to do this or that, how good her blood dumplings used to be, precisely what time she used to go to the barn and so on and so forth. My father-in-law and mother-in-law lived among us even though both of them were beneath the sod.

And Ásllat became just as religious as they had been and spent his time travelling around making speeches. He was often away for weeks at a time at prayer meetings, and then I had to run the farm and take care of the kids. We had a child almost every year, thirteen all together.

When Ásllat was at home, he lay in bed, or sat at the end of the table, preaching and talking with his brothers and sisters in the faith. I prepared the food and made the coffee and brought it to the table. I wasn't allowed to take part in the discussions. A wife was supposed to serve her husband just as Sara in ancient times was Abraham's servant. Ásllat never gave me help bringing up the children, couldn't even be bothered to change diapers when I was in the barn.

On top of this, Ásllat started telling me I couldn't talk with other women. He'd heard that we encouraged each other and badmouthed our menfolk, though all we really did was tell about what good husbands we had.

I was constantly tired during these years and often cross with the children. But after a while my self-denial and fear turned into anger. I could hardly bear looking at Ásllat's holy face anymore. Still, I was the wife on this farm, and half of everything fell to me. So I too should have a say. And that started to happen as well, almost by itself.

One evening when I came in from the barn, Ásllat was sitting by the wood stove with Vielte-Jovnnása Máret, a woman from a place not far from here. Red in the face, he sat lecturing on the Scriptures and the Word of God. They were so buried in the Word of God that they didn't notice I'd come in, in spite of the clanging milk buckets and the terrible racket I made when I banged them down on the table. Something started to seethe inside of me, like an overflowing pot of porridge that's about to boil, not just boil, but boil over. Then my eye fell on the water dipper that was just within reach. I reached down into the pail, filled the dipper with ice-cold water amd threw it at Ásllat and Máret, right in their faces.

There was a hell of a commotion! Ásllat shot up like an arrow, even though he was in the middle of the Holy Scriptures, and would have attacked me had he dared, but he wasn't about to start fighting with me with Máret looking on. He did say I was crazy though, and sputtered and snorted before he finally got away, leaving his spiritual girlfriend, Máret, behind.

I laughed, a brazen, devilish laugh.

Afterwards Ásllat hit me. At night when the children were sleeping. He could certainly have beaten me black and blue, but I scratched and bit my husband's face. Many years went by like this. I grew ever more hardened and I railed more and more. I didn't care about anything. I couldn't stand my husband. We fought, and I could have killed both him and me. But I didn't kill anyone, and so I became spiteful. Completely. When I was young, I had been so gentle and meek, but now I clenched my teeth and hated. And I did the work, the same as before.

Ásllat despised me and lorded it over me up until he got sick and was bedridden. He was an old man, but I was still young and vigorous, in my prime. Forty-two years gone to suffering, scolding and nursing my hatred. Why? Was this the meaning of my life? What should I have done? Called a halt to it, looked around and thought things over? Should I have grabbed hold of Ásllat's wings, looked him straight in the eye and asked why we were living as we were?

I didn't want to give in to Ásllat, not even when he still held me at night and I longed for closeness and a better life, away from the quarreling, away from the hate. I didn't want to, because I'd been hurt too badly, too deeply.

Underneath, Ásllat had a kind nature, but he'd hidden it behind his faith and the Scriptures; he was too busy trying to follow his parents' example, too busy looking at the sins of others to be aware of his own actions. Life could have turned out differently. I could have controlled myself, I could have kept myself from scolding. I could have been humbler. Ásllat doesn't deserve all the blame, but only now can I admit it.

Now.

Only now on the official day of mourning. Now that I'm starting to soften, now that my thoughts are starting to work free. I bring out my nicest clothes from the storehouse, the ones I wore when I was married. I haven't been allowed to use them, because dressing up was a sin. I put on my fancy jacket, drape the silk shawl across my shoulders, fasten the silver brooch, let the tassles swing. I'm an elf-woman, a fairytale-woman. White reindeer moccasins on my feet, black leggings. Fairytale-woman. Elf-woman. On the edge of fairytale, the forbidden boundary of fairytale.

How we used to tell fairytales when I was a child. On this farm storytelling wasn't allowed. That's how our children went out into the world, away from two evil people. They've scarcely been back home. Four died. Ánnemuorji is a drunk in Helsinki. Piera has been in jail three times, Ánde is a crook in Oalgenjárga, Sire wanders around in a madhouse. The others live normal lives, whatever that means. Only Katariinná and Máijá have had schooling and today they are teachers.

Official day of mourning. But where is my sorrow? Soon the relatives will be here. Soon I'll be ready to accompany you on your last journey, Ásllat. You've been lying in your coffin for a week already, but today you'll be consecrated to the earth.

I am dressed in my finery, I am ready to stand on the edge of your grave and watch them throw sand down on you. I am ready to leave you there, and I am prepared to start living my own life in the years yet to be given me.

Original title: *Eit attersyn*. Translated by Katherine Hanson

Inger Haldis Halvari

(b. 1952)
Inger Haldis Halvari lives in the Norwegian part of Samiland. She is from Tana, which is located in the northeastern corner of Finnmark, Norway's northernmost county. At this point in her career Halvari is best known as an author of books for children. For a people whose children were denied schooling in their mother tongue for so many years, children's literature has a particularly important role to play, not least in instilling a sense of pride in the children's own culture and language.

In "Little Lake, Hear Me!" Halvari is focusing on adult issues, but one senses the presence of the child throughout—both the child to whom the woman has recently given birth and the child within her. Ánne's lake is the lake of her childhood. It is her connection with a past that reaches back beyond her childhood, and with the natural world that has been home to her people as long as they have been a people. A cherished legacy of that past is the *joik*, the Sami's traditional mode of singing. The *joik* is both poetry and music; some *joiks* are epic, relating ancient myths, legends and history, others are much shorter and more personal. A Sami will respond to something or someone that has moved her by singing, or chanting a *joik*.

"Little Lake, Hear Me!" first appeared in the Sami journal *Sápmi* (1985-86). The translation below, however, was based on a Norwegian translation of this story published in the anthology *Vája vája nana nana* (1991).

Little Lake, Hear Me

So many sounds disturb your peace of mind on a Saturday evening, other evenings too, as far as that goes. Cars and motorcycles rush up and down the streets. All kinds of voices blend in with the noise of the traffic. A boat announces its arrival. Ánne has just put the baby to sleep. When she hears the boat's whistle she runs to the window, looks at the clock. Oh, here comes the boat from home, how I wish it were bringing visitors to me.

She looks out, knowing full well they're not expecting anyone now. But can you know for sure? She listens. To sounds outdoors, and sounds indoors. Above her, below her, there are people everywhere.

But she is so alone. She cries out: "Damn, dammitall! I wish I could say just one single word to another human being. I wonder what Biera's doing now?"

Ánne can feel the storm gathering again, and with it the scene from last night.

She walks from window to window, stops in front of the mirror. "Wedding gift!" She wrinkles her nose at her mirror image. "I'm going to do it now. If I don't do it now, I never will."

Slowly Ánne takes her clothes off. Takes off the sweater the baby spit up on. Takes off her pants and stockings. Surrounded by many different sounds, behind thick concrete walls, Ánne stands naked before the mirror.

"Wedding gift," she says through her teeth.

"You are getting this so Biera will have a pretty and stylish wife for years to come. For the mirror always tells the truth."

Those were the wedding wishes from Biera's uncle. And how the wedding guests had laughed—were some of them maybe still laughing?

The mirror doesn't lie!

Ánne covers her eyes with her hands, clenches her teeth, tenses all her muscles. When she takes her hands away, she sees her heavy, streaked breasts. Her nipples are red and sore. The baby suckles so vigorously. Or am I the one not doing it right?

Ánne gently strokes her nipples, but they're so terribly sore. She's never had breasts like her girl friends. They had pretty, pointed breasts. Hers were like two rising loaves of bread! She'd always been embarrassed and tried to hide them. Once a boy shouted at her: "You old cow!"

Ánne turns around in front of the mirror. Sees her round body. Squeezes her stomach, her hands are full of flabby, quivering skin. She feels and looks! The mirror doesn't lie, it tells that she has had a child. Only four weeks ago the baby was still in her womb. Then she was allowed to be round.

Raindrops start to splash. Ánne stiffens before the mirror. A scream is forcing its way out. Far off she hears an old cow coming closer and closer. Ánne has seen it for a long time. Its udder and stomach sag, its thighs are like mountains. She clenches her teeth again to keep herself from screaming. The cars driving by seem to be calling for stylish and pretty women too.

No doubt Biera remembers his uncle's words. That's why he's gone out now, to look for a stylish and pretty woman he can sit next to . . . lie next to, whom he can caress, kiss. Poor Biera has taken so many exams, he needs to be with other people. It's every person's right to go out on the town and have a beer.

"See other people!"

I'm not a person, I'm an old cow. When my breasts are full, the milk runs, and the baby has to suckle. If he came now, today, the poor tired man, I'd make him listen to me.

I want to go up north where you, my deep black lake, are. Tomorrow when the boat announces its arrival, I'll be standing on the pier, and with me I'll have the little baby I brought into the world. There will come a time when she, too, will have to wait for a tired husband.

Ánne sinks down onto her clothes. She claws the floor with her hands and cries. "You are so far away, my lake, I can't reach you, can't reach!" Ánne cries and repeats: "Can't reach." When the clouds lift a little, she sits up and whispers: "Little lake, you've drawn me to you since childhood, when I was alone, when poisonous snakes crept into my school work." Ánne stops and sighs. Her eyes are swollen. Her throat is sore.

"Little lake, if only I could come to you. I have gathered up so much that you could have kept for me. There are thousands of people here, but they just rush along, looking straight ahead.

"Little lake, hear me!

I'm so unhappy, I'm so alone. The worst was last night. I was taking care of the baby around midnight. Biera was awake too. He didn't like it that the baby was crying. And I was carrying her around so Biera could get some rest. I do that at night too.

But first let me tell about what made me happy. In the evening Biera bathed the little one for the first time. Oh, how it warmed my heart. It was so wonderful listening to Biera talk to the child.

Biera's eyes were beaming, and I thought to myself I do love you.

Biera sat down beside us, we were three. Father's strong hand stroked the child's head, the other hand stroked his wife's naked shoulder. All my sorrows disappeared. I was up north under the birch tree, and the moss underneath me was so soft. The summer breeze cradled us. And the depth of my love was as deep as you. Love had many depths.

We slept so peacefully. When the baby woke up again, the joy was still burning in me. Changing the diaper wasn't a burden. I hurried back to bed to let her breastfeed. Biera was awake. He watched and smiled warmly. I could have started to *joik* right there in the middle of the night, but I didn't dare. Biera would have asked me to stop. He didn't like my songs. He said they belonged to a bygone time.

I didn't want my happiness to end there. The baby, who was no longer only mine, suckled at my breast, Biera was behind us. Two warm hands took hold of me. He was so close to me. His body glowed.

Nothing was as good as his firm, warm body. I wasn't just a dishwasher after all. I nursed the baby, our little baby. At my back the man who also needed me, wanted me, was breathing.

Sweetly I said: "Biera, wait a minute, don't be in such a hurry!"

But he didn't have time to wait. Before my limbs could catch up with him on the steep slopes of love, he'd reached the top and gone out, and I didn't get to feel you, my lake, hold me gently in your depths.

Original title: *Lille tjern, hør meg!* Translated by Katherine Hanson

Merethe Lindstrøm

(b. 1963)

Merethe Lindstrøm saw her first short stories in print when she was eighteen years old, and since that auspicious beginning, she has published four collections of short stories and one novel. A story from her second book, *Borte, men savnet* (1988), was awarded first place in an international competition for short fiction in Germany.

Born in Bergen, Norway's second major city, Merethe Lindstrøm now lives in Oslo. She is an urban writer, though in the broadest sense of the word. Her stories do not evoke specific places but rather leave the impression they could be set in any European city. Even though "Mother Moon" is cast in a rural setting, the presence of the city is pervasive, and the young woman in this story is like so many of Lindstrøm's characters who are in their late teens or early twenties. Under a tough veneer, they are lonely and disillusioned, aimless and homeless. They belong to the generation that came of age in the eighties, born during the sixties to parents who were caught up in self-discovery and self-realization and whose marriages most often ended in divorce. Lindstrøm focuses on the child-parent relationship, from the child's point of view, at the same time as she explores the seeming inability of her young protagonists to find worthwhile goals or form lasting relationships.

"Mother Moon" is taken from *Kannibal-leken* (*The Cannibal Game*, 1990). In the book which followed, a novel titled *Regnbarnas rike* (*The Realm of the Rain Children*, 1992), Lindstrøm returned to the story of Ann's vagabond daughter.

Mother Moon

One day I woke up and discovered that everything around me had changed color. It wasn't only the furniture, my clothes, the curtains at the window, the pictures in their frames; it was the walls, the floor and the ceiling—every room I walked through. Whenever I looked in a mirror a frightening smile was hanging where my lips used to be, and even my face seemed to belong to somebody else.

There was no real color around me any more—there were contrasts—things looked gleaming white or shadowed and unclear. I felt no anxiety at the thought of it, no pain at the change, no confusion about the condition of things, but no joy either. I wasn't cold, but I wasn't warm. When I slept, I knew I would soon wake up—my dreams were also white—and I knew that when I looked around after I opened my eyes in the morning, everything would be white.

I'm taking the slow bus home. It's Christmas vacation and all the passengers are in high spirits. An old woman starts singing softly at the back of the bus, people clap when she's finished. Everything is strange. I'm frightened by all this overt joy over nothing. I look at the snow-covered roofs of the houses, little houses in quiet country towns. People are skating on a frozen lake. Several small houses in a cluster—here people aren't afraid to get too close to each other. Not like the city. I've lived too long in another place. I'm on my way to visit Ann. She lives alone in one of those houses, out in the country. She gets visits from old admirers and their faded wives. Sometimes she gets visits from characters who live out here. Ann collects people's eccentricities like other people collect stamps. There are plenty to choose from out here. It's not all idyllic. Centuries of inbreeding have left their mark, ax-murders and incest. Ann surveys them all, looks and listens, arranges the tidbits in her big card file. Ann is an actress. She is also my mother. Maybe I'm there, too, in her card file. Maybe she's borrowed a little from me, too. When I come home now she'll play the role of mother, everyone will take their places. There will be no talk about money.

Most important was the money. I needed money all the time. It was exciting in a way. Exciting to see what would happen when I ran out of money. But when I found out what it was like, it wasn't exciting any longer. It was just lonely. I thought about it a lot. White, I thought, like a bridal dress and veil. Like clean sheets on an untouched bed. Like old ladies' hair. It was white. It wasn't innocence any longer, but something else. Purity perhaps. I thought of it as a journey. It felt, in fact, like a plane ride. Like flying from continent to continent, time losing its significance, surrounding objects losing their function, like going through old memories when fog is remembered as more beautiful than clear sky, night seems clearer than day.

Mother is there to meet me when the bus stops. She is wearing the same old fur coat as usual. I look automatically for something of value: earrings, a necklace. Without wanting to, I notice a ring on her finger. Gold possibly. It might be worth something. Her admirers like to impress her. But I'm too tired to think about that right now. Tomorrow I'll think about that.

"Very becoming," mother says, trying to smother me in her fur. She means my hair. I've dyed it black. Just before I came, I had a couple of bad days. Some guy kept calling me up on the phone. He never left a message. Just his name, followed by silence. Even without it, I would have known it was him. A thin vibrating silence. I dyed my hair so he wouldn't recognize me.

"I've got everything ready, including your room. Last night I actually slept in your bed to see how it would be for you to sleep there."

We laugh together. A false laughter. When I answered the phone for her in the past, everyone thought I was her. I laughed like her, I talked like her. Once I cancelled one of her dates that way, so she wouldn't go out that night and would stay home with me. She never found out.

We walk across the field, a thin layer of ice crunching under our feet. It's getting dark. The houses glow on the edge of the field, perfect as little playhouses in a shop window. Mama is whistling. She owns the world. Remember all the nice people who never stop giving. Be thankful. Mother must think my days flow by, as simple and festive as an unbroken stream of champagne glasses.

When I was a child, I lay in the leaves under the biggest tree in the garden. I saw Mother through the window. She was bending over the old-fashioned paraffin lamp she insisted on lighting in the dusk, she was almost kissing the flame, her lips heavy like cherries, soft as a donkey's ear. A young man popped up beside her. Naked chest, thin and hairless. He licked the laughter off her lips before it reached the half-open window.

Yes, she's slept in my bed. But otherwise the room is exactly like it was before. My U2 poster is still hanging above the bed, a little boy's staring eyes and WAR written in blood-red script, passport photos of schoolfriends stuck in the frame of the mirror over the bureau, the lilac and blue patchwork quilt on my bed.

"How's life in the big cities of Europe?" Mama asks, smoothing my hair away from my forehead. I push my hair back in place on my forehead and shrug my shoulders.

"I need money," I say.

In the middle of the night I leap out of bed. The telephone is ringing. The telephone! The clock on the night table has a picture of Minnie Mouse on the face and silver hands that glow in the dark. Ten past two.

Mother shuffles out to the hall. She picks up the phone. From the low murmuring and laughter I can tell it's someone she knows well. She's apparently taken the phone into her room, because a door closes again and the murmuring continues, but now from a distance.

I can't get to sleep again. I lie there following the silver hands as they tick from point to point, until the morning light at last throws shadows against the walls.

The morning of Christmas Eve Mother goes to town to buy some last-minute Christmas presents, and I get to work. I ignore the jewelry and valuables, she's too likely to miss them right away. Instead I concentrate on locked drawers, chests, closets. People who live alone in the country, far from banks, always have a lot of cash lying around. And Ann is not the type to keep careful records.

If by some remote chance she finds something missing, I can always say I regarded it as a loan, or for that matter, say she'd promised I could have it. She doesn't remember things like that. She'll look at me blankly for a second and then shake her head. *I'm starting to get absent-minded.* And I'll repress the impulse to say: No Ann—you've always been absent-minded.

In the bureau I find two or three hundred kroner in an envelope. It's slim pickings. There's got to be more. But where? I just need a minute to focus.

I sit down on her bed. Ann's striped Marimekko nightgown is lying nicely folded on the bed. It smells like Ann. The whole room smells like Ann. Lavender and the baby soap she uses in the bath. On the night table are the same photographs that have always been there. One is of me—a childhood picture, and one is of me and Victor. At a dance. I remember that dance. Victoria, called Victor, the dark-haired beauty who used to work in the office at her father's gas station. She had every one of Gary Glitter's records and every morning she sat in front of a mirror and plucked her beautiful dark eyebrows. It was a dance at the hotel in town. I was fifteen. We used to go to town every other Wednesday and Friday to go to dance school.

We danced all night with boys a head shorter than we were and drank sickening-sweet cocoa from paper cups; eventually we went off to the bathroom and smoked the pack of cigarettes Victor had brought. The strong menthol taste made us gasp for breath, Victor danced the samba with her skirt pulled over her head and squeezed her shoulders coquettishly with her slender hands, she knelt on the polished tiles and let her dress fall back in place as she bent over an imaginary lover. I suddenly had the feeling we were not alone. And when I turned, the dance instructor was in the doorway. One of her two false eyelashes had come unstuck from its painted eyelid. She glared at us from the door. The loose eyelash quivered whenever she blinked. Finally she took it off and buried it in her thin, sinewy hand, but not before she'd sealed Victor's fate with the horrible words, "Victoria Lillian Hansen. You will never be a lady."

We were banished, of course, and had to go back through the town to the bus-stop without finding out who would be chosen queen of the ball. We laughed about it in the days that followed—we'd always been afraid we'd end up as ladies. But later on the episode had an aftertaste of sadness. Victor's thin ankles in torn pantyhose and Miss Eberson's, the dance teacher's, sinewy old hand pulling the eyelash off her black-painted eyelid. I look at the photograph. It was taken earlier in the evening. Before the scandal happened. It was sent to us afterwards without comment, wrapped in silver paper and delivered in a neutral business envelope. No return address. The photograph speaks for itself: we're both laughing—we've forgotten to close our mouths, as strictly instructed by Miss Eberson—we look like we're about to gobble up the world in one enormous gulp. We will possess and devour. It's easy to see that we'll never be real ladies.

I set the photograph down on Ann's night table. I still have cupboard drawers to go through.

Victor is married now, she lives further up the mountain with an automobile mechanic and their two sons. I won't be visiting her.

It's Christmas Eve. We open the gifts over a late breakfast, a tradition Ann introduced when I was a child because we were both equally impatient. Later in the afternoon we put on classical music and start to fix dinner. We take our time. Ann talks about a man she's just met, a sweet guy, she might invite him over so I can meet him. We'd like each other. Sure, I say.

I'm in the middle of peeling rutabagas for mashed rutabagas when the telephone rings. And suddenly my terror is back again. My hand is trembling so much I lose my grip on the knife. It falls on the floor, while I stare in fear at Ann.

"I'm sure it's nothing important."

She's already on the way to answer it when I stop her. "Don't answer it, don't answer the telephone."

I realize I'm shouting.

"What's the matter?" Mother says. She's trying to be calm, a studied calm. She can do it. Naturally. I wonder what play she got it from.

"It's him," I say, even though I know it can't be him. I don't know why I say it. "He wants his money."

Mother looks at me in fear. She's really frightened now. This isn't play-acting. I think: Now it's her turn to be afraid. When I was little and slept in the other room, she had visits from men with loud voices who cried out about "saving the world before it's too late," many skåls, and afterwards—silence. And in the morning: unshaved strange men at the breakfast table or snuffling, half-grown young men who gave me money as if I were a vending machine: stick in a krone and out rolls a smile.

Now it's her turn.

I'm sitting on my old bed, the patchwork quilt crumpled from my movements during the last half hour. I've taken off my black dress and lace bra. I loosen the lining of the bra and tear the little plastic bag away from the lining. At the top I cut a hole, find Ann's handmirror that I borrowed from the bathroom and put it on the night table. Carefully I pour a little of the powder out on the mirror and make two lines with a fifty kroner bill. I roll the fifty into a narrow pipe and bend over the mirror, where I can see part of my face as I sniff. The parts seem freed from any relationship, magnified. My eye stares steadily back at me.

Two days after Christmas I go up the old country road to the red house where Jarle lives. I used to come here a lot—we went all the way from grade school to high school together. He's wearing the same Shetland sweater he had on the last time I saw him, he doesn't look like he's shaved very often since then either. His hair is two colors: flaming red and black. Before, he used to have a kind of cock's comb. He gives me a hug and we go down to his apartment in the cellar. His parents are away visiting family. We have the house to ourselves. We keep an awkward conversation going. We mean something to each other, and like all old friends who haven't seen each other for a while, we don't have anything to talk about. We're like two creaking hinges that are holding up the same old door. A door of memories. When we discover we have nothing to say to each other, we begin to touch each other instead.

It's been a long time since I had sex with anyone. There's something about the whole ritual that repels me, sweaty bodies grinding against each other under equally sweaty sheets, panting like dogs toward something that is quite mistakenly called a climax. And afterwards, the inescapable evaluation of the body you have just used, pallid in the morning light. Skin that was slacker than you thought in the dark, memory of your own body which you haven't seen in a mirror for months.

But it's all right. We keep our clothes on, I hold his penis and caress him until he comes, or pretends to. I don't want to look. It makes no difference to me. Afterwards I feel more powerful than him, light one of his cigarettes, start to wander around the room. "I owe money, I've got a debt. There's a guy I owe money . . . for something. He keeps calling me. It's frightening."

Jarle nods. He doesn't ask questions. "You can stay at my house," he says, "if you need a place to live."

"Making organic bread, and wearing felt slippers all winter. No thanks."

We laugh at Jarle's parents. They are anthroposophists.

"Just a thought," Jarle says

"I'll manage," I say. I sound wobbly. Jarle sits on the bed and smokes. His hair is mussed up, he looks good in his longjohns. I still have a slight upper hand over him. I notice that it's shrinking every second I stay here. Pretty soon he'll be able to hurt me. I decide I'll just stay a little while and then leave.

Jarle runs his hand through his flaming red and black hair—it's starting to get thin at the temples.

"Just don't let it go too far, sister," he says.

It's already dark when I get back. The snow glitters out here where the snow is really white, not black or sooty like in the city.

Before, when I was young, Ann would be away many weeks at a time. She stayed at the theater. One of her friends looked after me and the house while she was away. When she was home, she was always full of energy—there was so much we had to get done together in the course of a couple of weeks. She was used to being admired. She wanted me to admire her too. But she was my mother. I was a dull admirer, she so special. Quiet, serene, cold—but always radiant. Sometimes invisible, but nevertheless there. I thought about her all the time, missed her. I look up at the dark heavens as I walk. Mother moon. It's a full moon. I see it now. When they rang from the theater and asked for her, I used her voice and said that unfortunately she wasn't home.

Mother moon. Casting shadows over the landscape I'm walking through.

I notice the minute I come in. Something has happened. The door of my room is open, mother stands on the threshold. She's holding something in her hand. I see now what it is. As soon as she catches sight of me, her shoulders droop a little and her mouth trembles like a child's. "You must tell me about it. I don't know about these things. You must help me," she says.

I see something behind her. It's exactly as if a wind has blown through the cracks in the walls and shifted everything in the house to new places. Something behind her back flutters for a second, then subsides. Things find their place. All is calm now.

"You must tell me about it," she says again. And I think: Now it's your turn, your turn to be afraid.

Original title: *Mor måne*. Translated by Judith Messick.

Marit Nicolaysen

(b. 1953)

Marit Nicolaysen was born in Oslo and has spent most of her life there, though after high school she did live in Paris for a time where she worked as an au pair. When she returned to Norway she enrolled at the University of Oslo and pursued her study of French and Portuguese. Combining her interests in literature and rock music, Nicolaysen wrote research papers exploring the integration of a woman's perspective with traditional rock, and the lyrics of female rock musicians. She has written articles on music for the press and worked for RadiOrakel, a local radio station started by women in the early eighties.

Her first book, a novel for adults, was published in 1985, and was followed in 1989 by *Tango med tiden* (*Tango with Time*), a collection of short stories which includes "Even the Most Loving Arms Get Cold When They Have to Reach Across the Ocean." Nicolaysen has also tried her hand at drama—a piece she wrote for the stage was recently performed at a drama festival in Oslo. In 1993 she published a novel for young adults and is currently working on its sequel. Set in the early decades of this century, the era of industrialization in Norway, these novels portray the itinerant laborers who built the nation's railroads. The protagonist is a fifteen-year-old boy who, like Stian in the story below, is growing up without a father figure.

Even the Most Loving Arms Get Cold When They Have to Reach Across the Ocean

I've been to the store and am dragging myself up the stairs with two full shopping bags.

"That's not cod. It's pollack."

Mrs. Olsen, Mrs. Mørk Olsen, points at the packages of Alaska green cod at 11 kroner 90 øre for 400 grams.

"I could see and taste that it wasn't cod. I'd been looking forward to filet of cod but filet of pollack I can do without. What nerve!"

Pollack or cod, I'm willing to be had at that price, and filet mignon it will never be, no matter how you turn the fish in the frying pan.

"We're having coffee at Karen's. Are you coming?"

"Maybe."

I continue up the stairs and hear that Stian is home. Every step I take, I hear it more clearly. The sound magnifies, along with my irritation.

The day's first meeting between mother·and son takes place as a battle of sound levels, in which my part consists of yelling: "Turn that damn music down!"

It's an uneven battle, but there's one place I'm master—in my own home. And he turns it down. Reluctantly to be sure, but he turns it down.

I go out to the kitchen which looks just as I expected. It's quite amazing how predictably a fifteen-year-old son behaves. Why didn't I have a daughter who would provide comfort and joy in my old age, now that I've turned thirty-five? Why didn't I have a daughter who took ballet and cleaned up the house? Why do you get sons, who break arms and legs as soon as they can walk, who dream about heavy motorcycles, soil their sheets and whose feet stink?

"Hi Mom. You in a bad mood or something?"

My offspring is standing in the doorway, tall and skinny. He's the spit and image of his father, something that's always irritated me. *That* little contribution, and not even face to face. *Nine months* in my stomach, and not a trace of me. Half of each, is what the books say. Her genes and his in equal measure. You heard right, in equal measure! Is it any wonder traditional medicine is losing ground?

"Yes, I'm in a bad mood," I say, helping myself to a slice of bread since the bread is out anyway.

I shove the Alaska green cod down into the freezer, saving it for a moment when I'm inspired to prepare something more complicated.

"What do you plan to do about harmonious fellowship?" he says, pulling at his upper lip.

I suspect he thinks it stimulates hair growth.

"About what?"

"Harmonious fellowship. Security within the family that's supposed to compensate for society's insecurity, the new development, rootlessness and the absence of ideals. You're responsible for future generations, you know."

I sit down, and luckily there's a chair.

"Repeat that," I say. "You sound like a tape recorder."

He repeats, and adds: "We had a substitute who told us about neo-Nazism and gangs of hooligans in Europe. Statistically they're boys between thirteen and twenty-five who are atheists, children of divorced parents, and who live with their mothers. I just thought that was something you should know."

"You can tell that substitute . . . You can tell him he stinks. The whole liberal-intellectual middle class stinks. Not only do they succeed in everything they do, but on top of that they puff themselves up with all these virtues. They have money and an open mind. They go out on the town and they collect modern art. We, I, have nothing, and then they come and tell me . . . "

"Relax. He wasn't like that. He was cool."

"He was undoubtedly very cool. But one thing he's never been is a single mother, and he could have put out a call for some of the fathers in that speech of his, you know. It's always the mothers who get blamed when something goes wrong. Hell! It's the same all over the world. Besides, isn't it German and math and that kind of stuff you're supposed to be learning in school? If you learned what you're supposed to learn, then there might not be so many problems for your mothers when you don't get jobs and just hang around getting into trouble."

'Take that,' I think, energetically chewing the slice of bread with peanut butter which is much too sweet. What's come over the people who manufacture food? Even mustard tastes sweet. When I eat hot dogs, I want mustard that tastes like mustard, not jam!

"It's no use telling you anything. You interpret everything in the worst possible way," says Stian, chipping paint off the doorjamb.

"Dear Stian, I love having you tell me things. I love having you tell me about your new friends who don't hang out at the shopping center, but who turn out for sports, that you dream of becoming an engineer and that rock musicians are actually pretty stupid, that you would like to fix up the kitchen and that's why you've already started removing old paint from the doorjamb, that you are eternally grateful to your mother who has provided you with the possibilities of becoming a decent human being, that . . . "

"Something must have snapped."

"Nothing has snapped. Quite the contrary—to be perfectly plain, I'm damned normal."

"*I* think that substitute really understood something about the problem with single mothers."

Stian is out the door, and not just the kitchen door, before I can catch him. The day is such a loss now anyway that I decide to go over to Karen's.

Karen opens the door. She is 5'11" and just about as wide. Karen is plagued with anxiety. She can't get rid of her husband even though he's been dead for two years, after twenty years of illness interrupted by occasional energetic periods when he would entertain the family with some classic domestic scenes like getting drunk and practice shooting at moving targets. But coffee and cakes are always on the table at Karen's, and you can always console yourself with the latest stories about who's died recently, about a relative who's both rich and beautiful and got cancer anyhow, about the old man in the neighboring stairwell whose clothes she washes, whose children never visit him, and who dirties his pants and uses a walker and barely eats, about Mrs. Pedersen who's got multiple sclerosis, and the children of the woman on the first floor who are unwashed and unfed, and two hundred casualties of catastrophic floods in India, or was it three hundred and was it in Mexico?

"How nice that you came," Karen says, and her rear end barely clears the doorway into the living room, where Mrs. Olsen sits leafing through a pile of magazines. Karen's son is in his room playing Elvis and filling out betting slips. Karen's daughter is reading *The Bobsey Twins* and watching "The Children's Hour" on TV, she's the same age as my son, but life has infinite variety.

"Listen to this," Karen says, reading from a newspaper: "With the aid of your date of birth, time of birth and place of birth, our astrologers can set up your personal horoscope, specially adapted for bingo. It is a fact that people have good and bad days. Astrology can tell you about your lucky days an entire year in advance."

Karen is skeptical and wants to hear my opinion, since I'm the intellectual among us and can type using the touch-method. Karen plays Flax, not bingo. Still, we agree they're all the same, and she starts filling out the coupon. Then my eye catches the small print at the bottom of the ad. "The horoscope can be used for all types of bingo, but not for Lotto, betting or other games of chance."

I'm not a pessimist, far from it. Contrary to most people, I believe in a life before death. Still, it seems to be my lot to be the one who discovers the small print at the bottom of the page. It's not my intent to squash people's hopes and dreams, but they have to build on a sound foundation. And you can't base your happiness on the rules for bingo when you're playing Flax!

Mrs. Olsen puts down the magazine. Her jaw hasn't moved for at least ten minutes, so it must be something really interesting. How to clean the corners under the bathtub, with photographs to illustrate, or the latest news from the divorce front on "Dynasty."

"Have you heard," she begins, and I stuff cakes into my mouth while I listen to incredible, but true stories from real life. Stories about kitchen curtains that hang crooked, about unwashed windows and single mothers on welfare, *who can afford to take taxis.* Stories about people who owe money and people who move and *the little girl ends up as a druggie or even worse.*

I don't know how long I sit there. I lose all sense of time in this way station before death where thoughts never lighten and the surest sign of success is symmetry with the window sill.

I thank her for the coffee, I've had my dose of female life, enough to last a long time. I want to go out and stand right in the middle of all the high-rise apartments and bellow: "Aren't there any decent men here? Any who aren't politicians, murderers, pederasts, any who don't commit incest or drink and drive. Someone for them to look up to, our sons who collect switchblades and watch *The Hangmen* on video and whose first encounter with men is when they come in contact with the police. I come up short, and I'm a poor father, a fate I share with many women."

I unlock the door to my empty apartment, sit down on a chair without turning on the light, and feel depressed. I wonder if I should call my mother, but she's a retired widow with grown children, living an active life, and I'm afraid of bothering her. The country is full of old people languishing away, neglected by their families. And I'm worried about being a bother! The last time I called Mother and asked if I could come over, I heard a man's voice in the background and my Mother's twittering apology that she was so terribly busy all week. What does she have that I don't? Besides a thirty years' head start? Here I sit believing in a life before death, but dammit, that doesn't mean I think a live dog is better than a dead lion.

"Take a course in personal development," said one of the women at work.

I realized that something had happened with the Experimental College since the last time I leafed through one of their catalogues. I see. So now it's no longer macramé, knots that are keeping neuroses in check. Now it's no longer the wooden bowl, but the personality that's getting a coat of rosemaling. Thanks for the offer, but my personality is developed enough as it is. What I lack is social interaction with intelligent people who are concerned with something other than birth, illness and death, these trivialties of life. Someone who's concerned with . . . Someone who's concerned with . . . What in the hell are intelligent people concerned with?

The thoughts race around inside my head trying to find something to hang on to, until Stian suddenly shows up.

"Gee, sure is bright and cheerful in here."

"I'm thinking. But that's probably a foreign word you don't understand."

I immediately regret what I say. It just slips out. Why can't I be a good natured and accommodating mama? Strengthen his self confidence with pats on the shoulder and cries of bravo.

He disappears into his room, and soon the wall is reverberating with the hard pounding of the bass. I feel empty and unhappy and sit down in the kitchen with a crossword puzzle and coffee. Talk about a loser! Talk about early retirement!

Hanging on the wall is one of those ceramic things in the series "Happiness is . . . " It makes me deeply unhappy. "Happiness is doing the dishes together." I got it from my mother. She is extremely taken up with trivialities. When I point that out she says: "Trivialities usually express things that are otherwise too large and difficult to notice."

"Paying too much attention to trivialities is a sign of narrow-mindedness," I say.

"Having no interest in trivialities is being removed from the realities of life," she says.

But when I call and say I feel like everything's going to hell, she says: "Trivialities! Problems of luxury! Lots of people are much worse off. Just look at the world, that's right, just look at the world. Take a warm bath and be glad you're healthy."

I try to concentrate on the crossword puzzle. Primitive becomes raw. Numbskull becomes dunce. Gnome becomes elf. I take a break at an insect with twelve letters and turn on the radio. "Stormy Weather." The vocalist's voice resonates with feeling. It's really pretty. It breaks down boundaries, it's international. Could have been Columbus Avenue in New York City outside, and here I sit. Nothing happens here. My life is as exciting as a dry vagina.

I decide to talk with my son. In spite of everything we have each other. I stand outside his door and try to convince myself of that.

"Can I come in?"

"Yeah."

It's unbelievable. The boy is sitting at his desk and appears to be doing homework. A sarcastic remark is loose in my mouth threatening to tumble out, but I press my lips together and swallow.

"What are you doing?"

The long hair hides his face. The pencil crunches between his teeth.

"Paper," he says spitting out splinters. "Due tomorrow."

Naturally, I think. Always at the last minute.

"What kind of a paper are you writing?"

There's something unreal about the whole situation. I feel like a bad amateur actor who's having trouble putting the right feeling into her voice. Or like a German shepherd who's trying to act like a poodle. My God! This is my child. A child I've had on my lap, for whom I've changed thousands of diapers, who put his soft cheek against mine and whispered mama. At that time all he could say was forty words, and then we really could talk to each other.

"This." He points, and I lean over his shoulder to see. "Tell about something or someone who means a lot to you."

"What are you going to write about? AC/DC? Samantha Fox? Motor sports?"

"You."

Now is when I should put my arms around him and cry while HAPPINESS streams through me. This is deliverance. This is the hour of destiny. My hands are shaking. Never have I been so near the conclusion of an American television film. All that's missing are the violins. NOW. But I wait. And wait. And some amazing forms hop out of my mouth.

"You're a strange one."

Hop, hop, hop.

And I'm out of the room. This is not America. And even the most loving arms get cold when they have to reach across the ocean.

Original title: *Selv de kjærligste armer blir kalde når de skal rekke over havet.*
Translated by Katherine Hanson

Laila Stien

(b. 1946)

The people and places in Laila Stien's fiction are firmly rooted in the ordinary, everyday world of women, children and men living in Northern Norway. Stien currently lives in a small town on Finnmarksvidda, the interior of Norway's northernmost county, but it is the region of her childhood, Rana in Nordland county, that is most clearly evoked in her stories. With an eye for the telling detail Stien captures the temperament and lifestyle specific to *nordlendinger*. Yet more than anything it is language—Stien has an uncanny ear for spoken language and renders all dialogue in dialect—that imbues her fiction with local coloring. She writes for children as well as adults (three books for children, four collections of short stories), poetry as well as prose (two books of poems). In 1993 Stien's masterful use of language was officially recognized with the *Språklig Samlings* prize, and that same year she was also awarded the prestigious *Kritikerpris* in the category of children's books for *Å plukke en smørblomst*.

In addition to her own work, Stien has translated several books into Norwegian from the Sami. Her qualifications as translator are impeccable: extensive knowledge of Sami language and culture (she has University degrees in ethnology and Sami) coupled with talent and experience as a poet and writer of fiction. Publications include poetry and prose, an anthology which she both edited and translated and a Sami reader for primary school.

"Blue Baby Buggy" and "Trip to Town", from the collection *Fuglan veit* (*Only the Birds Know*, 1984), are companion pieces about a single mother, Anita, and her little boy, Arne. The first story takes place a few months after Anita has given birth, the second when Arne is six years old.

Blue Baby Buggy
Anita and Arne

"One thing's certain—he's going to buy a baby buggy, the horny bastard and not an old piece of junk either."

She slams the kettle of potatoes on the stove so the water splashes and sputters on the hot burner. She's angry, her voice is gruff, a brand-new grandmother. Anita nods. Can see the buggy. Has seen it since the first day she felt sick and threw up in the sink. It's going to be blue. Skyblue. And it will have big wheels with shiny fenders. She'll push it down the road as soon as the ground is dry and the weather is nice. She'll wear new Wranglers, tight from top to bottom, and loosen her hair.

"Does he think he can prance around struttin' his stuff and not own up to the consequences like a man? No sir, we're not so low as to let some rotten ladies' man push us around."

Her mother has been carrying on like this for a long time now. She talks big as soon as there are more people in the room—her father, her brother and Stine, his wife. When it's just the two of them, she frets. Then Anita goes into her room and sits down. Looks at her little golden boy. His nose, curly hair, the dimple in his chin and those long fingers. He is so much like him. Will be just as tall too. Tall and loose-limbed, but with powerful muscles in his arms. He'll have the same hair too—brown and curly. And oh, the clothes she'll dress him in when he starts school. She thinks about Kirsti who had a baby with that long-nosed guy who works on road construction. The baby's got the same ski jump as his father. And Kirsti is so pretty. It's really too bad about Kirsti.

She hasn't decided on a name yet. For a long time she thought it would have to be Øystein or Ørnulf. She was positive it would be a boy.

"See to it that you choose something that begins with A. Should he have that pleasure too—of having the baby named after him!"

She'll probably decide on Arne. It's a perfectly good name. A lot of people in her family have names beginning with A. Her father's name is Anton. So he can have the pleasure of having the baby named after him. That should make him happy. Her father could frighten the devil himself with his bad temper. Every time she came home with a guy he clamped his jaw shut and didn't utter a word as long as the visitor was in the house. Just glared. Eyes like a raging bull. People won't put up with that. Not Øyvind anyway. Øyvind is sensitive about things like that. Doesn't like being harassed. He often talked about the foreman over on the pier. Thought he was a little too full of himself. If he didn't take himself down a peg or two, Øyvind would do it for him. For someone like Øyvind there was plenty of work.

Everywhere. He didn't need to go around bowing and scraping to someone who was slimier than a worm.

There had been some kind of a run-in over there. The foreman had been madder than hell. That was around the time she discovered she was pregnant. He'd been careful, he said. Was she sure? He'd jumped off in time. Did she think he had such a fat butt he couldn't manage that? No, she had said. No, but it had happened anyway. And then she'd started to cry, of course, even though she'd made up her mind that was one thing she wouldn't do. She would be happy. She'd even bought a split of vodka and snack food—potato chips and bananas. He'd downed a few and was a little high. Talked about the foreman. Went on and on. He'd show him, dammitall, that he was dealing with human beings. They weren't work animals, or cattle.

He was so sweet when she started to sniffle. Put his arm around her and patted her hair and her cheeks and . . . Then they made love and he was so good. Afterwards she'd asked if he'd help out with money. She couldn't manage everything alone. There were so many things she'd need. A buggy, for example. "Of course," he said. "Of course. And you'll get welfare, won't you?" "Well yes, that's true, but that just covers daily needs—that's what everyone says. Anne got a buggy from Erik and Brita got a buggy and a bunting from hers—real sheepskin." He asked if he could spend the night. Was so damned tired. Eyelids down on his chin almost. She said she didn't dare because of her father. He'd better go. And come back.

"Lazy no-goods, you can't believe 'em any farther than you can see 'em. We've seen 'em before! We've seen that nosey fellow of Kirsti's! All you saw was his backside. And off he went. Leaving her with a child who's so ugly it's a crying shame. Did she see any baby buggy? Not so much as the rim of a wheel."

Anita rocks her baby boy. Acts as if nothing's been said. Softly hums a tune from Abba—"Dancing Queen." Stine asks if she should bring her buggy down from the attic.

"There's no rush. It's still cold outside."

Arne. A nice name, as far as that goes. Arne. He started breast-feeding right away. Found his way with that soft, tiny little mouth and dug in. No trouble at all, and she has plenty of milk. He has a good strong grip too. When she puts her little finger in his fist, it's like having it in a vice. He'll be as strong as an ox. Stine has been great. Found all of Little Johan's clothes and gave them to her. You can't see that they've been used. Stine takes care of everything she owns. She and Johan are careful types. The buggy they have in the attic isn't very worn either.

"Tell me, don't you ever plan to give that child some fresh air?"

Her mother is constantly bringing it up. Good thing she has her room. She's fixed it up in there for herself and her little boy. Changes and dresses him on the bed and has a washstand and everything she needs. She bought the cassette player with her first paycheck from the shop. It's nice to have it now. A picture of Øyvind and her on the wall. Anne and Brita and Kirsti and a couple others came with presents. At first they just talked about babies, but when they saw she had a picture on the wall, they asked. Oh sure—he wasn't exactly the best letter writer, but she did hear from him regularly. His work is better now. Indoors. A machine shop. Noo—plans! Yes, of course she gets money. Naturally. As a matter of fact, he promised to send a buggy.

Anne and Berit have been over several times. Not Kirsti.

"Anton, if you had any gumption, you'd have gone to the sheriff a long time ago. We haven't seen a red cent and he must have been notified. They have his name, don't they? Anita, do they have his name?"

The father glances quickly over at the girl. Doesn't he crack a smile? Is she perhaps just imagining that?

He goes out. Slinks off to his work. Heavy and broad.

"Anita, did you hear what I asked?"

"Yes, I heard."

She takes the packet of porridge into her room. Pours water into a deep bowl, sprinkles the dry cereal on top, stirs. The baby is starting to cry over on the bed. Must be hungry now. She sets the porridge on the windowsill to cool off and picks the boy up. His neck is wet. Warm.

The sun is high now. Melts the snow. The wheel tracks leading up to the house are muddy. Along the side of the road are patches of dirty grey slush. Out in the meadow the snow is almost completely gone.

It won't be long before it's dry everywhere.

He must have received the letter a long time ago. She sent it to his home address. Please forward she wrote on the back. She didn't write much. Mentioned that she'd like it to be blue. The buggy. Enclosed a picture of the boy. He was almost a newborn, his face red and wrinkled, his eyes narrow slits. It couldn't be helped. There was no time to lose. Sincerely, Anita, she wrote. Not yours—nothing like that. And then: Write soon!

"Anita!"

Her mother's sharp voice reverberated through the wall.

"Anita, it's sixty degrees in the sun."

She touches the porridge spoon to her lips to feel if it's the right temperature. The boy swallows eagerly. Greedily. But then starts to shake his head and nuzzle in toward her armpit. She has to coax the last spoonfuls of porridge into him before she pulls up her sweater and lets him breastfeed.

Her mother lifts the latch on the door:

"Anita, shouldn't I talk to Stine?"

"No."

Anita pulls the baby closer to her. Her breast is beginning to empty. She settles him into the crook of her other arm. He can have as much as he can hold. His tiny lips relax around the nipple. Smack together. A thin stripe of milk dribbles from the corner of his mouth.

She takes out wool pants, a sweater, a cap and puts them on the baby boy. He's as round as a ball. Wraps a woolen blanket around him, slips into a coat and boots and goes outside.

The sun in her eyes smarts. She stands there squinting, her bundle pressed against her. Then she carefully pulls her coat underneath her and sits down on the top step. Shuts her eyes. Hears it seething under the snow by the steps. The smell of water-logged earth. From the cow barn she hears the clanking and clattering of buckets and pails. It's her mother gathering up the containers to be washed. She walks stiffly up the slight incline on her bony legs, stooped forward and carrying milk pails in each hand. Her face is narrow and angular inside the flowered kerchief.

"Well now, you're outside," she pants. Her lips pull upwards in a smile and reveal the large, blue-white teeth. She drops the pails on the bottom step. Reaches out with red, gnarled fingers and stands there for a short while. Shyly chucks the sleepy, contented baby boy under his chin. Picks up the pails and quickly climbs the steps.

"Don't freeze your rear end off," she says brusquely. "I'll throw out a pillow for you."

The pails bang against the door frame as she tromps in. A moment later she's back with a large, flat sofa pillow which she hands her.

"Here you go."

Anita wants to say something nice, but can't think of anything. Her mother ambles back inside.

The baby has fallen asleep. He's snoring like a grown man. Anne will probably show up again this evening, if she's not mistaken. Come and sound off for a couple of hours. It's a big job to keep up with her chattering. It's Erik this and Erik that. She's so sick of Erik she'd as soon he burn in hell. A blockhead and a lazy bum, but in Anne's eyes an absolute miracle. She holds forth about every crap he takes.

"Good Lord, isn't there ever a period in that bluestreak!"

Her mother usually holds her forehead and groans after Anne comes to visit. Even for her it's too much, though she otherwise loves visitors and news. For Anita it's way too much. And then all the fuss about the buggy.

The sun slips around the corner of the house and right away it's too cold to sit on the steps.

It's late in the evening when they hear laughter and voices out in the farmyard. Ice has formed and the footsteps crunch through the brittle sheets on the water's surface.

"You've got company, Anita."

She's already heard them. Can feel her heart beating faster. Why can't they leave her in peace.

"Good evening."

"Evening."

"We had to come over and see you, Kirsti and I. You've gone completely into hiberation."

"Hibernation—what do you mean?"

"You never show your face outdoors."

"Have a few things to do inside, you know."

"You could take the baby with you, now that the weather's so nice."

"I suppose so."

She turns toward the TV. The girls spread out, each in her own arm chair, and take out their tobacco pouches. They're buzzing and chattering. She forces herself to concentrate on what's happening on the television screen.

"Anita, set the cups on the table."

Her mother is measuring coffee into the kettle in the kitchen.

"Heard anything from Øyvind?"

"Yeah . . . sort of."

"Tobben ran into him."

"Oh really."

"At Steinkjer."

"I see."

"I thought you said he was working at a machine shop."

"Yeah, for a while. Not very long."

"How does he like military service?"

"All right."

"Tobben's been exempted. He was in for a week. Played crazy, screamed and carried on; I guess it was quite a circus. They were out on the town before he came home, Tobben and Øyvind. Celebrated."

Anita watches television. "Norway Today."

"Sounded like quite a celebration. Did Øyvind write about that?"

"No, he hasn't said anything about that."

Her mother comes in with the coffee and a packet of cookies. Sits down and asks for news from Nerbygda. Visits and jokes.

"Well girls, don't you have anything better to do on a Friday night than sit here and mope—are things in such a sorry state these days?"

Anita feels a heavy warmth spread through her body. Looks at her mother sitting on a spindleback chair at the coffee table, passing the packet of cookies around with a steady hand. The girls giggle and help themselves.

The woman on the television screen announces Mystery Hour. "Derrick". The girls settle comfortably into their chairs. Roll themselves fresh smokes and are soon drawn into the drama on the screen. The mother steals away unnoticed. Anita sinks deeper into the arm chair.

" . . . too good for those hussies . . . "

It's her mother's voice. It's biting and easily heard through the wall. Occasionally she can hear her father speak too. Just one word at a time. His voice is so deep. Kind of rumbles. Then it's quiet. The baby is breathing heavily over in his bed. Anita stretches and turns off the light.

"Should be here soon."

"Who?" Anita asks.

"Oh—just the delivery bus."

Her father has a boyish expression around his mouth. He turns and lumbers out to the entryway. Hands in his pockets, shoulders lifted almost up to his ears. Through the kitchen window Anita sees him walk with swinging steps down toward the milk ramp.

The baby is crying in the bedroom. Waiting for his food. Soon the water is bubbling in the little saucepan. She gets out the bowl and what she needs. Beats vigorously. There are beads of sweat on her nose. The child is screaming. She pours cold milk into the porridge to cool it off more quickly.

The baby is full and is dozing in her lap when her father comes and carefully lifts the latch of the bedroom door.

"You . . . you'd better come out and see."

Then he turns and is gone.

They're sitting on the steps. Her mother as straight as a board, her father round and broad across his back. They're smiling like the sun. At the bottom of the steps a new, bright blue baby buggy. High and modern. The hub caps shine.

She wastes no time getting herself and Arne dressed. She's down on the road in no time. Looks up toward the steps and waves. Her mother and father wave back.

The buggy has good springs and gently rocks. Anita takes her hand off the handle, pulls the band away from the tight pony tail and loosens her hair.

Original title: *Blå barnevogn. Anita og Arne.* Translated by Katherine Hanson

Trip to Town
Anita and Arne

Arne snuggles in as close as he can get. His mother is lying on her back, one arm up by her head in a soft arc on the pillow. Her hand is half closed. Arne has had his fist inside the warm hollow his mother has made with her hand. But just a little while. Then he took it away. Now he's lying with his head tucked under her arm, his nose touching the smooth body that smells . . . what does it smell like? Doesn't smell like anything else. Maybe a little like chocolate—and oranges and a little bit grandma. He's lying absolutely still. One foot's asleep, the one underneath when he lies on his side like this, but he doesn't move, doesn't even lift a finger. Light is filtering in between the curtains. Dances here and there on the wall. It'll be morning soon. She'll wake up if he's not quiet. Then she'll get dressed. Right away. Her pants and sweater are hanging over the back of the chair by the bed. Her tights are in a heap on the floor. She's just wearing a short-sleeved nightgown now. Nothing on her arms. There are green flowers on the nightgown. Green flowers! She's kicked the blanket off on one side so it's wadded between her legs from her feet all the way to her crotch. Her naked thigh is cold. Arne wonders if he should pull the blanket over them. He's cold too. Can't be helped. He'd only wake her. Then it would be over. Day. He tries counting the flowers on the nightgown. Gets to over forty. He can count to a hundred. Learned it from Uncle Johan. Has to stop at forty-four. The nightgown has worked its way up to her waist and is all bunched up. Her stomach goes up and down when she breathes. Her bellybutton is a little bud. His bellybutton is a hole. Completely different.

Now she's moving. Groans. Yawns and turns toward the wall. Doesn't notice him. Breathes heavily. Breathes so her entire body heaves. She's turned her back on him. Dummy.

He hears his grandma rattling around in the kitchen. The clattering of cups, chairs scraping across the floor. He's a little hungry. Very hungry. Bread with jam on it is best.

He touches her with his cold toes. She's sleeping. He pushes his knee against her rump, hard. She moves farther away. Sleeps.

"Mama."

"Mm . . . "

"Get up."

"Mm . . .

"They're playing along the side of the outbuilding. Have boxes for tables and big heavy birch logs for chairs. Kari's making beef stew from buttercups and red clover and ordering them down to the creek for water. Little Johan would rather throw the ball over the roof.

"Fix your mashed flowers yourself. It's just stupid."

Arne wouldn't mind getting water for the stew, but when Little Johan says it's stupid . . .

"I don't wanna either."

He wonders when he should tell him. Little Johan will turn green with envy. If he says it now, he'll just take off behind the outbuilding right away and start throwing the ball over the roof and Arne's not so good at that, doesn't get it over every time, has to try again and again. So it's better to wait til afterwards. Like when they're walking side by side toward the house on their way to eat. They almost always eat at the same time, the folks downstairs and Uncle Johan's family in the loft. When they're walking up the hillside and Little Johan is carrying the ball under his arm, then he'll say it. Or should he just tell Kari? She'll say lucky you or something like that. For sure. Little Johan always has to act so big. Like the time Mama brought that guy Rolf home; he could really dribble and had been in the newspaper and scored a whole lot of points. He played soccer with him and Little Johan and they had loads of fun. But after they'd taken the bus back to town, Little Johan was just grumpy and mean.

"He's not your dad if that's what you think."

"I know. Don't give a shit."

"Bet he won't come back either."

"He said he'd play soccer with us again sometime."

"Yeah."

"That's what he said!"

That was last spring. He was in the newspaper right afterwards. Arne got permission to cut him out. His shirt and hair were wet and he was holding his hands above his head and grinning. Grandpa said he was laughing his head off just because he'd managed to slam a ball into a net. A show-off was what he was. A show-off who farted around the country and worked up a sweat goofing around. What kind of a working man would that make? Would it put food on the table? Arne had kept the clipping in the drawer of his night table. For a long time. Showed it to Little Johan.

"Humph, him. That's no big deal, scoring in Fourth Division."

He had seen Dutte Berg big as life in the cafeteria in Bodø" when he was there for an ear infection.

Arne didn't know where Forthdivision was, but it definitely wasn't in Bodø.

The next time, his mother came on the bus alone. And the time after that. Arne would stand by the kitchen window every other Friday and watch the bus stop down by the ramp. He could have been really happy when she walked up the road carrying her bag if it hadn't been for Little Johan. She always brought candy or something. Donald Duck comic books and firecrackers. Running shoes. Lots of different stuff.

Aunt Stine is standing on the steps calling: "Diiinner."

Little Johan tucks the black and white checked ball under his arm like he always does. Arne runs alongside his tall cousin—a whole head taller than he is.

"I'm going to visit Mama in town . . . next weekend!"

There, he said it. Didn't mean to say it. It just came out. Darn, it just came out.

"You're as slow as molasses, boy. Have you seen a ghost?" Grandma smiles at him from the end of the table. "Eat up now, child."

He pokes in his vegetable beef soup with his spoon. Eats a spoonful and pokes some more.

"Is something wrong, Arne?"

It's his mother who leans over and asks. Her voice is so gentle. As if she were talking to a baby. She smells good too. When she comes real close. It gets to be too much. His eyes fill with tears. Has to dry them on his sleeve. Tears are streaming and it stings.

"Tell me what's the matter, Arne."

His mother asks so sweetly and that doesn't make it any easier. His lips twitch and he struggles to get it out.

"He says . . . he says it won't happen."

"What?"

"That I'm gonna go there. On the bus."

"Of course you are. I've said so. Next weekend."

"He says it's just a hoax that . . . "

"That?"

"That I'm gonna meet him . . . my dad."

He takes a few spoonfuls of soup. Swallows. Looks at Grandpa's enormous fist guiding the shiny spoon up to his mouth, down to the bowl, up to his mouth, down. He has hair on his hands. Sparse, black bristles. Grandpa never talks when he eats. "You can keep still while you chew," is what he says. Arne keeps still too. Vegetable beef soup is good.

"Has Little Johan said anything else?"

His mother poses the question gingerly. Arne glances up at her, just barely. Then it starts all over. The spoon drops to the floor when he covers his face with his hands. He's shaking all over."

"He says . . . he says I haven't gotten anything. Never."

"Gotten?"

"That the skis and skates and . . . and the baby buggy fell out of the sky."

It's quiet around the table. Grandpa stops eating. Reaches his enormous hand across to the boy's shoulder, quickly runs a couple fingers down his arm.

"You can punch that kid in the face next time. You've got permission. Say that you got permission from me."

Grandpa has finished eating. Places his chair silently up against the table. Walks with heavy steps into the bedroom. He takes a nap after dinner. He takes one every day.

A plump, sleek magpie is poking around in the dung heap by the fence. It's picking at potato peelings, scarfing down scraps of meat and greyish-brown bread swollen with coffee grounds and dish water.

They're sitting on the steps in the warmth of the sun, Arne and Anita, his mother. The flies are buzzing up against the side of the house. A couple of bumblebees too. The magpie's had its fill. Hops across the ground and flaps away. The kids from the loft are nowhere to be seen. It's dead quiet.

"Guess I'd better get my things together."

Anita stretches and stifles a yawn.

"Do you have to?"

"Yes, you know I do."

Yes, he knows that. She has to go to work. Everyone has to do that. No one can live on God's grace and the north wind, Grandma says. And besides, here it mostly blows from the southwest.

"Mama . . . ?"

"Yes?"

"Has he said so . . . ? Has he said that I should come?"

"Yes, sweetheart. He wants to meet you. He's said so. Many times. You're his boy, you know."

"Is he . . . Are you guys in love again?"

"Nooo, well, we . . . we're friends."

"I see."

She tousles his hair. Smiles. She has a large mouth and some curls. She's very pretty. Much prettier than Aunt Stine.

He stands by the kitchen window like he always does. Stands on a stool. Now she turns around. She does it every time. Right at that place. She sets her bag down on the gravel, lifts her hand and waves. Not the way Grandma does. Grandma shakes her hand like crazy up and down. Mama lets her hand glide slowly back and forth through the air. He tries to do it the same way, but he doesn't get it right. Then she picks up her bag.

He stands on the stool till the bus has gone.

"There goes the bus," says Grandma.

Just as if he hadn't seen it.

"Grandma, what day is it today?"

"It's Friday, you know that."

"Is it for sure she'll come and meet me?"

"As sure as Amen in church."

"Little Johan says . . . "

"Little Johan's a nincompoop."

He has his knapsack on his back. Won't start school until next year, but he has a knapsack and a pencil case too—in the chest of drawers.

"Make sure he gets there."

Grandma is fumbling with the end of her kerchief. The bus driver touches his hand to his cap and nods. He takes hold of the lever that closes the door, but Grandma is still standing on the step and doesn't budge an inch. She has taken his knapsack off and unbuttoned his jacket and felt in his pocket to make sure he has his wallet and handkerchief. She's standing there. Arne has nodded to her just like the bus driver, but nothing happened.

"Well, we're on our way," says Hans of the Hill who's been driving this route forever.

Then she's down. Arne didn't see that she moved her feet, but down she is. And Grandpa is standing by the side of the road, straight as a pole. He lifts his hand just a little when the motor starts up. Arne can see that he isn't happy. Grandma shakes her hand for all she's worth. That's the last thing he sees before the bus rounds the bend.

Sitting up front is a big deal. He's never sat up front before. But then he's never taken the bus alone either. And hasn't been Hans of the Hill's assistant.

"My assistant has to sit where I can keep an eye on him." And he winks, this man they call Hans Reverse because he's so amazingly good at backing up that he could back up all the way to Mo.

There's only the engine compartment between them. With a red hood. Arne has to hold on in the curves. It sways quite a bit. His wallet stays put. He can feel it the whole time. It presses against his thigh and is chock-full of money Grandpa has put in. Maybe he'll even go to the movies. If he's lucky there'll be a Disney film playing. If he wants to throw up, he'll use the bag Grandma found for him. The sun hurts his eyes so much he has to squeeze them shut when it's really bad, but he won't throw up, no sir.

There are people on the bus. They're talking and laughing. They're all old people, forty years old. The ones sitting closest have a thermos with coffee and a round green box. There are heart-shaped waffles in the box and they've asked him if he'd like some. He took one, but couldn't manage any more. Wonder what they eat in Mo. Wonder what they put on bread there. There was sliced egg on the waffle he got. There were ones with cheese too, but he took one with egg. He's really a super good driver, Hans Reverse. It looks like they could go crashing off the road any time at all, it's so narrow. And full speed. But he's not afraid. Not the least bit.

The old man way in the back has fallen asleep. When there's a bump in the road, he hits his head against the window. His mouth is open and he's snoring away, but there's a pause every time he thumps against the window. The downhill side of the road is due west. That's what Uncle Johan says. If you drive off the road there, it's over and out. Over and out, over and out. It's rumbling inside his head. The bus has a new sound when it's going uphill. And another new sound when it gets steeper.

His name is Øyvind. His father. He's seen a picture of him. But that's not the same of course. He's been at sea for a really long time. Been all over the world and seen everything there is to see. Mama has a picture of him smiling. He's gotta be nice. He gets a funny feeling in his stomach when he thinks about it. Thinks about . . . him. Like when he's waiting for the bus on Fridays. They have kiosks there too. Lots of them. He has enough money. And Mama has. And *he* . . . for sure. Kiosks and movie theatres and soccer fields and amusement parks and . . . The trees whish by. They're like roly-poly Teddy bears by the side of the road. One-two-three-four-five . . . Impossible to count. Must be a million.

"Well now, Assistant, did you nod off?"

Arne rubs his eyes with the back of his hand.

"We're just about there."

There's building after building outside. Brick buildings and ordinary wooden ones. Thick with cars and all kinds of shop signs. My God, they have everything here!

The bus turns into an open lot that's already full of busses. That's where she's going to meet him. If . . .

"There she is! There she is!"

His voice is loud and the others smile at him.

"Yes, there's Anita," replies Hans of the Hill, backing in between two busses as easy as one-two-three.

This is where Mama lives. The pillows she's embroidered on the weekends are here. She has her bed linen here and her cups and cassette player and everything. He doesn't know if he should sit on the sofa or in a chair. There's a picture of him on the bookshelf. He's here on a shelf and his mother can see him every day.

He sits down on the sofa.

"You must be hungry now."

His mother moves back and forth across the little room, setting things out and getting them organized.

"I have dinner. I just have to warm it up. It's hot dogs."

"Oh."

She makes a clatter with the plates and forks. The knife falls on the mat, she picks it up and her face is red and warm. It must be tough, working in the city.

Her mother asks for news from home about Grandma and Grandpa and everyone, even though she's just been there. There isn't very much to tell really. They eat grilled hot dogs and mashed potatoes.

"I have soda pop too, but you'll get that later."

He'd like to ask for some ketchup, but doesn't give in to it. He'd like to ask about other things too, but he can wait a while.

"You didn't get sick on the bus, did you?"

"No, wasn't sick at all. I got a waffle from a lady. I was Hans Reverse's assistant."

"Oh, were you really?!"

"It had egg on it."

"Oh boy, I bet that was good."

"Yes."

His mother clears the table as soon as they're done eating. Wipes the table with a rag. The kitchen is across the hallway. Several people share it. She carries out the frying pan and plates, stacked up high. Turns around in the doorway.

"Do you want to come and see?"

He jumps up. He's just in his stocking feet. His mother has slippers on. He looks down at his feet.

"You don't need anything on your feet. It's clean here."

In the kitchen three women are sitting and eating. They're having hot dogs today, too.

"Is this your pride and joy?"

He finds a sticker on a cupboard door and picks at it. Gets it almost loose, but then rubs it back on. It's a bird.

His mother flops down on the sofa when they come back. He sits down on the chair. She's bought a Donald Duck comic book. He leafs through it and looks at the pictures. Most of the time

Donald Duck is fun. His mother has a magazine too. She mostly looks at the pictures. They can hear the women in the kitchen all the way in here, talking and laughing and having a good time.

"Is it getting late?"

"It's just about five thirty."

"Don't you have TV?"

"No, but Turid does and she lives down the hallway—wanna go there?"

"No, I . . . don't feel like it."

There's a large birch tree right outside the building. Whenever there is a breath of wind it's as if someone is tapping at the window. Very lightly. With slender fingers.

She's made coffee for herself and brought out the pop bottle.

"I have potato chips too."

She smiles at him with her pretty mouth, but there's something a little strange about her. Her mouth, too.

"What time . . . what time's he coming?"

She turns around and starts going through the pile of cassette tapes, looking for something to play. She has a huge pile.

"He . . . he should be here any time, but something might have come up."

"Oh."

She's wearing a light blue sweater. She isn't as big as other women, his mother. Much thinner.

"Do you have the Hakkebakke tape?"

"Noo—wanna get one?"

"Yeah."

"We'll buy it tomorrow. For sure. We'll go and take a look at the shops. Won't that be fun?"

"Mmm."

"Eat some potato chips."

"I'm so full."

"Are you *so* full?"

"Yes."

"Would you like me to read Donald Duck to you?"

"Mmm."

"Come here . . . "

He sits down on the sofa. She moves right up close and puts her arm around him. That good smell of hers. She reads the comic book two times all the way through and he leans his head against her. It's so soft. She has a sweater on, but still. Her hair is long and it tickles the top of his forehead a tiny little bit when he sits like this. If he wrinkles his forehead, it tickles more. And if he stretches his neck, her hair comes down to his eyes. That tickles most. She peeks at him from time to time. He smiles because that makes her happy.

She wasn't up to reading Donald Duck one more time. He wasn't either, for that matter. His mother takes a turn across the floor. She glances quickly out the window—from the corner of her eye. And then she shakes her head as if she were searching for something. "The Children's Hour" was probably over a long time ago. They should've gone over to that Turid, or whatever her name is. It's too late now. He feels a tingling in his feet. He pulls them up onto the sofa and tucks them under him. There's not really very much to do. It's a pretty small room she has. Not much bigger than the pantry at home.

"Shall we look at the picture album?"

His mother doesn't wait for an answer. She takes out a red and gold album and brings it over. Here's Arne in the buggy and Arne in his sailor suit. Arne and Little Johan on the steps and in front of the Christmas tree and Grandma and Grandpa and Stine and Kirsti who is Svein's mother and then some people he doesn't know and then his mother and him. He's a handsome man. He's smiling. His mother keeps turning the pages. She's very quiet. Arne feels the quiet in his whole body. It's all tingling and prickly. There are lots of strangers in the album too. His mother looks at them. Arne looks at the leaf fluttering outside the window—and at the branch that now and then reaches over to the windowpane and knocks. He can feel his eyelids getting heavy. Can feel that he would like to sink down onto his mother's lap where the album is. But she keeps on turning the pages. He leans more and more into her side. He knows it's evening now.

"We'd better have a bite to eat, don't you think?"

"I don't know."

She goes into the kitchen to get things ready and he quickly jumps down from the sofa and is over at the window. There are people outside. Some are walking up the wide street and others are walking down it. But they don't stop. No one looks over here. Not one. He licks his index finger with his tongue and draws a circle on the windowpane. A circle with one, two eyes, nose, mouth . . . and then ears and hair . . . curly hair.

He eats a little bit. She wants him to. She doesn't say much, but he thinks she'll be happier if he eats. A half slice of bread, in any case.

She opens up the sofa. It gets very wide. Then she puts on a sheet and a blanket and a pillow and another pillow she has.

"I'm not tired."

"Of course you're tired—after your bus trip."

"Nooo, . . . you said . . . "

"Tomorrow we'll go to the movies. First shopping. That'll be fun."

"Will he come tomorrow then?"

"We'll see, sweetheart. Go to bed now. He . . . he'll come if he can."

She puts the covers over him, tucks them up under his feet the way he likes. Then she goes and sits in the armchair.

There are many sounds in this building. There's a whistling in the pipes. Sometimes there are people in the stairway. His mother doesn't make any sounds. She sits quiet as a mouse. As if she wasn't even breathing. She's pulled the dark green curtains shut. He can still see her. But she doesn't see him. She has her eyes open, but she isn't looking at anything.

After a long while she gets undressed. Slips under the covers with him. She's opened the window a crack. Arne can hear the noise of automobiles from the street. Voices too. Far away. And then there are the branches, rapping against the windowpane all the time now. His mother doesn't hear anything. She's lying as still as a cat, all curled up over toward the edge, breathing in the green-flowered nightgown. She's sung "Row, row to the fishing shoal" once, but she wasn't up to more because she's got a bad cold. She has a big handkerchief that she blows her nose into. The nightgown is tight across her back. He counts only nine flowers because she's pulled the blanket up so high. A start goes through him every time she blows her nose. He sings the songs to himself that she was too hoarse to sing. He sings "A sailor loves the billowing sea" and "Rock-a-bye-baby on the tree top." He can't remember any more.

He'll probably come tomorrow. Since he said he would.

A bang. Something heavy fell down. Arne blinks with one eye. Reaches his hand out for his mother. He's alone in the bed. The room is faintly lit. A harsh band of light is coming in under the edge of the curtains. In the middle of the floor he sees his mother. She's standing with her back to him. Above her head, another head. Arms on her back. Big arms.

"Let me go."

"Come on now."

His mother pulls away. Walks over and sits down on the armchair in the corner by the cassette player. He follows her. Arne makes a narrow slit with one eye. He stops breathing. And immediately he's full of air. Could almost burst from holding his breath.

He's squatted down in front of her.

"Anita,—don't be so . . . "

"Hush,—you'll wake him . . . You could have come earlier. He's been waiting so. You've no idea."

Now he bends his neck so that his head is on her lap, and his arms . . . he reaches his arms across her stomach. Up to her breasts. Strokes her breasts with his enormous hands. Strokes her over and over again on her nightgown.

He can't see the whole man because of the table that's in between. Just sees his back, neck, head, hands. Now he's stroking her farther down. And then up again.

"Stop it."

"Anita."

He has his hands under the nightgown now. They bulge out where her breasts are.

His mother has leaned her head back in the armchair. Her hands are hanging down along the side of the chair.

"Anita . . . "

"Be quiet!"

After a while she lifts her hands and rubs his neck, the back of his head.

Arne can feel his nose begin to tickle and itch. It's running. He wants to blow his nose. Can't. It runs down toward his mouth. He doesn't dare wipe his face with the blanket. The tears run diagonally across his nose, down onto the pillow. Make a wet, cold spot.

He's stood up. Takes off his clothes. Drops his clothes in a heap on the floor. Then he reaches his hand out to her, pulls her up from the chair. They lie down on the mat. One of his mother's legs is bent outwards. A strip of sunshine leaves a white light. He doesn't want to be here. Doesn't want to hear. See. Doesn't want to. His nose is all stuffed up. He can't breathe.

Her nightgown is rolled up like a sausage under her arms. He doesn't see the flowers.

Finally everything is quiet. His mother sits up, pulls a blanket down from the chair, and a pillow.

The ache in his stomach goes away. The snot doesn't itch any more. The wet spot on the pillow has gotten warm.

He can feel that he'll soon be asleep.

The curtains are pulled open with a snap. His mother is standing in front of the window wearing the blue sweater. She throws the window wide open. The birds are making a ruckus out in the tree. His mother leans way over and opens her mouth as if she's about to eat air. Arne turns his head cautiously and looks all around. There's only he and his mother. Just the two of them.

The blanket is rolled up in a heap at the foot of the chair.

"Are you awake, Arne?"

"Yes."

"We're going shopping today. Do you remember?"

"Yes."

"Hey Arne . . . Øyvind called last night after you were asleep. He was sick."

"Oh."

There aren't many others on the bus. Hans of the Hill asked if he wasn't going to sit up front with him. But he didn't feel like it. He would rather sit here.

The trees whiz by. If he squeezes his eyes almost shut, it looks like a coal-black wall. If he squeezes them all the way shut— hard—he sees Little Johan's sneer. Very clearly.

Original title: *Bytur. Arne og Anita*.   Translated by Katherine Hanson

Gro Dahle

(b. 1962)
When asked in an interview `Why did you begin to write?', Gro Dahle responded 'Because I wasn't good enough at drawing, and couldn't bring myself to work a regular job as a psychologist.' So after several years of study at the University, she entered a writing program at Telemark Regional College and the end result was her first book, *Audiens* (1987). In this and her four subsequent books, the reader is struck by the pictures, or images, in which Dahle expresses herself, and by her interest in discovering *who* the person behind the act is. Three of her works are books of poems, one a book for children, and one a collection of short stories called *Pelsjegerliv. Skjebnefortellinger* (*Life of a Trapper. Tales of Destiny*, 1991).

Dahle seems to have "borrowed" this double title from two well-known works in Scandinavian literature: *Pelsjegerliv* is the name of Helge Ingstad's account of his days as a trapper in Canada's Northwest Territories, and *Skjebnefortellinger* hearkens back to Isak Dinesen's *Anecdotes of Destiny*. Dahle's title may be purely coincidental. Still, the author does show a sense of adventure and a curiosity about uncharted territory in her use of language, and the stories in her book are indeed tales of destiny. *Pelsjegerliv* opens with a brief account of a birth and closes with a report of that same person's death, many years later. Birth and death form the perimeters of the stories in this collection. Against a background of small town or rural Norway, and in a cadence and tone reminiscent of folk literature, the sometimes mundane, sometimes bizarre twists of human destiny are related. In "My Father's Footsteps in the Room" Dahle reveals her fascination with the dark currents that threaten our equilibrium, desires and urges that suddenly erupt in acts of brutality.

My Father's Footsteps in the Room

My father watches me through the window. My father watches me from the door.

"Your hand is white. Your face is white. But your eyes are red," my father says, giving me milk to drink. He watches me across the table. He follows me across the room.

"Your hair is so red," my father says, "and your hands are so white."

"What's that streak there? What caused that mark?" His hands have broad fingernails. His hands have large knuckles and dry palms. His hands are crows or wood washed up on land. He watches me through the crack in the door.

He watches me from behind the curtains. He watches me from the shadows.

"What are you doing behind the storehouse, Daddy?" It's not the fox I hear on the hillside. It's not the mouse in the attic, scratching behind the wall. It's not the dog, running around the corner.

He watches me across the table.

"Your fingernail is broken," my father says.

He has grey hands that look yellow in the lamplight.

He has a watch that shines in the sun and blinds me.

"Don't hold the watch like that, Daddy. Put your arm down."

He walks along the river with his shovel. He walks up the mountainside with his ax. He follows me down the road.

"I'll just be gone an hour, Daddy."

The maple is turning yellow. The maple is turning red. He chops down the old family tree in the farmyard and lets it lie there.

"Why were you so long?" my father asks.

"Why is your blouse inside out?" my father asks.

"Why do you look away when I question you?"

His cheeks are red from his work. The tree blocks the farmyard driveway and stretches almost the length of the barn. Puffs of steam come out of his mouth. His knuckles are white on the hand holding the ax.

My father puts wood in the stove. He watches me as I walk by. He watches me when I bend over. The light slants in through the window.

"What's that on your throat?" my father asks.

"It's nothing."

"Why are you fiddling with the tablecloth?"

"No reason."

"Why have you changed your clothes?"

"I wanted . . .."

"Your hair is shiny," my father says.

I hang my head.

"You have your mother's hair," my father says.

I turn away to the left.

"You should leave your hair loose," my father says.

The beams in the ceiling have diagonal cracks. And outside the light runs across the field.

I'm sorting apples into two piles in the shed. My father is in the doorway. I have my back to him. The rotten apples I put in a sack for the horses. My father is in the doorway. The nice apples I wrap in paper and put in a box. My father is in the doorway. The wormy apples I put in pails under the workbench. When I turn around, I see his ears lit up by the sun. Red.

"I'm going out tonight, Daddy."

He divides the potato into six pieces and puts butter in the middle. The first snow covers the steps. The fields are white. They shine. Even at night.

"You have to tie your hair back," my father says. The carrot is green at one end. He slices it off and puts it on the table. Right between his plate and his glass.

I walk across the farmyard.

"How long is the tree going to lie there blocking the way?" He leans against the wall. I smell fir and birch and juniper. He's stacking wood in two rows. He watches me from the side. And the wind blows. And the wind blows.

When I make the beds he stands behind me. When I bend over the mattress, he stands behind me. When I shake the comforter with my arms stretched out, he stands behind me. He leans against the door frame in his grey sweater that's unraveling at the wrists. His arms are crossed on his chest. He watches me put the pillows in place, smooth out the folds, straighten the pillow.

I wake up and see my father by the bed.
"You look like your mother when you're asleep."
His hair is messed up from the night. Grey stubble on his chin.
"You look like your mother when you open your eyes."
"Open the curtains, Daddy."
Clouds are chasing each other from ridge to ridge.

"Who do you see when you're not here?" my father asks.
He eats a slice of bread with his left hand. The wind tosses the trees outside. Ash and oak.
He watches me from the side. His shoes shuffle under the table. He watches me from the side. His shoes scrape under the table.
"I'll be away this afternoon," I say. And the cat jumps from one chair to another.

My father meets me with an umbrella at the bottom of the road.
"You'll get sick," he says, lighting the way with his flashlight.
Our footsteps on the gravel. Like two elk crossing a marsh.

"You're wet," my father says from the wood stove. He lays wood on the fire. It sparks and crackles. He watches me from the door. He watches me from the end of the room. He walks up to me from behind and loosens my hair from its braid. He loosens my hair from its braid and lets it fall down my back.
"You're wet," my father says. He opens the stove and pokes the fire, while I change. While I change, he keeps one eye on the fire, the other roves.

It's not the cat walking across the rug. It's not the cat breathing in the room. It's not the cat turning on his heel.
He watches me from the tree. He watches me through the keyhole. He watches me from the shed.

"What are you doing in the shed, Daddy?"
"Why are you standing behind that hedge?"
It's not my foot snapping the twig I hear. It's not the wind moving the branches.

When he walks past, he walks close to me. And when he walks past, his arm touches me. And when he walks past, his arm rubs against my side. Sparks shoot out of the fireplace. I bend and pick them up before they singe the wood.

I'm lying in bed with a fever. My father gives me a drink of water. My father strokes my forehead with cool hands. My father strokes my hands under the comforter. And he breathes. And he breathes. His breathing fills the room. The whole room.

I'm lying in bed with a fever. My father spreads my hair out on the pillow. He takes hold of my throat with his broad fingers. He takes hold of my chin with his broad fingers. He strokes my lips with the back of his hand. He is very close. He is very close and he gets closer.

I'm lying in bed with a fever. The cat's sleeping on the comforter. My father puts his hand under the comforter. My father moves his hand along my thigh. His hand is on my thigh. His hand is on my thigh, trembling.

I'm lying in bed with a fever. My father touches my belly. My belly under the comforter.
His lips are sweaty and he doesn't look at me. He looks at the wall. He looks at the floor. He looks at the cat sleeping on the comforter. And the picture on the wall. While he touches.

We're sitting at the table. Vegetable soup beaded with fat. Cabbage floats to the surface. Carrots and celery. My father watches me over the bowl. My father watches me over his glass. I put salt in the soup. I eat bread with the soup. I blow on my spoon. My father watches me over the bread. The cat drinks some water. The cat drinks some water.

At night my father comes into the room. He's in the doorway. He's on the blue rag rug. He's standing by the bed. The clock in the living room chimes, strike after strike. He goes out into the hall pulling on his jacket.

I go away for three days and come back with my hair loose. "You smell like fresh bread," my father says coming close. The cat walks between my legs. The cat's body against my leg.

My father looks at the knotholes in the wall. He breathes in my eye. I close my eye against his breath. I close my eye against his mouth. I'm moist against his hand. And too soft.

The bull is loose, Daddy. Put the bull back in the stall. Oh Daddy, oh Daddy. Put the bull back in the stall.

Keep the bull on a tether, Daddy. Look, he's shaking his horn at me. The bull's in the farmyard, Daddy. The bull's on the steps. Oh, the bull's getting into the house. The door's open, Daddy. The bull's getting in.

And the floor rocks. The floor rocks when the bull comes.

And the horn blasts. It trumpets through the house. And the floor sways. And the floor sways. Because of the bull.

Until the bull is released from his hide. Until the swan sheds its down. The crows flee the trees. The crows flee the trees in big black clouds. The elks flee the forest and cross the marsh. Masses, masses of them.

And the wind in the fields. The grain bending softly to the side.

Afterwards I walk across the room with the milk pitcher in my hands. I put the pitcher on the table. Bring the cheese out. Cut the bread into slices. Fetch the butter from the cupboard. Hear through the wall the sound of someone chopping wood.

Original title: *Min fars skritt over gulvet.* Translated by Judith Messick

Sissel Lie

(b. 1942)

In 1986 Sissel Lie, a well-established scholar and professor of French literature at the University of Trondheim, published her first book of fiction which she called *Tigersmil* (*A Tiger's Smile*). An original collection of stories and short texts, Tigersmil was singled out as the best work by a new author, earning Lie the Tarjei Vesaas prize. Since that initial success, Lie has produced three novels, while simultaneously pursuing her academic projects and publications.

Women's history and women writers of the Renaissance are among the subjects Lie has researched and about which she has written extensively, and an important aspect of her literary project has been the integration of past with present, the incorporation of historical places and persons in fiction with a contemporary setting. In Lie's third novel, *Løvens hjerte* (1988; now available in English translation under the title *Lion's Heart*), the first person narrator perceives a solution to a problematic love relationship in the poetry of the 16th century French author, Louise Labé. Labé wrote love poems celebrating woman's erotic desire and in her own highly unconventional life she defied society's norms. Aided by an old map of Lyons, the narrator travels in time to Labé's home and meets the author and her circle of friends and lovers. The action switches back and forth between 16th century Lyons and present day Norway and through this remarkable journey the narrator learns that love, and love relationships, can be something different than she had believed, and that the same holds true for herself as a woman.

An interest in history and women who write is also apparent in the short pieces below which have been taken from *Tigersmil*. While many of the stories in this book are pure fiction with a modern setting, others are dedicated to women from history who recorded their lives in journals or memoirs, and in several the author/narrator explores her own history, or childhood. Common to all these women are problems of identity—the struggle to be a subject rather than an object, the difficulty of maintaining a separate identity in relationships with men

Puzzle Pictures

How will I be able to talk about childhood, when I don't have one; not a coherent childhood with episodes that form a chain of events and with prolonged exchanges that contain all the funny expressions and important information. Other people have childhoods where I show up as well, saying and doing things that don't exist in my glimpses from the other side of time.

My glimpses recur and are always the same, like when I was six years old and walked up the steps to the hospital to have my tonsils out and didn't cry. A huge stairway with many steps, mother and I walking up the middle. I've promised to be good. We walk without stopping and never reach the top of the stairs. Much later I came out of the anesthetic, and everyone explained that Mother wasn't allowed to come in, I might cry when she left. A doll with stiff arms and an angry celluloid face was placed on the bed instead—for a moment Mother was standing outside the door, which was open a crack, waving and acting like she cared about me. Later on I was all alone in the world and cried and threw up and had a sore throat. There was no rush for me to go back home from the hospital, I guess I stayed extra long on account of the flu at home. They finally brought me home—by that time I'd almost forgotten them and took care not to believe what Mother promised, and never cried. One day the apartment was full of people who were saying good-by to Father. He was leaving for the States and would be gone a long time. He lifted me up, my long legs almost touched the floor. "Are you sad that I'm going away?" Father might feel bad if he thought I felt bad. "I have so many other friends, Father." Soon I no longer had a father either.

Two photos have the same face, a foundling in a grey home-made coat, next to her a little sister with a round face. She's smiling. I look darkly at the observer, one hand on the armrest and my head tilted backwards, the garter around my brown woolen knickers barely showing. A pale, serious face that never forgave anything.

I continued to be a foundling at dance school, but there were so many ways we could pass the time while we waited. Some boys preferred us. They were the timid ones, the ones who couldn't compete with the more daring guys for girls with big breasts and narrow waists. I wore flats and a felt A-line skirt too, but it pretty much hung straight down, just like my arms and hair. "Jelly" has hands that slide in mine as we dance and dance. "Horse" leans toward me and looks like he wants to chew on me with those big teeth of his. The clearest picture captures me in a harsh light on the bench by the wall. I can't leave it, nor can I stand to sit there so visible. If I stand up and walk across the floor to leave, the music will stop, the legs of the others will freeze in midstep and their eyes will stare. I try to conceal my shame from the yellow light, and nothing ever stops.

The ones who came to school with hickeys on their necks lived more dangerously than the rest of us, plunging themselves into sex behind Pedersen's greenhouse as soon as the snow was gone. While I was reading Frank Yerby's titillating descriptions of slave breeding on brown leather benches—slender black women and strong black men—and my parents were giving away a stack of books I'd already read, my peers, to my horror, were getting pregnant in the nocturnal summer light and disappearing from childhood. It was simpler to see films with Debbie Reynolds in yellow oilskins. Afterwards I tap dance for all time on the veranda and wonder if anyone could fall in love with me. Maybe I was the one who had yellow oilskins, in any case it was raining.

In my confirmation picture I'm wearing pink pumps with high heels, gloves and hat. I look unhappy and tilt my head a little backwards so that my chin won't look so long in the picture. My new curls are carefully arranged under the hat, and my entire body is tense from being grown-up.

There was something even worse than dance school. Odd got my first kiss and rock-and-rolled so hard the chandeliers below nearly fell on top of Mother and Father. He dragged me back and forth across the floor—we'd only learned foxtrot and quickstep at dance school, but I was the one he wanted to dance with. I thought we were going steady after that evening, until he came out of the movies with Sølvi. Mons had been assigned to tell me that Odd was no longer interested. I'd had an inkling all right that I didn't have much to offer, flat as I was and serious, but I'd hoped he wouldn't figure it out so quickly. Sølvi was always laughing and let him feel her breasts, he'd never tried to feel mine. Nothing to do but clench my teeth and smile as if it was fine with me that Odd was chicken and no one wanted me. I'm still standing there with my kick sled in the square in front of the big grey stone building that was the Community Center, where they showed movies on the ground floor. Mons is riding with me and all the others are long gone.

There's a photograph from a masquerade ball in which Sølvi is a deck of cards, Kirsten a clown, and I an odalisque. We were girlfriends and stuck together. Sølvi is laughing out loud and Kirsten looks uncomfortable. Only my eyes are showing over the rust colored lace curtain, under harsh make-up they stare out into the world.

There must have been boyfriends after that, they form grey shadows on the periphery of memory, without faces, without lines, sometimes several at the same time, perhaps they were even unhappily in love. Sølvi says that I was cheerful and outgoing, actually popular.

But I myself couldn't have been there very long. It is others who have kept my childhood. They carry the years with them as a matter of course.

Original title: *Fikserbilder*. Translated by Katherine Hanson

Girl With Butterfly Wings

*To Marie Bashkirsteff (1858-1884)
who wrote thousands of journal
pages.*

The pale young women, who don't have much time left and turn away discreetly to spit blood in their lace handkerchiefs, peer anxiously in the mirror for the first signs of illness and go to balls with naked shoulders, silk shoes, and flouncing skirts. Graceful and untouched as porcelain dolls decorating a writing desk, they wait for the prince so that life can begin. Or perhaps that's not at all what they're thinking about?

Marie B. is rich and versatile, of noble Russian family, residing first in Nice, then Paris. With her grey eyes and her golden hair she thinks she resembles the heroine of a novel. Everyone expects that Marie will make a good match, but it isn't easy to find a suitable young man. The family has a bad reputation in the more genteel circles—an uncle has made a scandal with his drunkenness and adultery, some people think the fortune that supports them is not rightfully theirs and are bringing suit against them in Russia. Marie is never asked to the balls where everyone who is anyone meets. All the while, Marie casts sidelong glances at the experienced men about town, the ones who set up mistresses in apartments of their own and really know to appreciate women, but seldom marry them. But most of all Marie thinks about being famous. "Even if I die young," she writes in her journal, "everyone will know who I am. And if I live for a long time, I'll be celebrated for my song and my beauty." She can sing, draw, or publish the journals she's been writing since she was thirteen. "No woman has ever before written the whole truth about herself," Marie thinks contentedly and admires her round arms in the mirror. The white skin is perfect against the white dress, doesn't she look like Psyche with her red curls under the headband? Psyche who was so beautiful that no suitor would have her, and who was carried by the wind to the bed of the god of love. Psyche who the Romans portrayed with butterfly wings.

Marie wonders whether it will be Eros or Art that will make her immortal. She spits blood, the doctor calls it a sore throat. Perhaps she doesn't have all that much time at her disposal? If she's to experience love, she has to meet a rich man. Nothing kills love as fast as worrying about money, writes Marie. While travelling in Florence her aunt had to go to the pawnbroker with their jewels so the two could survive until the money from Russia arrived. Marie has not forgotten that humiliating journey. A lover musn't have any blemishes either. Who could love a man with corns?

Marie poses in front of the mirror, intent on making herself beautiful, in a specially made monk's habit with a cord around the waist for melancholy moments, as a peasant girl to please her mother and aunt, or in one of her many white dresses to be different from the other young ladies.

Marie poses by her writing desk and waits for real life, while she tells her diary about young men who don't dare and don't want to and bore her enormously. Marie prides herself on being eccentric, she can be pert and unpredictable—absolutely not a girl one chooses as a wife. She has read *Corinne* by Madame de Staël and takes comfort in the thought that if exceptionally bright women are not loved, it's because men are so small and frightened. But like Corinne she longs for love and looks for signs in herself that she's in love. Don't her cheeks turn red when he approaches, doesn't her heart beat harder when he takes her hand and presses it to his lips? Her lips burn for months after a kiss on a kitchen stairway in Rome. He was the nephew of a cardinal and wouldn't dare fight to get Marie. "Did he think that a woman who kissed one man would kiss them all?" muses Marie and almost feels like a fallen woman.

* * *

Marie travels to Russia with thirty Paris creations, to visit her father and scout out a Russian prince. In the evenings she organizes singing on the staircase to the second floor of her father's estate and revels in the admiring men who surround her. But even in Russia nothing ever happens. She's invited on a wolf hunt and, enraptured, discards her white dresses to put on men's clothes. But the wet seeps through her leather boots, she sleeps in the forest on her father's coat and shivers while she dreams about a life of adventure and waits for someone to scare up a wolf for them to shoot. There are no wolves and no Russian princes either. Marie is unspeakably bored. Three tallow candles burn in her room late one night and tell her that someone will die soon. When she is visiting the damp catacombs in Kiev, she feels a sharp pain in the lung that hasn't bothered her before.

Marie loses her voice and with it her dream of becoming a world famous singer. But she can still paint, and paint better than anyone, a female Titian? Marie with her golden-red hair and round white arms, always dressed in white—wool, silk, muslin, lacework, in studied shades of white against her light skin—enters a painting school for young women. The family breathes a sigh of relief that the moody Marie has found something to occupy her time. She sweeps into the atelier wearing an otter fur, with chaperone and dog in tow—no one knows that Marie is grieving over her own idleness and the energy wasted on family feuds and entertainment.

Marie wants to create a real life for herself—with repressed anger she works every day, annoyed at the family that pesters her with their demands. She never thinks she learns enough, never gets enough praise from her teachers, despairs and starts over. She paints the women working at the easels in the small crowded room and shows a painting at the big spring exhibition, but she doesn't think she's got it right.

Imagine being free to come and go as a man, mix with the other students in the Latin Quarter, go to a proper art school and learn the basics. Why wasn't she born a man? complains Marie to her journal. She wears a brown wig and secretly goes to feminist meetings, gives money anonymously, and dreads the family's ridicule if she is exposed. A moment later she orders a new white dress studded with white silk roses, and red-laced boots for her little feet that everyone admires so much. Marie makes herself into a work of art as well, and cannot be content with the dark blue artist's smock.

In the middle of her work she is sent to one of the upper class spas and must submit to healthy diets, cod-liver oil and goat's milk, baths and ineffective medicines. Marie puts up with everything, even though she has finally discovered how she wants to use her life, for she is in the process of losing her hearing and knows the tuberculosis can't be stopped.

Marie is full of ideas. She paints a young woman smoking and staring at a skeleton, she paints a woman dreaming under a blossoming tree and enjoying the spring, children in the street. She is planning a large picture of ordinary people on a bench. She wants to paint life as it is, but has so little energy.

When she finally achieves success, Marie is so weak that she can no longer climb the stairs to the atelier at home, she lies in bed, beautiful in white velvet and lace, scarcely smiling at the friends who bring news of her pictures. She is soon no longer interested in anything.

"The most cruel thing of all must be to die without leaving a trace," writes Marie and immediately consoles herself: "If I'm not famous for anything else, I'll be remembered for the journal, for I've told everything." But someone betrayed Marie when the journal was published, tried to make Marie into one of the other pale young women. Someone ripped out the pages on which she had written about her frenzied fear of death and her frustration, cut out the erotic dreams and toned down the despair at having a woman's body and a man's ambitions. Nevertheless thousands of pages still bear witness to Marie with the red curls and the white skin, who saw herself in the mirror as Psyche, the girl with the butterfly wings, forever bound to the insect's short life and yet exalted with the immortals.

Original title: *Pike med sommerfuglvinger*. Translated by Katherine Hanson

Notes on the Translators

NADIA CHRISTENSEN has published numerous translations of Scandinavian novels, short stories and poetry. She is currently Executive Director of the Nordic Center at Augsburg College in Minneapolis. Her most recent translation is *Dina's Book* by Herbjørg Wassmo.

JANET GARTON teaches Scandinavian literature at the University of East Anglia in Norwich, England. She has written extensively about modern Scandinavian literature—her most recent book is titled *Norwegian Women's Writing 1850-1990*—and translated numerous works from the Norwegian. She is co-director of Norvik Press Ltd and assistant editor of the literary journal *Scandinavica*.

KATHERINE HANSON has taught Norwegian language and Scandinavian literature at a number of colleges and universities, most recently at Pacific Lutheran University. In collaboration with Judith Messick she has translated three of Amalie Skram's novels: *Constance Ring*, *Professor Hieronimus* and *St. Jørgen's* (the latter two published in one volume titled *Under Observation*).

TORILD HOMSTAD has taught Norwegian at the University of Minnesota and has co-authored a study guide, *Scandinavia: Comparative Culture and Government*. Her translations from Norwegian include a children's novel as well as short stories for several collections. She is currently writing a dissertation on Nini Roll Anker.

BIBBI LEE is a planning consultant currently living in France. She has translated *Music from a Blue Well* and *Nothing Grows by Moonlight* by Torborg Nedreaas.

JUDITH MESSICK teaches writing at the Kellogg School of Management at Northwestern University. She received her PhD in English literature at the University of California at Santa Barbara where she also taught in the writing program. She and Katherine Hanson have collaborated on translations of *Constance Ring* and *Under Observation* by Amalie Skram.

JANET E. RASMUSSEN is Vice President for Academic Affairs at Nebraska Wesleyan University. She has published widely on Scandinavian women writers and immigrant women. Her most recent book: *New Land, New Voices. Scandinavian Immigrants to the Pacific Northwest*.

ELIZABETH ROKKAN has translated numerous books by Tarjei Vesaas and Cora Sandel, including *Krane's Café* and the *Alberta* trilogy. Her latest translation is of Johan Borgen's *The Scapegoat*. She is Welsh by birth, and until recently was Senior Lecturer in the English Department at the University of Bergen.

CARLA WAAL is Professor Emeritus of Theatre at the University of Missouri-Columbia. In addition to staging several plays by Henrik Ibsen, she has written biographies of the Norwegian actress Johanne Dybwad and the Norwegian-Swedish actress Harriet Bosse.

BARBARA WILSON's translation of the stories of Cora Sandel appeared in 1985 and was awarded a Columbia Translation prize. She has also translated a novel by Ebba Haslund, *Nothing Happened*. She is the author of several novels and two series of thrillers, one of them featuring the translator sleuth Cassandra Reilly (*Gaudí Afternoon* and *Trouble in Transylvania*). She was a founder of Seal Press in 1976 and of Women in Translation in 1989.

HARRIET BACKER (1845–1932), a detail of whose painting, "By Lamplight", appears on the cover, was one of an important group of women artists in Norway around the turn of the century. This group also included Oda Krogh, Kitty Kielland, Åsta Norregaard and Leis Schjelderup, among others, and is only now beginning to be recognized and re-evaluated. Backer was born in Norway but spent fifteen years studying and painting in the great art centers of Munich and Paris. She returned to Norway in 1889 to start her own art school, an academy where many women studied, including Cora Sandel. Backer began as a portrait painter but later developed an interest in interiors and figures. Her paintings of Norwegian farm dwellings and church interiors are well known, and can be found in the major and provincial museums of Norway.

Welcome to the World of International Women's Writing

How Many Miles to Babylon by Doris Gercke. $8.95. ISBN: 1-879679-02-7
Hamburg police detective Bella Block thinks she'll find some rest on her
countryside vacation, but after only a few hours in the remote village of
Roosbach, she realizes she has stumbled on to one of the most troubling
cases of her career.

Two Women in One by Nawal el-Saadawi. $9.95. ISBN: 1-879679-01-9
One of this Egyptian feminist's most important novels, *Two Women in One*
tells the story of Bahiah Shaheen, a well-behaved Cairo medical student—
and her other side: rebellious, political and artistic.

Under Observation by Amalie Skram. With an introduction by Elaine
Showalter. $15.95. ISBN: 1-879679-03-5
This riveting story of a woman painter confined against her will in a
Copenhagen asylum is a classic of nineteenth century Norwegian
literature by the author of *Constance Ring* and *Betrayed*.

Unmapped Territories: New Women's Fiction from Japan edited by Yukiko
Tanaka. $10.95. ISBN: 1-879679-00-0
These stunning new stories by well-known and emerging writers chart a
world of vanishing social and physical landmarks in a Japan both strange
and familiar. With an insightful introduction by Tanaka on the literature
and culture of the "era of women" in Japan.

Unnatural Mothers by Renate Dorrenstein. $11.95. ISBN: 1-879679-06-X
A compelling Dutch novel, by turns hilarious and heartbreaking,
Unnatural Mothers explores the oldest bond in the world: that of mother
and daughter.

Wild Card by Assumpta Margenat. $8.95. ISBN: 1-879679-04-3
This lively mystery is set in Andorra, a kingdom between France and
Spain. *Wild Card* tells the story of Rocio, a sharp-witted young woman
who devises a scheme to beat her sexist boss at his own game.

Originally established in 1984 as an imprint of Seal Press, Women in
Translation is now a nonprofit publishing company, dedicated to making
women's writing from around the world available in English translation.
We specialize in anthologies, mysteries and literary fiction. The books
above may be ordered from us at 3131 Western Avenue, Suite 410, Seattle,
WA 98121 (Please include $2.00 postage and handling for the first book
and .50 for each additional book). Write to us for a free catalog.